THEY TOLD ME I WAS EVERYTHING

THE FIRST QUARTO: PART I

GREGORY ASHE

H&B

Published by Hodgkin & Blount
https://www.hodgkinandblount.com/
contact@hodgkinandblount.com

Published 2022
Printed in the United States of America

Version 1.03

Trade Paperback ISBN: 978-1-63621-003-2
eBook ISBN: 978-1-63621-002-5

FALL SEMESTER
SEPTEMBER 2013

1

Auggie grabbed another box from the back of the SUV, eyed the distance to Moriah Court, and said, "Let's try to find a closer parking spot."

"Pussy," Fer said, elbowing Auggie aside and grabbing another box. "You're going to be walking your ass off for the next year. Might as well get used to it now."

Resting the box on the bumper, Auggie grabbed his phone and tried to get the right angle. He wanted himself, the box, and the outline of the college in the background.

"Five seconds," Fer snapped.

Auggie flashed a huge grin, took the picture, and posted it. He figured that was an easy mid-five figures for likes. He worked the pack of Parliaments out of his sleeve, tapped a cigarette loose, and patted his pockets for his lighter.

"Christ, you're a poser," Fer said.

"I wasn't going to smoke it right now," Auggie said, sticking the Parliament behind one ear.

Fer grunted, grabbed the heaviest box and plodded off across South Quad.

Wiping sweat from his forehead—this place was the middle of fucking nowhere, hot as the fucking tropics, and had two-hundred percent humidity—Auggie grabbed a box and followed. Even though classes didn't start for another week, the quad was busy in the mid-morning: kids tossing a frisbee, three girls in overalls taking turns playing the dulcimer, a shirtless kid with killer abs walking a rope he'd tied between two trees. He fell a couple of times while Auggie was throwing him sidelong looks—killer abs, just really spectacular, and Auggie could make a sweet-ass gif of him tumbling off the rope, so he slowed to grab the video—and then Fer shouted, "Dickcheese, get your ass moving," and Auggie jogged to catch up.

Moriah Court was one of the oldest residence halls on Wroxall's campus; the college itself dated back to the 19th century, and Moriah Court looked old enough to be original. Since it was an official moving day, a cinderblock propped open the heavy security door. They passed the desk, where a black woman in a uniform was on the phone; she waved at Auggie and mimed a pen in the air, and he nodded; he never forgot a chance to give away his autograph. Fer led them to the elevator, where four boys who looked like they'd crawled out of a basement were stacking boxes and bags. The boys looked at each other, looked at Auggie, looked at Fer, and tried to shuffle the bags and boxes to make room.

"We'll take the stairs, fellas," Fer said.

Auggie tried not to groan.

"Pussy," Fer called back.

"This is why I said I was totally fine moving on my own," Auggie said.

"And because you thought Mom would let you keep the car."

"I don't see why I can't have it out here."

"Because you are a dick and a tool and a fuck up," Fer said kindly.

They climbed the rest of the way in silence. On the fourth-floor landing, Fer stepped aside and let Auggie take the lead; when Auggie got to the room, he worked the key in the lock and went inside. It was a small space: two twin beds, two desks, a narrow window that only opened an inch, and two cramped closets. One bed already had sheets and a thin plaid coverlet; a pile of sneakers toppled out from the closet, and clothes and boxes were stacked on that side of the room— and, for that matter, on Auggie's desk.

"That dickbreath is still in the shower," Fer said, nodding at the strip of light under the bathroom door; Auggie and his roommate, a guy named Orlando, shared the bathroom with the two guys in the next room. "That's like thirty minutes, Augustus."

Auggie dropped the box on his bed and sat on the mattress.

Shoving aside Orlando's stuff, Fer set his box on the desk. "And his shit is on your side of the room."

"Yeah."

"You can't let him get away with that kind of shit."

"Ok, Fer."

"Give him one fucking inch, and he's going to be all over your shit."

"Ok."

"Tell him your schedule. Tell him when you need the bathroom so you aren't late for class."

"Yeah, I know."

Fer wiped his hands on his jeans, taking another look around the room. He was darker than Auggie, his skin a rich brown, and he was taller and bigger. Taller was the part that really bugged Auggie. Why couldn't his own dad have been taller?

"You probably think college is like all that porn you read."

"Oh my God."

"You probably think you're going to be banging chicks in the library and then coming home and banging some more of them here and then going to class and getting some chick to jerk you off under the desk."

"You are so stupid."

"You probably think that whole pretty boy makeup channel you've got on YouTube is going to be your pussy key."

Auggie grabbed his phone again; Fer's rants often hit six figures of likes, and this sounded like a good one. Auggie would have to do some editing, but the raw material was solid.

"Point that thing at me," Fer said, "and I'll shove it up your chute."

Rolling his eyes, Auggie pocketed the phone, unfolded the cardboard flaps of the box, and took out a stack of t-shirts.

"Hey, dongbait," Fer said, shoving his shoulder. "I'm talking to you."

"I'm listening, Jesus."

"College isn't just about getting girls, ok?"

"I didn't say that. You said that."

"Yeah, well, Mom's paying for this shit, ok? So you need to take it seriously."

"I am taking it seriously."

"You've got to be a man now. You can't just be a kid, ok? You've got to learn how to stand on your own two feet."

"You've got to learn not to talk in clichés," Auggie muttered.

"This asshole?" Fer thumbed at the bathroom, where the steady drone of the shower continued. "He's going to be jerking off into your jockeys if you don't set some limits."

"You are so twisted."

"I'm serious."

"So am I. You are messed up in the head."

Fer mimed jerking off.

"Goodbye, Fer. Just leave the rest of my boxes and get lost."

Fer started to moan as he pretended to stroke himself. Two girls passed the door, paused, and glanced in before hurrying away.

"Oh my God," Auggie said, grabbing Fer's arm and trying to force him out of the room.

Laughing, Fer dragged Auggie with him toward the stairs. "Come on, asswipe. Let's get the rest of your stuff."

After the third trip, when Orlando was still in the shower, Fer stopped in the middle of the quad and said, "Christ, I got the whole thing fucking backwards."

Auggie glanced at where they had parked the Escalade, and then he looked back at Moriah Court. "What?"

"It's gay porn, dude. You're living out your gay porn fantasies."

"Fer."

"That's like a staple of gay porn, Augustus. You're moving into your dorm, the new roommate steps out of the shower, he's naked, he's a fucking stud, he bends you over that stack of cardboard boxes and you guys do the two-boy bucking bronco."

"You know an awful lot about gay porn."

"Sexuality is a buffet," Fer said, stopping again to point a finger at Auggie. "Gotta get a little of everything on your plate, little bro."

"Hold still," Auggie said.

"What? Why?"

"I'm hoping this truck will hit you and kill you."

Fer slapped him on the back of the head before Auggie could get away.

There was only one box left in the back of the SUV. Auggie hoisted it, balanced it, and stepped back while Fer shut the door.

"You want me to come up and make your bed?"

Auggie rolled his eyes.

"You want me to count your socks?"

"Bye, Fer."

Fer surprised him by pulling him into a hug, kissing him on the cheek, and then giving him a noogie so hard that Auggie thought he had a traumatic brain injury.

"Love ya," Fer said.

"Love ya," Auggie said.

"You call me if any assholes give you trouble," Fer said. He hesitated, shoved his hands in the pockets of his jeans, and looked up the street as he added, "Especially about, you know."

"Nobody even knows about that here."

"I'm just saying. I'll drive all the fuck back and kick some fucking ass."

Auggie smiled and adjusted the box. "Yeah."

"I'll tell mom you said you missed her."

"Do not," Auggie said. "Don't you dare."

Fer threw him the bird, got into the Escalade, and backed out of the parking stall. A moment later the SUV was turning at the corner, the California plates winking out of sight. Then Auggie was alone with a Missouri sky, Missouri kids, and the un-fucking-bearable Missouri heat. Surrounded by people swarming to move into dorms. Surrounded by kids his age laughing and playing. Surrounded, virtually, by hundreds of thousands of fans who wanted to see his latest video or his next joke. Surrounded in just about every way imaginable, and feeling oh-so-fucking alone right then that he thought he might cry. He pulled a sad face, snapped a few pictures of himself—had to get the jawline right—and scrawled *wish you were here* on the bottom of the best one. He posted it and figured that it could easily hit high five figures.

He carried the box back to Moriah Court, climbed the stairs—this time, two girls were moving an electronic keyboard and a brass monkey the size of a Doberman—and let himself back into the dorm room.

His first thought, upon seeing Orlando for the first time, his roommate standing with a towel around his waist, nothing but muscle on muscle on muscle and a thick pelt of hair on his bare chest, was: oh, fuck, he's hot.

His second thought was: fucking Fer, being fucking right again.

And his third thought, seeing the slight shift in Orlando's expression when he noticed the elongated moment of attention, was that he, Auggie Lopez, was fucked.

2

When Theo got to Liversedge Hall, campus was busy, and he realized that the first official move-in day was in full swing. He arrived later than he would have liked. He had gone to Downing first that morning, just as he went every day now. It was too far for his bad leg, even on the bike, so that meant the bus, and the bus meant being late. Everywhere. All around him, kids—eighteen, most of them, but with eyes and hair and skin like babies—were everywhere: carrying hampers full of clothes, toting bedding, one boy with thirty shirts on hangers slung across his back, a pair of girls carrying what looked like a brass monkey. The damn thing looked tall enough to reach Theo's knees. And parents. Don't forget the parents. Moms whipping back and forth between cars and dorms, lugging suitcases and beanbag chairs and posters of teen pop stars. Justin Bieber? Theo had never heard of him, but then again, he wasn't sure he'd read the name right. The dads, for the most part, puttered around, obviously feeling very important and just as obviously trying to figure out how to look busy. One poor guy was walking in a circle with a screwdriver until a woman with a Jackie O bouffant put her hands on her hips and screamed, "Peter, get the lead out."

Once, on the farm, Theo's dad had had to put down an old mule. The look on Jackie O's face was eerily similar.

Theo went inside Liversedge. He filled up his water bottle at the fountain. He checked his bag for pens and pencils and notebooks and for the little Disneyworld keychain that he'd hooked to the inside of the D ring. The front of the keychain's plastic rectangle showed Sleeping Beauty's Castle; on the back, Theo had an arm around Ian, and Ian was holding Lana, who'd been two at the time and way too young to appreciate the experience—an argument that had dragged on and on before the trip. In hindsight, Theo wasn't sure he'd ever admitted that Ian had been right.

He ducked into the ground-floor men's room, checked his hair, tried to flatten his beard, which looked absurdly poofy today, and washed his hands. He ended up at the elevators, staring at the brass plate, the up button, the smudged fingerprints.

Theo was still standing there when Peg walked up, looking a bit like a carnation in her pink summer dress, and delicately pressed the up button with her matching pink nail.

"Well, Daniel," she said, her face almost as pink as the nail. "Hello!"

"Hi, Peg."

Her eyes slid to the cane, and Theo wasn't fast enough to stop himself. He shifted his weight, trying to hide the support.

"Well," Peg said. "Aren't you looking great?"

"Thank you."

"And after everything that happened."

Theo nodded.

"Daniel, I'm really just so terribly sorry."

"Thank you. That means a lot."

"We were all just so devastated."

Theo nodded again. He figured he'd better get it right while he was still in the warmup round.

"Such a tragedy," Peg breathed, her pink nails splayed against her pink dress, the whole effect like one giant pink carnation expressing its deepest sympathies.

"Yes. Yeah."

Peg blinked. Her eyeshadow was turquoise, which Theo thought might be a complementary color. The elevator dinged. The doors rattled open. Peg was still frozen with her nails spread against her chest.

Theo had almost forgotten his line. "It's, uh, been hard."

"You poor dear," Peg said and started to sob.

After that, Theo had to help her onto the elevator, and they rode up together to the third floor, where Theo guided Peg into the English department's main office and got her seated at her desk. Peg ripped tissues out of a box like a magician with handkerchiefs up his sleeve, and Theo filled a paper cup with water and set it by her elbow. By then, Ethel Anne had arrived, and she started crying while she was taking off her coat—never mind that it was September and almost ninety degrees outside. Ethel Anne had to hug Theo, and he had to repeat his performance from the elevator, and then Ethel Anne and Peg had to hug each other, both of them still calling him Daniel for the simple fucking reason that they'd read it on his student account, and somewhere in the middle of the whole fiasco, Theo had to soothe himself by imagining Liversedge Hall imploding and the three of them buried in the rubble.

When he finally extricated himself, he made his way to his office at the end of the hall, glad that the light was off behind the pebbled glass. He shared the office with two other grad students, and while Dawson rarely showed up to use the space, Grace spent most of her waking hours there. Technically, the semester didn't start for a week, and Theo was hoping he'd have that time to settle in and—well, adjust was a pretty small word for it. Normalize? Somehow feel like the universe still made sense?

He let himself into the office. He hadn't been there since the accident; it smelled the same, a mixture of chai and pencil shavings and old books. Grace had hung four cardigans, one on top of the other, across the back of her seat, and her desk was covered with vinyl clings shaped like flowers and ducks and a Visigoth with a period-appropriate battle axe. Dawson's desk had only an aging computer, supplied by the department, with what Dawson probably considered a discreet 4/20 sign taped to the side of the CPU. Theo's desk was bare. Grace had been very thoughtful about that. She had taken down all the pictures, framed and unframed; she had removed all the trinkets from vacations and all the holiday gag gifts. Everything was in a banker's box shoved into the desk's knee hole. Theo caught the back of the box with his foot, balanced on the cane, and dragged the box free. He shoved it to the side. He'd have to deal with it eventually.

Theo had barely powered on his computer when a knock came at the door. The pebbled glass made it impossible to tell who it was, but the spikey hair made him think of Ethel Anne. He considered the window. This was an old building; they had safety proofed everything. And anyway, he was only on the third floor, and he figured a jump would probably only land him in the hospital, and then he'd have to start this whole fucking terrible process over again.

"Come in," he said.

It wasn't Ethel Anne.

The kid who stepped into the room was definitely not here for move-in day. He was older, that was part of it, but Theo had been late to college himself—and even later to start grad school—so it wasn't the only factor that influenced his judgment. No, this kid didn't move like he was new to the school. He waited respectfully in the doorway, yes, but he didn't have the freshman timidity that made the kids buzz so fast they were almost hovering. Theo put the kid's age in the early twenties; the kid had unkempt hair and small, dark eyes.

"Hi," he said. "Dr. Stratford?"

Theo nodded but said, "Mr. Stratford. Actually, just Theo, if you're comfortable." Wheeling over Dawson's chair, Theo pointed to the seat. "What can I do for you?"

"Thanks. This is kind of awkward, but—" He produced a pink slip. "Is there any way?"

Taking the slip, Theo glanced at it. Robert Poulson, senior. Fall 2013. Civ 1: Shakespeare in the World. Theo raised his eyebrows. "It's already full?"

Robert's eyes shot down to his hands, which he clasped between his knees. "Uh, yeah. Guess so. Everybody registers in the spring."

"Yeah, but I've never had people lining up to take Shakespeare in the World."

Now Robert released his hands, and he scrubbed at his shorts. That was it. Nothing else. But somehow, Theo knew it had to do with the fucking accident. Everything in his life had something to do with that fucking accident now.

"Robert? Or Robbie?"

"Robert's fine."

"We're not supposed to add students. They cap the class sizes for a reason."

"Yeah, I know. I'm really sorry. I realized over the summer that I could graduate in December if I took this class, but then it was too late to register online, and when I called the secretaries, they told me I had to talk to you in person and get you to sign it."

Theo laid the pink slip on his desk.

"So, um," Robert said. "Mr. Stratford. I mean Theo. I'd really appreciate it."

"Sure," Theo said.

"Oh, man." Robert grinned and looked up. "Thank you."

"As soon as you tell me what they're saying about me."

"Mr. Stratford, I don't—"

"This is an easy deal. And I won't hold it against you."

Robert named one of the most popular rate-the-professor sites; he was scrubbing his shorts again.

"All right," Theo said, signing the slip and passing it back. "Have a great day."

"Thanks, Mr.—um, Theo." Robert paused in the doorway. "And, uh, I'm really sorry."

"Yeah. Thank you."

Theo logged on to the computer, navigated to the site Robert had mentioned, and found his profile. It had ratings for classes he'd taught before—as well as the highly sought-after fire emoji that meant he was hot—and a section for general comments. There it was, laid out in staggered time stamps from June and July.

—nearly died—

—boyfriend decapitated—

—husband, dummy, not boyfriend—

—little girl didn't make it—

—she did, actually, but she lost her legs, I think, or—

—just saying I had a class once where the professor killed himself and we all got A's—

—total bullshit, you stupid troll—

He closed the tab. His hand was sweaty against the mouse. His pulse beat in his fingertips. Then, for the first time since June, he opened his email.

Hundreds of unread messages waited for him.

He scrolled all the way down, opened it, and the words blurred together. He started typing the phrase he'd be using for the rest of his fucking life.

Thank you. That really means a lot.

4

Booze and pills didn't mix, Theo had learned, but since June, he had also learned that knowing something in his head had very little connection to the stupid shit he kept doing. But it had been a long week of prepping lectures, recycling slides, and digging himself every day out of the bullshit hole of sympathy only to find himself neck deep again the next. Long days of biking to campus at dawn, taking the bus to Downing, then hopping a second bus back to campus, and then biking home long after Liversedge emptied. Long days of trying to figure out what the hell he was doing. Plus, classes started on Monday, and that was a good reason to drink on a Saturday night. A good reason, but not the top of the list.

Theo was sitting in the kitchen of the little house he and Ian had bought west of campus, practically at the city limits. They'd had to stay inside the city for Ian's job—if you worked on the Wahredua police force, you'd better live in Wahredua—but Ian had been even more of a country boy than Theo. They'd found a spot in what Ian called the boonies, even though it was five minutes to a CVS and seven minutes to the Piggly Wiggly. It wasn't a trendy house. It wasn't old in a fashionable way—no mid-century design, no period craftsman detail. The tuckpointing needed work, the chimney was on its way down, and in May, Ian had stripped the floors and sanded them and now, of course, they were never going to get finished. Now when Theo walked around the house, he picked up wood dust on his socks, the cotton sticking occasionally where something—whatever Ian had used to strip the stain, maybe—left the boards tacky.

At the kitchen table—thirty-eight dollars at the flea market outside St. Elizabeth, chairs included, everything the color of Pepto-Bismol until Ian had refinished them—Theo swallowed a Percocet because his leg never really stopped hurting and then cracked open a can of Southside Blonde. They'd been in St. Louis, stopped at

Perennial, and picked up a few four-packs of the beer. Ian had wanted the IPA.

If history were a roadmap, Theo thought, you could see exactly where your life went off course. Exit 2 when you were supposed to take Exit 1. Left instead of right. Highway instead of surface streets. If history were a roadmap, you could take a pencil and trace a new route: jink back at the next intersection, cut up this alley, merge onto the ramp, and you're back on track.

For example, instead of telling Ian that you didn't have time to go back and pick up some four-packs of Hurry On Daylight, you shut your fucking mouth, let him take the McCausland exit, and flip around. Then you're not hitting I-270 at rush hour. Then you're not right in the path of that semi when it blows a tire, the trailer slews, and however many fucking tons of steel hit you like a slapshot.

He drank two of the Southside Blondes; his mouth tasted like sweet malt and lemon and hops, and it seemed like a good idea to be outside. What did he have inside? Inside was the unfinished floors, the flea-market table, Lana's plastic train that he stumbled over on the way to the door, and it flashed its red lights and made electronic chugging noises. Inside was a fucking tomb.

The September night was sticky and warm; they didn't have streetlights in the boonies, but the light pollution from Wahredua dissolved into a haze, particles overhead like huge grains of pollen drifting in the blackness. Theo made his way down the front steps, stumbled again, and fell. He was wearing a Blues t-shirt and mesh shorts; he scraped his knee on the cement walk. From inside the house, the train's cheery little song chased after him. He used the Malibu to get to his feet—the only thing the car, new in 2010 and with fewer than thirty thousand miles on it—was good for now that Theo refused to drive. As he limped down the street, he realized he'd forgotten his cane. By the end of the block, his hip would be screaming at him. Who cared, though? Let it scream.

When Theo got to the end of the street, his prediction was right: his hip was on fire, his whole leg ablaze. He stopped at the state highway, glanced left, glanced right. No headlights. He had this vision of hobbling out into traffic, lights, the blare of a horn. He knew, firsthand, the momentum behind a tractor-trailer. A lot of times out at the farm, they had to shovel up roadkill—deer occasionally, but more often raccoons or possums or skunks. Shovel was the right verb; usually, what was left was a mess of bones and flesh and organs, some of it already mashed into a paste. If you used a snow shovel, those had the best edge on the blade, you could get some of them in one go.

He turned and headed toward the city, toward Wroxall, toward the light. A pair of headlights appeared, racing toward him. He was on the right-hand shoulder, walking with traffic, and now he took a step up, toeing the white line on the asphalt. A second later, the truck blew past him, a wall of air rattling sticks and leaves across the highway, the receipt from a Conoco sticking to his sweaty calf. He kept going. He was on the white line now.

When the next pair of headlights came into view, he staggered a few steps to the left. He was winded now, out of shape after barely more than a month, his leg bitching like crazy. He was in the middle of the lane, his gait uneven. The sedan was lime green; the windows were down, and Kanye was pumping steadily out of the speakers. Somebody shouted, "Get off the road, asshole," and laughter chased the sedan into the night.

Theo trudged on. The world was underwater now; part of his brain knew that was from his homemade cocktail. Everything was undulating, flexible, pulsing closer and then retreating. Light, when it appeared on the horizon, shimmered. Two lights. Headlights, the edges of the beams marked by iridescent cones. The thrum of the wheels transferred through the asphalt and vibrated in Theo's ankles.

He closed his eyes and leaned left.

Brakes screeched. A horn blared. The sound of tires fusing to pavement came with the hot stink of burning rubber, and then there was a loud crash. Theo hadn't felt anything; part of his brain informed him that was shock. He wasn't ever going to feel anything again. He could just drift away on that underwater current.

But he didn't drift away.

He took a deep breath of burning rubber, now laced with exhaust and the hot, humid greenness of the trees.

A door opened.

"Jesus fucking Christ," a voice said. "What the fuck were you doing?"

It took Theo a moment to realize someone was talking to him.

Footsteps came closer, and Theo opened his eyes. The kid coming toward him wasn't cute or hot or attractive or pretty. He was stunning. Gorgeous. And Theo felt shitty even through the Percocet and the beer for thinking something like that. Dark hair in a crew cut, lean and toned, soft brown eyes; it was hard to tell in the darkness if the kid was really tan or had light brown skin. Whatever it was, it was perfect on him.

Then Theo's eyes moved past him, to the Porsche 911 that had skidded to a halt in the drainage ditch. Another kid was climbing out, holding his head, and things started to become real again. Theo recognized the second kid as Robert Poulson, who had come to his office earlier that week.

Then he saw the wreck, and in his mind, he was back on I-270, trapped in the car, Ian's blood all over him.

Some asshole driving too fast.

Theo charged the driver. He was vaguely aware of his leg pinging, a hot electricity that made him sick, but he was so furious he didn't register it completely.

"You stupid son of a bitch," the driver was saying. "You could have—"

Theo punched him. "What the fuck were you doing?" Theo swung again, and the kid stumbled back and went down on his ass. "Driving like a fucking maniac, what the fuck do you think you were doing?" He punched again, but this time the kid pulled back, and Theo just grazed him. "People live out here." Theo could hear himself screaming. He could hear the sobs stitching his words together. "Kids live out here."

"Hey," Robert shouted, and he tackled Theo, forcing him away from the driver. Theo and Robert went down, rolling together on the highway. Robert was a surprisingly good grappler, and he got Theo pinned in a matter of moments. Broken pavement bit into Theo's cheek; the cement was still hot from the September day. He could taste motor oil on each ragged breath.

Sirens broke the stillness.

"Shit," Robert said, releasing Theo. He jogged to the edge of the road and glanced back. "Dude, come on."

The driver sat twenty yards down, near the Porsche, pressing the back of his hand to a bloody lip. He'd only moved far enough to grab a pack of smokes that had fallen out during the scuffle. After a moment, the driver just shook his head at Robert's words; he was staring at Theo.

Robert waited a moment and then ran off into the scrub.

When the patrol car stopped, Theo was sitting on the gravel shoulder, massaging his bad leg. Theo studied the cruiser, hoping he'd get lucky this time, although he thought he'd stretched his luck pretty thin already. He recognized Peterson, the only black man on the force, getting out of the driver's seat. And then he saw Peterson's partner for the evening and groaned, dropping his chin to his chest.

Howie Cartwright had been Ian's best friend on the force. His boots crunched on the gravel. He dropped into a squat, shaking his head as he looked at Theo. And then he said, "For the love of God, Theo. What would Ian say about all this shit?"

5

Auggie got to class early because it was the first day, and no matter how he played it cool in snaps and posts, he had a minor case of nerves. Civ 1: Shakespeare in the World was a GE, and from the reviews Auggie had read about the instructor, it would likely be an easy A—either the guy would blow his brains out, or he'd have some sort of mental breakdown, and another professor would come in and give them all full points because he didn't know what to do.

His first class was in Tether-Marfitt, which from the outside made him think of Notre Dame with its flying buttresses and elaborate stonework and stained-glass windows. One of Mom's boyfriends—Perry? Terry? Larry?—had flown them to Paris for a weekend, and the bozo had given Fer a wad of cash and told him to keep Chuy and Auggie busy—and away from the hotel. They'd walked around a lot. Fer had been pretty free with the money, probably because it wasn't his, buying Chuy eclairs and splitting a bottle of wine with them. They'd seen Notre Dame, just the outside. When they'd gotten back to the hotel late that night, the bozo had told them their mom wasn't feeling well, and they hadn't seen her until the flight home.

On the inside, Tether-Marfitt still had stonework and dark wood and brass finishings that were worn and softly glowing, but it also had a student newspaper rack and a payphone and those industrial all-weather mats near the front door. The classroom, when Auggie found it, was just an ordinary room, not the grand lecture hall he'd imagined. It had high-traffic carpeting, tablet-arm seats, and it smelled faintly like curry. Auggie glanced at the blackboard, which was covered in curling script about the history of jazz, and took a seat in the back.

His phone buzzed, and he passed the minutes before class posting a selfie, his face exaggeratedly serious and thoughtful, making sure to capture the desk in the background. Responses popped up almost immediately—*oh my god, ur face! what happened?*—but he ignored them for the moment. He scrolled through his feed. Lots of congratulations from the bid party at Sigma Sigma—*you deserve it, honey,* and *oh my god, ur so perfect,* and, *they are lucky to have u i love u,* and on and on like that. A lot of new followers, too, which was great. And thinking about followers made him pull up his list. He wanted to find Robert and block him. Unfortunately, a lot of people didn't use their real names, and based on a quick scan, he didn't see which one might belong to the asshole who had almost gotten Auggie arrested on Saturday night.

It could have gone so much worse. If Auggie hadn't been just sober enough to lie. If the asshole in the middle of the road hadn't, for some reason, backed up Auggie's story that Robert, who had run off, had been driving. If Auggie hadn't been quick enough to explain that Robert had said the car belonged to him.

The drunken haze of the night made it hard for Auggie fully to trace his thinking. He remembered the surge of pleasure at Orlando complimenting him, the prickling heat in his gut that told him something was happening between them, and then the disappointment when Orlando vanished. He remembered wanting to fuck things up after a week of pretending to be someone else—after a week of rush, trying to be the human equivalent of a cardboard cutout. And of course, for Auggie, fucking things up always involved a car.

He remembered Robert suggesting stealing a car, and Robert coming back from the Sigma Sigma house with a pair of keys. Auggie had been driving like a total dick, determined to mess things up somehow. He'd spotted the asshole on the road at the last minute, swerved, and crashed in the drainage ditch. The asshole had hit him a few times and left him on the ground. And then—this was the part where things got messy—Auggie had realized he didn't want to keep fucking up his life.

Maybe those punches had knocked something straight in his head. Maybe it was the very real possibility of having to face his mom so soon again. Maybe—this felt the strongest, plucking a chord deep in Auggie's gut—maybe it had been the genuine terror in the asshole's voice, the realization that Auggie had scared him past reason, maybe even past sanity. Whatever the reason, Auggie, drunk and hurting, had wanted not to be himself anymore. He had wanted something new. So when the cops asked him about the car, he had lied, instead of embracing the shit show he had gone looking for. And for some reason, the asshole had backed him.

Sober, on a Monday, he could explain to himself that he was starting fresh, that he was done with that kind of stuff, that he was finished with what his mother called *making a scene*. He just needed to watch the tequila. Even the stuff with Orlando had been a one-off mistake; Orlando had been out of the dorm most of Sunday, and the few times they had crossed paths, he was polite and distant, so Auggie must have imagined whatever had happened at the Sigma Sigma house.

Today, moving forward, no more mess ups. Auggie was on track again. He had a chance to fix everything. A year here, and he could go wherever he wanted. He'd have the money he needed. He'd have the life he wanted. No stupid stuff with cars. No stupid stuff with . . . well, with anyone.

Students were making their way into the class, navigating the competing demands for personal space while still fitting everyone into the room. Auggie got one more picture, this time of his hand holding a pen above a page where he'd written *Notes on Being A Genius*, tagged himself, and posted it.

Another phone dinged in the room. Auggie looked up; a girl with pigtails was checking her phone, and then she glanced around, locked eyes with Auggie, and stared. He smiled and gave a small wave. Her face turned bright pink, and she jumped back on the phone and started typing like mad.

A comment showed up on his *Notes on Being A Genius* post: *oh my god it's u.*

Auggie sent a thumbs up, and then he sent the emoji with nerdy glasses.

The girl giggled, looked at him, and went back to the phone.

oh my god, the next comment said. *i'm in the same class as @aplolz.*

Comments poured in—expressions of envy from other followers, a show of excitement, and demands for details. By the time Auggie noticed that the class had gotten quiet, the professor was already at the board, writing his name and email.

The guy looked distractingly cute from behind. Great ass filling out chinos, nice shoulders, the sleeves of his gingham shirt rolled up to hint at some quality biceps. He had a bro flow of strawberry blond hair, the strands tucked behind his ears, and Auggie could see in profile the thick beard.

An alarm bell started inside him.

"I'm Mr. Stratford," the man was saying as he wrote. "You can call me Theo; that's what I prefer. Here's my email, and if you need—"

As the professor turned around, Auggie said, "Oh, shit."

The other students had already been silent. Now, Auggie didn't think anyone was even breathing.

It was the asshole. The asshole who Auggie had almost hit with the car.

Mr. Stratford—Theo—was staring back at Auggie. Then he crooked a finger and stepped out into the hall. Auggie wormed out of his seat, stumbled over his backpack, and made his way to the door. He heard the shutter sound of a camera app, and when he glanced back, Pigtails was blushing even harder and trying not to look at him.

When he got into the hall, Theo shut the door. The professor crossed his arms. Auggie's first impression had been right: really nice arms. His eyes moved up: the thick beard, the prominent cheekbones, the bro flow of strawberry blond with just the tiniest wave to it.

"Get your stuff," Theo said. "You're dropping this class."

It wasn't just the words. It wasn't just the tone, clipped and assured. It wasn't just the fact that this guy belonged in the same age bracket that Gabby Lopez drew all her new boyfriends and husbands from.

"Nah," Auggie said, reaching for the door. "I don't think so."

"There's nothing to think about." Theo planted a hand on the door. "There's a conflict here; we have a previous relationship. You need to be in another class. I'll transfer you out myself if I have to."

"Conflict?" Auggie said, tugging on the door. He couldn't even budge it. "What conflict?"

"Grab your backpack and go. Add/drop runs through the third week. You have plenty of time to find another class."

"Oh, conflict. You're probably talking about this." Auggie touched his split lip. "And this." The bruises near his hairline. "And the fact that you were walking in the middle of the road and just about got me killed."

"You were driving a stolen car."

Auggie raised his chin.

"You were drunk," Theo said.

"So were you. I wonder what your supervisor or administrator or whatever they're called will think when I tell them about how I almost hit you because you were trashed in the middle of the road. And then you attacked me. Do they keep guys like that on faculty here? It'd make a great news story."

"Wow," Theo said. "I felt bad for you. Bad about what happened. I lied to the police for you so you wouldn't get your ass hauled off to jail. And now you show up here and you're going to blackmail me?"

"I'm not—"

"Fuck. You. Go tell your fucking story to whoever you fucking want."

"I'm not trying to blackmail you," Auggie said, his chest tingling, and then the tingle moving up into his neck, into his face. "Ok, I guess—I didn't—I just want to stay in the class, ok? I've got my whole schedule the way I want it. I'll earn my grade. I won't say anything about the other night."

"You're making a mistake. You'll do better in another class, with an instructor where there isn't a . . . history."

Auggie met his eyes and waited.

"Fine," Theo said, dropping his hand from the door. "For your information, this is one of the many reasons I hate freshmen: you think the whole world revolves around you."

Auggie shrugged, opened the door, and slipped into the classroom. The other students were still silent and watching, all except Pigtails, who was tapping like mad on her phone.

"No phones," Theo snapped as he took his place at the front of the room. He grabbed a stack of papers and began handing them out while Pigtails shoved her phone in her bag. When Theo reached Auggie, he didn't even look at him, just thrust the packet in his direction and kept moving.

After handing out the syllabus, Theo stood at the front of the room and read through it. All of it. After about a minute, Auggie's eyes were drooping; the adrenaline from confronting Theo was dripping out of him, and the morning class meant he'd been up way earlier than he wanted. He was fighting to keep his head off the desk when his phone buzzed in his pocket.

It was loud enough in the quiet room that Theo paused in his reading and glanced up, locking eyes with Auggie.

"Sorry," Auggie whispered.

But his phone buzzed again. And then again. And then again.

Theo lowered the pages, resting them against one muscled thigh.

"I'll turn it off," Auggie said.

"Please."

Auggie fumbled with the phone and saw that someone he didn't recognize had tagged him in a post. It was getting comments. A lot of comments.

"Mr.—" Theo paused. "What's your name?"

Auggie opened the app and saw a video he'd been tagged in. A flutter of dread ran through his stomach. Was it something from the Bid-ness Party? Him doing shots? Him and Orlando? Christ, anything like that could have major fallout for his internet persona.

Could it be something with the car and Theo? Nobody could have seen that, right?

"Auggie Lopez," Pigtail offered. Auggie looked up long enough to give her the snake eye, and she blushed again.

"Auggie," Theo said, moving down the aisle now. "No phones in the classroom. Do you understand me?"

"Yes, yeah, I'm putting it away."

The video had finally loaded, and now it played. Auggie stared, not quite believing what he was seeing in the montage: first, a wobbly shot of him behind the wheel of the stolen car from Saturday, obviously drunk, screaming, "I fucking hate you," at the windshield; then a cut to another clip, with Auggie and Theo standing close together on the road, Theo shouting something indistinguishable on the video; and then a third clip that showed someone being dragged by the arms, a bag over his head, and strangled cry of, "Help!" The final part of the video was just white text on a black background: *you just saw a murder.*

Auggie was tagged in the comments with his business account, @aplolz. The poster had also tagged @theouponavon, which Augge guessed was Theo Stratford. The post had been made by wroxall_deepthroat. It was the only post from that account.

The comment feed was exploding.

"No phones," Theo said, taking the phone from Auggie, locking the screen, and putting it in his pocket. "You can have it back at the end of class."

He held Auggie's gaze; Auggie stared back, barely seeing him.

you just saw a murder

"As I was saying about revisions," Theo continued, moving back to the desk at the front of the room.

Auggie didn't hear anything for the rest of the fifty minutes. When it was over, he took his phone and stumbled out of the room. He thought he should talk to Theo, try to figure out what the hell was going on, but he knew it didn't matter. The video had already been posted. All he could do now was damage control.

6

Theo got home to find Howie Cartwright on the steps.

"Risers are rotted out," Cart said. He was out of uniform, wearing athletic shorts and a Budweiser t-shirt with the frogs from that one commercial. With his heel, he tapped the steps. "These things are going to go, and they're going to go bad."

"I'll get around to them."

"You could break your neck."

Taking out his keys, Theo moved past Cart and unlocked the front door. He turned on the window unit, and wisps of lukewarm air stirred the dense, sticky heat of the closed-up house. Cart had followed him in uninvited, and now Cart came after him into the kitchen, where Theo ditched his satchel and helmet. He opened the refrigerator, took out the last two Southside Blondes, opened one for himself and held out the other for Cart. Cart took it but just held it. He was one of those skinny country boys who stayed skinny forever, kind of like Ian. His hair was perpetually buzzed at a zero, and when he wiped the can with his shirt, he had those crazy, skinny-boy abs with a dusting of dark brown hair.

"How are you?" Theo asked. He glanced at the clock; half-past seven. "You eat?"

"I ate."

"You mind if I grab something?"

"It's your house, Theo."

So Theo got the loaf of bread from the refrigerator, pasted two slices together with peanut butter, and took a bite. It immediately stuck to the roof of his mouth, which was the sign of a good peanut butter sandwich.

"Did you use the whole jar?" Cart said.

Theo shrugged and took another bite. He washed it down—most of it, anyway—with the Blonde.

"That's about an inch of peanut butter," Cart said.

"What do you want, Cart?"

"Not a peanut butter sandwich, thanks. I like a really thin layer. I like grape jelly, too. Concord, if you have it."

Theo finished the rest of the sandwich, and Cart didn't say anything else. He rinsed the plate in the sink, stuck the knife and bread in the refrigerator, and brushed the loose crumbs on the counter into the trash can.

"Jesus," Cart said, still staring at the refrigerator.

"I'm going to use the knife again," Theo said.

Cart just sighed, popping open the Blonde and settling into a seat at the table.

"You want to talk about last night," Theo said.

Cart sipped the beer, made a face, and took another sip.

"I was just out for a walk," Theo said.

"This is some girly beer, you know."

"So that's it, ok? Just a walk."

"Great."

"Is that all? It was a long day. A . . . a fucking weird day, actually, right from the first class. And I want to go to bed."

"Sit down."

"Cart, whatever this is, can we do it another time?"

"Sit your ass down."

Theo took a long pull, killed the Blonde, and crumpled it. He tossed it in the trash. When Cart still hadn't moved or said anything, Theo sat at the table.

"If this is about Ian—"

"You want to tell me about this?" Cart said. He took out his phone, tapped something, and handed it to Theo.

A video played on the screen: the boy from class, Auggie, behind the wheel of a car screaming, "I fucking hate you," and then Theo and Auggie arguing in the street, and then someone being dragged off, shouting for help, and then white words on a black background: *you just saw a murder.*

"What is this?" Theo said.

"That's what I'd like to know."

The old house creaked; a fat drop of water hanging from the tap finally fell and splatted in the sink. In the front room, the window unit chugged, trying desperately to stir the air.

"You're kidding me, right? You think I killed someone?"

"Don't be stupid," Cart said. "But I want to know what this is about."

"I don't know."

"I think you know something."

"I don't know, Cart. Jesus."

"Ok," Cart said. "Let's pretend I didn't pick you up for public intoxication on Saturday night. Let's pretend you didn't lie to my fucking face about that kid driving the car. Let's pretend none of that happened. Why the fuck did someone post this video and say that you murdered someone?"

"They didn't say I murdered someone. They said—"

"I know what they fucking said," Cart shouted, slapping the table. "Don't fucking play that game with me. The person who posted this tagged two people: that dumbass kid and you. Why?"

"I don't know," Theo said. "I don't even know that kid. That was the first time I saw him, and I'd only seen the other boy once before, and—"

He heard the admission before he could call it back.

"Ian would be fucking humiliated right now," Cart said quietly. "Any other lies you want to get off your chest?"

Theo dropped his gaze to the table.

"You knew the other kid? The one you claimed was the driver?"

"He came to my office. He was supposed to be in my class." Theo shook his head. "He didn't even show up, so I figured he'd changed his mind after Saturday."

"And you didn't think this was important?"

"I didn't even know about the video. I have this," Theo said, dragging out the flip phone he kept in his satchel. "Ian made those stupid social media accounts so he could tag me in things. I've never even used them. Look, the kid, the driver. He just looked so messed up. It made me think about Luke, all the times I had to pull him out of the same kind of trouble, and I just . . . did something stupid. I know I shouldn't have lied for him. I know it was stupid."

For a moment, it looked like Cart wanted to keep fighting. Then, blowing out a breath, he sat back and took another pull of the Blonde. He said, "So you don't know anything about this?"

"I don't know anything about anything. I was out for a walk. That kid almost hit me. The end."

Cart shook his head. "You're not lying to me again?"

"I swear to God."

"This is weird, Theo."

"Am I . . . I don't know, should I get a lawyer or something?"

"For this? Come on, Theo. I'm pissed because you lied to me, but this is just somebody dicking around. Some weirdo edited together a few clips and posted an ominous message. It's not a serious accusation. It's just weird." Then Cart blushed, a trace of red in his cheeks. "I follow you, so I get alerts whenever anyone tags you. I saw it, and I got worried."

"Why would someone do something like this?"

Cart shrugged. "Maybe it's just some shithead trying to stir the pot. Maybe it's a kid who doesn't like you. Was there a third person in the car? Who could have filmed you fighting with that kid?"

"I don't know. I didn't see anyone else."

"What was the name of the one who was supposed to add your class?"

"Do you think he's dead?"

"Calm down, Miss Marple. What was his name?"

Theo dug through the satchel, found his roster, and saw the name scrawled in blue ink at the bottom. "I forgot—he didn't show up on the printed one, so I had to write his name here."

"Is that important?"

With a shrug, Theo said, "Maybe he had changed his mind and already dropped the class."

"It's probably nothing, but it's weird. I want to check it out."

Theo passed over the roster, and Cart folded and pocketed it. Then he sat there, staring at Theo, his thumb chasing condensation around the rim of the Blonde.

"I don't want to get a call to scrape you off the road," Cart said.

Face heating, Theo focused on the wall behind Cart. "I told you: it was just a walk. I had a couple of beers and stumbled."

Cart let a moment pass and then another. Then he stood and said, "No more late walks, Theo. No more drinking alone. No more mixing shit with your pills. No more stumbling. No more, ok? You find yourself suddenly needing to go for a walk, you find yourself swimming in Bud Lite, you find yourself wobbly and liable to have another accident, you call me. Understand?"

Theo raised both hands.

Cart grunted and tossed his can in the trash.

As Theo walked Cart to the door, he said, "You're sure I don't need to worry about that video?"

"Did you kill someone?"

"Not yet, but it's only the first day of classes."

"Then I think you're ok." Cart stepped out onto the porch. "But I'll look into it anyway."

"Cart, uh. Thanks. I know Ian would really appreciate this. He liked being your partner. He liked you. I know this would mean a lot to him."

Cart ran one hand back and forth over the stubble on his scalp. Then, his eyes locked on Theo's, he said, "I'm not doing it for Ian, dumbass."

7

Damage control for the murder video—as Auggie was now thinking of it—had been surprisingly effective. wroxall_deepthroat hadn't made any additional posts or comments. Auggie had apologized to his followers for the bad language, explained that it was an early cut that someone had leaked, and spun a story about a Halloween video he was already working on. Reactions ranged from mild reprimands—nobody liked internet Auggie to have a foul mouth—to frustration on his behalf that someone had leaked an early video.

As soon as the damage to internet Auggie had been contained, Auggie pushed the video from his mind. He didn't like thinking about what it meant. He didn't like thinking that someone had been filming him. He didn't like thinking about the words at the end: *you just saw a murder.* So he did what he did when his mom and Fer fought, or when his mom and her flavor of the week fought, or when his mom came home wasted, or when his mom came home with a Tinder hookup. He went online.

On Instagram, Auggie's feud with Chan was heating up. His ex-girlfriend had been a total bitch ever since she had broken up with him at graduation, but until this morning, she'd limited herself to nasty texts. Now his phone was blowing up with notifications, and it didn't take him long to find out why: Chan had reposted the video of the so-called murder, and she had tagged him again and added a single comment below: *bad boyfriend. psycho. murderer. bye bye.*

After that, shit got real.

Internet Auggie didn't get involved in trolling or flame wars. He let his followers do that. Instead of responding to Chan, he cleared a spot near the window, got a picture of himself looking out at campus, his face sad, and the caption: *u can love someone, and somehow they still keep hurting u. no h8.*

Chan lost her mind.

Auggie, now on the bed, squirmed to find a more comfortable spot against the pile of pillows. It was late Friday morning, the end of the first week of classes, and Shakespeare in the World had been canceled today. Orlando had left already, which meant Auggie had a few solid hours by himself to watch that bitch get eviscerated on social media. Messages kept rolling in on his own post:

ur perfect, don't listen to that cunt

ur so sweeeeeeeet

i luv u A, don't ever change

He scrolled through the messages a few times; he felt loose, relaxed, a hot pool of satisfaction in his belly. On his laptop, he pulled up an episode of *Community*, the one with the trampoline, and he half watched while keeping an eye on the shitstorm. Chan was going berserk, and Auggie's followers were coming back at her even harder. He wished he had popcorn.

The knock at the door startled him.

A couple of the guys on the floor had come by for autographs, and a lot more of the girls on the floor above. Auggie paused the video, arranged his face in an expression of sadness, and opened the door.

The guy standing in the hall was ancient. He had to be in his fifties at least, and he was short and squirrelly, wearing a summer suit shiny at the cuffs and knees. Two features dominated his face: an enormous gray mustache, and equally enormous glasses in yellow plastic frames.

"Yeah?" Auggie said.

The blow wasn't a punch. It was a slap, but the combination of physical violence and surprise made Auggie stumble back. The man followed him into the room, kicking the door shut and setting the lock, and then he kept coming, hitting Auggie again, another slap, and then another, and then he knocked the phone out of Auggie's hand.

Auggie shouted something, he didn't know what, and took a swing.

The guy stepped back, pulled back his jacket, and put his hand on a gun.

"Think really carefully about what happens next, kid."

Breathing hard, Auggie tried to process. His brain kept skipping, though, and all he could input was the flurry of blows, his phone, the gun.

"Sit down," the man said.

"Who the fuck are you?"

"Sit down, or I'll break your nose."

Auggie's eyes were locked on the gun. The guy's hand was steady on it. He looked really comfortable with that gun. After another heartbeat, Auggie sat.

"See? We're already off to a great start. Don't ruin it." The man bent and grabbed Auggie's phone; Instagram was still open, and he scrolled through the feed, one eye still on Auggie. "Hey, look at all these likes. I get five likes, tops. I post a picture of a hamburger, my mom likes it, that's about it. How'd you get so good?"

Auggie's cheek was starting to sting; he touched his face, checked his fingers, and saw no blood. "What do you want? I don't have any money. My laptop's right there, and you've already got my phone."

"I want Robert," the guy said. He waggled the phone at Auggie. "You know, your buddy from Saturday."

Auggie stared for what felt like a full minute. "What?"

"Where's Robert?"

"I don't know what you're—"

The guy, whom Auggie had started to think of as Glasses, tossed the phone on the bed, and Auggie reached for it. That was a mistake. As soon as he shifted his position, Glasses moved in, grabbed Auggie's shirt, and punched him once, hard, in the mouth. It wasn't a slap like earlier; it wasn't even like the angry, wild punches from Theo on Saturday. This was meant to deliver maximum impact and cause maximum damage. Auggie's head rocked back, the crown clipping the cement blocks behind him. Blood washed his teeth, his tongue, filling his mouth.

"That was the turning point," Glasses said. He was breathing harder now. "Did you feel it?"

Auggie swallowed blood. His hand crept across the mattress toward the phone.

"You are goddamn determined to do something stupid, aren't you?" Glasses said. "Where's Robert? The next time, it won't be my hand. You ever been pistol whipped? It does a lot more damage."

"I don't know him. We met at that stupid party, and I was drunk, and we took that car. That's it. When I wrecked the car, he ran off." The car, Auggie thought. This had to be about the car. That was the only thing that made sense. "Look, I'm sorry. I'm sorry about the car. I'll figure out a way to pay you back, I swear to God. He told me it was his car. That's what he told me. He said it was his. I swear."

Glasses reached for his gun.

"Jesus Christ," Auggie shouted, trying to pry Glasses's hand off him. "I'm telling you the truth. I don't know him. I don't know anything about him."

"They can do pretty good things with knees these days," Glasses said, drawing the pistol, settling the muzzle against Auggie's kneecap. "Replacements, I mean. Pretty amazing stuff. You'll definitely walk again. You'll probably walk without a cane. But you're not going to be playing frisbee on the quad, you know."

"Please!" Auggie didn't even recognize his own voice. "I'm trying to tell you, I'm trying."

"The video," Glasses said.

"The video," Auggie repeated.

"The fucking video with Robert getting dragged off. Talk about that."

Auggie blinked. "That was . . . that was Robert?"

"Fuck this," Glasses said.

"No, I swear to God, I don't know. I don't even know who filmed it. I thought it was just a prank. I thought it was a bad joke. Oh, shit. Shit, man. Please do not do this."

For a moment, Glasses's expression was blank. Auggie's panic had a kind of wild clarity to it. This guy looked like an accountant or a mortgage broker. He looked like he pushed pencils for a living. But the muzzle of the pistol was cold and heavy and real on Auggie's knee.

"I can find him," Auggie said. "I can find Robert. Or I can find who posted that video, I mean, and you can . . . you can ask them what happened to Robert. That's the only thing that makes sense, you know? That's the only thing you can do. You can talk to them, I can find them, and you can talk to them, and you—"

"Shut up."

Auggie shut up. Sweat ran down his back. His head was starting to ache where he'd hit the wall, and the punch had reopened the split lip Theo had given him. Blood was cooling on his chin.

"August," Glasses said, holstering the pistol. "I'm going to be honest. You seem like one dumb shit. I don't think you can do this. But I'm going to give you a chance. How's that sound?"

"Thank you. Yes. I will find him. Thank you so much."

"I want to make sure you understand something, August. Are you listening to me?"

Auggie nodded. The taste of blood was making him sick now; he was worried he might puke.

"August, if you go to the police about this, I will find you, and I will kill you. Do you understand what I just said?"

Auggie nodded.

"Say it."

"I understand."

"What am I going to do if you go to the police?"

"You're going to kill me."

"Do you believe me?"

Auggie couldn't help it; tears burned the corners of his eyes.

"Say it," Glasses said.

"I believe you."

"Good. I'm going to leave now. And you're probably going to start having some crazy ideas. You're going to think that the police can keep you safe, or you can run away, or you can ask your family to bail you out, or something really stupid. When that happens, I need you to remember something: I walked right in here without anybody looking at me twice, and I could have killed you and walked away, and nobody would have said boo. I'll check in with you soon. Please be smart about this, August." Glasses suddenly smiled, exposing yellowing, uneven teeth. "You've got a bright future ahead of you."

Then he left, shutting the door behind him.

As soon as the door clicked shut, Auggie grabbed the phone. Then he stared at it. He opened the phone app. He closed it. He opened Facebook. He closed it. He opened Twitter, Instagram, Snapchat. A hundred thousand followers, and nobody he could ask for help.

For a moment, he considered his family. He thought about Fer, who would be busy with work. He thought about Chuy, who would be busy with whatever fuckup he'd gotten himself into now. He thought about his mom, who was on a cruise with Nicholas, the current boyfriend. He could already hear her, hear the mixture of disappointment and exhaustion, as she explained that her youngest was *making a scene* again.

It was laughable, unbelievably ridiculous, because he knew he should call them. He knew whatever he was involved in, it was worse than anything he'd gotten into before. But he kept hearing Glasses say *or ask your family to bail you out*, and he pictured Fer, the butt of the pistol cracking across his face.

Auggie staggered into the bathroom. He made sure the door to the other suite was locked, and then he washed his face and rinsed out his mouth, spitting pink water into the basin, where it swirled away into the drain. His eyes stung worse and worse, and then he was sobbing, bent over the sink, his whole body shaking as he tried to be quiet, tried to calm himself down. Bits and pieces of it kept coming back: the humiliating slaps that had driven him across the room, the sudden powerlessness as he was forced onto the bed, the fist cracking against his teeth, the cold steel of the gun against his skin.

"Holy shit," Orlando said from the doorway. "What happened to you?"

Auggie shut the water off, grabbed his towel, and pushed past Orlando, drying his face as he went.

"Hey," Orlando said, his thick brows drawn together as he caught Auggie's shoulder. "Who the fuck did this?"

"I gotta go," Auggie said, trying to twist away.

"Like hell. Tell me who did this. I'm going to murder the son of a bitch."

"Get the fuck off me," Auggie shouted, slapping Orlando's hand away.

He plunged out into the hallway. Brad, from two doors down, was standing in his doorway staring. Auggie ignored him and rushed for the stairs, but he could hear Orlando coming after him, the murmur of low voices. Great, Auggie thought. Perfect. They'd all heard him shouting at Orlando, but nobody had heard a fucking peep when Glasses had been threatening to kneecap him.

When Auggie got outside, he was so wrapped up in himself that he didn't hear the voices until he'd covered almost twenty yards of the quad.

"Hey, kid, I said hold the fuck up."

Auggie glanced over his shoulder. A man and woman were coming after him. The man was huge, his head shaved, a Celtic cross tattoo taking up most of one forearm. The woman was tall and thin, bleached hair in a ponytail, a swastika tattoo on her cheek.

"Yeah, you," the woman shouted. "We want to talk to you."

Auggie turned and ran.

8

The bus getting to Downing had been late. Then the bus coming back had been late too. Then Theo had gotten distracted by *Astrophil and Stella* and missed his stop, and he'd gotten off half a mile north of campus. He'd had to walk the half mile because there wasn't a bus that would take him back—not for another half hour, anyway. The September day was hot; his clothes were soaked with sweat by the time he reached Liversedge Hall, and he could already feel the beginning of a sunburn. Worse, the bus had smelled like BO and fire-lime Takis, and now the smell clung to Theo as he limped onto the elevator and wiped sweat from his face. A moment later, one of the Philosophy Department secretaries got into the car—prissy, gangly Solomon, who looked around the car and wrinkled his nose. When they got to the third floor, Theo limped off the elevator; he heard Solomon say, "Absolutely disgusting" as the doors closed.

Theo considered calling the elevator back. He could ride up to the Philosophy offices. He could find Solomon, who kept a row of faux Art Deco figurines on his desk, all of them vaguely resembling Cher. He could smash those little ceramic Chers one by one. And if Solomon made a fucking peep, Theo could shove the Chers down his fucking throat.

Instead, he decided on his second-best option for dealing with a shitty day: reading poetry.

After the half-mile walk, Theo needed the cane more than usual as he made his way down the hall to his office. Light shone behind the pebbled glass, and he braced himself for Grace, for the questions, for the concern, for the long, lingering looks of sympathy. When he opened the door, the fragrance of microwaved masala met him, and a plastic TV tray steamed in front of Grace's computer, but Grace was miraculously absent. Dawson's desk and computer still looked like they hadn't been touched this year; Theo figured that Dawson was on track to finish the PhD sometime in 2030 at this rate.

Settling himself at the desk, Theo had just propped his cane against the wall and stretched out his aching leg when someone hammered on the door.

"Go away," Theo shouted. "This is not office hours."

The door flew open, and Auggie Lopez tumbled into the room. He looked around, his dark eyes wide, and then he shut the door and leaned against it.

"Please," Auggie said. "Please tell them I'm not here."

"What? Who?" Theo struggled to get to his feet, but his leg was starting to stiffen. He grabbed the cane. "What's going on?"

"Please," Auggie whispered.

The door thumped as someone tried to force it open.

"Hey," Theo said. "What the hell is going on out there?" He limped toward Auggie, pushed him into the corner behind the door, and threw open the door.

A big guy with a buzzed head stumbled, off balance without the resistance of the door. Next to him, a blond woman with a swastika on her cheek had one hand behind her back. Theo had been married to a cop. He'd grown up in a rough part of a rough county. He'd worked the first five years after high school logging, and loggers—the guys he'd worked with, anyway—were some of the biggest assholes in the world. He knew when a fight was a fight, and he knew when a fight was something else. This was something else.

"I've had a really bad morning," Theo said. "So get out of here, right now, before I take it out on you."

The big guy recovered his balance. "Out of the way, teacher." He put a big paw on Theo's shoulder, already shoving forward. "We've got business with that little bitch."

"Get out of my office," Theo said, fetching up against Grace's desk. Masala slopped out of the TV tray, spattering his hands, the superheated sauce burning him. Theo felt it at a remove; his blood was up. He kept his eyes straight ahead, so as not to draw attention to Auggie, hidden behind the door now.

"Where is that little pussy?" the man asked. "Auggie, where the fuck is Robert?"

"How many lines does a sonnet have?" Theo asked, pushing up from the desk.

"What the fuck are you—"

Theo headbutted him. The key to a good headbutt was to use the solid bone of the forehead as the point of impact. Theo had been in a lot of bar fights. Theo had an asshole younger brother who had dragged him into a few more serious scrapes. And Theo had lived and worked with guys who carried knives and didn't think twice about using them. For Theo, the only good fight was the one that ended absolutely as quickly as possible. A headbutt was a really good way of doing that.

The big guy was still turning, drawn by the strangeness of the question, when Theo connected. Theo felt the bridge of the man's nose crumple. The man screamed and went down; he had his hands over his nose, and he was kicking, his legs catching in Grace's chair as he pinwheeled on the ground.

"You're dead," the blond woman screamed. Her hand came out from behind her back, and she charged into the office with a gun.

"Now," Theo shouted.

Auggie barreled into the door, and it caught the woman completely by surprise. She crashed up against the doorframe, pinned between the jamb and the door. Theo swung the cane as hard as he could. It connected with her hand, and the woman shrieked. She dropped the gun. Auggie was still bearing down on the door, which was real wood, heavy and solid, and Theo swung the cane again and caught the woman across the face. She screamed again. Somehow, she slipped free of the door and back into the hallway. Auggie stumbled over the big guy and grabbed the gun. The dark-haired kid was panting, his hands shaking as he dragged the door open and pointed the weapon at the woman.

"Ok," Theo said, his voice sounding distant over the rush of blood in his ears, and he touched Auggie's shoulder. The kid flinched. "Don't do anything stupid."

It wasn't just Auggie's hands that were trembling; the kid was shaking all over.

"Auggie," Theo said quietly. "Get your finger off the trigger, please."

The whoosh of Theo's heartbeat made it hard to hear; he felt like they were in a vacuum, just the two of them, and nothing he was saying was reaching Auggie. Theo let his fingers slide down Auggie's arm, bump over his wrist, and wrap around his hand. Then he freed the gun from Auggie's grip.

"That's good, Auggie. You did really good."

The woman had stopped screaming, and now she crouched on the floor. One hand was over her face, covering where Theo had struck her with the cane. The other hand hung at her side; several fingers were obviously broken. On the floor of the office, the big guy had stopped pinwheeling, but he still had both hands over his broken nose, and blood streamed between his fingers.

"I'm calling security," Theo told the woman.

She stared at him for a moment. Then she stood. "Jerome," she said. "Jerome, get your fucking ass off the fucking floor. Right now, Jerome."

Somehow, the big man got to his knees. He crawled to the doorway, past Theo and Auggie, and the woman helped him to his feet.

"You stupid fucks don't have any idea—" she shouted.

Theo slammed the door and locked it. Then he grabbed the phone on Grace's desk and dialed campus security. The dispatcher promised to send someone over right away and told Theo to stay in the office. When the dispatcher asked if Theo wanted to stay on the line, he said no and hung up. Then he finally got his first good look at Auggie.

Something bad had happened to the kid. A bruise was darkening on his jawline, and his lip was split again—Theo felt a flash of guilt for that—but mostly it was the terror in his face. The kind of scared look Luke had worn too many times for Theo to count: when he'd dealt bad weed in high school and had Billy Schoening and his gang hunting him down; when he'd gotten Tammy Kluth pregnant, and the Kluth boys were hunting him down; when he'd cut baggies of crystal meth with Pop Rocks and had the Ozark Volunteers hunting him down.

"Sit down," Theo said, touching Auggie's arm, intending to steer him toward a seat. "You look like you're—"

And then, before Theo knew what was happening, Auggie was stepping forward, obviously having mistaken the movement as the beginning of a hug. He wrapped his arms around Theo and buried his face in Theo's shoulder as he shook.

"Ok," Theo said. He stood there with no idea what to do. Luke had never wanted a hug. Luke had never wanted anything but for Theo to fix it. After a moment, Theo felt stupid standing with his arms out to the side, so he patted Auggie's back. "Hey, it's ok. You did good. You handled yourself really well."

Auggie started to sob.

"All right," Theo said. It sounded very stupid, but he had no idea what else to say. "It's going to be all right."

They stood like that for a few more minutes, Auggie crying, Theo alternating between patting his back and rubbing slow circles.

"I'm so stupid," Auggie said, pulling away. "Oh my God, I'm so fucking stupid. I'm sorry. There was this guy, and he—I don't know, and then they were waiting outside, and they started yelling, and I just ran. I . . . I don't even know why I came here, I just didn't know where else to go."

"Auggie."

"I'm sorry, I shouldn't have gotten you involved, I shouldn't have come here. I'm so sorry. Please don't tell anyone about this."

"Auggie—"

"Please, oh my God, my mom will kill me. Please. You cannot tell anyone."

"Your mom? This is way more serious. Anyway, it's too late for that, ok? I called campus security. They're on their way."

"Oh my God," Auggie said, his voice rising with panic. "He's going to kill me. He said if I went to the police he'd kill me."

It was Luke all over again. Theo wanted to scream. He knew every line in this fucking performance by heart.

He had found Luke in the hayloft, shot up with enough heroin to kill a horse. What Theo remembered, when he remembered that day, were the flies crawling on Luke's eyes.

Auggie's eyes were very brown and very wide. Helpless eyes.

Theo said, "Sit down. I need you to tell me everything, but first we have to get our story straight."

9

When campus security left, Auggie was alone with Theo in the office; a girl with a cloud of brown curls had stopped by briefly to pick up the microwaved meal on her desk. She'd tried to hang around until one of the security guards asked her to leave. Now, Auggie sat next to Theo's desk, replaying snatches of the day—the *Community* theme song, the pile of pillows squished behind him, the fragrance of Orlando's soap, the sun hot on his neck as he ran across campus, the weight of the gun in his hand. His eyes moved to Theo's desk.

Theo seemed to sense his thoughts because he put a hand on the drawer.

"Why did you lie to them?" Auggie asked. Theo had spun a story about meth heads trying to steal the computers. He hadn't said anything about the distinguishing tattoos. He hadn't said anything about the gun. Now that the guards had left, from time to time he rubbed his head, and Auggie remembered the sudden, brutal viciousness of the headbutt. Theo wasn't excessively tall or big, but he was definitely strong, and he also apparently knew how to beat the shit out of white supremacist gang bangers. Not exactly what Auggie had expected from his Shakespeare professor.

"You told me this couldn't go to the police," Theo said. "If I tell campus security that two white trash assholes with a gun broke into my office to abduct a student, they're going to take it to the police."

"I mean, why are you helping me?"

"I'm part of a freshman transition-to-success program," Theo said. "We're supposed to handle this kind of stuff."

"Oh," Auggie said.

"That was a joke."

"Oh," Auggie said again.

Theo sat back; his chair bumped a banker's box on the floor behind him, and he flinched without seeming to realize it. "You gave me the reader's digest version while security was on the way over. I want to hear the whole thing."

So Auggie told him. When he'd finished, he said, "And now this asshole is going to kill me, or those people he sicced on me, they're going to kill me, or Christ, I don't know. I am in such deep shit."

Theo said, "It's not the same group."

"What?"

"The guy who was in your dorm room, he works for someone else."

"Those guys were literally waiting outside my building after he finished knocking me around."

"Exactly," Theo said. "If they were working for that guy, why wouldn't they have come upstairs with him and really put a scare in you? Why wait outside and do the whole show a second time?"

"Because—I don't know. Because they're not that smart. Because they thought it would send a message. Fuck, I don't know, because they forgot to get my organ donor info for when they blow out my brains."

"Nope. They're working for somebody else. And that means two groups of people are ridiculously interested in the disappearance of a college senior who's graduating in December."

"Robert's a freshman."

"No," Theo said. "He told me he was a senior."

"He's definitely a freshman. He rushed with the freshmen. He's a Sigma Sigma pledge too."

Theo tightened and relaxed his hands, knuckles popping. "Whatever. Drugs. It's got to be drugs."

"I don't do drugs. I mean, I smoked some weed, but that's basically legal in Orange County. What?"

"This isn't about weed."

"No, you made this little face. I mean, your mouth. I don't know. What does that mean?"

"Of course Orange County," Theo said. Then, before Auggie could ask what that meant, he said, "Does your roommate do drugs? Could he be involved in this somehow? Never mind, that doesn't make any sense. They wanted to know about Robert. Why do they think you're involved with Robert?"

"I don't know. I don't even know him."

"Do you always do fun things with strangers like steal a car and drive drunk and almost kill somebody?"

"I didn't steal—"

"Jesus Christ. Just don't, ok? I'm trying to help you, so don't insult me by lying to me."

Face hot, Auggie stared past Theo, looking out a window that had a great view of South Quad.

"I'm not just talking about almost killing me," Theo said. "I was being stupid, I get that. I shouldn't have been in the road."

"You were trying to kill yourself," Auggie said. On the quad below, a girl with a yellow backpack had spilled her books, and a guy with a man bun had stopped to help her pick them up. She was laughing. He was laughing. They were taking a lot longer than they needed to, just to pick up a few books. And Auggie wondered what that would be like, to just be able to have things happen like that. He realized the silence had dragged on.

"No," Theo said like he was explaining a difficult passage. "I wasn't. Anyway, my point is that you could have hit another car, you could have crashed into pedestrians on the sidewalk, you could have hit a tree or a building and killed yourself and Robert."

"I don't need another dad, for the love of fuck."

Theo's blond eyebrows arched slightly. The hum of the computer's fan sounded like a tornado.

Auggie let his gaze slide back to Theo. "Look, I get it. I screwed up. It's not going to happen again. I'm here to get my life back on track; I'm not going to let it happen again."

"Get your life back on track? What does that mean?"

"Nothing."

"If I'm sticking my neck out to help you on this, then it means something, and I want to know."

"Who the fuck asked you to stick your neck out?" Auggie couldn't help it; his voice slid into a mockery of Theo's tone on the last words.

"You did, when you barged in here and said something like 'Please don't let them kill me.'"

The heat in Auggie's face flashed into pinpricks. "That's not what I said. But, yeah. Ok. Thank you, again. And . . . and I'm sorry. I'm freaking out."

"What do you mean, get your life back on track? Were you involved in some kind of trouble back home? Could these guys have followed you here?"

"No. Look, I've got this . . . business, I guess. On social media."

Theo's expression was blank. "Like, Facebook?"

For the first time in what felt like days, something loosened in Auggie's chest, and he laughed. Pulling out his phone, he opened Instagram and passed it over. "Facebook, Instagram, Twitter. There's a new one called Snapchat, and I think it's about to explode. Here, this is one of our most popular videos ever."

Theo watched it and said, "You're a pretty good dancer. Who are these other guys?"

"Oh, my buddies Logan and Devin."

Scrubbing a hand through his thick beard, Theo said, "How do I watch it again?"

Auggie tapped the screen.

When it finished this time, he said, "I don't get it."

"There's nothing to get."

"You try to eat a slice of pizza. Then your buddies drag you away before you can get it. You guys dance to 'Walk Like an Egyptian.' Then you eat pizza and pretend to spill it on each other. Then it shows an empty pizza box."

"Yeah."

"And that got six hundred thousand likes?"

"Yeah, I told you, it's one of our most popular."

"What in the world?"

"Ok, well, some people like it," Auggie said, snatching the phone back. "And I was on track to get this huge sponsorship deal in South Korea—I'm really big in South Korea—and then, um, something happened."

"What?"

"Can we not talk about this? I promise it's got nothing to do with these guys showing up or Robert or drugs or whatever the hell this is about." Auggie blew out a breath, wagged the phone at Theo, and said, "Old guys aside, a lot of people actually like what I do, so I've just got to keep my name out of the news, build my brand, and my agent is sure we'll get that deal in the spring."

"You swear you're telling me everything about Robert? You met him by chance at the bid party, you guys decided to do something stupid because you were drunk, that was the end of it?"

"That was the end. I haven't seen him since. I thought about blocking him, because he said he followed me, but I couldn't figure out which handle was his. That's it."

For a moment, Theo just scratched his beard. Then he said, "The responsible thing to do right now, the right thing to do, is tell you to take this to the police. I know, you already told me you don't feel like you can do that."

"That guy was not joking. He'll know. And he'll kill me."

"I said I know, but I'm also telling you, I still feel obligated to say you should go to the police."

Auggie's heart had begun to thump. He scooted closer in the chair; his knee bumped Theo's.

"But?"

"But I was married to a cop for almost five years. And Ian was really frustrated by the fact that police work is almost always cleaning up after the mess happens."

"Meaning?"

"Meaning this guy might be telling you the truth."

"Wait, you were married to a cop?"

"Yes." Theo rolled his eyes. "Believe it or not, not everyone finds me so boring they fall asleep on the first day of class."

"I didn't fall asleep, I just—if you were married to a cop, you know how to do stuff like this. You can help me find Robert and get these assholes off my back."

"Oh, sure," Theo said. "Just like if I'd been married to a surgeon, I'd be fully qualified to take out your gallbladder."

"Theo, I swear to God, if you help me with this, I will do whatever you want. Please. You're smart, you saved my ass, and you're literally the only person who can help me with this." A flash of inspiration washed over Auggie like goosebumps. "And they might come after you too. You're tagged in that video, right? And you beat the shit out of those guys today; they're not going to forget that."

"We can go to the police together, Auggie. That's what we should do."

"Please," Auggie said, crowding closer. He could smell something that Theo must have put in his hair and beard—a musky, woodsy scent. Cedar and moss. Heat coiled like a spring in Auggie's gut, and he heard himself saying, be careful, be careful, and then he put a hand on Theo's thigh, a little too high on his leg to be mistaken for anything else, and said again, "Please?"

Theo's face was neutral as he leaned forward, caught Auggie's wrist, and moved his hand away. He met Auggie's eyes, pointed at himself, pointed at Auggie, and said, "Is that part clear?"

"Yeah, ok." Auggie took a breath. "Please?"

"Fine. Yes. Christ, you are worse than Luke, do you realize that? At least Luke didn't try to seduce me."

"Thank you, Theo. Thank you. Thank you so much."

"I'll talk to a friend and see what I can find out. I think we can wrap this up by Monday."

"Oh my God, you are amazing. Thank you."

"Give me your number; I'll text you when I've got an update."

He slid a piece of paper to Auggie, and Auggie scribbled down his number.

Theo folded the paper and put it in a pocket. He looked at Auggie. Someone was walking down the hall, heels clicking.

"Right now," Theo said, "I should probably get some work done."

"Yeah," Auggie said. "Sure."

Another long moment ticked past; something happened inside the computer, and it made a series of soft beeps. The knot of tension inside Auggie tightened. He would have to walk across campus alone, head up to his dorm alone, stand in that room again, alone, even with a hundred thousand followers. He'd be alone, unless Orlando popped in, if Glasses came back. He'd be alone if someone else was already there, waiting for him.

"So," Theo said, nodding at the door, "if you want to—"

"Can I do something? Do you want me to grade quizzes or make copies?" Auggie tried to grin. He tried to look casual. The roil of fear, floating above the mixture of embarrassment and disappointment at having Theo move his hand aside so casually, made his face twitchy. "I'll sharpen pencils. Do you need me to sharpen pencils?"

"This isn't a 1950s schoolhouse," Theo said. "Look, I've got a lot to—oh."

"I swear I can make copies. I had to make copies all the time when my mom was selling real estate."

"You know what?" Theo said, grabbing his cane. "I could use a walk. You mind going with me?"

"Sure."

"And maybe you could show me your dorm room. I'd like to take a look. You know, in case this guy left any forensic evidence."

"See?" Auggie said. "You even sound like a cop."

Theo grabbed a satchel and limped after Auggie toward the door; Auggie hadn't remembered the limp being that bad in class.

At the door, Auggie paused and looked Theo in the eyes. "I know what you're doing."

"Yeah?"

Auggie nodded. "Thanks."

He had only known Theo a short time, but he thought he was seeing the first genuine smile behind that beard: soft and reserved and very, very cute.

"It's that freshman transition-to-success program," Theo said, pulling the door shut as they stepped out into the hall. "We're full service."

10

Theo left Liversedge earlier than usual that day. His leg was on fire as he biked to the Piggly Wiggly. Walking across the quad to Moriah Court, taking the stairs up to Auggie's apartment to make sure the kid felt safe, and then walking back had been torture on his already throbbing leg. At the store, he got brats and a packaged potato salad and one of those bagged salad kits. He also got beer. He started with three six-packs of White Rascal, and then he realized he was being stupid and added a fourth.

The little brick house was dark and waiting for him, the September sun low enough to frame the chimney when he got home. Now, every time he took the front stairs, he thought of Cart bitching about the risers, and he thought he could feel the treads sagging. He carried the groceries into the kitchen, locked the front door, and went out to the deck to get the grill ready. While the coals started in the chimney, he stretched out on the couch, an ice pack on his hip, another on his knee.

His weekend plans, ever since June 9, 2013, had been easy and simple: Percocet, beer, and the closest thing to a coma that he could manufacture inside the walls of his own home. As soon as he had some food in his stomach, he'd begin Operation Get the Fuck Out of His Own Head.

But, stretched out on the couch, he found his mind was restless. Instead of thinking endlessly about the pills and the White Rascal, he kept thinking about stupid stuff from the day. The visit to Downing, that morning, of course. But then other things. The way his blood had sung in his ears when he'd busted that motherfucker's nose. The way his whole body had reacted when Auggie's knee bumped his own, something zipping through his chest. The boys he'd seen kissing on a bench when he hiked across the quad with Auggie. The hot smell of the mulch. The way Auggie had said thank you. Luke.

The icepacks softened as they melted. The throbbing in his hip and knee faded. In the front yard, a robin sat on a branch of the cherry tree, and Theo ran his hand through the condensation beading on the icepacks, watching. There was a whole world out there. And then the robin was gone in a fluttered-up movement, its reddish-orange breast twisting away, and Theo blew out a breath he hadn't realized he'd been holding.

Outside, as he shifted the coals, he called Cart.

"What do you want, you miserable son of a bitch?" Cart asked in his politest voice.

"Do you like brats?"

"Does the pope wear a funny hat?"

"I'm grilling brats."

"Is that an invitation?"

"You're the cop. Call for backup if you can't figure it out."

Cart was laughing when Theo disconnected.

The September night cooled off a little as the sun set, and a breeze picked up, carrying the smell of old-growth forest from the tree line. It mixed with the charcoal, the searing meat, the taste of coriander from the beer. Theo thought maybe he could do just half a pill tonight. Half a pill seemed really reasonable.

"What are you doing, asshole?" Cart asked as he came around the side of the house. He was carrying a six-pack of Big Wave; droplets glistened on the bottles. He must have showered and changed after work because he looked fresh in spite of the heat and he was wearing mesh shorts and a Tigers tee.

Theo pointed the tongs at the grill.

"Finish that one," Cart said, nodding at the White Rascal, "and then no more of that girly stuff."

"Because Big Wave is butch."

"Damn straight."

Cart disappeared into the house; when he came back, he had two beers uncapped, and he held one out to Theo. Theo set it on the deck railing while he finished the can he was working on.

"You being a stupid shit again?" Cart asked after his first long drink.

"Probably."

"I saw those pills in there. If you're drinking, you sure as fuck better not be thinking about taking those."

"Then I guess I'm not thinking about taking those."

Cart watched him over the neck of brown glass. "Maybe I should take them with me."

"Cart?"

Cart eyed him as he set the bottle to his lips.

"Go fuck yourself," Theo said.

"Aww," Cart said. "There's the English professor."

"Go get the salad ready. Potato salad's in there too if you want it."

"Does the pope wear a funny hat?"

"Fuck if I know, but I do know you're sure as fuck not going to eat if you don't do some work."

"I brought the beer."

"I had beer. What I don't have is somebody fixing the salad."

Cart pulled a face and went inside, and Theo crushed the empty White Rascal and switched to the Big Wave. He pulled the brats off, went back inside, and turned on the window unit. Lukewarm A/C drifted through the house.

"Hotter than a whore in church in here," Cart said.

"You ought to know."

Cart grinned. He had this crazy, wonderful, shit-kicking grin that never got old.

They ate at the flea-market table, and the Piggly Wiggly's potato salad wasn't bad.

"So," Theo asked when Cart was slathering yellow mustard on his third brat. "You hear anything about that kid, the one who stole the car?"

Cart was eyeing the brat carefully, trying to make the zig-zag of mustard perfect. "Now, here I thought I was just getting invited to a friendly dinner."

"You did get invited to a friendly dinner. Now I want to know about that kid."

"Why?"

"Because the whole thing is weird, and you got me freaked out about it."

Cart took a bite of the brat, chewed slowly, and washed it down with Big Wave. Then, pointing the mouth of the bottle at Theo, he said, "Ian always said you couldn't bullshit."

"What's the bullshit?"

The window unit had developed an ominous rattle; Theo didn't want to think about what would happen if it gave out. Between paying for Downing, paying the hospital bills, paying for everything until the insurance kicked in, he'd be lucky if he could afford the mortgage next month. Outside, a bat cracked, and kids screamed with excitement. The Rudock kids, the only ones out in the boonies, were playing baseball, Theo guessed.

"I looked into it," Cart finally said.

"And?"

"And I didn't find anything."

"What do you mean? Like, no priors?"

"No, I didn't find anything. That's what I mean. I got nothing."

Theo shook his head.

"No Robert Poulson," Cart said. "At least, not living in Wahredua city limits, and not with a Missouri driver's license."

"Ok," Theo said slowly. "So he's from out of state. He's a student, right? Wroxall gets kids from all over the world."

"What part of the world is this kid from? China?"

"Don't be an asshole."

"Look, I told you: I didn't find anything on that kid. I asked around about that video. No, don't have a hissy fit. It's not like I went around asking the other guys if they thought you'd killed someone. I asked a couple of people I know, people who hear things. They didn't know anything about it. Hadn't seen it before. If you ask me, it's like I said: a prank. Maybe something to do with rush week. Those kids do some dumb shit, you ask me."

Theo nodded, but his mind was racing. Yes, kids did dumb things during rush week—and after, during their time as pledges. But this was something else. People were looking for Robert Poulson. Dangerous people. And they were focused on Auggie, for some reason.

And on Theo, he realized with a dark suddenness. Auggie had pointed that out, but it hadn't really sunk in. Theo had been tagged on that video too. People would want to talk to him too. The same kind of people who had wanted to talk to Auggie.

Theo grabbed his satchel from the chair next to him, dug out his laptop, and booted it up.

"Please tell me tonight is dinner and a show," Cart said, sliding into the empty seat, his thigh pressed along Theo's.

"Sorry," Theo muttered as he opened up the faculty resources for Wroxall. "I don't watch straight porn."

"Neither do I," Cart said, leaning in until their elbows bumped. "I mean, not exclusively."

A part of Theo's mind dinged an alarm, but he was too focused on his search. He found the student directory—the secure database, only available to faculty and staff—and typed in Poulson. A list of hits came up, and he scanned down them. No Robert.

"How's your hip?" Cart asked. "I saw you walking in here with those brats; still got a limp. I give a hell of a massage."

Theo tried again, this time searching for Robert Poulson. No matches. He tried again, R Poulson this time. Nothing.

"What's got you so freaked out?" Cart said. "It's just a massage. Make you feel a lot better."

Theo barely heard him. No Missouri driver's license. No record of him in Wahredua. Nothing at the school.

Robert Poulson didn't exist.

11

Saturday morning, Auggie lay in bed, pretending to sleep until Orlando was finally out the door for practice. Auggie had avoided his roommate the night before, knowing Orlando would want to talk about what had happened. Auggie also knew he could only keep to himself for so long. They were living in a room small enough that Auggie could reach out and touch Orlando's bed without getting out of his own; at some point, they were going to have to see each other and talk.

After Orlando left, Auggie washed his face, did his hair, tested the natural light in the room and eventually lowered the blinds and positioned a lamp. Then he got back in bed, dragged the sheet into place—internet Auggie only showed nips when he was swimming, thanks—and checked himself on the phone's screen. He was lucky that Glasses had only hit him on one side of the face; he turned that side away from the camera, gave himself sleepy, sexy eyes, and snapped a few pics. He tried some filters, settled on one that made his cheekbones pop, and scrawled *morning, boo* before posting it across all his feeds. Likes and comments began to rush in.

He showered. He checked his phone. He brushed his teeth. He checked his phone again. As he searched for something to wear, a pack of smokes tumbled free from the stack of clothes. Auggie grabbed it, intending to set it aside to roll in his sleeve later. Then he stopped. These were Kools, not Parliaments. He vaguely remembered picking up the pack last Saturday night, when he'd almost hit Theo with the Porsche. He tossed the pack to the back of the drawer—in case of emergency—and kept looking.

He picked out running shorts and a tank, put them on, thought about what Theo had been wearing every time Auggie had seen him, and dug through the drawers until he found his best pair of jeans, the kind that practically looked painted on, and a salmon-colored polo. He changed, fixed his hair again, and snapped another picture. After popping his collar, he got a fun, meta shot of himself glowering into the mirror. He scribbled *look out, world* across the center of the picture, posted it, and then went back to his previous post.

At the beginning, when Auggie had first been building his brand, he'd made a lot of mistakes. Bad lighting. Bad hair—God, that faux hawk. Bad jokes. But one of the biggest mistakes had been taking time to reply to every single follower every time they posted. For a while, it had been sustainable, if only barely. He'd spend an hour or two after every post, catching up on comments, writing thoughtful, meaningful replies. He wasn't sure, now, if that had helped build his brand or if it had just been a waste of time. Internet Auggie was sensitive, maybe a little vulnerable, maybe even a little shy. Internet Auggie was kooky and funny. Taking time to reply had really accentuated the sensitive side.

As time went on, though, it had become impossible. A hundred thousand followers, with five or six thousand comments on even the stupidest posts—a picture of bacon and eggs arranged into a smiley face, for example—meant that it simply wasn't possible for Auggie to respond to everyone. He also realized it wasn't effective. If people got a response every time, they expected a response every time—and, worse, the value of those responses shrank over time.

Now, propped up against the mound of pillows, he worked his way through the feed the way he had learned to do: after a significant number of responses from his followers, he began scrolling through the first half of the comments. He might come back and look at the second half of the comments later, but it was important to reward people who commented early, and it was also important to show that he didn't necessarily have time to get to the end of every comment section. Out of that first half of comments, he had to find the ones that stood out. A million *love u* and *miss ur face* and *ur so hawwwwwwt* didn't give him much material to work with. He liked to hit the trifecta: sad, sweet, and silly.

He found the sad one right off: *thank you for posting my mom just left my dad and we don't have anyone to watch my little bro and just seeing ur face made me smile for the first time this week so thx.* He hit reply and typed: *thanks for sharing that. my dad left me before I turned one, and my mom did all the work. shout out to super moms everywhere. ur gonna get through this. i'm here for u.*

Sweet was always a little tricky. Auggie had to hit the middle ground between accessing his sex appeal and acting too much like a bro. His followers didn't want an overly confident jock who knew he was hot and a heartbreaker; these people had signed up for a sweet, quirky hot boy who just might be into sweet, quirky girls. He lucked out today and found another comment early in the feed. The way this one was formatted made it sound like it'd been written by someone over twenty-five: *You are so cute and funny. Has anyone ever told you that you should do modeling? I'm a photographer, and I would really love to see you succeed!* Auggie typed back: *thanks! checked out your portfolio link—u r really talented! can't believe anyone would want to see this mug on a runway though.* At the end, he added a skull emoji and a laughing face.

Silly came easiest to him. He found a comment near the middle where someone had tagged MikiLuvs2Sing, a girl who did acoustic covers out of Los Angeles and who was, to judge by what her followers said about her, one of the kindest, most encouraging internet personalities out there. The comment said: *o my god! can u imagine if @aplolz and @mikiluvs2sing got together? their babies would be* and then a series of emoji fireworks. Auggie had cultivated a one-sided, pretend feud with Miki over the last year, one that Miki liked to play on too by pretending to be innocently confused and somehow managing to instigate him further. He immediately wrote back a series of emojis, skulls and knives and guns, ending with the throw-up icon.

Ok, he thought. Morning work was done.

Now he had to decide what to do about the hot professor.

Auggie was pretty sure that Theo would keep his word; Theo had, after all, headbutted one asshole and broken the hand of another. He'd protected Auggie when the woman had drawn a gun. That was serious stuff; Auggie didn't think Theo would balk now. And Auggie knew that showing up at Theo's door—he pictured one of those gingerbread brick houses near campus, where most of the faculty lived—might seem a little crazy. A little . . . stalkerish.

But he kept thinking about what it had felt like for someone to see him, the real him—scared out of his mind, without special lighting or filters or a hundred different shots to get it right, touching Theo's thigh, gayer than God and not knowing what to do about it, no poise, no charm, no clever comment—someone seeing him like that, the real him, not the cardboard boy in all his pictures, someone seeing him and still liking him. When he'd first started building his internet persona, the dopamine rush of all those likes had left Auggie feeling high, floating for a while until he crashed and needed it again. He'd done his research, learned about social media and the dopamine loop, and moved past that, seeing the interactions now for what they were: his business. But those early dopamine highs were kiddy stuff compared to the rush of Theo's arms around him, Theo's breath hot on his ear, Theo's voice low and rumbling in his chest. *You did good. You handled yourself really well.*

And so, knowing he was stupider than anybody in the history of the world, Auggie opened up a browser and started searching for Theo's address.

12

On Saturday, Theo went to Downing, the way he did every morning now. He biked to the closest bus stop. When the bus came, he chained his bike and boarded. He spent an hour at Downing, and then he took the bus back.

"Fuck," he said.

Someone had stolen the back wheel off his bike.

He considered unchaining the thing and lugging it back home; his hip and knee throbbed just at the thought. So he hiked back home, out into the boonies. It was nearing noon, and the September sun was high and hot. The late morning traffic on the road kicked up dust, and by the time Theo got to his street, his oxford was stained with sweat, and the chinos had spatters from where an asshole had hit a pool of standing water right when Theo was passing it.

When he got to the brick house, he stopped at the end of the driveway.

"Fuck," he said again.

Auggie was sitting on the steps. He was in jeans and a polo, and somehow he managed to look like sitting on the broken-down steps of a house in the middle of Missouri was some kind of photo shoot. When he saw Theo, he stood, grinned, and waved.

Theo felt something he couldn't name pressing down on his breastbone; he whispered, "Oh, fuck."

"Auggie," Theo said when he got to the steps. "What are you doing here?"

"Hi," Auggie said, his grin getting bigger. "Good morning."

"Good morning. What are you doing here?"

"You're all dressed up for Saturday morning. Did you have an important meeting or something?"

"Yes," Theo said. "I'd like you to answer my question, please."

"Oh, sorry. I know this is weird. Please don't think I'm crazy. I just . . . I was thinking about Robert. Thinking about this whole, weird mess. And I realized I didn't thank you for helping me yesterday."

"Yes, you did," Theo said. "You said thank you."

"But, I wanted to show you how much I appreciated it. So I thought I could stop by, we could talk things over, see what our next move is, and then I could buy you lunch." Auggie opened his arms innocently: "Just lunch. Just a thank you."

Theo wiped sweat from his forehead. Down the street—which was saying something, out in the boonies, where the next house was on its own acre lot—Mrs. Rudock was calling for Barnabus, their dog. She sounded royally mad.

"Auggie," he finally said.

"Please don't say no. Look, I couldn't stand the thought of sitting in the dorm all day, and I'm freaked out because those guys might come back, and I know if we work together on this, we can find Robert. And then it'll be over, and I'll leave you alone." Auggie flashed another smile, more tentative this time. "Please?"

"I'm your instructor."

"Please, Theo."

"This really isn't a good idea."

"Please. I swear, I will not take advantage of you."

In spite of Theo's best efforts, an eyebrow went up.

"I mean—no, I didn't mean—" A blush worked its way across Auggie's face. "Oh my God, that is not what I was trying to say."

"So, my honor is safe?"

Auggie tried the smile again. "I meant, you know, with grades. This is separate from class, I get that."

Suddenly, it was hard for Theo to remember why the morning had seemed so bad. Downing, the bike, the long, hot walk—they all seemed smaller now.

He passed Auggie on the steps, unlocked the door, and went inside.

"Uh," Auggie said from the doorway, playing with the screen door, the thin aluminum making its sing-song warble as he worked it open and shut. "Am I supposed to stay out here?"

Theo kicked off his shoes, gave the living room a glance—chaotically messy, yes, and he shoved some of Lana's toys into the corner—and then took the stairs. He called back as he went, "You already stalked me this far. I don't think it really matters what I say at this point."

Upstairs, two bedrooms were tucked under the eaves: a larger room that Theo and Ian had shared, and the smaller room that had been Lana's. Theo unbuttoned the oxford, tossed it in the hamper, and checked the white undershirt, which looked pit-stain free and probably cleaner than anything else at the moment. He tossed the chinos in the hamper as well, tried to decide appropriate wear for an extremely hot eighteen-year-old student who had tracked him to his home, and settled on running shorts. He ditched his socks, looked at Ian's clutter still taking up the top of the dresser and half the bed. A t-shirt Ian had taken off at the last minute before they left for St. Louis. A pair of Under Armor socks Ian had balled up and forgotten to pack. Ian's cologne—something Burberry. The polished wooden tray where Ian had kept his watch and wallet was empty now; the mortuary had returned them, of course, but they were in plastic baggies somewhere in the basement; Theo hadn't been able to stand the thought of touching them again. He turned off the light and headed downstairs.

Auggie was perched on the edge of the couch, in between a stack of books of Shakespeare criticism on the one side and, on the other, the crown jewels: empty Big Wave bottles, a bottle of Percocet, and half a joint.

"Jesus Christ," Theo said, grabbing the pills and the joint and throwing them in a drawer.

"This is a really nice house," Auggie said, still sitting on the couch like he thought it was spring loaded and might launch him into the air if he sat back any farther.

"Don't," Theo said, flipping on the window unit.

"It's cute," Auggie said.

"I said don't."

Auggie stared at him, his expression slightly hurt.

Theo went into the kitchen, got a glass of water from the tap, and drank it. He looked out at the deck. He looked past the deck to the tree line of old growth. A fox darted behind a blackberry bush, the branches waving, and then Theo thought of the beers he had picked up with Ian, the table Ian had refinished, the floors Ian had stripped and sanded. He pressed the glass, cold and empty, to his forehead.

"Do you want me to come in there?" Auggie said.

Theo went to the opening that joined the kitchen and living room. "I think this was a mistake. You should go."

"What? Why?"

"Auggie, please. This is not a good idea."

"Is it about the joint? Because I don't care. And I won't say anything."

"I've had a really, really bad day. This morning, I had to—you know what? Never mind. It doesn't matter. But then I came back, and somebody had stolen the wheel off my bike, and I had to walk. And I'm so fucking sick of walking, but the minute I sit down behind the wheel of a car, I have a fucking panic attack. And I'm realizing, right now, that you are my student and I am talking like a crazy person." Theo rubbed his hip, where it was already aching. "It's been a really bad year, ok? I'll help you on this stuff because I know you need help. But I think it'd be better if you go."

Auggie's gaze went to the plastic train in the corner, the dolls in their misbuttoned dresses, the toy shopping basket with plastic carrots and milk cartons and muffins. When he looked back at Theo, his dark eyes were wet.

"Please don't say you're sorry," Theo said, unable to stop himself. "If you say that, I'm going to lose my mind."

Auggie's adam's apple bobbed, and he wiped his eyes.

"Hang out in the library," Theo said. "Or at the student union. Find somewhere you feel safe. In a few days, we'll figure this out, and it'll be over, ok?"

Auggie stood and held out his hand. "Keys."

"What?"

"Give me your keys."

"Why?"

"I'm going to get your bike."

"I don't want you to get my bike. I want you to leave."

"You can either give me your keys, or I can walk to a hardware store, buy bolt cutters, and do it that way."

"This isn't about the bike, ok? I just—that was just an example."

"Ok, but it's something I can help you with. Give me the keys. I won't steal your car." Auggie offered a sloppy, slanted grin. "Promise."

"I really—"

"Ok, I'll find bolt cutters."

Auggie was pushing open the screen door when a strangled, "Fine," escaped Theo.

Auggie looked back.

"Fine," Theo said again, a little more coherently. "Fine. Thank you. But that's it. Then you go home or go to the library or go somewhere else, ok?"

"Yeah," Auggie said, holding out his hand again. "Sure."

13

Auggie had passed the bus stop on his way in, and he remembered seeing a bicycle chained up, a wheel missing. He backtracked now, tossing the keys in one hand, trying to keep his attention on the jangle, the sudden weight, the sharp edges. Instead, his mind kept going back to Theo in an undershirt and running shorts. The September day was hot; that probably explained why Auggie was sweating so much.

When he got to the bus stop, a heavyset young woman was sitting on the bench, raking back her hair from where it stuck to one sweaty temple. Two little kids, a boy and a girl, were playing on the asphalt shoulder, chasing each other and giggling.

"Not on the road," the woman called to them. "What's your daddy going to say if I tell him you were playing on the road?" With mock severity, she smacked her hands and said, "He's gonna spank you."

The boy shrieked with laughter, obviously having heard the empty threat before, and the girl, who must have been a year older, caught up with him and screamed, "Tag." Auggie dropped into a squat, undid the lock, and worked the chain free from the bike's frame. He hoisted the bike over one shoulder, the remaining wheel bouncing against him and threatening to unsettle the load, and then he got his balance. When he caught the woman's eye, she smiled and waved and looked back at her kids.

As Auggie made his way back to Theo's, he told himself the same thing he told himself every time he saw something like that: not everybody grew up the same; just because it looked perfect didn't mean it was. He knew better than anybody the power—and convincing illusion—of a moment frozen in time. Maybe that little family went home and that woman beat the hell out of those kids. Maybe they went home and she locked the kids in their room. Maybe that woman was having an affair because she wasn't happy, hadn't ever been happy, except these tiny moments of feeling spotlighted and special that were the brain-chemistry equivalent of dope. Not that Auggie wanted anything bad for that family; sometimes it was just hard for him to see stuff like that.

When he got back to Theo's little brick house, sweat was pouring off him, running down his ribs, dampening the cotton boxers at the small of his back. Auggie carried the bike around the side of the house, spotted the freestanding garage built at the end of the driveway, and headed for it. The roll-up door was closed, but he spotted a door on the side that might get him inside.

Before he could get inside the garage, the sound of tired springs drew his attention; Theo stood on the back deck, propping open a screen door with his elbow.

"Just leave it there."

Auggie nestled the bike against the roll-up, where the slight overhang of roof would offer a little protection from the elements, and jogged over to the deck. He tossed the keys as he came up the steps; Theo snagged them out of the air.

"Thanks," Theo said. "You really didn't have to do that."

"I don't mind."

"Auggie, Christ."

Auggie shot a glance back at the bike. "What?"

"Your shirt."

The chain and gears had left greasy smears along the polo.

"It's fine," Auggie said.

"It's a really nice shirt. Hold on. I'll give you some money to buy a new one."

"I'll just wash it."

"Good luck," Theo said. "Hold on. I'll get some cash."

"I don't care about the shirt."

"This is why I didn't want you to get the bike."

The sun was pounding down on them now, radiating back from the brick, making Auggie feel like he was caught in an updraft. Something moved in the tree line, and a branch popped. The mildly cooler air from inside the house smelled like peanut butter and toast.

"Fine," Auggie said.

"No, I'm sorry."

"No, you asked me not to do it. I should have listened."

"Auggie, I'm sorry. I shouldn't have said that. I'm . . . not being very kind. Thank you for getting the bike. Thank you. That was really nice of you."

"Yeah," Auggie said, suddenly not sure how to stand, restless and frozen in place at the same time, a smile trying to break free. "Yeah, you're welcome. So, um, can I come inside?"

"I thought we agreed this wasn't a good idea."

"But we haven't even talked about Robert."

"I'm handling Robert. You just take care of yourself until I figure this out."

"I just want, you know, an update. That's it. Then I'll take off."

The next moment was long; then, sighing, Theo elbowed the door open wider and moved back, letting Auggie into the house. As Auggie passed him, he smelled Theo's hair, like cedar, and clean sweat, and he felt something compress inside him, a kind of wild, potential energy just waiting for release.

The kitchen was small, like the rest of the house, and like the rest of the house it looked like it needed some serious attention. Empty pots and pans were stacked on the electric range; more rested next to the sink. A single plate sat in a drying rack. The refrigerator had a lot of magnets on it. Magnets, but nothing else. Auggie remembered the toys piled in one corner of the front room. He wondered where all the drawings and craft projects had gone. He had a mental image of Theo taking them down one by one, Theo stuffing them into a trash bag, Theo doing all of it alone.

"The bad news," Theo said, shutting the door and leaning against it, "is that it's not going to be as easy as I thought. Robert gave me a fake name when he tried to enroll in my class. That name isn't showing up anywhere in the area: nobody with utility bills in that name, no driver's license, and nobody registered at the college."

"Wait a minute," Auggie said. "He was going to add your class? Which one?"

Theo brushed his beard and looked away.

"No fucking way," Auggie said.

"We don't know if it was a coincidence—"

"It was not a coincidence," Auggie said. "Think about it. He shows up to add your class, but he gives you a fake name. Why didn't you tell me this when I was in your office?"

"Before or after I gave myself a concussion keeping you safe?"

Auggie's face heated. "I just mean, this is really weird. He shows up to your class, asks to add, gives you a fake name. He's got to realize you'll figure out the name's fake when you can't add him, right? Wouldn't you get some sort of notice?"

"All I do is sign the card. He takes it to the registrar after that. Of course, he wouldn't have done that because he's not really a student, and so he never showed up on my roster."

"So why do it at all?"

"I thought about that," Theo said. "I think he wanted a window. An opening. He could come to class for the first week—honestly, the first three weeks, through the whole add/drop period—and if he didn't show up on my roster, I wouldn't think twice about it. I'd just wait for add/drop to close, and then I'd print a new roster."

Auggie shrugged. "Yeah, but, why?"

"He made up a fake name to add the same class you're enrolled in," Theo said. "He approached you at a party and buddied up to you."

"You think this is about me?"

"What else is it about?"

"I don't know. I think it's just . . . it's just a weird misunderstanding. I mean, why would he be interested in me?"

"I can think of a few reasons," Theo muttered. He must have seen something on Auggie's face, though, because he said, "I mean, I already mentioned drugs."

"That's not my scene, ok? I told you that."

"Or this could be a setup: blackmail, extortion, something like that. These guys show up, scare the hell out of you. When they come back next time, they want some money."

"I don't have any money."

"You're literally covered in Vineyard Vines."

"Right, but, I don't have a lot of money. Not worth ransom or extortion."

"Maybe they know about that sponsorship deal. Maybe they know there's money down the road."

Auggie spread his hands. "It's just too weird. Why not come right out and accuse me of killing . . . killing whoever that was? Why that weird edited video that doesn't really show anything? Why tag both of us? And then why show up and start asking me where Robert is? People are looking for him, and they're freaking out because they can't find him. Now, because of that stupid video, they think I know where he is."

"You know who would have answers to all these questions?" Theo said.

"Robert."

"So the first question we need to answer is: where's Robert?"

Auggie shook his head. "No, actually, the question now is who's Robert, right? Because you told me he used a fake name, and so we can't find him until we know who he really is, and that means digging through what we already have to try to figure out the answer."

From the next room came the droning of the window unit; Theo shifted, his feet sounding sticky against the stripped floorboards.

"What?" Auggie said.

"That's really smart," Theo said.

And there it was again: heat and light like a flower blooming in Auggie's chest.

"You'd better make me some of that peanut butter toast," Auggie said, locking eyes with Theo. "We've got a lot of work to do."

Theo combed his beard with one hand. He had dark blue eyes that made Auggie think of wildflowers.

"Let me get some stain spray," Theo said. "And a t-shirt you can borrow. Your polo's going to be ruined otherwise."

Auggie waited until Theo was out of the room before releasing the breath he'd been holding. He turned himself out of the polo, the lukewarm air brushing the bare skin of his chest. With every second that ticked past, the goosebumps got worse.

"You can change in the bathroom," Theo said, returning to the kitchen with a t-shirt held out while he read the label on a spray bottle. "It's right over—"

His head came up. He saw Auggie. And he stood there, his face expressionless.

Auggie held out the polo. Theo took it and handed over the tee.

"Bathroom's right over there."

Auggie was already squirming into the shirt. "It's a shirt. It's not like I'm naked."

"If I can see your nipples, it's too close to naked."

When Auggie's head popped through the collar, he found Theo at the sink, alternating between blotting the grease stains and spraying stain remover. Auggie glanced down at the tee and saw that it was for Iron Maiden.

"Bread's in there," Theo said, not looking up. "Peanut butter too."

"Is this a knife you already used for peanut butter?" Auggie asked, grabbing it off the refrigerator's shelf.

"Yes. It's fine. It's just peanut butter."

"Ok."

"There are clean knives over there if you want."

"No, it's ok."

"Plates are in there."

Auggie plucked at the shirt. "You like metal?"

Theo gave a half shake of his head that could have meant anything.

"Just going to slide past you," Auggie said, touching Theo's back as he tried to reach the toaster. Theo's whole body was rigid, every muscle taut and defined under Auggie's fingertips.

"What other bands do you like?" Auggie asked.

Theo let out a strained breath, balled up the polo, and pitched it in the sink. "Just make your toast, please," he said as he left the kitchen again.

Auggie made toast, and he used the knife that was on permanent peanut-butter duty. He put everything back in the refrigerator just the way he'd found it. He filled a glass with tap water because he figured Theo would lose his shit if he tried to score one of the beers, although Auggie saved that thought for later. Theo had gone upstairs—the old house made it easy to keep track of his movements—and now it sounded like he was up there getting ready for a 5K: lots of rapid walking, the joists protesting.

At the table, which was maybe the ugliest part of the whole kitchen, Auggie ate his toast and started doing what he did best: trawling social media. Robert had been at the Sigma Sigma bid party. He'd been wearing a pledge sash. And that meant somebody at the party had gotten pictures of Robert. He probably wasn't a real pledge because he probably wasn't a real student. But someone might know Robert or recognize him. And Auggie was going to find that person.

He'd gotten through most of the Sigma Sigma Bid-ness Party pictures when Theo came back down. Auggie was careful to keep his eyes on the screen, but he still noticed: the pallor, the slight redness around Theo's eyes, the translucent spots on his shirt where he had splashed water—or, the thought came to Auggie like thunder—where tears had fallen.

"I'm going to apologize because I feel like I'm acting crazy today," Theo said, his voice a scratchy attempt at normal. "But this isn't a good idea. I need you to go, Auggie. If there's anything else we need to talk about, I'll be in touch."

"I found him," Auggie said.

"What?"

"I mean, I found a girl who knows him. She says he deals weed and meth to some of the girls in her house."

"She told you that?"

Auggie looked up and blinked. "Yeah. I'm famous, right? And I'm looking to score."

"You aren't famous."

"I've got over a hundred thousand followers."

"Yeah, but you're not a celebrity."

"I looked you up, you know. You know how many followers you have?"

"I'm just saying, internet famous isn't the same thing as really famous. You understand that, right? I know it's different for people your age, but it's an important difference."

"You have two," Auggie said. Holding up two fingers, he repeated, "Two followers."

"Really famous people are known outside of a limited medium and are known to most of the population—"

"My grandmother has three hundred followers."

"And famous people are known—wait, really?"

"Well, like three hundred and eighty, which is closer to four hundred, but I said three hundred because I didn't want you to feel bad."

"Oh my God," Theo said, putting his face in his hands.

"It's ok," Auggie said. "Let's go look at what you've got in your closet."

"No. You're going home. Or to the library. Or hell, wherever you want to go. Anywhere but here."

"We've got plenty of time to pick out something good."

"What are you talking about?"

"She said she'd meet us at the Alpha Phi Conjunction Junction party tonight. She promised to get Robert's contact info from her friends."

"I'm not going to a Greek party. Why can't she just text you the information?"

Auggie sighed, stood, and grabbed a handful of Theo's long, strawberry-blond hair. He tugged and said, "Come on, Goldilocks. Unless you have something better to do tonight?"

"Do that again and I'll kick your ass all the way out to the curb."

"Besides Percocet and half a joint, I mean," Auggie said with a grin.

Smacking Auggie's hand loose, he said, "This is why I hated Luke too, just so you know."

"Who's Luke?"

"My brother. Just like you. Always acted like I didn't have anything to do except bail him out."

When the refrigerator's fan cut off, a soft, tick-tick filled the silence.

"We're going separately," Theo said. "And we're not talking to each other while we're there. I'm only going to make sure you don't get into trouble."

Auggie raised an eyebrow. "That doesn't make any sense."

"We go, we get the information, and we get out."

"Yeah, of course."

"This is to save your ass. We are not going to a party together for fun."

"You sound very worried about the prospect of having fun."

"For the love of God, Auggie."

"Yeah, ok. Sure. This is to save my pathetic, scrawny ass. I get it."

Theo scrubbed at his beard, made a face, and said to no one in particular, "I fucking hate freshmen."

"My innocent ears," Auggie said.

Theo made a noise that sounded a little like a scream.

14

They had hours to kill before the party, but no matter what Theo did, Auggie refused to leave. Theo said he needed to work on his thesis. Auggie asked if he could borrow a copy of *King Lear* to do some homework "for this asshole who keeps assigning more reading." Theo said he needed to clean the house. Auggie offered to start in the kitchen. Theo explained about doing the laundry. Auggie suggested throwing in the polo to see if the stains would come out. Theo pulled out the big guns: it was time to cut the grass. Auggie said he'd do it.

"I won't even get grass on your shirt," he said, already wiggling out of it, grinning and smoothing his hair down after his head came free. "I cut the grass with my shirt off at home all the time."

"For the love of Christ," Theo said, "I need you to literally keep your shirt on."

"It's not even my shirt, it's—"

Theo locked himself in the bathroom, sat on the toilet, and tried to figure out how he could get to the remaining half of the joint without Auggie noticing.

He decided the least problematic option was working on his thesis, so he found a copy of *Lear,* gave it to Auggie, and took his spot on the couch. Auggie sat at the other end, legs up on the cushion between them, his feet brushing Theo's thigh.

"No," Theo said. "This is my spot."

Auggie had his tongue between his teeth as he stared at a page of *Lear.* "What?"

"I do my thesis work on the couch. Right here. This is my spot, this is where I work."

"Ok."

"Auggie."

Auggie tore his eyes away and looked over the top of the book. "Yes, what?"

"This is my spot."

"Oh my God," Auggie said, and then he shifted until he seemed to find a comfortable position, his toes burrowing under Theo's leg.

Theo stared at him. He stared at the paperback of *Lear*. He said, "Am I talking to myself?"

"Whoever you're talking to," Auggie said as he turned a page, "could both of you keep it down? I'm trying to do my homework."

Theo considered the bathroom again: the blessed silence, the locked door. He considered finishing his thesis from the tub.

Somehow, he got to work. He'd coordinated his teaching with his research, hoping for a degree of synergy. Civ 1: Shakespeare in the World dealt with a single Shakespeare text—*Lear*—and translations, adaptations, and editions of it throughout the last four hundred years. Not coincidentally, Theo was trying to finish his chapter on *Lear*. Until he'd met Auggie Lopez, he'd considered that teaching might actually make his life easier. He grabbed the book of critical essays he'd been working on, flipped it open, and tried to disappear inside.

Auggie made that surprisingly difficult. He was only reading. But somehow, that reading seemed to require a lot of noise and energy and movement. He mumbled words under his breath. He paged back and forth. He tried reading on his side. Then his other side. Then his back again. Then his stomach. His butt was—Theo snipped that off. It was a student butt. That's all that mattered. Auggie lay prone, his legs up, crossed at the ankle. Student butt. That's all.

But Theo had to swallow before he swatted Auggie's calf and said, "Get your feet out of my face, please."

Auggie rolled onto his side, already wedging his feet under Theo's thigh again. Then he did some more furious paging. Then he grabbed his phone and started typing. After a moment, he threw it down with a noise of disgust and did some more frantic flipping back and forth.

"Jesus God," Theo said. "What? You didn't get a million likes on your last video of you milking a cat or whatever it was?"

"Huh?"

"What's the problem?"

"What does 'With my two daughters' dow'rs digest the third' mean?"

Theo reached over, mindful of the heat of Auggie's body, and folded back the book. He tapped the facing page with notes.

"I'm not dumb," Auggie said. "I already looked there."

"Well, what do you think it means?"

"I'm not dumb—"

"If I thought you were dumb, I'd just tell you the answer."

For a moment, Auggie was silent, his thumb rubbing the page. Then he said, "Digest sounds like eating, I guess. And a dower is like their inheritance."

"Close enough."

"Ok, so these two daughters are going to eat the other dower. Like the crops or something?"

"A little less literally," Theo said, not able to stop a small grin.

"They're going to take it over."

"Yeah, pretty much. Eat it. Kind of a figurative way of saying consume it. Absorb it."

Auggie's thumb stilled on the page. "Huh."

And then they both went back to reading.

Ten minutes later, Auggie had flopped onto his back again. He laid the book open on his chest, grabbed his phone, and then tossed the phone back down.

"Why haven't I heard of this?"

"What? *Lear*?"

"Yeah. The introduction is about all these people who say it's Shakespeare's best tragedy. I've seen *Hamlet*. Ok, just part of it. In high school. And we read another one about a black guy when I was a sophomore."

"*Othello*."

"I've never heard of this one."

"That's a really, really good question," Theo said. "Actually, that's one of the most interesting questions in scholarship on *Lear*. People are seriously divided about it. About seventy-five years after Shakespeare died, a man named Nahum Tate made his own adaptation—which we'll be reading, so you can look forward to that. It has a happy ending, and it was way more popular than Shakespeare's version." Theo stopped. "Sorry, you're getting a reader's digest version of my thesis."

"No," Auggie said. "I like it. I haven't seen you look like that before."

"Like what?"

"Glowy," Auggie said with a shrug. "Excited."

"Yeah, well, about five more minutes would have put you to sleep, trust me."

Auggie didn't answer, and they both went back to their books; after a minute, though, Auggie's leg slid down, resting across Theo's good knee. Theo knew he should say something, got ready to say something, had it all perfectly clear in his head. And then he didn't say anything. He just tried to read essays and called himself every kind of fucker imaginable.

They spent the rest of the day like that. Auggie ordered Chinese delivery without Theo realizing, and then he wouldn't take any money from Theo when it came. They ate orange chicken at the table Ian had refinished. Theo considered a White Rascal, but he decided against it. It felt weird, drinking in front of a student. That was the reason at the top of his brain.

"Let's see your clothes," Auggie said as he dumped the paper cartons in the trash.

"No way," Theo said.

"I'm not going to a party with you looking like I got you out of a nursing home."

Theo decided the best answer was no answer as he made his way to the stairs. He could hear Auggie coming after him.

"Set one foot on these steps," Theo said, "and see what happens."

"Are you always this grouchy before a party?"

Theo tried to go faster on the stairs.

"Is it social anxiety?" Auggie called after him.

Parties, in Theo's life, had mostly consisted of getting wasted with Luke and their high school friends, usually in Eddie Scharf's basement, usually with a keg that Eddie's older brother had bought for them. When Theo had finally gotten to college, he'd been too old for Greek life, and he'd met Ian quickly, and then partying had seemed like a kid thing to do.

Standing in the closet, he slid hangers along the rod. All his clothes were dirty because, of course, his life had been a time-lapse landslide for the last two months. Now he was looking at Ian's clothes, and his stomach was sour, and his heart was hammering in his chest.

"I can come help you," Auggie shouted.

Theo grabbed one of Ian's shirts, one that he'd really liked on Ian, navy with pink flamingos, and he did up the buttons and then had to redo them because his hands were shaking and he'd done them all wrong the first time. Ian's pants were too small for Theo, so Theo dug out a pair of relatively clean jeans and pulled them on. He found chukkas that Ian had told him to wear when they went out to dinner, and he even found a pair of clean socks. He caught a glimpse of himself in the mirror and asked himself what the fuck he was doing.

Auggie was on his phone when Theo got downstairs. When he glanced up, he cocked his head, and then he stood. He came across the room and reached for Theo like he wanted to hold his hand.

Theo jerked his arm back.

"Ok," Auggie said, drawing out the word. He moved more slowly and caught Theo's sleeve. Then he began rolling it up until it was cuffed neatly above the elbow. He repeated the process with the other sleeve. Then he stepped back and nodded. "Yeah, ok."

"A ringing endorsement," Theo said.

"You look hot," Auggie said. "That better?"

"Not in the slightest."

"Come on, I need to stop by the dorm and change."

Theo shut off the window unit and locked the door behind them. Auggie was on the driveway, rocking on his heels. He glanced at the Malibu.

"If you want," Auggie said, "I could—"

"No."

Auggie nodded.

The night had cooled off considerably, and it was starting to smell like autumn, the crisp air that Theo associated with the season. The sky ran from purple to black. Across the dome, stars blurred into the town's light pollution.

Auggie had that look in his eyes, like he wanted to say something about how sorry he was.

Before that could happen, Theo started walking, and Auggie joined him.

They were halfway to town before Theo realized he hadn't even thought about the Percocet.

15

Auggie stopped Theo a block away from the Alpha Phi house; even at that distance, music thundered from inside, and expensive cars clogged the street. Guys and girls, some in groups, some alone, headed toward the party. Some of them looked twice at Auggie and Theo, but they were the normal, just-a-second-glance kind of looks Auggie was used to getting. He focused on Theo instead.

"Sleeves look good," Auggie said, tightening the cuffs. "Hair—"

"Auggie."

"Ok, ok. I'm not going to touch. It looks good. Beard is on point. Umm, if you'd just let me undo this top one—"

"If you touch that button, you're going to fail Civ 1."

"Hey!"

"We get in and we get out, ok?"

"Oh, wait. Is that the plan?"

Theo crossed his arms; he had very nice arms, and the cuffed sleeves accentuated them.

"That thing you've been saying since like two o'clock this afternoon," Auggie said. "That thing about getting in and getting out. That thing you wouldn't stop saying the whole way back to campus. The first thing you said to me when I came down from my dorm. That's our plan?"

"Auggie."

"Don't worry, I'm locking it in." Auggie pretended to type something and made a few computer noises. "Yep, got it."

"A million people think this kind of stuff is cute? They actively seek out this kind of behavior from you?"

Grinning, Auggie, pulled out his phone and displayed the picture of Samantha Kretzer, the girl he had contacted on Instagram after finding Robert featured in several of her photographs from the night of the Bid-ness Party.

"This is who we're looking for?" Theo said.

"No, she's just really pretty." Auggie was fighting to keep the grin under control. "That was a joke."

"A million people. That's what I'm supposed to believe?"

"So," Auggie said, "if I remember correctly, our plan is to get in and get out, but I just wanted to confirm—Theo! Wait up!"

When they got to the Alpha Phi house, the party was already going strong. Auggie gave the guy at the door cash for him and Theo, and he barely looked at them before waving them inside. Like the Sigma Sigma house, the main floor of the building was divided up into common areas: an industrial-size kitchen, two rooms with TVs, a room clearly designed for studying, and then all-purpose rooms with vinyl-upholstered furniture and high-traffic carpet. Tonight, every space had been adapted for the party. Webs of fairy lights were clipped to the ceilings, providing the only illumination in much of the house. From speakers mounted in every room, the thump-thump of a Pitbull song pounded in time with Auggie's heartbeat. The air smelled yeasty from too much beer, underscored by a hundred different perfumes. People were everywhere: dancing, making out, drinking. A girl was handling a glow-in-the-dark beer bong like a champ, while the guys and girls around her shouted encouragement.

The press of bodies was so thick that Auggie grabbed Theo's wrist, towing him through the crowd. He passed a dollar bill to a guy at a folding table, took one of the red plastic cups filled with beer, and kept going. Theo reached past him and took the beer.

"I paid for that," Auggie shouted over the din.

"Great," Theo shouted back. "I'll give it back when you're twenty-one."

Auggie rolled his eyes and kept going. They had made a complete circuit before Auggie let out a frustrated breath.

"Did you see her?"

Theo shook his head; he was still holding the beer.

"You can drink that. My treat."

Theo gave another slight shake of his head.

It was a really good party. Auggie got out his phone, found the right angle—a shot of his face, bemused but happy, and over his shoulder, the throng of bodies and the fairy lights and the rotating, multicolored spots near the DJ's table. He snapped a few pictures, tried a few filters, and finally settled on one that he liked. He posted it with a caption that said *i wanna dance with somebody . . . wish u were here* and watched the likes and comments begin pouring in.

"What does she say?" Theo shouted.

"What?"

"Did you message Samantha? Where is she? What did she say?"

"Oh, yeah. Um. Still haven't heard from her."

He tapped out a quick direct message and heard Theo say something like, "No, really, I'm ok."

When Auggie looked up, he almost dropped his phone. A girl who looked barely eighteen—Auggie recognized, distantly, the irony—had pulled Theo into a knot of dancing bodies, and now she was grinding up against him. She was pretty: blond, with big, dark eyes and a quirky way of smiling. Theo was still trying to say something to her— probably explaining something about Shakespeare, Auggie thought— and he was trying to juggle the beer and get himself loose. The girl wasn't taking no for an answer; she was holding Theo's free hand, pulling him tight against her, and thrusting back into him like she had a serious itch.

Auggie's phone buzzed, and he saw a message from Samantha: *upstairs, 2nd bedroom on right.*

Theo was bending down, talking into the girl's ear, and she said something back. Theo laughed. He threw his head back like she'd said the funniest thing all year. And then he took a long drink of the beer.

Pushing between a pair of upperclassmen, Auggie went to find the stairs. The music was too loud; it was a shit party, he realized now. The fairy lights were stupid. The strobing, sweeping colored spots at the DJ's table were stupid. This many people in one house, everybody crammed together, that was stupid. Hadn't they ever heard of a fucking fire code?

He dug more cash out of his wallet. When he got to another drink table, he bought himself two shots of Jose Cuervo Silver, shook his head, wondered if he was breathing fire. He wondered if Theo was bi. He wondered about a third shot.

Instead, he kept moving, found the stairs, and went up. The crowd thinned a little; a guy was shirtless, pressed against the banister by a girl kissing him all over; a pair of girls, both of them looking like they'd borrowed their outfits from Stevie Nicks, were making out hard on the top step. Auggie skirted them, turned right, and rapped on the second door. It opened, and Samantha stood there in a pink skirt and a flimsy white top.

"Hey, this is so cool," she said. "Come on in."

When she shut the door behind him, the noise from the party died off substantially.

"So much better, right? Thank God they paid for good soundproofing when they renovated. Do you want something to drink?"

Auggie was feeling the tequila filter into his bloodstream, hot little tendrils of it, and he nodded. "What do you have?"

"Barry brought up beer. Here, have mine." She passed him the red cup, and Auggie took it, drank, and pictured Theo wrapped around the blonde. His memory was playing tricks on him; he kept seeing Theo rock into the girl, returning the movement. He kept seeing Theo kiss her neck, even though part of his brain knew Theo had just been trying to talk into her ear.

"Barry?" Auggie said and then took another drink.

"My boyfriend," Samantha said. "It's totally not serious. So, like, you're really here. That's so cool. Why did you come to Wroxall?"

"Scholarship," Auggie said. "And they've got a great communications program."

"Not that you need any help," Samantha said with a giggle. She kept brushing her hair back over her ear. Right now, she was standing at the built-in desk, swaying her hips so that the pink skirt whisked against her thighs. "I didn't follow you before you messaged me, but you've got such a good platform. You're really funny. That one with the cat in the box is hilarious."

"Thanks."

"Seriously. And you're so cute with your friends."

"Thanks."

She was still playing with her hair, but now she drifted across the room, her hips still moving to the muffled beat of the music, the pink skirt still swishing.

"You are so cute," she said, and now she was close enough for Auggie to smell the sweet, candy-like perfume.

Auggie smiled a cardboard smile. He knew how to sit, how to hold his head, how to hold the beer, how to breathe. Cardboard, all the way through. So fucking cardboard you could stand him up and walk away. Cardboard was what everybody in the whole fucking universe wanted from him.

"Hey, I should have said this earlier," Auggie said. "But I was wondering if you'd want to be in a video with me."

Samantha stopped. "Are you serious?"

"Yeah."

"Are you fucking serious?"

Laughing, Auggie nodded.

"Yes, I would love that."

"Great. But, here's the thing. I'm kind of, you know, in a slump. Robert was supposed to hook me up, but I didn't get his number."

"Yeah, totally, I've got it." She was tapping through her phone. "So, like, what's best? You know, for being creative. Because I've got some Adderall if you want to do that, and I swear it helped me pass Econ."

"Adderall's good," Auggie said.

"Ready?"

"Ready."

She read off the number, and Auggie typed it into the phone.

Sliding a hand onto Auggie's knee, Samantha said, "And what do you like to do when you party?"

Before Auggie could answer, the door opened, and a massive guy with dark, shaggy hair was standing there, carrying a bottle of Bacardi in one hand and a bottle of Coke in the other.

"What the fuck?" he said.

Snatching her hand away, Samantha said, "Barry, just calm down. Jesus Christ."

"What the fuck is going on?"

"Nothing," Auggie said, pushing off from the wall and heading for the door. "Nothing at all."

"It sure as fuck didn't look like nothing," Barry shouted. Then he threw the bottle of Bacardi, and it shattered against the far wall. "Samantha, what the fuck is wrong with you?"

Auggie tried to slide past him.

Instead, Barry grabbed a handful of his t-shirt. Barry was a big guy, with probably six inches and a hundred pounds on Auggie. He smelled like rum and coconut, and Auggie had a vision of this guy beating the shit out of him while drinking a pina colada.

"Were you hooking up with her?" Barry said, yanking him by the shirt and tossing him against the wall. "What app? Tinder?"

Samantha grabbed Barry's arm. "Barry, you are fucking wasted. What the fuck is wrong with you? We were just talking."

Spinning toward his girlfriend, Barry said, "Talking with your hand in his crotch. Yeah, I can fucking see you were talking. Hey, you little shit, get back here."

Auggie sprinted down the stairs. Theo was on the bottommost step, and those strawberry blond eyebrows went up when he saw Auggie.

"What—"

Catching Theo's arm, Auggie dragged him into the mass of bodies.

"Get the fuck back here!"

Barry had some healthy lungs.

For the moment, the chaos of the party provided cover. Behind Auggie, Barry was still shouting, but the music and the fairy lights and the crowd kept him from catching up. Even through the tequila, though, Auggie knew that the real problem was once they got outside of the Alpha Phi house. Barry would have buddies; guys like Barry always had buddies. Theo had handled one guy easily. He might even be able to handle two. What about five frat bros showing up for the same fight? Worse, once Auggie and Theo were outside, they wouldn't have a quick means of escape. They'd walked here, and they'd have to walk out of here. Outside, without the crowd, Barry would spot them in an instant. And he and his buddies would have cars. He and his buddies would be able to catch up even if Auggie ran—and Auggie wasn't even sure Theo could run.

When they got outside, the late September air felt chilly in comparison to the sweltering heat of the party. Theo turned, obviously planning on heading the way they had come, but Auggie grabbed his wrist and pulled him twenty yards in the other direction, following the wall of the Alpha Phi house. A dense line of boxwood ran under the windows. Auggie dropped onto his back, squirmed until his head and shoulders were deep beneath the boxwood, and pulled Theo down on top of him.

"Fuck," Theo yelped.

"Are you ok?"

Theo nodded, but he was pale, and he had one hand pressed to his knee.

"I'm sorry, Christ, I'm so sorry. Look, we've got to sell this. Fast. That asshole wants to beat the shit out of me."

"I can—"

"Theo, please." Auggie didn't wait for an answer before grabbing his shirt and pulling Theo toward him. Their cheeks were touching; Theo's beard was softer than Auggie had expected. Auggie whispered again, "Please."

"Where the fuck is he?" Barry shouted. He sounded like he was standing right next to him. "Where the fuck did that prick go? Get the fuck back here!"

Theo whispered, "This is going to be in my nightmares for the rest of my life, just so you know."

Auggie didn't know what he was talking about until Theo began to pump his hips, pistoning back and forth, supporting himself on his elbows, never quite making contact. His breath was hot, licking Auggie's collar bone where the t-shirt had slid aside. He smelled like cedar and musk and hops. On Auggie's cheek, the friction of Theo's beard built into a blaze, and the fire spread down into his chest, between his legs. Upstairs with Samantha, he'd felt like Pinocchio, dancing on strings he'd hung for himself; this, in contrast, even with Theo faking every moment of it—this felt real.

Auggie squeezed his eyes shut. The tequila in his blood fueled the fire. He caught Theo's rhythm, felt it in his pulse, knew that this would be what it was like if they were together for real: the confidence, the steadiness, the control. He could imagine, if they were really together, Theo's hand on the inside of his thigh. He could imagine Theo's hand at the small of his back, guiding. He could imagine Theo's hand between his leg. Auggie knew could rut up right then, matching Theo's rhythm. He could make contact. Even the tequila couldn't convince him, though, that he wouldn't just be fucking everything up.

"Jesus Christ," Theo whispered. "My knee."

"Oh, sorry," Auggie put a hand on Theo's shirt, the sweat-damp cotton rough against his fingertips. "You can stop. I think—I think he's gone."

With a groan, Theo flopped onto his back, pulling his knee to his chest, massaging it.

"Are you ok?" Auggie whispered, inching out from under the boxwood.

"Yep, great. Just don't look at me. Maybe you shouldn't look at me ever again."

"Well, you saved our asses. So, um. Thank you."

Eyes shut, Theo nodded.

"How bad is your knee?"

"My knee is royally screwed up," Theo whispered. "I'm more worried about which circle of hell I'm going to."

"Do you want me to call a cab?"

"No. I can—I can walk. I just fucking forgot my cane, which is so fucking stupid that I fucking deserve every fucking step I'm going to have to walk tonight."

"I'll call you a cab."

"Did you get the number?"

"What? Oh. Yeah."

"Well, call it."

Auggie glanced around; they were alone on the Alpha Phi lawn. He placed the call and put it on speaker.

"Yeah?" It wasn't Robert; this voice was older, raspier, probably a smoker.

"I want to talk to Robert."

The breathing on the other end of the line altered, quickening with what sounded, to Auggie, like panic. And then the call disconnected.

Theo's eyes were opening, wildflower blue looking black in the shadows. He shrugged and said, "Try again."

Auggie placed the call again. It rang twelve times before going to a generic voicemail.

"Once more," Theo said.

This time, the phone rang once before being shunted to the generic voicemail again.

"He turned it off," Auggie whispered.

"Yeah," Theo said. "But who the hell was that?"

16

The next morning, Theo didn't hear the alarm go off. He woke hours later, his knee throbbing from overdoing it last night, his head throbbing because he'd come home from the party and finished off the White Rascal. Lying in bed, with a stack of Ian's neatly folded t-shirts next to him, Theo considered puking. He remembered the feel of Auggie beneath him, the slim musculature, the smell of tequila, the smoothness of his cheek. He remembered what it had felt like to stare at the hollow of his shoulder, soft brown skin taut over bone, to have his mouth inches from Auggie's, to feel like he was burning up in spite of the cool evening. Rolling onto his side, Theo buried his face in Ian's tees, knocking over the pile. All he could smell, though, was laundry detergent.

Eventually, he had to get up. He took a Percocet, drank as much water as he thought he could stand, and toasted the heel of a slice of bread. The late-morning sunlight came in across the sink, picking out motes of dust in the air, highlighting tiny fuzzies that clung to the door of the oven. The Rudock kids were screaming at the top of their lungs, and Theo wondered how much a box of plastic bullets would cost. A hangover of this magnitude seemed like a reasonable excuse for riot gear.

Cart called, and Theo sent it to voicemail. Cart called again. This time, Theo let it ring until it went to voicemail on its own.

When he didn't think he was going to puke anymore, he showered, dressed, and grabbed his cane. He made his way to the bus stop and did his daily pilgrimage to Downing. He got lucky on the return trip—the bus came on time—and he trudged home. His leg was on fire again. With every yard, Theo wondered why he had forgotten everything that was important last night: the cane, the Percocet, Ian. But that question was so messed up that Theo shoved it aside to focus on something more straightforward. They'd tracked down Robert's phone number and gotten a stranger. What was the next move? How did they find Robert before those assholes came after Auggie again?

Lost in that question, he didn't notice that the front door of his house had been forced until he was halfway up the steps. Theo paused, the keys hanging from one finger, and then he made a fist with the keys sticking out. He eased his weight up to the porch, wincing as the cane thumped against the wood. He examined the jamb and saw where wood had splintered around the strike plate. He listened, heard nothing, and stepped inside.

Someone had destroyed his home. The TV lay on its back, the screen shattered, a faint whiff of burnt electronics in the air. Theo's piles of books had been dismantled; books lay everywhere, some of them with pages ripped out, many with spines cracked and bindings torn. Wads of batting spilled out of the couch where someone had slashed the cushions. Lana's toy train had been smashed. The red light flashed weakly in the plastic wreckage.

He moved slowly into the kitchen, trying not to rely on the cane too much, trying to keep his steps quiet. The damage was bad here too: the back door was open, and the table Ian had refinished lay at an angle, two of the legs having been kicked off. One of the chairs formed a broken heap at the base of the wall. Another was on its side. He could see two more out on the back lawn, where someone must have pitched them off the deck. The faucet had been broken, and water fountained up; the only good luck Theo could see was that the water was falling into the sink and going down the drain.

A step behind him made him turn, and he saw the big guy with the shaved head and the Celtic cross on his arm. He had a splint across his nose, two black eyes, and a look like he planned on returning the favor. Theo slid into the kitchen and heard movement on the deck. When he glanced over, he saw the blond girl with the swastika on her cheek. She was wearing an eyepatch today, and she had her arm in a sling, with several fingers splinted. In her off hand, she carried another pistol.

"Jerome, right?" Theo said to the big guy. To the girl he said, "And who are you?"

"Sit the fuck down," Jerome said.

"You broke all my chairs," Theo said, running his thumb along the edge of a key, the metal greasy under his touch. He resisted the urge to look upstairs at the bedroom, where he'd stashed the gun he'd taken from the blond girl the last time they'd run into each other. "And if you come any closer, I'm going to gut you, you big dumb shit. Understand?"

"And Mae will shoot your brains out."

"Mae better not take one more fucking step inside my house," Theo said, glancing at the blond woman. "Or I'll take out her other eye. What are you two dumbasses doing here?"

"Where's Robert?" the woman—Mae—asked.

"Come a little closer," Theo said. "I'll whisper it in your ear."

"Mae'll shoot you," Jerome said, but he'd stopped in the middle of the front room. "She'll shoot your fucking face off."

"She'll have to hit me first," Theo said. "Did you two rehearse your Three Stooges routine? Last time was pretty good. I liked the part where she got stuck in the door. Classic Curly."

"Put the cane down, faggot," Mae said. "And drop the keys. I don't have to be a good shot to hit you from right here."

"Who's Robert?"

"He's—" Jerome began.

"Shut up, Jerome," Mae shouted. "Jesus Christ."

"See, I figure this is drugs," Theo said. "You two look like you've had your brains fried at some point, and you're clearly of the homophobic, racist, white nationalist shit-eating breed. So I figure this is drugs, and it has to do with the Ozark Volunteers. What I want to know is who's Robert. Why are you looking for him? Why the fuck are you bothering me?"

"Last time I'm going to ask you," Mae said. "Put the cane down. Drop the keys. We're going to have a nice, long talk."

Eyeing the distance between himself and Jerome, Theo judged his odds. Getting away from the gun was his best chance, but fighting Jerome wasn't going to be easy. Theo had had the advantage of surprise last time, and the guy looked like he could take a punch. Theo drew in a few deep breaths, preparing to launch himself into the front room.

Sirens blatted. Jerome shot a look over his shoulder, called, "Cop," to Mae, and then swung his gaze between Theo and Mae.

"Come on, dumbass," Mae said, disappearing outside.

Jerome sprinted past Theo, and a moment later, both of them had disappeared into the tree line.

"Theo?" Cart called from the front door. "Holy fuck. What happened? Theo? Are you ok? Theo?"

"Yeah." Theo limped into the opening to the front room. "Hey, Cart. I'm fine."

"Shit, man." Cart rubbed his buzzed head. He was in uniform, and behind him, the patrol car's lights spun while the siren wailed. "What the fuck?"

"I don't know. I got home and found the place like this."

"Did you call the cops?"

"No. I just got back."

"Jesus, I could tell something was wrong, which is why I ran the siren. But this is insane." Cart fixed a look on Theo. "I thought I saw somebody in here."

Theo thought of what Auggie had told him: *He said if I went to the police, he'd kill me.* Then he shrugged. "Just me."

A long moment passed before Cart said, "Did you check upstairs?"

"Not yet."

"Come on. Get out of the house."

So Theo followed Cart outside, and at the cruiser, Cart called in his location and then turned off the lights and siren. Drawing his service weapon, he waved Theo back toward the street and went into the house again. He was gone for maybe five minutes. Theo stood in the September sun; the heat had broken, and the day was cool and crisp and clear. The Rudock kids had gathered on the other side of the street to watch the action.

When Cart returned, he was holstering his gun. "House is clear. I checked upstairs and the basement. Back door is ok, but you're going to have to get somebody out here to fix the front door."

"Fuck," Theo said.

"Let's take a look and see what's missing."

The problem, of course, was that nothing was missing. Theo took advantage of the search to make sure the pistol he'd taken from Mae on their first encounter was still safely hidden inside the box spring, but other than that, he mostly followed Cart around the house and said the same thing over and over again: "It looks like everything's here."

"Well, fuck, man," Cart said when they had made their way through the house and were standing in the kitchen. He was rubbing his head again. "Why the fuck did they break in here? They destroyed this place."

"Maybe it's an angry student," Theo said.

Cart barked a laugh. "They were definitely trying to find something."

"Like what?"

"Like anything valuable, dumbass. That's kind of the point of a burglary." He toed the broken table. "Shit. Some of this, they did it just to be nasty."

Theo surveyed the damage again. Then he pinched the bridge of his nose. "What a fucking mess."

"You want me to dust for prints?"

"Is it a waste of time?"

"Not necessarily," Cart said.

Theo stared at him.

"Ok," Cart said. "It probably won't go anywhere. But I'll do it just in case."

"Fuck it," Theo said. "It doesn't matter." He played the back door open and closed, and then he left it open, staring out at the chairs on the back lawn. "I guess I'd better get started. I can just board up the front door for now, right? And the rest of this stuff—" He stared at it, trying to figure out where to start.

"I knew you were country trash," Cart said. "I didn't know you were bottom of the barrel trash."

"What?"

"Boarding up your door? You're not living with Ma and Pa Hillbilly, all right? Have some fucking self-respect."

"Fuck off. I can't afford to pay a carpenter, and I sure as fuck am not—"

"Dumbass," Cart interrupted loudly. "I get off in a few hours."

"What the hell is going on? Am I having a stroke?"

"I own a drill," Cart said with a grin. "And I own a saw. And fuck, buddy, I even own a few of these fancy things called screws."

Theo stared at him.

"Just ask me, dumbass," Cart said.

"No way, you've got a job, and you don't want to spend your Sunday fixing my problems."

"How about you let me decide what I want to do?" Cart said, his smile fading. "Just ask me."

"Really? You'd do that?"

"I only accept payment in beer."

"Yeah, ok." Theo felt himself smile. "I can pick up some Big Wave."

"You going to be all right for a little bit? I was just stopping by to see if you were ok; you weren't answering your phone."

"Sorry," Theo said. "I was out at Downing, and, well, you know."

Cart squeezed his shoulder. "I'll call you when I'm on my way."

"Thanks. Thank you, Cart. Seriously."

Rubbing his buzzed head, Cart gave an embarrassed grin and headed for the door.

Something Cart had said turned in Theo like a key, and he said, "Cart?"

"Yeah?"

"You know that kid. The murder video. That whole weird thing. You remember?"

"Yes, motherfucker. I'm not senile."

"What about fingerprints?"

Cart paused. "What?"

"The car they stole. Did the police dust it for fingerprints?"

"Who the fuck cares about the car? What the fuck are you talking about?"

"Robert Poulson. I don't think that's his real name. But what if you ran his fingerprints from the car? Maybe he'd show up, right?"

Cart had turned to face Theo again, thumbs tucked behind his belt, studying him. It was a cop's face.

"Now just what the hell is going on? You think this, what happened here today, has something to do with that?"

"No. I don't know. I just—I just thought of it."

"You lying to me again?"

"No."

"For fuck's sake," Cart muttered, his eyes still locked on Theo.

Outside, a string trimmer whined. Theo shifted his weight, massaging his hip; his hand slid along the cane.

"I'll check," Cart finally said.

"Thank you."

"When you're ready, you going to tell me what's going on?"

"Nothing's going on."

Another moment passed; the string trimmer's whine rose in pitch and cut off abruptly, and one of the Rudock boys let out a string of shits, damns, and hells.

"For fuck's sake," Cart muttered again, shaking his head as he left.

17

After the Alpha Phi party, Auggie found himself coming up with reasons not to see Theo—except in class, of course—and three weeks rolled by.

During the first week, Theo had stopped Auggie after class to ask about the search for Robert, suggest new strategies, and update Auggie on his own efforts. Auggie had nodded, answered as politely as he could, and left as quickly as possible.

During the second week, Theo had tried to stop Auggie only once, and Auggie had said something about a friend waiting, and he had seen, in Theo's face, that he had heard the lie.

During the third week, Theo hadn't said anything that was related to class.

Auggie had great reasons for avoiding Theo: first and foremost, to avoid fucking up everything he'd worked so hard to build. He'd come close to making a huge mistake that night outside the Alpha Phi party, and he didn't want to risk it again. Besides, he was a freshman in college, he was making new friends, he was pledging Sigma Sigma, he was branching out, he was exploring new interests. Every once in a while, he would trawl Instagram or Twitter, looking for a clue about Robert's identity. But nobody showed up to ask any more questions, and with every day, the whole thing seemed like a weird nightmare that was slowly dissolving.

To fill the time, Auggie did exactly what he thought he was supposed to do: he made friends. It was easy enough; internet Auggie made waves at the college, and all Auggie had to do was pick the right people. He made adjustments to fit in: he talked about girls, he stopped rolling the pack of Parliaments in his sleeve, he drank more than he used to. Once he had his circle of friends, most of them guys from Sigma Sigma, it was easy to start pumping out content again. Funny videos, sweet videos, dorky videos. The biggest surprise was finding that Orlando was really funny, and more and more often,

Auggie found himself asking Orlando to be part of his videos, and more and more often, Orlando said yes.

And, of course, Auggie's free time was rapidly swallowed up by Chan's escalating feud with him. His ex-girlfriend apparently hadn't learned her lesson from when she had reposted the murder video. She had created a new account, exclusive to Instagram, and every day she posted a new video of her defacing or destroying a picture of Auggie: she cut them up and burned the pieces; she made voodoo dolls and stabbed them with pins; one of her favorites was to ink over a picture of Auggie so it looked like he was giving a blow job. And during each of these videos, she would tell a story about Auggie being an awful boyfriend—most of them made up, a few of them true. The account's handle was thisisurex2, and the worst part was that it was incredibly popular.

So Auggie figured he had his hands full: classes, new friends, making videos with Orlando and the gang, dealing with Chan. He felt busier than he ever had in his entire life. And at night, before he fell asleep, he'd remember Theo's body framing his, remember the smell of cedar and moss and beer, the raspy burn of whiskers against his cheek, Theo's breath hot where his neck joined his shoulder.

"No," Auggie said. It was a Friday in October, late afternoon, and he and Orlando were finishing up a video. "You have to look seriously mad."

Orlando had the perfect face for looking mad: the heavy brows, the heavy scruff, the strong jaw. The problem was he kept breaking character and giggling.

"Ok, ok, ok, ok, ok," Orlando said, shaking the box of Cookie Crisp so the cereal rattled inside. "I got it, Augs."

"You're smiling again."

"No, I'm not!"

"Think about a dead puppy. Or a dead kitten. Or a dead puppy inside a dead kitten."

"Oh fuck," Orlando said. "You are so weird."

"Yes, that face."

Auggie started recording and then moved into the frame. He pretended to sneak toward the mini fridge under Orlando's bed. He opened it, got out the milk, and then walked over to the boxes of cereal lined on the windowsill. He ran his finger down them, stopped at the spot where a box was missing, and made a face for the camera. With a shrug, he pretended to settle on Apple Jacks, hooking the box with one finger.

Orlando stomped into the frame, grabbed Auggie by the shoulder, and tossed him toward the bed. Auggie was ready, and he jumped into the movement so it looked like Orlando had thrown him across the room. Then Orlando poured himself a bowl of cereal, added milk, and let out a satisfied noise as he crunched the first bite.

Auggie burst out laughing as soon as the scene ended. He had landed on Orlando's bed, and now he rolled onto his back, laughing even harder.

"You are so bad at this."

"Fuck off," Orlando said, grinning around another mouthful of Cookie Crisp.

"You are. You don't look angry at all."

"Oh yeah?"

"Yeah," Auggie said. "You look like a little kid. You're just so excited to get that Cookie Crisp."

"That's the whole point, dumbass."

"But it's funnier if you look mad the whole time."

"I'll show you mad," Orlando said, crowding up against the bed and slotting himself between Auggie's legs, leaning over Auggie, propping himself on one elbow so that they were inches apart. He screwed his face up into a grimace and chomped another bite. "How's this for mad?"

"You are so stupid," Auggie said, laughing.

The change, when it happened, was instantaneous: Auggie's laughter turned to stone in his chest, and it was suddenly hard to breathe. Orlando seemed to feel it too. His chewing slowed and then stopped. He swallowed. Then, without taking his eyes from Auggie, Orlando set the bowl down. His hand slid along the mattress, his thumb grazing the side of Auggie's thigh.

A knock came at the door. Orlando froze, and then a blush rushed in behind that thick, dark stubble, and he grabbed the bowl and stumbled back. Milk sloshed over the rim, and he swore.

"I'll clean that up," he muttered.

Auggie slid off the bed, staring at Orlando. Orlando stared back, sucking milk from the back of his hand. Then he blushed even harder and hurried into the bathroom.

The knock came again.

When Auggie opened the door, he thought, for a very short moment, about slamming it shut again. The rational part of his brain told him that wouldn't solve anything in the long run, so instead, he set his shoulder against the door to keep it from being forced open, and spoke through the gap.

"Yeah?"

Glasses hadn't changed much in the month since Auggie had seen him. Same huge glasses in yellow plastic. Same huge mustache.

But he looked younger, rested, refreshed. He smiled with his uneven teeth and placed a hand on the door. Just looking comfortable? Or ready to force his way into the room? Auggie's heartbeat accelerated.

"Let's take a walk," Glasses said.

"Hey," Orlando said, emerging from the bathroom, "uh, I just wanted to say—"

"I'll be back later," Auggie said, grabbing his phone and stepping out into the hallway. Again, by some miracle, Glasses had chosen an opening when no one was wandering around—which seemed impossible in a place like Moriah Court, where people were up and going at all hours.

On the quad, a beautiful fall day was waiting: the sun high and bright, the sky crisply blue. It was warm, threatening to tip over into hot again. A maintenance team was working on a fountain, and the smell of wet leaves and dead grass was not exactly unpleasant. Auggie glanced around, looking for the big guy and the woman who had been waiting for him last time. He didn't see them, and he wondered if Theo had been right: maybe they really were working for someone else.

"August, how are you doing?" Glasses asked as they walked around the quad's perimeter. A frisbee hit the sidewalk ahead of them, skittering along for another yard before stopping against a crack in the cement. Glasses bent and tossed it back to the girls who were waiting; he was grinning when he looked at Auggie for an answer.

"I found someone who knows him," Auggie said. "I found—"

Glasses hushed him. "I mean, how are you? You're young. You're on your own for the first time. College is a difficult transition."

"You're asking me if I'm ok?"

"Well, it seems to me like someone should. For example, I noticed that your brothers don't call. They only text. Fernando and—how do you say it? Chuy?"

I nodded.

"And your mother hasn't even texted. I suppose she's busy with Timothy." Glasses smiled under the mustache. "That's the latest one, by the way. Nicholas is old news. They're in Greece. Have you been to Greece?"

"I found a girl who knows him," Auggie said. "I—"

"When I want to know what you found," Glasses said. "I'll ask you. Until then, answer my fucking questions."

The same frisbee, bright yellow and orange, skipped across the grass. This time, it dead-ended right at Glasses's loafer. He bent and tossed it back with another huge grin.

"No," Auggie said quietly. "I haven't been to Greece."

"It looks beautiful. I'd love to go someday. How are your classes?"

"Fine."

"How's Shakespeare in the World?"

"Fine."

"How's Mr. Stratford?"

"I don't know. Fine."

"August, we can find a private place to continue this conversation." Glasses didn't touch his jacket, didn't pull it back, didn't display the pistol holstered at his hip. But he didn't need to; Auggie's eyes went there anyway.

"No." Auggie thought, suddenly, of the milk in the mini fridge. His throat was so fucking dry he couldn't even swallow. "No, this is fine."

"Now, I'd like to hear what progress you've made."

"A phone number. And a girl who knows him."

"How does she know him?"

"He deals to her friends."

"Does she know where he is?"

Auggie shook his head.

"Then she's useless," Glasses said gently. "What about the phone number?"

"It doesn't work. I mean, it does, but it goes straight to voicemail. The first time I called, a man answered. Older. Smoker, maybe. He wouldn't say anything about Robert."

They were passing one of the narrow walkways between Wroxall's old buildings, and Glasses grabbed Auggie's shoulder and steered him away from the quad. Auggie tried to lock his legs by reflex, but Glasses had a tight grip, and he forced Auggie to keep walking. A service passageway opened to the right, and Glasses shoved Auggie ahead of him until they ended up in a small space with a bike rack, a steel security door, and two orange buckets turned upside down.

"See, I was worried you were too stupid to find out what I needed to know."

"I'm not," Auggie said. He stumbled back until he hit the stone of the building behind him. "I'm not, I'll find him, I just need more time."

"Really? Because I think you've lost motivation."

"No, I swear to Christ. No. I will find him."

Glasses shook his head. "Does Fer still like mountain biking?"

Auggie gaped; he couldn't even find words for an answer.

"Do you think," Glasses asked, "he could still bike if I broke every bone in his leg, all the way down to his toes?"

"Please don't do that," Auggie said. "Please don't hurt him."

"Stand up straight," Glasses said.

"Please don't—"

"Stand up, August."

As soon as Auggie straightened, Glasses punched him. It was an easy, perfect punch with a lot of force behind it, and Auggie felt the breath whoosh out of him.

"Up," Glasses said. "Stand the fuck up."

Somehow, Auggie managed, and Glasses hit him again.

This time, Auggie went to his knees, and a moment later he was puking onto the concrete pad.

"Just because I've been generous with my timeline," Glasses said, toeing Auggie with a loafer while Auggie continue to gasp for breath and heave, "does not mean I've forgotten. I want results, August. Next time, I'll just buy a ticket to California." A folded scrap of paper fluttered down next to Auggie. "Call me when you have what I want."

His shoes made soft whicking noises as he left.

Auggie knelt there, the concrete rough against his bare knees, smelling his own puke and his own fear. When he had enough breath, he started sobbing. He cried until he could pull himself back together, and then he went looking for Theo.

18

When the knock came at the door, Theo checked the clock and decided there was no way Cart had decided to pick him up two hours early. He wedged a pencil into the book to mark his place, shifted the stack of articles to the side, and got to his feet. A second knock came while he was making his way across the room. The knock went on and on, faster and harder, until Theo opened the door.

"Jesus fuck, what the—oh."

Auggie stood on the porch. He looked like shit: his face waxen, his dark eyes fixed on the ground, his shoulders hunched.

"What?" Theo said.

"I need to talk to you," Auggie said without looking up.

"Great. Office hours are eleven to noon—"

"Move the fuck out of the way so I can come inside," Auggie shouted. "I need to fucking talk to you."

"Who do you think you are?" Theo said. "I tried to talk to you. Every day after class. And you looked at me like you'd never met me before, like I was some crazy guy from the bus station. And then you wouldn't even do that. You gave me bullshit excuses and ran away. So, you know what, Auggie? If you need to talk to me, you can do it during office hours. Get the fuck off my doorstep."

Theo slammed the door. He made his way back to the couch, sat, and gathered his papers and book. Then he shoved them all aside again. Covering his face, he counted every fucking way he was an idiot, and then he got up and went to the kitchen. He ran the water, and then he turned it off because he had no idea why he'd started it in the first place. He opened the refrigerator and stared at the bottles of Big Wave, the mostly empty jug of orange juice, the half sub sandwich Cart had left the last time he'd been at the house—two nights before, helping Theo with the floors upstairs. When Theo slammed the refrigerator door, the bottles rattled inside.

This time, Auggie was sitting on the porch steps. He was crying—quietly, sure, but still crying.

"Up," Theo said, grabbing his arm. "Come on."

Auggie let Theo lead him into the kitchen. Theo got him seated at the table, which Cart had found some miraculous way of repairing. Two of the chairs had been a loss, but Cart had stopped by with replacements that were a pretty close match. He'd picked them up at a flea market, he said. Cheap.

"I'm a piece of shit," Auggie said, wiping his face. "I tried not to come; I wanted to leave you alone because I knew you'd be mad at me."

"Oh my God, I just don't have the stamina for this. What do you need?"

"I'm sorry I avoided you."

"It's your life, Auggie. If you don't need my help, that's fine."

"I do need your help," Auggie said. He landed the words pretty dramatically, but they were ruined by a fantastic snot bubble that popped right when he was finishing.

In spite of himself, Theo laughed, and then Auggie laughed too. Theo got up, found a box of tissues, and pulled out a few for Auggie. They sat there for a while, Auggie mopping his face.

"Christ," Auggie said after a few minutes. "If Chan could see me now, she'd be so fucking happy."

"Who's Chan?"

"My ex-girlfriend."

Theo couldn't help it; he made a noise.

"Yeah," Auggie said. "Most of my audience is girls."

"So, your dating life is another part of this internet persona?"

"I know you think it's stupid, but I'm really good at it, and it's . . . it's important to me. If you're going to make fun of me, can you wait until I'm gone and you can do it with your smart, cool, hipster friends?"

Theo dragged his knuckles back and forth across the table, bumping over the uneven layers of paint, and finally said, "What makes you think I have any friends?"

For some reason, Auggie found that hilarious.

"You don't have to put a label on yourself," Theo said when Auggie had finished laughing, trying to pick the right words, "but did you stop . . . needing my help because of what happened at the Alpha Phi party?"

"No."

"Because you understand that nothing's going to happen between us, right? If you think I'm making a move on you, I'm not. That was a performance. Camouflage. And it was your idea."

"Ok."

"I'm not into you."

"Great."

"I am gay, though," Theo said.

"Oh my God," Auggie said, slipping down in the chair like he was trying to slide under the table. "You are so fucking awkward."

"I just thought I should—"

"Yeah, Theo. I know. You were married to a guy; I kind of figured it out. Oh shit, sorry."

"No," Theo said. "It's fine. Nobody wants to say anything about Ian around me. They all want to say they're sorry, but then they also desperately want to pretend nothing happened. I'm not going to fall apart if you remind me I was married."

Auggie slowly squirmed upright again, passing the ball of wadded tissues from hand to hand. Then he said, "Does anyone ask you how you're doing?"

Theo dragged his knuckles over the uneven paint and then stopped. "Not really."

"How are you doing?"

"Ok. Not great." Theo cleared his throat. "Better, before a freshman showed up on my porch trying to knock down my door. What's going on?"

"He came back again. The guy with the glasses."

"Are you ok?"

"I guess. He . . . hit me. I'm fine. But he also threatened my family. He said next time he's going to fly out to California and hurt my brother."

"Damn," Theo breathed. Then he asked, "Why did he wait so long?"

"What?"

"It doesn't make sense. When Robert disappeared, those guys came after you fast. They wanted to find him, and they were acting like it was time sensitive. The Ozark Volunteer assholes came here and asked about him, but that was more about revenge, I think. And this Glasses guy hasn't contacted you since the first time, right?"

"Wait," Auggie said. "Those guys came here?"

Theo shrugged.

"Shit, they cut up your couch and you used . . . duct tape to fix it? Why didn't you say anything?"

Theo raised an eyebrow.

"Oh," Auggie said, a blush working its way under his light brown skin. "Sorry."

"They haven't been back, though," Theo said. "Why? What's changed? Why was this so pressing at the beginning, but now it seems like it's not time sensitive anymore? Like maybe this guy just wants to tie up a loose end?"

"I have no idea." Auggie massaged his chest. "But I don't want him to hurt Fer. Or you. Or anyone. And I don't know what to do, because the pictures from the party were a dead end, the phone number was a dead end, and I'm completely out of ideas."

"Robert McDonald."

"What?"

"That's his real name. That's another thing I was going to tell you, but I . . . I didn't learn it until last week, and by then I was kind of angry at you."

"How did you get his real name?"

"I asked a friend who's a cop—no, don't freak out, I didn't tell him why. I just asked him to check the Porsche that you were joyriding in for prints. Passenger side. He lucked out and got a clean set from the dashboard."

"But those could be from anybody that rode with the owner."

"Maybe," Theo said, "but it's pretty unlikely that a lot of guys with charges for possession and distribution were riding in that Porsche."

"Robert McDonald," Auggie said, dragging out his phone. "Shit, that's incredible. Thank you."

"I asked him about the full record, but he wasn't sure he could get it." Theo checked the clock again. "I'll ask him again tonight."

"Holy shit," Auggie said, dropping the phone. "Are you going on a date?"

"I'm sorry, what?"

"You actually look excited for once, and you're going out with a guy, and is it a date?"

"Oh my God. I wish Cart could hear you right now."

"And he's a cop. Is that, like, a thing for you?"

"Goodbye, Auggie. I'll tell you if I get that record."

"You should put out for him. You should definitely put out. Then he'll give you Robert's file."

"It's not a date," Theo said, laughing as he stood. "Now goodbye. I have to get ready."

"You're getting ready," Auggie said, ticking it off on his finger. "You look happy. He's picking you up, right?" Auggie held out three fingers. "It's a date."

"He's Ian's best friend," Theo said, shoving the chair back into place because the joke wasn't funny anymore. "And it's my birthday, so will you fucking drop it?"

"Yeah," Auggie said. "Sorry. I was just—"

"I'm going to shower."

Auggie spoke when Theo was moving into the front room. "Hey, um. Theo?"

"What?" When Auggie didn't answer, Theo looked back; Auggie was staring at the table, shredding the tissues, the fear shrouding his face again. "Oh," Theo said, blowing out a breath and trying to smooth out his voice. "Yeah, ok. You can hang out here until I get back."

"Thanks."

"But don't go upstairs, don't mess up my papers, and don't even fucking think about touching my beer."

19

After Theo left, Auggie tried to get comfortable on the couch. There were three problems. Problem one, his shirt kept sliding up, and the duct tape on the cushions irritated his bare skin. Problem two, the couch was either too long (if he tried to sit up), and he felt like he was sinking into it, or too short (if he stretched out the whole way), and he remembered that he had fit just perfectly on the couch when Theo had taken up part of it for his thesis. Problem three, though, was the doozy. Problem three was that Theo was on a date.

Theo might not know it was a date. Theo, in fact, might even claim he didn't believe it was a date. But Auggie knew it. He could tell. The way Theo looked when he came down in a black tee and jeans and bright white sneakers. The care Theo had taken with his hair and beard, the bro flow gleaming, the thick beard groomed, and the smell of cedar and moss following him. The beers—beer after beer, until he looked like he was in high school and afraid of getting cut off—while he waited for his ride. Mostly, though, it was the way Theo had shouted when Auggie had teased him about it.

And no matter how Auggie squirmed and twisted and flopped on the couch, his brain was squirming and twisting and flopping even more frantically. He'd picture Theo at some fancy restaurant with a big, handsome guy—for some reason, he looked a little like Orlando—pulling out the chair. He'd picture Theo smiling that tiny, gentle smile when the guy poured him a glass of champagne. He'd picture the static spark when their hands touched for the first time that night, and the handsome guy tried to laugh it off, and Theo just did that quiet teacher thing that made every bone in Auggie's body resonate like he'd hit a new frequency.

Then Auggie would flop onto the couch, remind himself he was an idiot, and go back to his phone, searching for Robert McDonald's social media profile. He didn't find anything on Facebook, so he switched to Instagram. On a second set of tracks at the back of his head, his brain was replaying the first time he'd shown Theo one of his videos, and the confusion on Theo's face when he said, *You're a pretty good dancer*, because he'd missed the whole point of the video, which only made it cuter.

Groaning, Auggie tossed his phone aside and buried his face in his arm. He was such an idiot.

He called Fer.

"What, dickcheese?"

Based on the background static, Auggie guessed Fer was driving. "Hey, what's up?"

"You called me. What do you want?"

"I just wanted to talk."

"Bullshit."

"Come on, tell me what you're doing."

"Are you lonely?" Fer asked.

"No."

"Are you bored?"

"No."

"Are you doing your homework?"

"God, Fer, yes."

"Because Mom is paying a shit ton of money for you to go to college."

"I know. I'm doing my homework, ok? This is why I don't call you."

"I thought you joined a frat."

"I did join a frat."

"Why are you being a lonely fucker and calling me? Don't you hang out with those guys?"

"If you watched any of my content, you'd see I do all sorts of stuff with them. A few of them are regulars. We hit it off pretty well."

Fer grunted.

"So," Auggie said. "What are you doing?"

"I'm driving to the county jail to bail out your assturd brother."

"Isn't every turd an assturd? And anyway, he's your brother too."

Fer grunted again.

"What is it this time?" Auggie asked.

"Possession. Again. Bail is going to be a fucking fortune."

"I thought Chuy was in rehab."

"Yeah, well," Fer said, and for a moment he didn't sound like Fer at all; he sounded tired and alone and hopeless.

"Are you ok?" Auggie asked.

"I'm not in a bathtub of Dom Perignon getting a blowie from Selena Gomez."

"You are so weird sometimes." Auggie blew out a breath. "Hey, um, Fer. I kind of forgot someone's birthday. I mean, I didn't even know it was their birthday. What do I do?"

"You forgot someone's birthday? Who? What's her name? How long have you been dating?"

Auggie fixed his gaze on the wall, a crack in the plaster, and wondered what it was like to just say things, not always having to think about the next lie and the next and the next. He felt himself becoming cardboard again. "We're not dating."

"What does she like?"

"Books, I guess. Shakespeare."

"Drop her."

"Fer!"

"She sounds like a drip."

"Will you just help me, please?"

"Is she super fucking hot?"

"Yes, sure, whatever."

"Is she funny?"

"If it'll move this conversation along."

"She likes books?"

"Yes."

"So get her a book."

"Never mind. You're useless."

Fer laughed. "Tell me why you like her so much."

"Goodbye."

"Tell me one thing, and it's gotta be the absolute fucking truth, and I will give you the secret to a perfect birthday present."

Auggie's gaze was still fixed on the crack; his vision blurred. "When we hang out, I feel like I can just be me."

Something changed on the end of the call—the car had stopped, maybe. Fer's voice was clearer when he said, "I've never heard you talk about a . . . girl like that before, Augustus."

Fer's pause hung between them.

"What about Chan?" Auggie said.

"You never talked about Chan like that."

"Ok, well, what's the secret?"

"Give that bitch the little spaghetti noodle between your legs."

"I hate you so much, Fer."

He was laughing again. "Ok, here's the deal. It took me a long time and a lot of wasted money to figure this out. Anybody worth having around, they're not going to care if you can buy them the most expensive jewelry or the fanciest clothes or whatever the fuck some assholes want. If . . ." Again, that pause. "If she's worth your time, all you have to do is buy her something that shows you know who she is, really is, and that you care about her and like her."

Auggie stared at the crack in horror. "How the fuck am I supposed to do that?"

"Bye, Augustus."

"You are absolutely no fucking help, Fer. That's a fucking impossible request. Don't you fucking dare hang up on me, don't you—"

Fer was laughing as he disconnected the call.

Great, Auggie thought. Just buy Theo something personal and intimate and that fully recognizes his personhood and his value and, also, if it's not too much of a stretch, apologizes for your being a total dick and, you know, just maybe also expresses that you can't stop thinking about him no matter how hard you try to keep yourself busy.

"I am fucked," Auggie said to the crack in the wall.

Then he got his shoes and walked to the Piggly Wiggly.

The grocery store was quiet at this hour. He found an ice cream cake, and he found streamers. The only remaining birthday banner was rainbow letters on white vinyl, saying HAPPY BIRTHDAY TO MY FAVORITE SON. He put it in the cart anyway. Then he wandered up and down the aisles, looking for something that could be a singular, meaningful gift that represented how much Theo had come to mean to Auggie over the last month. In a Piggly Wiggly. Auggie stopped in one aisle, stared at a bottle of hoisin sauce, and thought maybe it'd be easier if he just never ever saw Theo again.

He found a few things, though, and a card, and he bought them and lugged them back to Theo's house. He stored the cake in the freezer, hung the banner and streamers, and because he didn't have any wrapping paper, he just used the shopping bags as best he could to hide what he'd bought. Then, staring at the setup on the kitchen table, Auggie smiled. Something unknotted in his chest, and he went back to the couch, and for the first time all night, he could focus.

On Instagram, he scrolled through his list of followers. A hundred thousand was a lot, and he did not want to go through them one by one. But he also felt sure that Robert's name would be on that list. Robert had told him, at the Sigma Sigma Bid-ness Party, that he followed Auggie. It was entirely possible that Robert had been lying— after all, he'd lied about being a student, lied about being a pledge, lied about his age, lied about his name. Lied about almost everything, in fact. But the reality was that, for some reason, Robert had approached Auggie at the party. And Robert had come up with the idea of stealing the car. And Robert had enrolled in the same Civ class as Auggie. And someone had tagged Auggie in a video where it looked like Robert was being murdered. So Auggie thought it was likely that Robert had been following him on social media. For the first time, Auggie realized how much of his life he exposed on the feed. Even the carefully controlled pictures, the filters, all of it—they still told a story about where he'd been, who he'd been with, what he'd been doing. No wonder it had been easy for Robert to find Auggie.

Digging a pen and a scrap of blank paper out of Theo's clutter, Auggie worked his way through all the Instagram usernames that started with *rob*. If the account was locked, he sent a follow request and wrote it down on the paper. If the account was unlocked, he checked the profile picture and scrolled through the feed, looking for anyone that looked like Robert. Eventually, the *rob* usernames bled into the *robert* usernames. When Auggie had finished them, he glanced at the clock on his phone and saw that it was almost eight. He had a list of twenty accounts he needed to check when—if—they accepted his follow request, but he hadn't found Robert McDonald.

He switched his tactic, starting now with the *mc* usernames. He knew that his approach wasn't foolproof; Robert could have unfollowed him already, or Robert could have created an account with a completely random username. Robert McDonald could be hashluvver1996 or mctwinkiehole or bigeyeddoeppppp. Auggie guessed that, if worse came to worst, he could work his way through every single account in his list of followers, but he really hoped it wouldn't come to that. He followed the same routine, examining unlocked accounts, requesting access, and writing down the names of the ones that were locked. Another hour dragged by; a low headache had started behind his eyes.

Caught up in the rhythm of the search, Auggie almost missed it. mcdaddyr, which had to be one of the stupidest usernames in the history of the world, was unlocked, and the profile picture showed a guy with a godawful center-part haircut and frosted tips. It took Auggie half a second to realize, behind the different hair, Robert McDonald, aka Robert Poulson, was staring back at him. He grabbed the pen and jotted down the username. Then he worked his way through Robert's feed.

The best luck of the night was that the account was unlocked, and Auggie had access to years of photos. He went through chronologically, beginning with the most recent, which had been early September—right around the time the murder video had been posted and Robert had disappeared. Before that, Robert had posted regularly. He had clearly imagined himself as a kind of artist—lots of pictures of sunsets and abandoned buildings—but also as an actor: video clips showed him doing monologues or reading lines against a partner. In a video from 2012, he opened an acceptance letter from Wroxall and announced that he would be studying theater, but nothing in the feed showed any evidence that Robert had followed up on the plan. Many of the still photographs displayed Robert with friends, and Auggie began a list of recurring characters, sometimes jotting down the names and nicknames in the comments, sometimes adding his own descriptions, like (meth teeth).

Several of the pictures and videos showed Robert in the same room: off-white walls, a sagging couch, a CRT television with broken rabbit ears. The far wall had a sliding glass door that opened onto a balcony. Auggie assumed it was Robert's apartment; it was the most frequent setting for his pictures, and sometimes Robert was alone and in comfortable clothes, a good sign that he had taken a selfie while relaxing at home. Unfortunately, there was nothing helpful like a closeup of an envelope with an address or a street sign visible through the glass slider. Auggie ran through the pictures again. The closest he could come to a landmark was an orange plastic sign visible on the building opposite. Auggie could only make out part of it, and it looked like half of the letter V.

All in all, it was much, much more than he had expected to find. He squirmed, still trying to find the right spot on the sofa, and started looking up corporate logos.

20

"Have some more champagne, dumbass," Cart said.

Laughing, Theo tried to cover the flute. He was drunk, definitely, and it was mostly a game. He was willing to be talked into more champagne. He felt willing, for the first time in a long time, to be talked into just about anything.

"Have some more," Cart said. He looked like an adult tonight, and he looked good too, his wiry frame shown off by fitted chinos and a polo. He shook the bottle. "Come on, we've got to finish it."

They'd almost closed down Moulin Vert; only a few other diners remained, including a middle-aged couple arguing about the tip, and a group of ten, all of varying ages, all with the same chin, loudly debating the merits of *Insidious: Chapter 2* versus the original. The candle on the table had burned low; their waitress drifted by like she was on the trade winds, always with the bright optimism of a woman waiting to hear that they were ready for their check.

"I don't even like champagne," Theo heard himself saying, still covering the flute.

"Fuck," Cart said, drawing out the word scornfully. "Fuck, this fucker says he doesn't like champagne when he finished a bottle all by himself."

"Did not."

"Fuck," Cart said again, with that ridiculous way of drawing it out. He shook his head. "You are a fucking liar."

"Dessert," Theo said. "Let's get dessert."

"Oh God," Cart said. "I told you, I've got your birthday cake back at my place."

Theo blinked. "You did?"

"You are so wasted," Cart said, laughing. He took Theo's hand, the calluses on his fingers throwing off sparks, his thumb sliding half an inch until it rested at the knob of Theo's wrist, and pulled Theo's hand away from the flute. "Drink, motherfucker. It's the only time you'll turn twenty-eight."

Cart finished the champagne bottle in Theo's flute, and Theo drank.

"God, I like bubbles," Theo said, melting into his seat. "Is that cause I'm gay?"

"Everybody likes bubbles," Cart said. He flagged their waitress, who sailed over like the place was on fire.

Theo reached for his wallet.

"Not on your fucking life," Cart said.

"It's my—"

"Not a fucking chance," Cart said, counting out bills. The waitress snapped the vinyl book closed and scurried away. "Come on," Cart said, grabbing Theo's arm. "Cake."

"Cake," Theo said, stumbling once, glad when Cart put an arm around his waist. "It's my birthday," Theo informed the bartender, who looked eighty and so surprised by Theo talking to him, Theo was worried for a minute that it might finish the guy off. For some reason that was so funny that Theo started giggling and couldn't stop while Cart loaded him into the truck.

"For a guy who keeps so much beer in his fridge," Cart said, snugging the belt across Theo's lap, "you are a real fucking lightweight."

"It's the bubbles," Theo said.

"Christ, again with the bubbles."

"And I drank a lot of beer before you picked me up because I was nervous."

They drove to Cart's place with Eminem on the radio. Theo rested his head against the glass. Wahredua became a blur of sodium lights, a fog of orange that rolled in and buoyed him up.

"I'm gay," Theo said.

"I remember."

"I told Auggie I was gay."

Cart's hands shifted on the wheel. "And who's Auggie?"

"He's just a kid. He's just a nice kid. He's just a really sweet kid."

"Yeah? Why'd you tell him you're gay?"

"He's just so fucking sweet. I mean, he's an asshole sometimes, but he needs somebody." Through the champagne, a thought swam up to Theo. "Hey, Cart, did you get the record on Robert McDonald?"

"No. I don't think I'm going to be able to get it."

"That's ok."

The wheels hummed under them.

"You're a great guy, Cart."

"Ok."

"And I am really drunk."

"I'm starting to get that."

"Am I a widower?"

"What?"

"If a guy's wife dies, he's a widower. But Ian wasn't my wife. He was my husband. Does that make me a widow? Or am I a widower?"

They drove a hundred yards without talking, and then Cart turned off the radio.

"I still have Ian's stuff all over my bed," Theo said.

"You want to talk about Ian?"

"No."

Cart's hand came to rest on the nape of Theo's neck. He worked his fingers lightly there, tickling the sensitive skin. "If you want to talk about him, we can talk."

"No, I just. I don't know what I'm saying."

"Maybe you just let him go tonight. What do you think about that? Just for tonight."

His fingers felt very good; it had been a long time since anyone had touched Theo like that.

When they got to Cart's apartment, he had to help Theo inside.

"One slice of cake," Cart said when Theo stumbled on the steps and almost took them both down. "And then we're getting your ass home. Why the fuck did you drink so much?"

"I was nervous," Theo said, and he started to laugh again.

"Sweet Christ," Cart muttered.

Theo had been inside Cart's apartment plenty of times. They'd come for barbeques, come to watch the game, come to hang out when Cart had a girlfriend, for game nights. A framed poster of a Ferrari—Cart could tell you which one—and a massive TV, leather furniture you could disappear into, a fully stocked bar.

"I'm going to make a Manhattan," Theo said, heading for the bar.

"Not a chance," Cart said, steering him toward the kitchen. "I'm serious: cake, and then we're taking you home. Sit."

Theo sat.

When Cart brought over a slice of fudge cake from the Wahredua Family Bakery, a single candle stood on top, already lit, the flame flickering.

"I'm not singing to you," Cart said. "And you can take the rest of the cake with you."

"I love fudge cake."

"So blow out the candle."

"It's my favorite cake."

"Just blow out the candle, please."

"You knew my favorite cake."

"Jesus, Theo. Make a wish."

Theo bent; the wish was dark and unformed, exploding in his chest like antimatter as he blew out the flame. Then Cart got a piece for himself, and they sat and ate and talked, the way they always did.

"That was so good," Theo said when he'd finished, scraping the tines of the fork against the plate, the stainless steel ringing out against the ceramic. "That was so, so good."

"Well, you'll be eating it for a week," Cart said, picking up both plates. "I'm glad you liked it. Let's get you home."

"I need to pee."

"Christ, then pee. I'm not going to hold your dick for you."

To get to the bathroom, Theo had to pass through Cart's bedroom: the bed neatly made up with a blue comforter, a particleboard dresser supported on one side by a cinderblock, a picture of Cart's family taken at a wedding for one of the siblings. A desk. The last time Theo had been here, a handful of pictures had covered the desk, but one was gone now. Theo knew why: it was a picture of Cart and Ian from the time the *Courier* had run a story about them. They'd literally rescued a woman from a burning building. And now, Theo knew with drunken clarity, Cart had put it away for exactly this moment, so Theo wouldn't see it if he needed to use the bathroom.

A few minutes later, Theo found it under the bed. Ian and Cart were a matching set: both of them with that skinny country boy build, both of them with their hair buzzed short, Cart with that shit-kicking grin, Ian handsome in a sharp, angular way that still cut Theo to ribbons. Theo stared at it for a while before shoving it back under the bed. His hand brushed something else: cardstock. More by reflex than anything else, he tugged it out from under the bed to see what it was.

It was a manila folder. And inside, it held Robert McDonald's complete criminal record.

For a drunken moment, Theo couldn't believe what he was seeing, but he connected the dots in a few sloppy lines: Cart had gotten the record, Cart had lied about it, and Cart had kept it and hidden it because he didn't want Theo to see it. Theo tried to think through the haze and gave up. He was just too drunk. Instead, he took out his flip phone, which, thank God, had a camera, and started snapping pictures. Then he returned the file, peed, and washed his hands. He stared at himself in the mirror: the bro flow of strawberry blond hair, the beard that was always too poufy, the flush from the alcohol, the bleary eyes. He splashed water on his face. He remembered Cart's fingers tickling the back of his neck. He told himself that Ian was dead, and that things were never going to get any better.

When he got back to the kitchen, Cart was reading something on his phone. "Did you take a dump or something?"

Theo grabbed his collar, dragging him up from the chair, and they stumbled back until Cart was pressed against a wall. He was leaning into Cart—leaning on him, actually, barely standing on his own. Cart's breath came in tiny, explosive puffs. Theo brought his head closer. He could smell chocolate and champagne. He ran his fingers over Cart's cheek.

Cart cupped the back of his head and kissed him.

For a moment, Theo felt nothing. Then he was hard, rocking into Cart, yanking on the polo.

"Hey," Cart said, grabbing his hands, "hey, hey. Slow down."

Theo stumbled back.

"Hey," Cart said. "Theo, man, hold on."

"Oh my God."

"Calm down. It was just—it wasn't anything, ok. That wasn't anything. That was nothing."

"Oh my God."

"Ok, let's just talk about this."

"I've got to go home," Theo mumbled, and he staggered out into the October night, chased by Cart's shouts.

21

The key in the lock woke Auggie, and for a moment, he didn't know where he was: there was only the hazy glow through unfamiliar windows, the smell of old upholstery, and his heart hammering in his chest. Then the light came on, and realizations trickled through him: he was at Theo's; Theo had just gotten home; it was past midnight; Theo was wasted. The strawberry-blond bro flow was mussed, hanging over the left side of his face, and his eyes were glassy and dilated. When he saw Auggie, he grunted, and a wave of boozy breath washed through the room. Then Theo tried to step forward, grunted again, and sagged against the jamb.

"Are you ok?" Auggie asked, scrambling up. He knocked over some of the books, but Theo just stared at him. "Hey, um. Happy birthday."

Theo laughed.

"I bet you're ready for bed," Auggie said.

"Yeah," Theo mumbled. He pushed off from the jamb again, and this time he managed two steps before hissing and locking up. "Shit, shit, shit."

Auggie, still waking up, felt pieces falling into place. "Where's your cane?"

"Dunno."

"Why didn't I hear a car?"

"Cause I walked."

Theo tried another step; his face screwed up with pain.

"Ok, what can I do?"

"Pills."

"What?"

"Where are my goddamn pills?"

"I don't know. I didn't touch them." Auggie looked around, saw the prescription bottle on the TV console, and grabbed them. "I don't think you're supposed to mix these with alcohol."

"Give 'em."

"No, I really think that's a bad idea."

"Auggie!" Theo drew himself upright, trying to make his face stern. "I said gimme those goddamn pills right now."

"How about I help you sit down?"

"Those are mine. My pills."

"I know. Let's sit down, and then we'll talk about your pills."

After a moment to consider this, Theo gave a bleary nod.

Slipping an arm around Theo, Auggie helped him the remaining steps toward the couch, and then he used his body as a counterweight to lower Theo slowly onto the cushions. Theo hissed again. His eyes closed, and when they opened next, it was only halfway.

"Please, Auggie."

"Why'd that asshole make you walk?"

"Didn't make me."

"Then why'd you walk?"

"Dunno. I'm a stupid fuck, guess."

"I saw some ice packs in the freezer. You want those?"

Nodding, Theo said, "And my Percocet."

"Yeah, right."

In the kitchen, Auggie found a glass and filled it with water. Then he dug through the cabinets until he found a bottle of ibuprofen and dumped out two pills. He grabbed the ice packs and headed back to the kitchen.

"Open up." Auggie didn't give Theo a chance to look at the pills before pressing them into his mouth. Theo's beard was soft and bristly at the same time under Auggie's hand; his lips were full and lightly chapped. "Drink. Good. Now drink all of it."

Theo was halfway through the water when he let his head fall back. "Two," he muttered. "I don't take two anymore."

"You need two tonight," Auggie said, settling one ice pack against Theo's hip and the other against his knee, "because you walked so much. I ought to beat the shit out of that guy for letting you walk so far. Who was he?"

"Cart."

"Why'd he let you walk?'

"Didn't. Followed me in his truck all the way to my street."

"Jesus. Guess your date didn't go the way you wanted."

Those half-open eyes fixed on Auggie. "Nope," Theo said quietly.

"I'm sorry."

To that, Theo didn't respond. His lidded gaze remained fixed on Auggie as the seconds ticked past, and Auggie was suddenly aware of the tightness of his own skin, of the slight quickening of his own breathing.

"I don't think we can get you upstairs," Auggie said. "Can you sleep on the couch?"

Theo mumbled something.

"What?"

"'Bout you?"

"Oh, it's fine. I should get home anyway."

Theo started mumbling again, and then he levered himself upright, grimacing through the whole process, batting away Auggie's hand when he tried to push Theo back into his seat. Once upright, Theo began tearing cushions off the couch.

"So you're kind of a crazy drunk, huh," Auggie said.

"Ta da!" Theo grabbed a handle set into the couch's frame, tugged, and howled as he pivoted.

"Ok, ok, how about I do this part?" Auggie said, pulling out the bed. "Sheets?"

As Theo sagged forward onto the bed, he waved at the stairs.

Auggie waited for some sort of warning, like the one Theo had given him before leaving—*don't go upstairs*—and when nothing came, he sprinted up the steps. There were two bedrooms with sloping ceilings: one had pink and white striped wallpaper, a toddler-sized bed, a dresser, and a rocking chair. Auggie's heart gave a lurch when he saw the room. The other obviously belonged to Theo; clothes were folded and stacked on one side of the bed, while the other was rumpled and unmade, and Auggie's heart gave another lurch.

He found sheets and a blanket in the linen closet and carried them back downstairs; Theo was watching him through that slitted gaze.

"You see Ian's stuff?"

"I didn't snoop," Auggie said.

"It's all his stuff. Don't have any fucking idea what to do with it."

Auggie worked the fitted sheet over the mattress. "You don't have to do anything with it right now. You can take as long as you want."

"And Lana. Don't have any idea what to do about Lana."

"Can you get up for a minute? I need to finish putting the sheets on."

Instead, though, Theo rolled onto the half of the mattress Auggie had already made up.

"That's great," Auggie said. "That's very helpful."

"Leg," Theo said into the bedding.

"Yeah, yeah."

When Auggie finished, Theo tried to kick off his sneakers. He'd get as far as catching the heel of one shoe with the toe of the other, and then he'd slip and start the whole process over.

With a sigh, Auggie reached down and tugged them off. Then he settled the ice packs in place again.

"Ok," Auggie said. "Just so we're clear, I'm not taking your pants off for you."

"Clear."

"I guess I'm going to go."

"Don't go."

"Yeah, you're going to be asleep in five minutes, and you've got everything you need."

"Don't go."

"Theo—"

"I hate this fucking house. I hate this house. I hate it. Please don't go."

Auggie had that feeling again of too-tight skin, of breathlessness.

Sitting up, Theo tried again for a serious expression. "I will burn this fucking house to the ground if you leave. I will."

"Ok."

"I'll do it."

"Oh my God."

"I've got gasoline in the—in the—" He screwed up his face. "What's it called?"

"Honestly, you are the worst drunk I have ever met."

"In the garage!"

"I would rather be at a frat party with a bunch of asshole upperclassmen who can't stop talking about all the pussy they get."

Theo didn't seem to be listening; his focus was turned inward, and he was mumbling about burning down the house.

"Enough about the gasoline, you dumbass pyro," Auggie said. "Hey, cut it out. Fine. I'm staying. I'll get some blankets and sleep on the floor."

"No," Theo said, flopping back onto the mattress and patting the open space next to him.

"You will cut my balls off in the morning."

"Right here," Theo said, slapping the mattress again.

"You made it perfectly clear, about eighteen times, that nothing's going to happen."

"I will burn this house—"

"Oh my Christ, ok. Just shut up already."

Auggie kicked off his shoes, turned off the light, and crawled onto the mattress. He was at the very edge of it, one arm hanging off, the exposed springs cold against his fingers. The sleeper's frame creaked as Theo wiggled, and a moment later, Theo's hand landed on Auggie's belly. Through the cotton, the touch was hot and heavy.

"Go to sleep," Auggie said.

"I want to look at you."

"You are looking at me, perv. Go to sleep."

Theo tugged on the shirt, though, until Auggie rolled onto his side. As his vision adjusted to the darkness, he could make out the lines of Theo's face, the glitter of his eyes.

"You are funny," Theo said, like he was testing a piece in a puzzle.

"Nice try, but I remember you watching my video."

"I watched all of them. You are really funny. And you're a good dancer. And you're smart. And you're a good person." Theo's breath hitched, and in a rush he added, "And you're cute."

Auggie's eyes burned. "Go to sleep, Theo."

"I want to kiss you."

Blinking furiously, Auggie said, "You're drunk."

Theo's hand cupped Auggie's face: a strong hand, bone without much padding, the calluses rough on Auggie's cheek. "I want to kiss you."

"Not tonight. Maybe another time."

That seemed to satisfy him. His thumb skated back and forth over Auggie's cheekbone, and then he grinned and rolled onto his back and fell asleep.

Auggie didn't fall asleep, though. He stayed up in the darkness, wrestling with the thing trying to crack his breastbone, until dawn slipped through the curtains.

22

Theo woke to a chain of memories: mistake after mistake after mistake. The inside of his mouth seemed like the clearest register of those lapses in judgment: it tasted furry and brown. And then there was the headache splitting open the back of his skull. And the low, throbbing heat in his hip and knee, which told him he'd really screwed up his leg last night. Drinking too much, Cart, dinner, the kiss. Auggie. Everything with Auggie was a blur, but Theo remembered, vaguely, coming home and finding Auggie still in his house. After that, things fractured.

Then he felt the wet bedding and realized he'd peed himself.

"Oh shit," he muttered, plucking at the sheet, trying to figure out how—and why—he'd managed to make up the sofa sleeper.

"Ice packs," Auggie said from the opening to the kitchen.

"Oh," Theo said, at first overwhelmed by relief that he hadn't, in fact, peed himself. Then he noticed that Auggie was in the same clothes he'd been wearing yesterday. In Theo's kitchen. In the morning.

"Oh shit," Theo said again.

For a moment, Auggie looked confused. Then he laughed. When Theo winced, he zipped his lips, and he added in a whisper, "Calm down, nothing happened."

Groaning, Theo buried his head under the pillow.

Auggie's footsteps padded away.

The smell of hot cast iron and carbs floated in the air, and Theo's stomach gave an ominous lurch. When footsteps came padding back, he fully intended to tell Auggie that this was wildly inappropriate, and as much as he appreciated whatever Auggie had done for him last night, this was out of line, and the best thing right then would be for Auggie to go home. He had the whole scene recorded in his head. He got ready to press play.

"Water and ibuprofen," Auggie whispered, and glass clinked against the coffee table. "And your stomach probably feels like shit, but I made pancakes, and I'll fry some eggs when you're ready. You'll feel better after you eat."

Fuck the pre-recorded scene, was Theo's last coherent thought before he drifted off again.

When he woke, he felt a tiny bit better. Enough that he was able to get the pillow off his head, swallow the ibuprofen, and drink the full glass of water. He sat on the edge of the mattress, head in his hands, and decided he would never touch a beer again. No champagne, either. Never again. He thought of Auggie. Thought of facing Auggie like this, still messed up from the night before, and wondered if this was the grown-up version of the walk of shame. He could crawl out the window. He could live in the woods. Just give up the house, grad school, all of it. God, that sounded so much better.

Auggie's footsteps sounded tacky against the unfinished boards. He leaned in the opening to the kitchen, grinning. "I can hear you thinking all the way in the other room, so I'm going to save you the effort: totally inappropriate, won't ever happen again, hope it doesn't affect our professional relationship, etc. Did I pretty much get it?"

Theo rocked a hand from side to side.

"Come eat," Auggie said. "You can yell at me after."

Somehow, limping heavily, Theo made it to the kitchen table. Streamers hung from the ceiling; a limp banner over the back door said HAPPY BIRTHDAY TO MY FAVORITE SON.

"Where's your cane?" Auggie asked as he brought over a plate of pancakes and fried eggs.

"Upstairs, I guess."

"I'm going to get it. Don't freak out."

After a moment, Theo nodded. Auggie had already been upstairs the night before—he must have gone upstairs, because someone had made up the sofa sleeper. And that meant Auggie had already seen the wreckage of Theo's life. Had already seen how fucking pathetic Theo was. Big deal if he went up there again.

"Leaning it in the corner," Auggie said when he came back.

"What's this?" Theo said, cutting into the egg on his plate and poking a Piggly Wiggly bag.

"Oh, um. Birthday presents."

Theo focused on the fork. Focused on the egg. Focused on the bite of pancakes, heavy with syrup.

"They're just for fun," Auggie said.

"Thank you."

"They're just little things."

"Thank you for a lot of stuff, I guess. Last night—"

"Hey, Theo?"

"Hold on, I want to say this."

"Actually, um, could you not? I know what you're going to say. I understand. I get it: we're already walking this weird line because you're helping me with the stuff with Robert. That means a lot to me, and I don't want to mess up, you know, our friendship, or whatever this is. So I just thought maybe we could forget about last night."

"I don't want you to think I'm taking advantage—"

"Ok, this is why I said let's just forget it. Pretend it didn't happen."

"I think you're a great kid—"

"Didn't happen. Nothing happened. Hey, hi, good morning."

After a moment, a grin tugged at the corner of Theo's mouth. "Hey. Hi." Around a mouthful of pancakes, he said, "Good morning." He swallowed, tried to think of the best thing he could say, and asked, "What are my presents?"

Auggie smirked. "I'm only telling you one; you have to open the rest yourself. Aspirin."

"Because you're a headache?"

"Jesus, Theo!"

In spite of the pounding behind his eyes, Theo laughed.

"Not nice," Auggie said.

"Sorry."

"Aspirin because you headbutted that asshole."

"Right."

"Not because I'm a headache."

"Definitely not."

Auggie grinned. "Want to hear what I found last night?"

"What?"

Auggie told him about searching Robert's social media accounts, and when he displayed the picture of the room he thought was part of Robert's apartment, he tapped the screen and said, "That sign you can see outside his building. Does that look familiar?"

"Kind of. But I don't know what it is."

"Damn," Auggie said. "I searched through all these lists and images of corporate logos. I couldn't find it."

"We'll keep looking. It's a really good lead. You did a great job."

A dusting of scarlet worked its way over Auggie's cheekbones, and Theo would be lying if he said he hadn't noticed: the tiniest bit of praise, just an ordinary kind word, made Auggie light up. Theo couldn't help himself, now that he knew how it worked. He liked that look on Auggie's face so damn much.

"These pancakes are really good, by the way. And the eggs are awesome."

"They're fried eggs, Theo. It's not exactly rocket science." But he was glowing again.

"Yeah, but I make pancakes all the time, and they're not as good as this."

"It's Krusteaz. You literally just follow the instructions."

"What instructions? You just dump in water until it looks right."

"Oh my God."

"Are you being serious? There are instructions?"

"Oh my God. How are you my professor?"

"Christ," Theo said, fighting a grin. "How does an Orange County kid learn about Krusteaz? I figured your personal chef would be whipping up buckwheat hotcakes with organic, free-range eggs and—"

A piece of pancake hit Theo in the forehead. Laughing, he dodged the next one.

"Ok, ok," he said, raising the fork in surrender. "But seriously: these are fantastic."

"Because you're a sloppy drunk and you're dying for food," Auggie said. But he was shining like a star. "And, uh, I kind of had to learn how to cook for myself pretty early, actually. I didn't grow up in Orange County. And it's not all rich people, you know. We just moved there last year."

"Oh yeah?" Theo asked, cutting into the egg again.

"Yeah. My mom wasn't around much. I mean, I guess she was. It's hard to explain. I have two older brothers. Fer, Fernando, he's the oldest. And Jesús is in the middle, but we just call him Chuy. We all have different dads, and they're all gone. Fer's died. Chuy's is in prison. Mine just upped and left. I think I found him on Facebook, but the asshole never paid a dime in child support, and I'd rather see him get hit by a truck than make first contact. Uh, ok, I'm kind of hearing myself there. Sorry about that."

"You don't need to be sorry," Theo said, but he remembered the raw edge of fury in Auggie's voice when Theo had tried to offer advice and Auggie had said, *I don't need another dad.*

"Anyway, Chuy went off the rails in middle school. He got into drugs pretty bad. He's messed up, and he blames all of it on our mom. And Fer tries to hold everything together. He's got a great job in pharmaceutical sales, he's super smart, and he's seriously the only reason I'm not as messed up as Chuy. Fer has this weird way of babying me where he's also a giant tool at the same time. I don't know how to explain it. When I was really little, he did everything for me:

made my meals, packed my lunch, helped with my homework. But when he got this job, he didn't really have time, so I had to figure a lot of it out myself."

Theo thought about all the ways to respond: to tell Auggie he was sorry he had grown up like that, to tell Auggie that he understood what it was like to feel invisible and unwanted and unloved. The echo of *I don't need another dad* rang in his ears, though, so he chewed slowly and tried to think his way down other paths.

After swallowing a bite of pancakes, Theo said, "So, I have this huge family. Extended family, I mean. And I have four brothers."

"Oh shit."

"Jacob, he's the oldest. Abel, number two. Meshach, number three. Daniel Theophilus," he jerked a thumb at himself.

"You're shitting me."

"No shits."

"You have got to be shitting me."

Theo rolled his eyes.

"I am literally going to call you Theophilus for the rest of my life."

"Easy there, August."

Auggie's grin crinkled his eyes.

"And Luke," Theo added. "He was the baby. I think I told you about him; he died a few years ago."

"Oh. I'm sorry."

"It's ok. It was his own damn fault. Hard to be mad at anyone else."

Auggie moved his fork around his plate. He was losing ground to a grin. "But seriously, Theophilus?"

"Well, dumbass, I grew up using Daniel. But when I came out, things got bad for a while. It felt like the right time to make the switch. New name. New life. New chance."

"Lot of Bible names in your family."

"Yep," Theo said. "Doesn't matter. It was the right thing for me to do. I've never regretted it."

"I get that," Auggie said. "It's nice to be . . . who you feel like you really are, I guess."

Theo waited.

"I don't really know, um, what my deal is," Auggie said, staring at his plate; his fork dragged to a stop. "So it's not like I've had to, you know, tell my family anything."

"That's ok."

"It's just hard, you know? I've got a million girls in my fan base. Fuck, I sound like a fucking asshole. Never mind."

"Do you want to talk about it?"

"No."

Theo nodded. He let a moment pass, and then he said, "Do you ever use your family for your content?"

"Oh my God," Auggie said, the hard line of his shoulders relaxing, and he grinned as he tapped at his phone. "Fer gives these epic monologues, and then I edit them or remix them."

"That sounds familiar," Theo said. "Jacob likes to give speeches. Pretty regularly, actually. I think it's an older brother thing."

"There's this one where Fer totally loses his mind," Auggie said.

"Let's see," Theo said.

Auggie started explaining the backstory of the video, and he slid into the seat next to Theo without seeming to realize it.

23

October turned into November. November turned into December. Auggie grabbed minutes of free time to dig through websites and image galleries, looking for anything that might match the half-sign he could see in the pictures of Robert's apartment. He even went to the library, for the love of God, and had a lame excuse about a history of marketing project. The librarian helped him find a few reference books and an industry magazine for corporate signage, and Auggie spent hours, nights, and weekends digging through the stacks.

At least, he did at the beginning.

As the weeks rolled on, though, and Glasses didn't make contact again, Auggie found himself losing momentum. From time to time he'd remind himself that Glasses had threatened his family, and then for a week or four days he'd hit the library regularly, working through a few more issues of trade magazines, trying to find anything that might match what he had seen in the photographs. But school interfered with homework and tests and projects and papers. And life interfered with pledging Sigma Sigma and hanging out with his friends and filming crazy-as-shit videos with Orlando and a few other guys. They did one where Auggie pretended to be desperate for Orlando's friendship, and instead Orlando ignored him and found excuses to play Xbox with Pranav and Chad, and Auggie finally threw himself across their laps to get attention. The video ended with Orlando pushing Auggie off, and the guys leaving to go hang out somewhere else. They broke five hundred thousand likes with that video. Auggie's agent called three times that week.

And, of course, there was Theo. For the first few weeks after Theo's birthday, they had been busy running down addresses from Robert's police record and from internet searches under Robert's legal name, all of which Theo had somehow gotten from Cart. All the addresses turned out to be dead ends. Auggie had used the pretext of searching for Robert as a way of firmly establishing his right to come and go at Theo's house whenever Theo was around. Then it settled into a routine: Theo working on his thesis on the sofa, Auggie sprawled next to him and reading or doing homework or managing his accounts.

Every once in a while, random texts with a green bubble would show up on Auggie's phone, formatted with irritating attention to spelling and grammar: *How did your calculus test go?*

And Auggie would write back: *just say calc.*

And Theo would write: *Well? How did it go?*

Or sometimes a grainy picture would show up, and Auggie would have to squint, and eventually he'd give up and type: *is that an octopus in a ballroom gown?*

And of course a message would come from Theo at the exact same time, because his timing over text was atrocious, and it would say something like: *I think you could use this in one of your videos.*

what? like dancing with the stars

It's an installation at the Norell.

wtf is an installation?

What is dancing with the stars?

They could go for hours like that, with Theo always half a step out of sync, and Auggie grinning harder and harder as the disjointed answers rolled in.

Thanksgiving break was the longest five days of Auggie's life. It was weird to see Logan and Devin again, but of course, they had to get together and do some reunion videos. Chan floated just under the surface of every conversation. Her thisisurex2 account had blown up, and she was now posting new content that users submitted—pictures, stories, flames—but Auggie still featured regularly as the whipping boy for shitty boyfriends everywhere. Auggie saw her once, at a party Friday night at Jenny Reed's house, and it only took him a moment to feel the vacuum in the room as everyone got sucked toward her. He ended up standing alone by the foosball table, with everyone else crowded around Chan. Letting himself out through the sliding door, Auggie stood in the brisk chill that passed for an Orange County winter. He thought about going back and getting wasted. He thought about confronting her.

His phone buzzed, and it was a picture from Theo, so blurry that Auggie honestly had no idea what he was seeing.

wtf is that? did u barf?

Got a TV! was Theo's staggered announcement.

ohmygod is it like six inches or something?

A half-second off: *It's not very big.*

Auggie waited, leaning on the rail, having totally forgotten about Chan and the party. Sometimes he liked to give Theo a few seconds to catch up; it was like when you let a little kid win a race just, you know, because it was cute.

Theo: *Hey! It's 24".*

Auggie: *now u can watch all ur dirty shows again*

Theo: *Maybe you could do something like this for your blog?*

Auggie: *still not a blog so quit calling it that*

Auggie: *something like what? buy a tiny TV?*

Theo: *Why isn't it a blog?*

Auggie gave him another few seconds of lead time.

Theo: *Hey! This TV got great reviews!*

Auggie leaned out over the balcony, staring at the spread of lights below him, tasting the cool, dry air that he'd missed in Missouri. He thought Theo would like this place. Not to live. But for a visit, maybe.

The phone buzzed again.

Theo: *You could do a spoof of A Charlie Brown Thanksgiving.*

Auggie: *ohmygod how old r u*

The semester rolled on like that until finals week, and Auggie was shocked to realize that he'd be going home in three days and wouldn't see Theo for almost a month. Their final in Civ 1 was an in-class, timed essay, and Auggie needed the whole time. Apparently so did everyone else. When Theo asked everyone to turn in their work, there was a lot of groaning, scribbling, frantic pawing at volumes of *Lear*. After a few grace minutes, Theo asked for the essays again, and students began packing up their bags, handing in the essays, and filing out of class. A few of them thanked Theo for the class, shaking his hand. Theo got a little pink in the cheeks and had his little smile and rubbed his beard like he had no idea what to do, and Auggie had to squeeze his eyes shut so he wouldn't explode from watching the whole thing.

Then Auggie was the last student in the room.

"What are you grinning about?" Theo said, shuffling papers.

"What? Nothing."

"Essay time's over, Mr. Lopez."

"I figured you'd be willing to make an exception. Give me a few extra minutes."

"Not a chance."

"What's the point of being friends with the professor," Auggie said, grabbing his essay and taking it up to Theo, "if I don't get any perks?"

"The perk is that I let you eat chips on my couch and get crumbs between the cushions."

"And I like that perk very much. Want to go ahead and just put an A on there right now?"

"Very funny."

"It's good."

"Uh huh."

"It's going to be the best one."

Theo packed the essays in his satchel. "I guess I'll see."

"Probably bump my ninety-seven in this class up to a ninety-eight."

"If I didn't see how hard you worked and how many bags of Doritos you ate, I might think you were a little cocky."

"I like Cool Ranch. Sue me."

Theo's gaze moved to Auggie's face, and those strong, hard hands played with the strap of his satchel, winding it around his fingers, undoing it, winding it again, then letting out the slack.

"Auggie, I wanted to talk to you about something now that the semester is basically over. I'm not going to be your instructor anymore, and I guess I think now is the best time to say this."

"Oh." Auggie reached back, trying to find a desk, a chair, anything that would keep him upright. "Um. I guess I, uh, kind of wanted to talk to you too."

"Ok," Theo said. "Go ahead."

"Uh, no, you first."

"I think you should change your major."

For a long moment, the hiss of blood in his ears was the only sound Auggie could process. He knew that he managed to say something like "What?" but it was somebody else saying the word.

"I'm not trying to diminish the importance of your internet thing, but I think you're wasted in a Communications major."

Auggie stared at him.

"You're really good at this stuff." He touched the satchel. "Really, really good. I'm not saying you should exclusively be an English major, but it's an easy one to add as a double."

The heat bloom at the words *you're really, really good at this stuff* helped Auggie over the worst of the pain. He smiled. "Oh, yeah. Thanks."

"I just wanted to tell you officially, as your instructor, that's how I see you."

"Yeah," Auggie said. "That's how you see me. As my instructor."

"Right."

"Ok," Auggie said. "Thanks. I'll think about it."

"If you want to talk about—"

"Yeah, ok. Let me just think about it."

Theo blinked. "Sure."

"I guess I'd better go."

"Actually, there was one other thing," Theo said.

Auggie hated himself for hoping. Auggie hated himself for that electric zing that started low in his belly and ran up to his lungs so he couldn't breathe. He hated himself for the way he felt when Theo smiled, when Theo said *you're really, really good,* hated himself for the way he kept playing it on a loop because it made him feel so good. And so shitty, too. At the same time.

"Oh," Theo said. "Wait. What did you want to say?"

"What?"

"You said now that it was the end of the semester, you wanted to say something."

"Oh, yeah. That. About the major. I wanted to ask you what you thought."

"Really?"

"Absolutely."

Theo was scrubbing his beard again. "Ok. Well, I wanted to tell you: I drove home over the weekend, and I found it. Actually, that's not right. I figured out what it's for."

"Sorry," Auggie said, and it was like a delayed explosion was happening, his chest crumpling, his face stinging, his eyes hot as the full extent of what Theo hadn't said began to sink in. Auggie hadn't even known, until now, what he'd been hoping for. He hadn't even put it into words. "I'm kind of—my brain's somewhere else. What are you talking about?"

"Are you ok?"

"Yeah, yes, God, what are you trying to say?"

"I matched that sign," Theo said. "The one outside Robert's apartment. I know what business it belongs to."

24

Another class needed the room in Tether-Marfitt, so Theo led Auggie back to his office in Liversedge. Snow had come earlier that week, and it lingered as slush on the sidewalks. Theo had to be extra careful; his knee and hip were getting better, but he still relied a lot on the cane, and he didn't want to slip and have to start the whole thing over again. They rode the elevator up in silence, and it wasn't until they were halfway down the hall to Theo's office that he realized Auggie hadn't said a word since leaving the classroom. He looked over, expecting to see Auggie absorbed in his phone, but instead Auggie just stared straight ahead. His dark eyes were dead. His face held a patchy flush. He kept biting his lip and blinking.

When they stepped into the office, the smell of chamomile met them; a mug of tea, now cold, sat on Grace's desk. Theo shut the door, waited until they were both seated, and said, "What's wrong?"

"Nothing."

"Auggie, you're obviously upset." Theo cast back, trying to remember when things had changed. Auggie had been bragging about his essay, and they'd been joking about Doritos or something, and then Theo had said something about adding a double major with English. "Hey, if I made you feel like I didn't think your internet thing was important, that was not what I meant."

"No," Auggie said, but he was sniffling now, and his voice was thick with the need to cry.

"Then what? Come on, I did something or said something, right? Is this about the sign? Are you mad I didn't tell you? Did that asshole—did he come back, and you didn't tell me? Did he hurt you again? Your family? Geez, Auggie, you've got to tell me because you're freaking me out."

"For fuck's sake," Auggie said, wiping his eyes, "can you just not be so fucking nice about it? Fuck. Fuck, fuck, fuck."

"Nice about what?"

"Never mind."

"Auggie—"

"I'm fine. I am totally fine. This is a personal thing, and it doesn't have anything to do with my major or with Robert disappearing or anything. It's just something I'm dealing with."

After a slow breath, Theo said, "Do you want to talk about it?"

Auggie burst out in a wet laugh that was more like a sob. "Oh fucking Christ, no. Please, no. Tell me about the sign."

Someone on the quad shrieked with laughter; even through the window, the sound startled Theo, and he shifted in his seat as prickles ran down him.

"What company is it?" Auggie said.

"It's a chain of gas stations. They're all out of business actually. Gas 'n Guzzle." Theo browsed on the computer for an image and showed Auggie.

"That's not the same," Auggie said, wiping his face and leaning closer. "It's the right color and the right size, but—"

"But, here's the thing. Show me that picture of Robert's apartment again."

Auggie held up his phone next to the monitor. "See, they're not—"

"Flip it in your head."

"What?"

"In Robert's picture, that's a reflection. From the windows on the other side of the street, see? So you have to flip it. And it's cut off, so we couldn't even see the whole thing."

Auggie zoomed in on the picture. "Holy shit."

"Right?"

"I am so fucking stupid."

"I didn't see it either," Theo said. "But I drove home over the weekend, and I passed one of these. I saw the sign in my rearview mirror and boom. I recognized it immediately."

"Where is this place?"

"Well, like I said: it's a chain. And they're out of business. I tried searching Google Maps, but nothing shows up."

"So we've got multiple possible locations and no way of knowing where they are."

"I taught you better than that. We had lessons on research and scholarship."

Auggie rolled his eyes, but he said, "Ok, this isn't exactly the same thing as doing a search in JSTOR. What do you mean?

"We know what we're looking for. We know the general location. We just have to do the work to find it."

"You want to wander around until we find one of these Gas 'n Guzzle places, just by sheer luck, and then match it to Robert's building, by sheer luck, and then get into his apartment, by sheer luck. Is that it?"

"Research is two things. Ok, three. One: smart choices. Two: hard work, just grinding it out. Three: luck. You did it when you were looking for the signs, right? You narrowed down to a set of archives, and you plowed through them."

"And I didn't turn up anything."

"Luck," Theo said. "Take a look at that picture again. Narrow it down. I'll give you a clue: Gas 'n Guzzle was a chain of truck stops."

"Ok," Auggie said, looking at the picture of the inside of Robert's apartment again. "So he's near a state highway, or, also possible but less likely, a major road."

"Good."

A little of the shine came back into Auggie's face, and he looked more carefully at the picture. "You can count the floors on the building across the street. His apartment is on the third floor. And we know it faces the street."

"Very good."

"It's an older building; I can see a radiator. And it doesn't look like it's been kept up. The fire escape has a lot of rust, the outlet plate is missing. I'm guessing it's low rent. No, hold on. He's running an extension cord through the window. So, what? He doesn't have power and he's stealing from somewhere nearby? He's squatting in an apartment that doesn't have the electricity turned on. Maybe the whole building is abandoned."

"Very, very good."

Auggie flicked a glance up; for a moment, he was glowing. Then he said, "So where are we going?"

"A neighborhood called Smithfield."

"Uh, I've heard about Smithfield."

"You'll be fine."

"I'm not worried about me. I'm worried about you limping around on your bad leg when somebody tries to knife us."

Theo had practiced this part; a fist was crushing his chest, but he managed to keep his voice even. "I think it would make sense for you to drive us."

"Theo—"

"It'll be fine."

"No. I can go to Smithfield myself."

"Absolutely not."

"This isn't a good idea."

"Why not? I've ridden in cars since the accident. I don't have a panic attack every time." Theo managed a brittle smile. "And I trust you. You're smart, and you can be careful."

"I don't have a good track record with cars."

"Auggie, I trust you."

In that moment, with a huge smile breaking over his face, Auggie Lopez had never been more beautiful. He was studying the floor, rubbing his knees, and he said, "Yeah, ok. I can be careful."

So they walked back to Theo's—or rather, Theo coasted on his bike, and Auggie walked. And Theo grabbed a bag of tools from the garage, and he got the keys from Ian's nightstand and the gun from where he'd hidden it. He tossed the keys underhand to Auggie when he got back outside.

"Please tell me you're sure about this," Auggie said, the keys jingling as he caught them.

"I'm sure."

They drove toward Smithfield. Auggie followed Theo's directions, handling the car like he had a brick on the brake: stopping hard at every intersection, barely getting the Malibu over thirty. To be fair, the Malibu was making an awful grumbling noise, but Theo didn't think that was the problem.

He squeezed Auggie's shoulder as they idled at a light.

"You're a good driver," Theo said.

Auggie blew out a breath; his shoulder was tense under Theo's touch.

"And I understand that you are now living out your nightmare of *Driving Miss Daisy*."

With a shaky laugh, Auggie nodded.

"How about you relax a little and try going five over?"

"Five over."

"Five over is fine."

"I got in a crash."

"What?"

"Last time I drove I got in a crash."

"I remember, I was—"

"No, not that. A bad one. A really bad one. Theo, I just want to pull over. I'm going to go to that parking lot."

The light changed, and Theo said, "No, keep driving."

"I really don't want to—"

"Keep driving, Auggie."

So Auggie kept driving.

"I didn't want to tell you," Auggie said. His voice was on the verge of breaking. "Because, you know. Christ, I should have told you."

"You're doing great."

"I didn't kill anyone. I swear to God, Theo. I didn't. I would never have gotten behind the wheel again if I'd killed someone."

"Ok, let's do this. You're going to take a really deep breath, and then you're going to let it out slowly while I count. How's that?"

"I would have told you but—"

"Here we go."

So Theo counted. And Auggie breathed. They did that for a while, with Theo interrupting to provide directions. They cruised the streets of Smithfield: strip malls of yellow brick, tattoo parlors, bars, walk-up apartment buildings, a boarded up Lutheran church, an elementary school where kids played on the playground. In some places, Victorian houses still stood, remnants of another time, their wood mildewed, their windows dark. They passed a White Castle, and the smell of sliders made Theo's stomach rumble. They passed a mercado, and Auggie mumbled something that sounded like, "Tamales."

"Better?" Theo asked, his fingers massaging the hollow of Auggie's shoulder.

"Holy shit."

"It's just a breathing trick, Auggie, it's not magic."

"No, holy shit. It's right there."

And there it was: a Gas 'n Guzzle with the pumps ripped out, the convenience store boarded up, sitting right on the state highway's business loop. The orange plastic sign towered over the street.

Auggie turned at the next intersection.

"It's this building," he said, pointing. "I know it's this one."

Theo peered through the windshield. "Maybe."

"I know it is. That one is the one across the street. I've looked at that picture so many goddamn times. This is his building. Come on."

The Malibu died with a rattle that did not sound good, but it was a problem for another time; Theo got out, grabbed his tools, and limped after Auggie. The walk-up's security door was chained shut. It also had an electronic lock that had probably been connected to the intercom system; when Auggie yanked on the door, though, it opened until it caught against the chain, and Theo could see where the latch had been broken.

"Hold on," Theo said. "Nobody's supposed to be living here. We don't know which unit might have been his."

"It's a third-floor apartment facing the street, just like the picture. And I know this is the building. Trust me."

So Theo cut the bolts; there was nobody on the street to object. As soon as they stepped inside, Theo smelled it: putrefaction.

"You should wait here."

Auggie shook his head.

They took the stairs to the third floor. Theo needed the cane more than he would have liked; stairs were still hell for him. The building was like so many other low-rent housing places Theo had been in his life; he'd grown up with friends who lived in places like these. In his mind, he associated them with the smell of too many bodies living together and hydrogenated fats, like frozen toaster pastries. Here, though, the smell of decay overpowered everything else. When they passed the door to 3C, a mouse scurried along the baseboard, its claws ticking against the carpet, and Auggie jolted and grabbed Theo's arm.

3D was at the end of the hall.

"Windows facing the street," Auggie said. "It's got to be the right one. God, I need a mask."

Theo nodded, checked the stolen pistol at his waistband, and knocked.

"Are you carrying—" Auggie asked.

Theo put a finger over his lips and knocked again.

"Nobody could be in there," Auggie said. "It reeks too bad."

Theo took out a wrecking bar and a mallet from his bag of tools. He wedged the wrecking bar between the door and the jamb, right where the latch would be.

"Is that seriously going to work?" Auggie asked.

"Not if someone set the deadbolt," Theo said. "But it's worth a shot."

He gave an experimental tap, and the latch popped free of the strike plate. The door swung inwards.

"Why didn't he set the deadbolt?" Auggie asked.

Theo took a breath, and the smell of corruption rolling out of the apartment was even stronger. He had scraped up too much roadkill in his life not to recognize that stench.

"Stay here," he whispered.

"Like fuck."

"Auggie—"

"No, no fucking way. This is my mess. I'm going with you."

His fingers were biting into Theo's arm, and Theo covered Auggie's hand for a moment before working them loose.

"Sorry," Auggie whispered.

Theo nodded and eased into the apartment. He drew the gun, although he knew, already, that no one was here. The empty building was the only possible reason the stench hadn't been reported yet. And this was Smithfield; the people who might have broken into this building weren't likely to report anything.

Living room, empty. Kitchen, empty. Bedroom, empty.

The dead man in the bathtub might have been Robert McDonald once. Months of decomposition had robbed him of recognizable features, but the clothes looked familiar. Theo thought they were what Robert had been wearing the night he and Auggie stole the Porsche.

Covering his nose and mouth with his sleeve, Theo stepped back slowly. Auggie had pulled up his shirt to breathe through the fabric, and his eyes were wide; when he moved to get past Theo for a look, Theo planted a hand on his chest and shook his head. He steered Auggie out of the apartment and whispered, "Call Glasses."

"It's him?"

Theo nodded.

"Thank Christ," Auggie whispered. "It's over."

Theo pulled the door shut and carried the tools back to the car, and Auggie placed the call. They waited until Glasses arrived; it was Theo's first look at the man, and he recognized Al Lender, detective for the Wahredua PD. Lender spotted them, waved, and headed into the building.

"It's over," Auggie said again, and then he pressed the heels of his hands against his eyes. "Oh thank God. Thank God."

But it wasn't over; Theo knew it wasn't over. Someone had murdered Robert McDonald. Someone had wanted to frame Theo and Auggie for it. And dangerous people, including a dirty cop, had been determined to find out what had happened. Robert's body wasn't the answer; it was just the next question.

"Come on," Theo said. "Let's go home."

25

The semester officially ended on Thursday; Auggie booked his ticket for Saturday, because Friday was the Sigma Sigma induction ceremony, followed by the Final Judgment party. Auggie dressed in a blazer and tie; Orlando, who had pledged Sigma Sigma too, wore a simple black suit. The induction ceremony was about what Auggie had expected: dry and limping along, tailored for proud parents and grandparents. When it was over, Auggie got pictures with friends, met some parents, and found a quiet moment alone. He posted a selfie with the comment: *officially a bro . . . WHAT HAVE I DONE?!!!* While the responses were pouring in, he sent a picture of himself and Orlando to his mom. A bubble popped up, showing that she was composing a reply. Then the bubble disappeared. Then the screen timed out. Auggie unlocked the phone and sent the same picture to Fer.

Good job, dickbreath.

Auggie sent back the middle-finger emoji.

Who's your boyfriend?

Auggie was typing a response that explained exactly how much he hated Fer.

A string of eggplant emojis interrupted him.

Then: *Did you get straight A's?*

Christ, Fer. Don't worry about it.

I will fucking beat your ass if you didn't.

Yes, I got straight A's.

A thumbs-up emoji came back.

Then more eggplants.

Auggie sent back skulls, knives, and middle fingers.

"Come on," Orlando said. His tie hung loose now, and for the first time, Auggie realized that Orlando had shaved. He looked five years younger without the perpetual scruff.

"Where are your parents?"

"Who the hell knows? Let's party," he said with a grin, shoving Auggie toward the door.

The Final Judgment party, the annual celebration for pledges who had been inducted into Sigma Sigma, also doubled conveniently as an end-of-the-semester blowout: finals were over, classes were finished, and nobody, with the exception of a few dummies like Auggie who had booked early flights, had anywhere to be the next day.

At the Sigma Sigma house, he and Orlando got blue wristbands marking them as inductees, and that meant comped drinks. Auggie hadn't forgotten the Bid-ness party, though, or how close he had come to messing up his life again, so he stayed away from the tequila and stuck with a red plastic cup of beer. Every Sigma Sigma brother in the chapter was there, plus friends, plus girlfriends or, in a few cases, boyfriends, plus guys who had graduated but were still in the area or were back in town for the holidays. It meant that the Sigma Sigma house was full to capacity: it was more people at one party than Auggie had ever seen, bigger than the Bid-ness Party, bigger than the Alpha Phi Conjunction Party.

Auggie had fun.

He danced; he ditched his jacket and tie, and the heat of bodies made him sweat until his shirt stuck to his ribs. He drank—just beer, but even beer started adding up. He ate slices of pizza in the Sigma Sigma kitchen with a couple of the other inductees, and then eating pizza turned into an impromptu pop-and-lock competition, and before Auggie knew it he was dancing in a clearing with a crowd screaming encouragement. The competition ended when one of the other inductees did a back flip, and the crowd surged into the tiny opening, everybody shouting congratulations and admiration.

One of those invisible currents that run through parties carried Auggie to a quiet spot in the hall, and he checked his phone.

No new messages.

He checked the picture to his mom to make sure it had sent, even though he had seen the composition bubbles appear and then disappear. He could picture her right now, drinking Chardonnay with Brandon or Nicholas or Jefferson or whoever the fuck it was this month. He could picture her checking her phone, beginning to tap out a reply, and then when Jefferson or Brandon or Nicholas said something or refilled her wine or brushed her knee, the phone went back in her clutch.

"Shots!" It took Auggie a moment to recognize Josh Krewet, the chapter president, who was pressing a glass into his hand.

"No, man, I think—"

"Dude, that's your drink, right?"

"I'm ok with beer."

"No way." Josh was grinning, weaving slightly, his eyes glassy. "I read your interview, Augs. You like Drake and One Direction, your drink is tequila, and you're a fucking bona fide internet stud."

"Yeah, I'm just sticking with beer tonight," Auggie said.

Josh shrugged and moved off, shouting, "Shots!" again.

"Dance," Orlando said, coming out of nowhere to grab his arm and steer him back into the melee.

"Hey, do you remember doing an interview?"

"Just dance, Auggie."

For a while, Auggie danced, but now he was tired and sweaty and thirsty, the taste of beer gummy in his mouth. For a while, he was grinding up against a blond girl with tinsel earrings and a Santa Claus necklace. Then, for a while, it was a black girl with a short, sequined dress. Then the blond was back. Then a redhead who kept groping him through his pants. She grabbed too hard, and when she got hold, she just kind of mashed him.

Auggie finally got free and stumbled into a dark, empty room. He was surprised that any rooms in the house were dark and empty. He was surprised it was past two in the morning. Some of the alcohol had worked its way out of his system, and he dropped down onto a sofa and stretched out, glad for a moment of quiet. His brain kept going back to what Josh had said about an interview. He remembered it now, vaguely. The chapter secretary had interviewed them at the Bid-ness party. He'd tracked down everybody with a sash, asked the same questions, put their answers on a form. Lying there, Auggie took out his phone again. No new messages. He squeezed his eyes shut and thought maybe he was still pretty drunk because he felt himself drifting.

"What the fuck are you doing in here?" Orlando swatted his legs until Auggie moved, and then he sat next to Auggie. "It's hookup time, man. The redhead was seriously into you. She's still out there."

"Yeah," Auggie said. He kept thinking about the interviews. Some part of his brain wouldn't let go of it. The chapter secretary had done interviews with everyone wearing a pledge sash. Everyone. The poor guy had been making his way through the crowd at the Bid-ness party, which seemed like a pretty stupid time to do an interview, but that's what had happened. Everybody with a sash. Every single guy with a sash.

When Auggie sat up, his vision swam.

"So, um, is it weird if we both take a girl back?" Orlando said. "Honestly, it won't bother me. Just kind of, you know, keep your eyes on the prize."

Every single guy with a sash. And Robert had been here. Robert had been wearing a sash. Robert had stolen one or bribed someone to give him one.

Auggie tried to figure out why it mattered. The beer cloud made it hard. Robert was dead. They had found him, and he was dead, and it was over. Auggie could just move on with his life. He had to do one more semester at Wroxall, and then he'd have money, have a life, have everything he ever wanted.

But Auggie still didn't have the answers that mattered. He didn't know why Robert had singled him out. He didn't know why someone had tagged him in a video of Robert's murder. He didn't know why any of it had happened. And he wanted to know who had been trying to fuck up his life.

"If that's weird," Orlando said, "my buddy gave me a key to his apartment; he already went home. I can—"

"No, just, you know. Go ahead. I'm going to do something."

"What?"

Getting to his feet, Auggie shook his head. "Nothing. You danced with that girl with curly hair for a long time. You should see if she's still around; I think she really likes you."

When Orlando stood, his face was inches from Auggie's and his breath smelled sweet like rum. After a moment, he grinned and shook his head. "Nah."

"What do you mean, nah? You're the one that came in here talking about hooking up."

"I don't know. I want to see what you're doing."

Auggie was too drunk to parse that, too drunk to argue the logic of it, so he just nodded.

The party was thinning out quickly, and it was easy for Auggie and Orlando to blend into the people leaving as they made their way to the chapter president's office. It was the only room on a short hallway, and the lights were off. Just a few feet away, partygoers streamed past them. Most of them seemed oblivious to Auggie and Orlando; the few that looked, Auggie thought, probably assumed they were just a couple who had found a dark space to make out. The thought closed around his chest like a fist.

When Auggie checked the door, it opened.

They stepped inside, and when Orlando shut the door behind him, Auggie flipped on the lights. He had been in here once for an interview during rush; it was the college boy's dream of the executive office: dark wainscoting, wingback chairs, a massive desk. Auggie made his way to the filing cabinets and stumbled once. The drawers were locked.

"Shit," Auggie said.

"What are we doing?" Orlando said.

"Those interviews they did the night of the party. I want to see them."

"Why?"

"I don't know. I just do."

"You are so fucking strange."

"Yeah, fine."

"You do such dumb stuff."

"Ok."

"Is this why you've been acting so weird all semester?"

"Orlando, focus: either help or shut up."

Orlando's jaw tightened, but he said, "The guy who did them, he had a binder like that."

When he pointed to the shelves behind the desk, which were filled with binders, Auggie remembered it too: the secretary stuffing the form into the binder when he'd finished the interview. Auggie started pulling binders from the shelves. Some of them held chapter and regional growth plans: outreach initiatives, market studies, demographics, branding ideas. Others held policy handbooks, documents approved by the national board, official positions that the fraternity was expected to uphold. Some held financial documents, but they were all chapter-specific and minor, often detailing local fundraising activities; Auggie guessed that the locked filing cabinets held the more substantive information.

"Here," Orlando said, sliding an open binder toward Auggie.

The front page said 2013 PLEDGE PROFILES.

"Lemme see yours," Orlando said, leaning into Auggie, the line of his body hot against Auggie's shoulder.

Auggie flipped through the pages.

"I bet you like Taylor Swift," Orlando said; he'd brought up one hand, and now he squeezed the back of Auggie's neck. "I bet you love Katy Perry."

And then Auggie saw it: Robert Poulson's pledge interview.

Footsteps moved in the hall outside the office.

"Why the fuck was the door unlocked?" Orlando whispered.

Auggie ripped out the sheet, shoved it into his waistband, and replaced the binder.

The latch turned.

Grabbing Orlando, Auggie dragged him down. They wedged themselves into the desk's knee hole as the door opened, and drunken voices—one of them Josh's—filled the room.

"Why the fuck is the light on?"

The answer came from the hall and was muffled.

"Christ," Josh said, "I can't leave things for five fucking minutes."

His steps moved around the room; Auggie tried to judge his location from the soft brush of his soles against the carpeting. In the cramped space, Auggie was suddenly painfully aware of how much bigger Orlando was: a semester of hard workouts on a college wrestling team had added density to the layers of muscles Orlando already carried. He was staring at Auggie, Auggie realized. That dark hair, those heavy eyebrows, those shoulders trying to split his jacket. He had one hand on the inside of Auggie's thigh, and maybe you could explain that with how quickly they had rushed to hide. His breathing was slow and steady; the smell of rum and something else, something distinctly Orlando, made Auggie swallow.

"Here it is," Josh said, and then he stumbled out of the room. The light went off, and the door shut behind him.

In the darkness, Auggie couldn't see Orlando anymore. All he could feel was where they touched: knees and elbows, and that blaze of a handprint on Auggie's thigh. The hand slid down. Auggie's breathing, in the darkness, sounded like panic.

Their noses bumped, and Orlando kissed him. His hand slid lower, and Auggie couldn't help himself: he was hard, and he made a noise when Orlando touched him.

"Is this ok?" Orlando whispered. "I've wanted to do this since the bid party."

Auggie's breaths were short, sharp whistles.

"I can be discreet, dude," Orlando said. "Lots of guys don't want it getting around. I know you've got your reasons."

"I can't."

"You know you make me crazy," Orlando added in a whisper. "Crazy about you. Crazy about touching you. Crazy when I see you messing around with other guys. I've been crazy fucking jealous since the first time I touched you. All those people you joke around with. Every time you're laughing and bullshitting with your friends. Crazy, crazy, crazy jealous. I want you all to myself for one night. I want to take care of you. I want to protect you. I want this."

His hand moved again, and Auggie gasped. He wanted this too. He hated how much he wanted it, hated feeling like he was standing on a cliff and he was dumping everything he'd worked for over the edge. He wanted, just once, to feel like himself and not like the fucking cardboard boy he'd been all night. He remembered the redhead groping him. He remembered all the nights with Chan, high school dating and high school making out and high school mistakes.

Orlando kissed him again and said, "I want to take you home tonight."

"Yeah," Auggie whispered, his throat tight. "Yes, please."

26

By the time Theo reached Moriah Court, the wine was hitting so hard that he had to lie down on a bench. It was a cold night, but several glasses of red offered a very pleasant layer of insulation; he even unbuttoned his coat. When the breeze picked up, dead leaves skittered across cement, the sound like running steps, and several times Theo had to open his eyes to make sure he was still alone.

The English department's holiday party had been a shitshow this year. In all fairness, it was the same every year: Dr. Wagner had gotten drunk and stood a little too close to the female grad students; Dr. Shuffield had worn a slinky top that she was thirty years too old to wear, and she'd followed poor Alan around the room, leaning in to ask him about his thesis; Grace had brought her non-binary partner, Eckhart; Devon had shown up because there was free wine, and he'd brought his latest girlfriend, whose name had disappeared into the sea of red in Theo's brain. Dr. Delaney had sung a song that was marginally racist against the Irish. The same things every year.

Only this year, Theo had been alone. And the questions, once they started, didn't stop. Would he be spending the holidays with his family? Would he visit friends? Did he have anyone nearby? Did he know that the holidays were especially difficult for someone who had recently lost a loved one? No, Theo wanted to say. No, he'd had absolutely no fucking idea. So many questions. Did he know how sorry they all were? Did he know that he could just tell them if he needed anything, anything at all? Did he have somewhere to go on Christmas? He wouldn't spend Christmas alone, would he? Then Theo made a game of it. He filled up his glass with every fucking question. And he kept filling it up and filling it up.

On the bench, Theo let his head roll to the side and wondered how long it took to die from the cold.

After a while, he got up and staggered to the door of Moriah Court. It was past two. A very small voice warned him he was doing something stupid—stupid and, quite possibly, dangerous. He buzzed at the door; the security guard on the other side was a young guy with zits all over his face, and Theo had barely started his explanation of why he needed to see Auggie before the guy turned off the intercom. Theo buzzed again. Tried to explain again. It was a really thorough explanation, starting with the accident, no, going back further, starting with Luke, trying to tell this asshole with the zits why he needed to see Auggie right this fucking minute.

"Sir, if you don't move along, I'm going to call security."

Theo started looking for a brick. He was pretty sure he could break the glass with a brick, and then he could explain in person. The guy would definitely understand if he just heard Theo out.

Laughter and footsteps made Theo pause; he recognized that laugh. He'd been hearing that laugh, on and off, for the last four months. He'd heard it in class. He'd heard it on long walks. He'd heard it in his house, when two-thirds of his couch were being taken up by a lanky eighteen-year-old. Then the laughter stopped. Theo waited, but it didn't move any closer. No more footsteps either.

Moving toward where he had last heard those sounds, Theo walked around the side of Moriah Court. He saw two shapes in the darkness. They were pressed up against the wall. Two frantic sets of breaths. Hands moving. Bodies thrusting against each other.

"Auggie?" Theo said.

Both figures startled.

"Holy shit," Auggie said, stumbling free. He was the smaller one, the one who had been pinned against the wall. He jerked at his coat and his pants. "Holy shit."

"What the fuck?" the other one said. "Who the fuck are you?"

"Auggie," Theo said. "Auggie, Auggie, Auggie."

"Jesus Christ. Theo?"

"You know this asshole?" said the other guy.

"What are you doing?" Auggie demanded.

"I came to talk to you." Theo took a step, but the darkness made everything uncertain, and he stumbled and hit the wall of Moriah Court. "I just need to say one thing to you. I just came to say one thing. I just need to say one thing, one thing. Just one thing."

"Oh. My. God." Auggie put his face in his hands. "Are you drunk?"

"He's wasted," the other guy said. "Come on. Let's go inside."

"Hold on," Auggie said.

"This asshole is acting super weird. Let's go inside, Augs."

"That's cute," Theo said. "He calls you Augs. That's really cute."

"Just give me a minute, please?" Auggie said to the other guy.

"You're kidding."

"Just a minute." Auggie moved closer, his features resolving in the shadows. "Can this wait until another day, please?"

Theo held up a finger. He wasn't sure if his finger was moving or if he was, but everything looked like it was trembling and out of focus. "One—" He had to take a breath and hold it for a moment. "One thing."

"Jesus," Auggie said. "You cut your head open on the wall. You're bleeding all over."

"I just need to say one thing," Theo said.

"For fuck's sake, just say it," the other guy said.

Theo pointed at him. "No. No. No."

"What?" Auggie said. "Tell me what you need to tell me, and then you need to get home and clean up that cut."

"No." Theo managed to point again at the other guy, although it was hard to tell because everything was moving around. "He's listening."

"You are honestly unbelievable," Auggie said.

"I just need to say—"

"Oh my God, stop. Ok. Orlando, just, hang out by the door, please?"

"For fuck's sake, just leave him," Orlando said. "He's so trashed he doesn't even know what he's saying."

"Go wait by the door, Orlando. Fuck, I'm trying to handle this."

Orlando muttered something under his breath and left.

"I just need to say one thing," Theo said.

"I am going to kill you if you don't spit it out. I will be the first student at Wroxall to murder his professor. Do you understand me?"

"I'm leaving."

"What?"

"I'm going to London."

"What are you talking about?"

"I'm going to London right now, and I'm not coming back. Ever."

"Ok, Theo, you need to go home and sleep this off. Can you get home? Fuck, it's so cold."

"Not going home. Going to London."

"Let's get you home," Auggie said, taking his arm.

"No." Theo twisted away, staggered, and hit the wall again. This time, he felt his head rebound. "Not going home. Going to . . . going to burn that motherfucking house to the ground. And then I'm going to London."

"What is it with you and burning down that house?"

"Gonna burn it down. And then I'm—"

"Ok, yes. I heard you." Auggie let out a frustrated breath. When he took Theo's arm again, Theo let Auggie lead him around the building.

"Jesus Christ," Orlando said. He had a strong brow and a strong jaw, and right then, he was frowning.

"I've just got to get him home."

"Fuck that. Let him take a cab."

"He's out of his mind," Auggie said. "And it's freezing. I'm not going to leave him alone like this."

"Who the fuck is he? And how old is he? Forty? Fuck, Auggie, what the fuck is going on?"

"I'll take him home, and I'll be right back. I swear it won't take very long."

"Not going home," Theo said, trying to yank his arm free.

Auggie held on. "It'll be an hour, tops. I'm sorry. I'm really sorry."

"Not going home," Theo shouted. "Gonna burn that place to the ground."

"Will you shut the fuck up about that already?" Auggie said, shaking his arm.

"This is so fucking weird," Orlando said.

"I'm sorry," Auggie said. "I'll be as fast as I can."

"Fuck this," Orlando said. "I'm staying at my buddy's tonight."

"Orlando, come on. I didn't want this to happen. But I can't just leave him."

Shaking his head, Orlando moved off across the quad. Pools of light dimpled the darkness; the next time Theo could see him, he was halfway gone and jogging.

"Gonna burn that motherfucker—" Theo mumbled.

"Stop it," Auggie said, shaking him again. "Jesus Christ, Theo. Why the fuck do you have to ruin everything?"

Theo stumbled back, breaking free, and tried to regain his balance. "I'm going to London. I'm going. I'm going. I'm never coming back. Not going to . . . not going to be alone on fucking Christmas."

Auggie ran a hand through his short brown hair. His breath whooshed out; it sounded like he'd been punched.

"Come here."

"Just came to say goodbye."

"Fine, ok. I understand. Come here."

"Going to London."

"I know. Come on. Let's go clean up that cut. We'll go upstairs, get you ready to go. When's your flight?"

That was a stumper. Theo finally settled on, "Tomorrow."

"Ok, so we've got plenty of time."

That made sense. Theo took a step forward.

Sighing, Auggie took his hand and led him toward the door. He keyed past the electronic lock, signed Theo in at the desk, and led him toward the stairs. The guy with the zits watched them the whole way. They went up four flights, and Auggie held his hand for every step. The fourth-floor hallway was dead, and Auggie was still holding his hand. He only let go to unlock the door, and then he took it again and led him into the room.

"Sit," he said, pointing to one of the beds.

Theo sat. He studied the pictures: Auggie with his brothers, Auggie with friends that Theo recognized from his videos, Auggie with a woman who must have been his mom. She had the same dark eyes.

When Auggie came back, he had a wet towel, and he began cleaning the side of Theo's head.

"Ouch," Theo said.

"Hold still, you big baby," Auggie said, but he worked more gently after that. "It's already stopped bleeding. I don't think you need stitches."

Auggie's hands were still very cold. Some of that cold seemed to work through Theo, and he felt suddenly sober, seeing everything more clearly now: the clean lines of Auggie's face, the soft eyes, his mouth.

"You are a cockblock," Auggie said. "You know that, right?"

"You were going to fuck him," Theo said.

Auggie pulled away the wet towel. He was quiet for a moment, and then he said, "You can sleep in my bed. I'll sleep in Orlando's."

Leaning forward, Theo slipped his arms around Auggie and pulled him between his legs.

"Theo," Auggie said.

"Eighteen-year-olds don't know anything about fucking," Theo said.

Auggie's breathing accelerated.

"They all think it's a sprint." Theo drew one hand back and ran it slowly over Auggie's chest. Through the dress shirt, he traced ribs, sternum, and then he zagged right and circled a nipple. "I could make you feel so much better than that dumb kid."

"Yeah?" Auggie said. And it sounded like he was going to say more, sounded like he was going to be a smart aleck about it, and his nipple was stiffening as Theo's finger ran circles around it, so Theo leaned in and bit lightly through the fabric.

The noise Auggie made was so fucking hot it was indescribable.

Theo's hands worked the buttons on Auggie's shirt, and Auggie tried to help, fumbling out of it. Working together again, they stripped him out of the undershirt. Theo locked his legs behind Auggie and used both hands to explore his chest: tracing the hollows just at his hips, limning the slight swell of his stomach, counting his ribs. Theo's mouth closed over a nipple again. Auggie gasped. Theo switched sides, and Auggie grabbed his hair—not in control, but in a kind of helplessness that made Theo dizzy.

"Up here," Theo whispered when he broke away.

"What are you doing?" Auggie said. "What do you want?"

"I want you. Come up here."

"No. You . . . you told me no, and you wanted to talk about my major, and Christ, Theo, you told me never."

Theo rubbed his thumbs along the ridge of Auggie's hips. "I don't know how to be around you. I don't know how to sit or stand or talk. I can't think around you." He shook out his hair. "Come up here."

Auggie slid up onto the mattress.

Flattening Auggie to the bed, Theo straddled him, working Auggie's pants down to expose gray boxers. A wet spot marked the fabric. Theo mouthed along the cotton, leaving wet prints where he closed around Auggie's shaft. Auggie was shaking. He clutched helplessly at Theo's hair again. His breath came in tiny, stuttered explosions.

Theo moved back up, kissing across Auggie's chest, biting his nipples, using his tongue. His hand settled on Auggie's dick and stroked him through the cotton.

"Uh," Auggie said, the pitch of his voice shooting up. He let go of Theo's hair and tried to push himself up. "Uh, uh, oh God, Theo, I'm going to come."

Theo kept stroking him through the boxers, feeling Auggie jerk beneath him. Auggie's eyes were huge and locked with Theo's through the orgasm.

"Oh shit," Auggie mumbled as he began to drift back. "Oh shit."

Theo used the boxers to wipe the warm wetness from his fingers.

"Oh my god," Auggie said, turning into the pillow. "That's so embarrassing."

Nuzzling the side of Auggie's neck, Theo whispered. "It's not embarrassing. You're hot. You're beautiful. I could watch you get off all night."

Auggie groaned, but then he said, "No, it's definitely embarrassing. I'm not fifteen, ok? I cannot believe I just did that."

Theo kissed his way up Auggie's neck, down his jaw, and then once on his lips. Sitting back, he said, "Can I take it as a compliment?"

"Um, yeah. Definitely a compliment." Auggie looked up at him. "I've never—I mean, that was incredible. You're incredible. I can't even believe that just happened. Oh, shit. You didn't—"

Catching Auggie's wrist, Theo said, "I think I'm a little too drunk. Kind of, you know, out of order down there right now."

"I could try—"

With a laugh, Theo shook his head. "No, thanks. This was what I wanted. You're perfect. You are so fucking hot. The way you grabbed my hair."

Auggie glowed with the praise.

Groaning, Theo settled down on the pillow next to Auggie, and they squirmed around until Auggie was inside Theo's arms, with Theo's chin on his shoulder. Within moments, Theo felt blackness drifting in across his vision.

"Getting—" A yawn interrupted. "Getting kind of sleepy."

Auggie laughed. "Let me just wash up before we go to bed.

Theo had slipped into sleep before Auggie was out of his arms. He woke only once, when Ian came back to bed, and he couldn't remember if he'd turned off the light.

"Ian, did you check the porch?"

There was an answer: a sharp intake of breath. But Theo was already asleep again.

He woke in the morning with a hangover and pounding headache. He vaguely remembered coming up with Auggie, vaguely remembered the sex, and looked around, trying to figure out where Auggie had gone and just what the fuck he'd say to the student he'd just all but molested.

But Auggie was gone. His dresser drawers were open and empty, and the suitcase Theo had seen under the bed was missing. Then he remembered his confusion, Ian coming back to bed and Theo asking him something about the porch light, and he muttered, "Oh fuck."

SPRING SEMESTER
JANUARY 2014

1

For Auggie, the three and a half weeks of winter break passed in a blur. Three and a half weeks of California days: sun and a breeze, warm enough to get by without a jacket until evening, the faint dustiness to the air that made him think of manzanita and Mrs. Gutierrez's Indian paintbrush flowers next door. Three and a half weeks of making reunion videos with Logan and Devin, three and a half weeks of dodging Chan—she kept messaging and Snapchatting him, probably trying to apologize—three and a half weeks of Fer watching *Pardon the Interruption* in his underwear, and three and a half weeks of Mom coming back loaded, every single night, with Brendan.

"Why do you put up with this?" Auggie had asked. "You make the money. It's your house."

Fer had chucked the remote at him and said, "What the fuck did you just say?"

Auggie decided he hadn't said anything.

Three and a half weeks of no contact from Theo. Three and a half weeks of nights where Auggie remembered the drag and burn of Theo's beard across his chest and belly, the feel of his hands, the warmth of his mouth. Three and a half weeks of remembering getting back into bed, and Theo calling him Ian, and then packing in a hurry: everything from his clothes to the pack of Kools at the back of the drawer, like he was a little kid running away.

On the day Auggie's plane landed, he got his first text from Orlando since the Final Judgment party: *where r u? we need to talk*

Auggie dismissed the message, snapped a picture of himself in Lambert-St. Louis, and then found a GIF of Billy Madison's back-to-school montage. During the shuttle ride to Wahredua, Auggie replied to comments, snapped a few silly selfies, and sent a few experimental jabs at MikiLuvs2Sing, more out of boredom than anything else. Two more messages came from Orlando during the shuttle ride; Auggie dismissed both of them.

When Auggie got down from the shuttle at campus, he worked his bags lose from under the bus and set off toward Moriah Court. His phone buzzed as he was halfway across the quad, and he stopped to check it.

Orlando: *u r being a real prick this is important.*

Auggie shoved his phone back in his pocket and wished he'd gotten his coat out of his bag; Missouri winter was very real, and his hands were already going numb.

Across the quad, it looked like everyone was more or less on the same journey as Auggie: kids were coming back from wherever they had spent the winter holidays. Some of them had obviously traveled quite a distance; most of them had probably stayed within a day's drive; and a good percentage had family in Wahredua. A pair of boys who had to be freshmen were carrying an air hockey table, cutting across the snow-covered lawn, the cord trailing behind them. For the next week or so, the air hockey table would be wedged in their dorm, and they'd have to crawl under it or over it to get to anything else, and then the RA would come along and make them dump it in the trash. It actually wasn't a bad idea for the start of a video, but then Auggie thought of how badly things had ended with Orlando, and he decided most of his videos would have to be with his other Sigma Sigma friends from now on.

He was a hundred yards from Moriah Court when he saw Orlando charge out of the building. He had his head down, his hands shoved into his coat pockets, and he was headed toward the pathway along the side of the dorm.

As Auggie keyed himself into the building, the security guard—a thin-faced Korean-American girl named Elizabeth—stopped him.

"You're August Lopez, right?"

"Yeah."

"The police are waiting for you up there."

When Auggie asked for details, Elizabeth just shrugged, so he lugged his bags toward the elevator, but of course, the assholes with the air hockey table were taking up the whole thing. Swearing under his breath, Auggie dragged his bags to the stairs and started up all four flights. The luggage swung awkwardly, clunking against each riser and pulling him off balance. By the time he got to the fourth floor, he was sweating. Sure enough, the door to his room was open.

Auggie stopped in the doorway and examined the sight in front of him. His room had been torn apart. Literally. Both dressers lay on the floor. The drawers were scattered across the carpet; several of them had been smashed, the particle-board bottoms splintered and caved. Both mattresses had been cut open and springs and fill pulled out. The closet doors had been ripped off. Orlando's poster of the 2013 Wroxall wrestling team, himself included, had been torn from the wall. Auggie's tripods and lamps had been smashed. Where he'd taped monthly business goals and projections, ideas for skits or posts, the wall was now bare; Auggie saw some of the pages on the floor, trampled by wet and muddy shoes.

Two men stood in the room, both of them in suits. One was older, probably in his late thirties; his hair was thinning on top, his face was freckled, and he had a little tummy going. The other guy was probably Theo's age. And this guy was hot: he had a swimmer's build, and his short, blond hair was messy, but his eyes, crystalline blue, were what really made him stand out. He didn't have that same vibe as Theo, of course. But it wasn't agony to look at him.

"Are you August Lopez?" the older man said.

"Yes, I'm Auggie Lopez. What's going on? What happened?"

"I'm Detective Upchurch with the Wahredua Police Department. This is my partner, Detective Somerset."

"I don't understand. Are you searching my dorm room? Don't you have to have a warrant?"

Upchurch's eyebrows shot up. "Well, that's interesting. Why are you worried about us searching your room?"

"I'm not worried. I'm just asking."

"Your roommate called this in," Somerset said. "Apparently, he got back into town today and found the room like this. The door had been forced."

"Auggie, why don't you come in," Upchurch said. "Let's clear a place by the door for your bags, and let's talk."

Glancing up the hallway, Auggie tried to think what his other options might be. He had absolutely no idea. Aside from a security guard at a Target stopping him once when he and Devin had been making a video, Auggie had basically been a model citizen his whole life. He dragged his bags into the room, and Somerset helped him find a spot for them, and then Upchurch closed the door.

"Auggie," Upchurch said, "how old are you?"

"Eighteen."

"Do you have ID?"

Auggie got out his driver's license and passed it over. Upchurch studied it and handed it to Somerset, who took a picture of it with his phone and jotted down something in a notebook.

"Eighteen years old," Upchurch said. "Kind of a new phase in your life, right?"

"What is going on?" Auggie said. "Do you know who did this?"

"Well, Auggie, I'm going to explain a little police organizational structure to you. You don't have to take notes," Upchurch laughed, an easy laugh, "but I think it'll help you understand why we're here. You see, the police department is kind of like a pyramid. Up at the top, you've got the chief. That's Chief Cravens. In the middle, you've got two sets of detectives. And down at the bottom, you've got the patrol officers. That's where this guy was not too long ago."

Somerset grinned and waved as he handed back the license.

"Patrol guys, they handle the routine call outs. So, when your friend called this in, a couple of patrol officers responded. With a burglary like this, the case eventually moves up to a set of detectives. This time, it should have gone to the other pair: Lender and Swinney. It was their turn."

"Why are you here?"

Upchurch smiled.

"You said it should have gone to those other detectives," Auggie said, "but instead you're here. And that's the whole point of telling me that organizational whatever, so why are you here?"

"See?" Upchurch said to Somerset. "I told you he'd be smart. Wroxall kids are always smart."

Somerset just smiled at Auggie; it was a really nice smile, inviting and genuine, but behind the smile, Auggie sensed some serious thinking was happening. A quiet voice told Auggie that Upchurch might be older, and Upchurch might do the talking, but the one he really needed to be careful around was Somerset.

"We're here," Upchurch said, "because Detective Somerset and I are working a murder case."

Auggie pictured the apartment in Smithfield, the smell of decomposition, the figure, mostly skeleton, that he had glimpsed over Theo's shoulder before Theo had forced him out of the bathroom.

"Did someone get killed here? I don't get it. Why are you here?"

"Who's Robert McDonald?"

"I don't know."

"Really? Do you want to think about it a little more?"

"I don't know."

"Auggie," Somerset said, "we're trying to help you."

"I have no idea who that is."

"Well, here's what's interesting, Auggie: see, we found a dead guy named Robert McDonald. Really, really nasty. He'd been dead for months. You know the body starts to liquefy if it isn't preserved? I mean, we're talking hazmat suits. Kind of stuff you'll see in nightmares. And Robert had pictures of you. He had your course schedule in his wallet. Are you sure you don't know him?"

"I do not know anyone named Robert McDonald."

"Auggie—" Somerset began.

"Me," Upchurch said, "I think you two were boyfriends. I think it was all hush hush. See, after we found Robert, we got a little curious about August Lopez, who had Civ 1 first thing Monday, Wednesdays, and Fridays. So we did a little digging. And we found that big old social media presence. And we found a video of you, where someone accused you of murder. We've been wanting to talk to you for a while, so when the call came in about the burglary, well, that was just the perfect opportunity."

"That video was a dumb prank. They didn't even say I murdered someone. It's just—it was just a stupid video."

"Here's what I think happened," Upchurch said. "I think you and Robert were fagging out—"

"All right," Somerset said. "Take it down a little."

Upchurch exhaled slowly and smiled again, "Isn't Detective Somerset a swell guy? You're lucky he's here. I'm not such a swell guy. I think you and Robert were fooling around, but you had to keep it a secret because of all those girls who follow you on social media. I think you've got a reputation. You've got a business. That's what this is, right?" Upchurch plucked a page from the ground, one of Auggie's more ambitious projections of how much he might make on endorsements and marketing deals over the next five years. "That's a lot of money. Maybe Robert wanted some of it. Maybe Robert just wanted you to kiss him in public. So you killed him." Upchurch flashed a smile. "Guys do a lot of crazy things when they're closet cases. The back of Robert's head was smashed in. That sounds like a lover's quarrel to me. You argued. He turned away. You were so mad you grabbed the closest thing and bashed his brains in."

"I want a lawyer," Auggie said.

"A lawyer?" Upchurch said, his eyes wide. "This is just a friendly conversation."

"I want a lawyer. I'm not talking to you without a lawyer."

"The smart thing for you to do right now, Auggie, is get your shit together and tell us exactly what happened. We can't help you if you don't tell us the truth."

"Get the fuck out of my room. Unless you're going to arrest me, just get the fuck out."

"He's a little tiger, isn't he?" Upchurch said, laughing as he picked a path over the wreckage. "Goodbye, Auggie. We'll be in touch soon.

You might want to find that lawyer you were talking about, just in case."

At the door, Somerset lingered. He spoke in a quiet voice. "You don't have to say anything, but just so you know, we do want to help you. If this isn't what it looks like, then I need you to figure out a way to tell me what it is. Tell me who we should be talking to, tell me what really did happen, tell me how you're all tangled up in this. Whatever it is, we can help you."

Another moment dragged by, and then Somerset sighed and stepped out of the room. Auggie wiped his hands on his joggers and, after another dazed look, began taking the broken drawers out into the hallway, trying to figure out what he was going to do.

2

This time, the destruction had been worse. Theo kicked aside broken plaster, wincing as his hip throbbed. Someone had taken a sledgehammer to most of the walls. They'd ripped up floorboards. They'd tipped over the refrigerator, and Theo wasn't sure if the damn thing was broken because he needed to let it stand upright for twenty-four hours before plugging it in again. They'd used the sledgehammer to smash Lana's crib to pieces.

He'd been on campus most of the day, prepping for classes that started Monday. It had been dark when he'd biked home, and the cold had left his face stinging and puffy. The door had been hanging from one hinge, and he'd gone inside to discover the wreckage of his home.

He'd called the police. Uniformed officers had come and taken a report. And now Theo stood next to the couch, which had been flipped over and had its wooden frame broken in several places. He could still smell the assholes who had done this: body odor and a stale, hot-oil smell he associated with dollar French fries. Knee protesting, Theo managed to set the couch upright, but the broken frame made it sag in the middle, and when he prodded it, it wobbled.

"Holy shit," Cart said. He stood in the doorway, a rigger bag in each hand. He set them down now and stared at the broken boards, the split laths, the plaster dust, the splintered furniture. He was wearing a Blues sweatshirt, a Carhartt coat, and a knit cap. When he met Theo's eyes, he said, "Hey."

"Go the fuck home, Cart."

"I know you're mad at me."

Theo grabbed the twenty-four-inch TV, a Black Friday purchase that was now broken into two pieces connected by a few wires. He carried it out the back door and tossed it in the trash. When he came back, Cart had a drill in one hand and was rummaging through the rigger bags.

"I said go home. Right fucking now. Get out of my fucking house."

"No."

"You son of a bitch."

Cart held up a bit, eyeballing it, and then fitted it into the drill.

"Hey," Theo said, grabbing his shoulder and hauling him upright. "Get out of my house right fucking now."

Face smooth, Cart stared back at him. "I'm sorry for what happened on your birthday."

"Fuck off."

"I wanted to apologize, and you wouldn't answer my calls, wouldn't come to the door when I knocked. Then I tried giving you space."

"So get a fucking clue, Cart. I don't want to see you. Not now. Not ever. Get lost."

"No. I'm not leaving, not until we make sure you can lock the door and sleep here tonight." Cart shifted his weight. "Was there something else?"

"I'll call the police."

"If you want."

"I'll tell them you kissed your dead partner's husband."

Cart flinched and paled, but all he said was, "If you want."

"What the fuck, Cart? I trusted you." Theo didn't know what he was saying, didn't even know what he was doing, part of him shaking Cart by the coat, part of him trying to shove him away. "I trusted you, you stupid piece of shit."

Gently, Cart reached up and prized his hand loose. Then he turned back to the door, and the drill whined.

Theo went into the kitchen and leaned on the counter, his face in his hands until the prickling flush died down and he didn't feel like he was coming to pieces. Then he started picking up the debris. Some of the furniture could be salvaged, but not much. He wasn't worried about the furniture right then. He was worried about an old house with the plaster and insulation ripped out, with the floor torn up, the whole place barely livable. There was nothing he could do about it for the moment, though. He focused on one thing, and then the next, and then the next: putting to rights the furniture that could be repaired, dragging the completely destroyed pieces down to the side of the road. After half an hour, his hip and knee had twisted themselves into fiery knots, and he could hear the uneven pitch of his breath verging on a whine.

He was on his way back from dragging another broken chair to the road when the front door opened and Cart said, "You want to take a look at this?"

As Theo limped up onto the porch, Cart worked the door open and shut. "I got a reinforced strike plate this time. It'll make it harder for these assholes if they decide to come back."

"Thank you," Theo said.

"They make pretty good stuff for home security now," Cart said. "Floor-mounted door blocks, full barricade systems. I thought about picking up some of it when they called and told me what had happened, but you've got all these windows. Windows make it pretty hard to barricade. I'll go get it, though, if you want it."

"No, this is fine. Thanks"

"I checked the back door. I put a better strike plate on that one too."

"Thanks."

"You're saying thanks an awful lot for a guy who still wants to kick my ass."

In spite of himself, Theo felt a flicker of a smile. "Yeah, well."

"I know it looks bad in there right now," Cart said, "but I learned how to do floors. Did them in my mom's house last month, so you get the benefit of all the mistakes she's got to live with. If you don't mind, I say we just rip out the rest of the plaster, reframe the walls, and hang sheet rock. It'll be faster, better in the long run, and a hell of a lot easier to keep up."

"No. I'll figure something out."

"Theo, pardon the redneck in me, but this part's not your fucking choice. I'm doing the floor. I'm doing the walls. If you want plaster, say plaster. That's about as much choice as you get." Cart fiddled with the drill, removed the bit, and bent to replace everything in the rigger bags. "When it's done, you can go back to hating my guts and calling me every kind of asshole you ever imagined."

Lights swept across the porch, illuminating Cart for a moment: the hard lines of his face, the brass buttons on the Carhartt jacket, his hands. A car pulled into the driveway.

"Guess you're getting priority treatment," Cart said. "Normally, they wouldn't send the detectives out this late."

The man coming up the walk was middle aged, with a bushy mustache and huge glasses in thick, yellow plastic frames. The last time Theo had seen Al Lender, the detective had been walking into an abandoned apartment building to inspect the dead body that Theo and Auggie had found. Lender's gaze swept from side to side, and when he came up onto the porch, he paused when he saw Cart.

"Officer Cartwright. Stopping by to lend a hand?"

"You know," Cart said with a shrug. "Ian would've done it for me."

Lender nodded; to Theo, he held out a hand and said, "Theo, I just wanted to tell you how sorry I am about Ian. Should've come sooner to tell you." He held Theo's gaze for an extra moment and said, "What seems to have happened here?"

"Come on in," Theo said. "Although I'm not sure there's much you can do. The patrol officers already checked for prints."

"You want me to hang around?" Cart said.

Theo shook his head. He hesitated, then said, "Cart, thank you."

"What's the fucking good of being a fucking redneck if you can't pull your fucking ivory tower friends out of the fucking shitter every once in a while?"

Theo was still trying to parse that sentence as Cart left. He led Lender inside, thinking about the best way to get to the gun upstairs without Lender suspecting, and glanced over his shoulder. He said, "Would you shut—"

The kick to the back of his leg set his knee on fire. He hit the floor hard, and then his hip went nuclear too. Theo had been in enough barroom brawls and worse fights, nastier fights, to already be thinking, already be reacting. He scrambled forward, trying to put space between him and Lender, already looking for a weapon.

The next kick caught him in the back of his head. It knocked him to the floor, and his face crunched against the boards. Blood filled his mouth. Theo pushed up, trying to get to his feet. A split lip was fucking penny stuff where he came from.

Before he could move, though, he felt a cold muzzle at the back of his head.

"Hello, Theo," Lender said. "I thought it was time we had a talk."

Theo spat blood onto the boards.

"Until now, I've been more or less satisfied dealing with Auggie. He's eager to please, you know. Highly motivated. But my situation has changed. You did a very nice job finding Robert McDonald. Now I want you to find a flash drive that Robert was in possession of. It's gone missing. As you've probably figured out, some dangerous people believe you have it. That's why they ripped this shithole apart. They're going to keep looking; I want you to find it first, Theo."

"Fuck you."

The barrel connected with the back of Theo's head, and his world went white. He came back together by degrees, aware of the nylon-polymer muzzle jabbing up under his jaw, Lender's knee on his back, Lender's hand in his hair, yanking his head back.

"You stupid motherfucker," Theo said; the words sounded bubbly through all the blood. "You don't have any fucking idea. Shoot me. What the fuck do I care? And if you don't kill me, I will fucking destroy you, I will—"

Lender shushed him, tugging on his hair, digging the muzzle into the side of his throat so Theo choked.

"Shush," Lender said again. "Just listen. God, you're every bit how Ian described you. I need you to pay very close attention right now, Theo. If you don't find this flash drive for me, I will visit Auggie again, and he'll need a double knee replacement. I'll even mess up his pretty face. And if that doesn't convince you, and you need further encouragement, I'll pay a visit to Downing. Am I making myself clear?"

Theo arched his back, writhed, tried to twist free. He was going to kill this man, even if he got a bullet in the head doing it.

But Lender bore down with his knee, pinning him to the floor, and jabbed the gun harder into Theo's throat. Theo gagged and choked again.

"Right now, son. Pull your shit together right fucking now. Tell me what you're going to do."

Theo's throat hurt when he spoke; the words were ragged. "I'm going to find a flash drive."

"And if you don't?"

"You're going to hurt Auggie."

With a little clucking noise, Lender said, "No, Theo. I'm going to torture the shit out of that boy and cripple him and make him look like a fucking monster. And if you still don't do what I want?"

"You're going to go to Downing."

"That's right. Now, convince me why you're not going to run off and tell Officer Cartwright, or anyone else on the force, about this?"

Theo's breathing was sheared off at the ends; black spots whirled in his vision, and he knew he wasn't getting enough oxygen.

"Be persuasive, Theo," Lender said gently, digging the gun into his throat again.

"Because you're a cop," Theo managed to say. "Who are they going to believe?"

"And because I will kill Officer Cartwright if you tell him, and then I will go find Auggie, and then I will go to Downing. I've been doing this longer than you've been alive, son. Please don't make the mistake of thinking I'm stupid." He stood with a grunt and said, "Getting old is a bitch, Theo. You have two weeks."

3

Auggie was trying to get ready for the day, and Orlando wouldn't get out of his way.

"You have to talk to me at some point," Orlando said quietly, filling the bathroom doorway.

Finishing with his hair, Auggie checked the button up and cardigan.

"I know I was an asshole," Orlando said. "But I really like—"

With one finger, Auggie pointed to the dorm room that shared their bathroom; the door was open, and no doubt Tyler and Chris could hear everything.

"I like hanging out," Orlando said with a faint blush. The heavy scruff was back, and he was wearing just his compression shorts and a ratty old Fox Wrestling tee. "I was drunk, and I was frustrated, and I acted like an asshole."

"Could you move, please?"

"Not until you talk to me."

"I'm going to be late for class."

Orlando's eyes narrowed, and he stepped into Auggie's space, sliding an arm around him, tugging him forward.

"Are you out of your fucking mind?" Auggie whispered, stiff-arming him.

"Come here," Orlando growled, and he dragged Auggie into their room and shut the bathroom door. He pressed Auggie up against it, his body outlining Auggie's, his mouth inches away. Then his grip eased, and he smoothed Auggie's shirt. "Why do you make me so fucking crazy?"

"That sounds like a bad line," Auggie said. "Get off me."

"I thought about you all break. I'm so fucking mad at myself for the way I acted."

His hand was still at the small of Auggie's back, and he tugged again; this time, Auggie let him.

"I want to make it up to you," Orlando said.

"Orlando—"

"I know you don't want anything public. That's fine; I mean, I'm bi, and I've told guys on the team, but keeping things private is honestly easier for me too. I really like you. I think you like me. I know how to keep my mouth shut." He grinned, pressing in where their bodies joined, and Auggie felt himself getting hard. "And I think we could have a lot of fun."

He bent in for a kiss.

"Oh no," Auggie said, sliding away. "No fucking way."

"Augs, Jesus, man."

"Now I've got to walk across the quad with a boner. How's that for discreet?"

Orlando just smirked and tugged at himself.

"This is worse than gay porn," Auggie said. "In gay porn they just fuck and don't have to talk to each other or ask their roommate to pick up his fucking Xbox controllers."

"Let me show you how nice I can treat you," Orlando said. "Let me make it up to you."

"Bye, Orlando."

"Dinner, tonight. Please."

Auggie rolled his eyes.

"That's a yes! That's a yes, Augs."

"I'll think about it."

"And think about where you want to go."

Halfway down the stairs, Auggie had to readjust himself; he'd never been with somebody who could toss him around the way Orlando just had, and it was having an effect.

Outside, the January weather—cold freezing the corners of his eyes, his breath exploding in white clouds—hadn't stopped the first day of classes from getting into full swing. Students filled the quad, all of them layered in heavy winter clothing, the snow crunching under their boots. Auggie realized immediately that he'd forgotten his coat, and the cold cut through his cardigan. Going back upstairs, though, meant another round with Orlando, and the wrestler was a little too persuasive for Auggie to be comfortable with that right now. Auggie had his first class in Tether-Marfitt again, although this semester, he had Civ 2: 1500-Present. The building wasn't far, and he could make it there without freezing to death. As he headed off across the quad, he caught a whiff of maple syrup from the dining hall, and then a stale, sour sweat smell. Somebody had been having too much fun last night and hadn't woken up in time to shower.

With so many people on the quad, Auggie didn't notice the sound of approaching steps until it was too late. A hand closed around his upper arm, and Auggie glanced over to see the big guy with the shaved head; a heavy coat hid his Celtic cross tattoo, and no sign remained of the broken nose Theo had given him. That had been months ago, Auggie realized distantly. Movement to the right drew his attention, and he saw the woman with the swastika tattoo on her cheek.

"Hello, August," the big man—Jerome, Auggie remembered now—said. "Long time no see."

"If you're thinking about making trouble," the woman said, "think really carefully. You can shout, sure. You can call for help. You can make a whole big deal out of it. But here's the question you have to ask yourself: how long will it take campus security to get here? Do you think it'll take longer than it'll take Jerome to stomp on your head until your skull cracks?"

Auggie missed a step, and only Jerome's hand kept him upright.

"We want it, August," the woman said. "We want that fucking flash drive. And wherever you've got it, you better dig it up and hand it over. Is that clear?"

"You were in my room," Auggie said.

Jerome jerked him to a halt at the center of the quad. Eight different paths converged here, and people milled around them, many of them obviously irritated at having to change course because Auggie and his new friends were standing in the way. Auggie guessed there were easily a few hundred people on the quad right then. He could have reached out in any direction and grabbed a backpack, a coat, a sleeve.

"What are you talking about? What flash drive?"

The hand on Auggie's arm tightened until he grunted. "Don't fuck around, August."

"I don't know what you're talking about."

"Robert had a flash drive. He was supposed to deliver it. Then somebody, maybe you, killed that stupid son of a bitch. You were the last person to see him alive. That means I think you have the flash drive."

"I don't. I don't have anything. I swear to God."

"Then you'd better find it," the woman said. "I'm not going to ask you again. You have two weeks."

"Did you know that the average chimpanzee is worth approximately fifty-seven thousand dollars, if you harvest and use all of its parts correctly?" the girl's voice was effervescent; Auggie had to blink to make sense of the girl his age, her blond hair spilling out from under a knit cap, proffering a clipboard and a pen. "And did you know that right now, millions of chimpanzees are going to waste, dying in Africa, their fur and organs sadly underutilized by local—"

"Get the fuck out of here," Jerome roared.

The girl squeaked, dropped her pen, and ran.

Jerome glanced at the woman with the swastika, his head dropping. "Sorry, Mae."

She didn't look at him. Her gaze was on Auggie. "Now, the last time we ran into each other, your friend really did a number on us." Her hand traced an almost-invisible scar that bisected her eyebrow. "I think you might need a little encouragement, and we do owe you some payback. So I want you to hold out a hand, and Jerome's going to break your fingers."

"What? No, I don't need encouragement. I'll find the flash drive, I'll—"

"If you don't pick, I'll let Jerome decide."

"They're going to hear. I'm going to scream, and everybody's going to hear. It's the middle of the quad." Jerome grabbed his hand, and Auggie twisted, trying to pull free. "You can't do this."

"But we are doing it," Mae said. "And by the time campus security gets here, we'll be gone. Go ahead, Jerome."

Jerome grabbed Auggie's pinkie.

"No," Auggie shouted. People were stopping to stare now, but nobody moved to intervene. Auggie twisted again, and Jerome's grip tightened as he forced the finger back. Auggie went up onto his toes.

"Auggie?" Orlando pushed through the crowd. "Hey, what the hell?"

Jerome was already releasing Auggie, and as Auggie settled back onto his heels, Jerome shoved him. After a few slippery steps, Auggie crashed into Orlando, who wrapped an arm around him to keep him from falling. More people had stopped to watch, but Mae and Jerome just turned and hurried toward the edge of campus; Auggie lost sight of them in the crowd after a few moments.

"What the fuck was that?" Orlando said.

Auggie realized he was still pressed against Orlando, still had Orlando's arm around his waist. He managed to stand up straight, massaging his pinkie as he stepped clear of his roommate, and then he shuddered.

"Well, there's nothing to fucking see here," Orlando said. "Move the fuck on."

As the crowd dispersed, Auggie realized Orlando was wearing Sorels and gym shorts and a coat over his wrestling tee. He'd obviously rushed out of the dorm without really dressing, and now, meeting Auggie's gaze, he blushed and held up Auggie's coat.

"Sorry, I thought, you know, you might want this."

Auggie's teeth were chattering so badly that when he tried to say thank you, it wouldn't come out. A small part of him was wondering how Orlando had known where he would be, but he couldn't get that question to come out either.

"Here," Orlando said, helping him into the coat.

Auggie tried the zipper a few times, but he couldn't get the zipper to catch.

"Let me," Orlando said, and he got it in one and zipped the coat. Then he met Auggie's eyes. "What the fuck was that?"

"Nothing," Auggie managed.

"That was definitely something. Something really serious. They were trying to hurt you."

"No," Auggie said. "It was just a misunderstanding."

"Come on, don't bullshit me. I'm trying to help you."

"I don't need help," Auggie said, too loudly. He took a step away from Orlando, shook his head, and said, "I don't. I'm fine. Thank you for the coat, but I'm fine."

And then he jogged west across the quad; he needed to talk to Theo.

4

Theo got lucky; the bus from Downing was on time, and he made it to Liversedge Hall with an hour to spare before his first class. He was teaching another section of Civ 1, and although he'd made some modifications to the course, the prep was much less substantial this semester. He rode the elevator up, sharing the car with Peg. It was his first interaction with anyone from the department since the holiday party at the end of December; judging by the way Peg's carnation-pink nails played with the buttons on her coat and the way she kept her gaze on the floor, Theo guessed nobody had forgotten his behavior yet.

"I had a great Christmas, Peg," Theo said into the stuffy silence and the smell of wet wool that filled the elevator car. "Thanks for asking. How about you?"

"Oh, yes," she said, addressing her comments to the third button on her coat. "We tried tamales. Too ethnic for me, but the boys gobbled them up."

"And I guess everybody now officially considers me the department drunk, as well as being the department pity project?"

"Well, you know, Theo, I had a great-uncle once who had a little too much to drink now and then. And, you know, like you, he'd suffered just so terribly."

Theo waited and realized that was the end of the statement. He drew a deep breath and pictured a meteor smashing into the elevator.

When the elevator dinged at the third floor, Peg said, "Once, the police had to take him away because he tried to make love to a jug of maple syrup." Apparently caught up in the power of storytelling, Peg seized Theo's hand. "But you will be happy to know he got the help he needed. And you can too, Theo."

"Yes," Theo said. "Thank you."

"Don't be like Great-Uncle Stephen, Theo."

"No, I don't think there's a risk of—"

"You have people who love you. People, Theo. You don't need things to comfort you."

Peg paused here to dab at her eyes, smile up at him tearfully, and give his hand a final squeeze before getting off the elevator. When the doors dinged shut, Theo was still staring after her, and he had to jab the open button to step out onto the third floor.

As he made his way down the hall, though, he groaned.

Auggie was sitting outside his office.

Theo tried to brace himself, but he didn't know what was coming. A fight? Blackmail? Tears? The last time he had seen Auggie, he had just jerked him off through his underwear, passed out, and called him the name of his dead husband. What was the Emily Post etiquette for the follow-up conversation?

Before Theo could reach Auggie, though, a door opened, and Dr. Kanaan poked her head out into the hall. She wore a loose hijab and an elegant black suit; her thick eyebrows drew together when she spotted Theo.

"We need to talk."

"Morning, Dr. Kanaan," Theo said. "How was your break?"

"Not great, Theo. My parents were in town. My husband was so anxious he went through a Costco pack of Tums." She shook her head. "You. My office. Right now. We're going to discuss how to keep you in this program after the holiday party."

At the end of the hallway, Auggie had gotten to his feet; when Theo looked at him, he gave a half wave and buried his hands in his pockets.

"I'm sorry, I've got a very upset student I need to talk to," Theo said. "Can we have this conversation in a little bit?"

"Sure," Dr. Kanaan said. "Would you like to have it before you get called into the chair's office, or after?"

"I promise I'll hurry. He's obviously upset, and I told him I'd talk to him first thing."

"Then hurry, Theo. I'm just trying to help because I want you in the program."

Dr. Kanaan shut her door, and Theo hurried down the hall. He had lied about arranging to talk to Auggie—that was a surprise—but he hadn't been lying completely; Auggie obviously was upset. His eyes and nose were red, and his shoulders were hunched, and even through the thick coat, it was clear he was clenching his hands in fists.

"Auggie," Theo said, his tone as neutral as he could manage. He unlocked the door and stepped inside; cardamom and ginger perfumed the air, and he saw a pot of tea—cold, when he checked— that Grace had left.

Auggie followed him inside and shut the door.

"How was your break?" Theo asked. "Sit down. I guess we need to talk."

"I'm not . . . I don't want to talk about that."

"Well, we have to talk about it eventually."

"No. We don't. I'm just here because—because I want to know if you picked up something."

"Like, an STI? No. And, anyway, we didn't do anything that would transfer an STI. I could go with you to a clinic, though, if you—"

"Oh my God," Auggie moaned, and he pulled his fists out of his pockets and pressed them to his eyes. "Just stop, please. I mean when we were at Robert's apartment. Did you pick up anything, take anything while we were inside?"

Theo was in the middle of powering on his computer, and he froze. Then, bracing himself against the plastic tower, he said, "He came to talk to you too."

"They both did," Auggie said. "And I'm fine. It's fine. I can handle it. I'm not asking for your help. I just need to know if you took something."

"What do you mean, they both did? His partner came too?"

"Yes, of course. I always see them together. I thought maybe that bitch would have lost her eye after what you did to her, but no, she's just got a little scar."

It took Theo a moment to understand. Then he said, "I think we should sit down. This is going to be a longer conversation."

"Will you just answer my fucking question?"

The shout rang through the small office.

"I know you're angry at me," Theo said. "I know you probably hate me—"

"Jesus Christ, Theo. Give me a little fucking credit. It was one night, we were both drunk, and we fooled around. It's a little fucking embarrassing that I was just some fucking stand-in for your dead husband, but it's not like you were the love of my life. Can we talk about something important, please?"

Theo sat down; his cheeks stung like he'd been slapped.

"Well?" Auggie said.

"I didn't take anything."

"Fine. Ok. That's all I needed."

"Auggie, please sit down."

"I've got shit to do."

"I want to talk to you."

"Sure, great. Text me sometime."

Theo was out of the chair before he realized it, slapping a hand against the door, holding it closed. He took huge breaths, trying to calm himself.

"What the fuck is wrong with you?" Auggie said, elbowing him, trying to clear him from the door. "I'll scream. Do you want your fucking professor buddies to come down here and find a student screaming in your office?"

"Sit down," Theo said quietly. "Right now."

Whatever Auggie saw in his face, it made him blink, and he slunk around Theo and dropped into a chair. For another moment, Theo stayed at the door, drawing deep breaths, fresh pain needling his knee. He limped back to his seat and sat carefully.

Auggie was staring at the floor, but he asked, "Are you ok?"

"I shouldn't have gotten up that fast."

"Oh," Auggie said. Then, "I'm sorry."

"No, I'm sorry. Someone came to my house last night. He threatened . . . me. It was the guy you called Glasses."

"He went to your house?"

Massaging his knee, Theo nodded. "Has he talked to you?"

"No. The other detectives came, Somerset and the other one."

"Why did they want to talk to you?"

"Someone broke into my dorm room and searched it. They tore it apart. I think it was those white supremacist assholes." Auggie explained the rest of it, and when he'd finished telling him everything through Orlando saving him on the quad that morning, he said, "They told me I have two weeks to find that flash drive."

Theo was still rubbing his knee, but he leaned back now, shaking his head. "What the fuck?"

Auggie giggled; he slapped a hand over his mouth, and his eyes crinkled.

"This is funny?" Theo said.

"No, it's just—that's basically the only thing I've been able to think. I've got cops in my dorm room accusing me of murdering Robert. I've got white supremacist assholes trying to break my fingers on the quad. I've got Orlando trying to turn me into his fuck buddy. And now you're telling me that there's a dirty cop who's threatening you."

Hand slowing, Theo tried to keep his voice casual as he said, "What about Orlando?"

One of Auggie's eyebrows shot up.

"Never mind," Theo said, his face heating. "Just be careful."

Auggie's other eyebrow shot up.

"I'm just trying to say, you can develop feelings for someone—"

"Theo?"

"Yes, please, God, say something."

"I don't need a dad, so shut the fuck up."

Theo considered pressing the point, realized how far up shit creek he'd gone, and nodded.

"So we're starting from scratch," Theo said. "I guess we go back to his apartment and search it, although the police probably already took anything that was there. Then we go back to trying to figure out who he was and where he might have hidden the flash drive."

"A dirty cop wants it," Auggie said, "and so do white supremacists. How does that work?"

"In Wahredua," Theo said, "that means drugs. The Ozark Volunteers control most of the meth production and trafficking, and they have their hands in just about everything else. Shit. I guess we could try to find a contact who might know why this is so important to them. That might give us some info about who Robert really was and where he might have hidden this stuff."

"I, um." Auggie flushed. "I actually might have somewhere we can start."

"Really?"

"Robert pretended to be a pledge, and he filled out one of these interview sheets. I've got the original. I kind of stole it. But I took a picture on my phone in case I lost it. Here, look." Scooting across the room, Auggie moved his chair next to Theo's, their knees bumping, and displayed his phone. "Can you read what he wrote?"

"Graduated from Wahredua High, plays lacrosse, likes fishing and water skiing, favorite place in the world is family condo at Lake of the Ozarks. Sorry, Auggie, but these are needle-in-a-haystack kind of answers. Every kid from Wahredua is going to have answers like these."

"That's what I thought. I figured he was just making up stuff. But take a look at this one: Favorite Place to take a Date."

"Frozen King on Route 50. Ok, that's kind of strange."

"I looked it up. It's, like, twenty miles outside of Wahredua."

"Yeah, it's . . . I mean, it's an institution, and it's been around forever. But it's far enough out that it's not exactly a place every kid in Wahredua goes."

"That's what I thought."

Even though he knew it was wrong, even though he knew he was going to hell for it, Theo couldn't help himself; he said, "Auggie, this is fucking fantastic."

It was like flipping a switch; Auggie squirmed a little in the chair, his whole face lighting up. He said, "So let's go visit Frozen King."

Theo grinned. "How about you go to class, and I go to class, and we go this afternoon?"

"This afternoon, ok. You promise?"

"Promise."

For the first time since Theo had spotted Auggie in the hall, the tension in Auggie's body eased. He pocketed his phone, moved to the door, and stopped with his hand on the knob.

"Theo?"

"Yeah."

"I don't blame you, you know. For what happened. And, well. Thanks."

5

That afternoon, Auggie met Theo back at his office.

"Let me just lock up here," Theo said, "and we can go get the car."

"The car?"

"Frozen King is twenty miles away. Were you thinking about giving me a piggyback?"

Auggie checked his phone. "Why don't I go get it?"

"What?"

"I'll run back to your house and get the car. I'll pick you up here."

"What's the rush?"

"No rush."

"Oh, you've got plans."

"Theo, please."

For a moment, he just combed his fingers through his beard. Then he shrugged and handed over his keys.

Auggie ran. It was after three already, and he was supposed to meet Orlando for dinner at six. They'd decided on a craft pizza place a few blocks off campus; low key, casual, and somewhere a couple of buddies could go without anybody thinking it was something else.

Outside, clouds blanketed the city, and a few flurries flitted through the gloom. The cold made Auggie's cheeks tingle, and his nose was running by the time he hit the state road. He jogged along the shoulder, slowed by the slush and the gravel. His sneakers were soaked by the time he'd made it halfway. Traffic seemed busier than usual, and Auggie guessed people were trying to get ahead of the storm. A red van shot past him. Its tires threw up a spray of snow, coating one side of Auggie, and his eyes stung as he blinked them clear. He thought about Theo doing this every day.

He unlocked the Malibu, climbed inside, and started it. The engine grumbled, and somewhere under the hood, a belt squeaked. The car smelled closed up, and a little bit like sour milk. Cranking up the heat, Auggie backed out and headed to Wroxall.

When Theo got into the car, Auggie said, "I think it's going to snow."

Theo stared straight at him, didn't glance at the steady fall of flurries. "Really?"

"I just meant, maybe we should go another day."

"We have two weeks, Auggie. We're going today. If you don't want to drive, I will."

"You will?"

Theo scrubbed his beard. "Uh, no. That was a pure bluff. Please don't make me drive."

Auggie smiled and pulled away from the curb.

They merged into traffic, heading out of the city and toward Route 50. Snow was starting to stick to the roads, enameling the asphalt for an instant before the tires of the car ahead of them erased it. Pools of slush on the side of the road were freezing over, glazed with thin layers of ice that rocked when one of the big trucks roared past. On either side of them, the quilted landscape of central Missouri replaced the town: stretches of dense woodland crowding the highway, and then patches of stubble fields choked with snow, and then pasture with split-rail fencing. They drove along two hundred yards of a cornfield where the shocks had been left to rot over the winter. They passed an old-fashioned water tower; the original lettering was gone, but Auggie could read the outline where it had been for many years: HARTFORD. On one side, someone had spray painted, HARTFORD BALL TUGGERS ANONYMOUS and a phone number.

"My friends and I climbed that," Theo said.

"You're part of the Hartford Ball Tuggers Anonymous?"

To Auggie's surprise, Theo burst out laughing. It was a quiet laugh, but a nice one, and when it ended, Theo had one of those smiles hiding behind his beard. "I did get a tugger up there, actually, but the graffiti wasn't there at the time."

"Maybe you were inspiration."

Theo laughed again.

"Maybe your boyfriend missed you and decided to write a tribute, like all those dumb sonnets you made us read."

"He was not my boyfriend," Theo said. "Believe it or not, he won the 4H sportfishing championship that year. He had this great girlfriend, Lou, and we both did a really good job convincing each other we were totally straight."

"What about your girlfriend?"

Theo looked at him, and the tires thrummed beneath them.

Running an arm over his face, Auggie said, "I know it's hot in here, but my feet are frozen solid. Sorry."

"I'm not hot."

The hiss of the heater filled the car.

"Do you want to talk—" Theo began.

"No, please, absolutely not."

"—about what it was like for me to come out, I was going to say."

"Oh. Um. I don't know."

"If you ever want to talk about that kind of stuff, I don't mind. If it would help you—"

"Help me what?"

"I don't know."

"Help me come out?"

"I just meant, if it would help."

"I'm fine, thanks."

"Good."

"I am."

Theo jerked on his seatbelt and stared straight ahead. "That's great, Auggie."

Ahead, a light marked the intersection where they hit Route 50, and Auggie slowed the car and signaled the turn. He had to swipe twice to turn off the signal, and then he had to run his arm over his face again.

"So," he said, trying for a normal tone, "I was thinking maybe I could do this on the days you teach."

"Go looking for a flash drive?"

"No, give you a ride. That's a really bad stretch of road to walk or bike in the winter. I could come over, drive you in, and give you a ride home at the end of the day."

Theo jerked on the seatbelt again. "That's very thoughtful."

"I guess that means no."

"I think we can talk about it later."

Once, when Auggie had been six or seven, Fer and Chuy had taken him to one of those indoor trampoline parks, and Fer had paid for it with the shit money he'd made mowing lawns. It had been awesome, just the three of them, and Fer and Chuy had known exactly how to time their jumps so that they shot Auggie extra high. The bottom of his gut would drop out. He would scream. And they'd catch him, every time. And at some point, Fer had gone to get slushies, and Chuy had gotten bored and wandered off, and Auggie had been alone, bouncing on the trampoline, thinking that everything smelled like feet. A bigger kid, maybe ten, had gotten on, and he'd made it his mission in life to knock Auggie down and keep Auggie down—never touching him, never hitting him, just bouncing at the wrong time, coming too close, doing everything he could to keep Auggie off balance and tumbling and scared. Fer had chased off the kid and screamed at Chuy for five minutes, and Auggie had sobbed on Fer's shoulder until he finally could calm down and drink his slushee. He still remembered what it was like to feel the ground go out from under him, his stomach flip, the helplessness over and over again.

"Oh my God. You're like—I don't even know what to call it. You're breaking up with me."

"That's an interesting choice of words."

"You know what I mean. And you definitely are. As soon as we find this fucking flash drive, you're going to cut me off or something."

"I think you're making a lot of conjectures right now."

"Oh my God. Don't you fucking dare talk to me like you're my fucking professor anymore."

"I think you need to take a step back from this and breathe."

"I don't need you to tell me what I should do. I don't need you to be my fucking professor or my fucking college counselor or my fucking dad. Do you understand that?"

"Auggie, can we please focus? Somewhere out there, there's a flash drive with something on it that a dirty cop wants and the Ozark Volunteers want. And that means it's got something bad on it, something really bad. And we're tied up in all of it for some reason I can't understand. So let's just focus on solving this problem first."

"This problem?"

"Jesus Christ," Theo muttered.

"So, what? I'm your other problem? The next problem?"

"That's not what I meant."

"It's ok for you to want to kiss me when you're wasted, is that it?"

"I thought you didn't want to talk about this."

"I want to talk about it right fucking now. It's ok for you to show up when I'm trying to be happy and fuck up everything, and it's ok for you to give me a handjob, as long as you're totally plastered, and it's ok for you to use me like a fucking replacement part for your dead husband. But once you're sober, I'm supposed to hit the fucking road and pretend nothing happened."

"I do not see you as a replacement for Ian," Theo said. "I was drunk. I was half-asleep. I didn't know what I was saying, and you know that. What you're doing now, it's a shitty way to hurt me, and you're better than that. Don't say it again."

They drove a mile of monochrome countryside; then Auggie mumbled, "I'm sorry."

"Frozen King is right there," Theo said, pointing to a low, white building that was almost indistinguishable from the increasingly heavy snowfall.

Auggie swore, braked, and turned into the lot. He parked near the door; it didn't make much of a difference, because there were only two other vehicles in the lot: an ancient Ram at the back, near the dumpster, and a beat-up yellow Bug. He killed the engine and held out the keys.

"Hey," Theo said.

Auggie dropped the keys in Theo's lap and stared straight ahead.

"Hey, will you please look at me?"

"No, let's handle this first problem."

"For the love of God," Theo said. His hand found the side of Auggie's face and turned him so they were looking at each other. The engine ticked once; on the highway, the slush of tires rose and fell. Heat prickled under Auggie's arms, across his chest, between his legs, a weird mixture of shame and arousal. Theo still hadn't said anything. Those blue eyes, wildflower blue, just held him. Saw him. The real Auggie, not the cardboard shit.

After a moment, Auggie blinked. Then he had to blink again, and he turned into Theo's hand.

"I'm sorry," Auggie said again.

"I don't know what to tell you that will make you feel better," Theo said. "I care about you. Do you believe that?"

"Yes."

"Can it just be that for right now?"

"I guess."

"I'm not saying this to be an asshole, but do you understand why this is hard for me?"

And Auggie realized he hadn't thought about that. Not really. Not in any depth, not for any length of time. A dead husband. A dead daughter. Ten years separating them. Theo was smart and hot and strong and brave. And Auggie was—he could see himself now from the other side—a kid not even all the way out of puberty. The trampoline went out from under him again.

He nodded. And he threw open the door and got out of the car before he could start crying.

6

Theo let Auggie get a head start. When a minute had passed, he grabbed the keys from his lap and headed into Frozen King. Originally a burger stand that also offered frozen custard, Frozen King had grown and evolved over the years into its current form. Like any other fast-food restaurant, it had easy-clean tables, tile flooring, red plastic trays and baskets. The only difference was that the employees wore paper hats that vaguely resembled crowns. On the far wall, a sun-bleached poster of the Frozen King himself, who looked kind of like Henry VIII and Jack Frost mashed together, pointed an icicle finger at the viewer and said, BY ROYAL COMMAND, YOU NEED TO COOL DOWN! The air smelled like seared meat, raw onions, and hot oil.

Auggie was standing at the counter, talking to a dark-haired girl who might have been Latina or, maybe, Native American. She was short, and she kept looking up at Auggie and smiling and pulling her braid across her shoulder. She was missing an eyetooth.

When the door chimed, Auggie and the girl both glanced at Theo, and Auggie gave a distracted wave. His attention was on his phone, which he was showing to the girl. She was nodding enthusiastically, and then she got out her own phone, and they each took a picture of them standing together.

"I'm going to post it right now," Auggie said.

The girl squealed with excitement and started tapping madly on her phone.

From behind a metal warming stand, which blocked the kitchen from view, a big guy with very hairy arms stepped out, obviously wanting to see what was going on. He wore a hairnet, and he wiped his hands on his apron, working the cotton around each digit individually. After a moment, his gaze moved to Theo, and he held Theo's gaze just long enough to tell Theo that he considered himself one tough fucker of a fast-food cook. Then he went back to the kitchen.

"Seriously," Auggie was saying, and both he and the girl were laughing so hard he could barely talk. "I am being totally serious."

The girl was wiping her eyes, she was laughing so hard.

"Theo, this is Lindsey. Lindsey, Theo. He's my lawyer. He's also kind of the ideas guy, you know. Anyway, this is going to sound super weird, but we need to find somebody who knew Robert McDonald."

"Like the clown?"

Auggie smiled. "No, Robert's a guy who lives around here. Well, actually, I guess he passed away recently. But he sent me some content that was fantastic, and I can't use it until I can negotiate with whoever inherited his estate."

"Like his family or something?"

"I guess. Unless he was married, then it might be his wife."

"You flew all the way out here for this?"

"No, I'm at Wroxall now. That's how I met Robert."

Lindsey shrugged, but her eyes were fixed on Auggie's phone.

"We'd definitely be willing to pay a finder's fee to anyone who could help us track down Robert's family, or maybe just where he lived, or anyone that knew him. This is great stuff, you know, and I really want it for my platform."

"I don't know Robert," Lindsey said.

"Really? Because he said this was one of his favorite places to go."

"Yeah, but I mean, lots of people come here."

"Ok, sure. What about your friend in the back?"

"Oh, no, Sal doesn't know anybody."

"Damn," Auggie said. "Theo, I guess it's a bust. We'll have to keep looking."

"Fine," Theo said. "You're throwing cash around like it's nothing. Paying way too fucking much for any scrap of information. I told you this was a bad idea, and I told you we'd get stuck in the middle of fucking nowhere doing it."

"See?" Auggie said to Lindsey. "This is why he's the lawyer and the ideas guy, and this is why I'm the one who makes the videos. Nice meeting you. Thanks for the picture—tag me for sure, ok?"

They were halfway to the door when Lindsey said, "I could call someone."

"I thought you didn't know Robert," Theo said.

"Calm down," Auggie said, putting a hand on Theo's arm. "She's trying to help."

"No, she's trying to get cash out of you."

"Jesus, Theo. Don't be such a dick. What are you talking about, Lindsey? You know how we can find his family?"

"Not . . . I mean, not directly. But if he's from around here, I can call a few people. See if I can find him."

"Seriously?" Auggie said

"This is bullshit," Theo said. "Let's go."

"Let me just make some calls," Lindsey said. "It's not like it can hurt anything."

"You are amazing," Auggie said with a huge smile. "Do you realize that? You are absolutely amazing!"

"I'll just—" she shrugged and nodded. "Do you want something while you wait? It might take a few minutes."

"I think Auggie needs to try the Frozen King Super Freeze," Theo said. "I'll have a chocolate malt. And fries."

Lindsey looked at Auggie for confirmation.

"Yeah, I mean. Gotta live a little."

She giggled, took Theo's money, and passed the order back to Sal. Then she disappeared to make her calls.

Theo sat at one of the booths near the picture window; traffic was still steady on Route 50, huge waves of slush splashing across the drainage ditch as cars and trucks fought through the snow. Darkness was settling over everything, and the world became a geometry of white: cones of light from the cars; arcs of slush glittering, suspended, in the beams; pale quadrilaterals cut out of the ground below the picture windows; and then Frozen King itself, clean lines of tile and glass.

Auggie kept checking his phone.

"What time is your date?" Theo asked.

For a moment, Auggie hesitated. Then he slid the phone back into his pocket.

"Six."

"What's her name?"

Auggie traced a circle on the tabletop; his finger left a smear on the plastic.

At that moment, Sal emerged from the back. He put two waxed-paper cups on the table and a basket of fries. He scratched his arms, staring at them.

"This looks good," Theo said. "Thanks."

Sal just stood there.

"Oh," Auggie said, looking up. "Yeah, thanks."

After a few more seconds, Sal stomped back to the kitchen.

"What's his deal?" Auggie said.

"Doesn't matter," Theo said, nudging one of the cups toward Auggie. "Try your freeze."

Auggie grabbed the cup, poked the spoon around inside, and said, "Do I want to know what's in it?"

"Just try it."

"It looks like dog food."

"Just try it."

"I don't eat a lot of ice cream."

"Auggie, please have one taste."

Making a face, Auggie shoved a spoonful into his mouth. His eyes went wide.

Theo laughed and said, "I know, right?"

"What's in there?"

"Peanut butter, marshmallow crème, hot fudge, I think they've got Reese's Pieces, chunks of brownie."

"Um." Auggie poked around with the spoon a few more times and took another huge bite. "Yeah," he said through a mouthful of brownie, "'spretty good."

Theo laughed again. He snagged a few fries and dunked them in the chocolate malt.

"Gross," Auggie said.

"You didn't think you were going to like your dog food."

"No, seriously, that's gross. French fries in a chocolate shake?"

"It's a malt."

"Same thing."

Theo shrugged.

"It's flat-out gross," Auggie said.

Theo shrugged again.

"Let me try," Auggie said with a grin.

Flicking the basket of fries toward Auggie, Theo offered the malt. Auggie took a fry, dipped it, and popped it in his mouth.

"It's not bad," Auggie said after swallowing.

"It grows on you."

"It's not good either."

"Then you should probably eat your freeze instead."

"Just a few more," Auggie said. "For science."

Two minutes later, Auggie had the malt, and Theo was digging around with a spoon inside the freeze, searching out the Reese's Pieces.

"This place is really good," Auggie said.

"Yeah."

I mean, really good."

"It's an institution for a reason. If you didn't have a date tonight, I'd make you get a burger."

"Good?"

"I think they're the best around here."

"Damn. We'll have to come back."

Theo nodded.

"It's a guy," Auggie said, his gaze dropping to the fry he was stirring the malt with. "Tonight."

"Oh. I didn't think you—"

"I don't know. I mean, I think you know, like, that's probably, um, yeah. My thing, you know? But I've got my business, so it's never really felt like an option."

"Well," Theo said, the spoon slowing now, and he trapped a chunk of brownie against the waxed paper of the cup. "I am going to go on the record here and say I'm not trying to sound like I'm your dad."

Auggie groaned and popped another fry in his mouth.

"I'm just saying this as a friend."

Another groan.

"Is that ok? Am I allowed to say things as a friend?"

"Whatever will make this moment end."

"First of all, I'm really happy you're trying something that might make you happy."

"Gross."

Theo tried to tamp down his smile at that. "Second, I hope you'll be careful—"

"I will literally gouge out my own eardrums if you say any of the following words: lover, pleasure, tender, intimate, protection, safety, satisfaction."

"If I could finish?" Theo asked.

"Oh, and don't say stroke, passion, bliss, caress, necking, or thrust."

"Sweet Jesus," Theo said, closing his eyes.

"Or lube, pelvis, cradle, velvet heat—"

"Ok, ok, ok!" Theo said, his eyes shooting open.

Auggie was grinning. "Go ahead."

"I hope you'll be careful of a few things. If you're not ready to be open about everything in your life, people can sometimes see that as a way of taking advantage of you. People can also pressure you into doing certain things that you're not ready to do—"

"Oh my God."

"Ok, ok. But mostly, I just don't want you to risk something you've worked hard for without really thinking about the consequences. Don't get me wrong: I think being authentic, being who you really are, it's very important. Coming out to my family was the best thing I ever did. But that doesn't mean it was an easy thing or a pleasant thing or that it felt good. It was hard, it hurt, and it wrecked me for a long time. So, there. Finished. Done. I will never say anything again."

With a massive eyeroll, Auggie popped a few more shake-coated fries into his mouth.

"Except," Theo added, "be sure to use lube and protection when your lover gives tender caresses to that velvet heat."

Auggie began to choke.

The door chimed, and a squirrelly guy with a thatch of brown hair stepped into the restaurant. He was wearing half-moon glasses with brass frames, and he swept a grinning glance across the empty dining room. After checking out the whole place, he made his way over to them. He had a walk that actually, literally looked like a mosey: a kind of arrogant, leisurely slowness to his movement. He slid into the booth next to Auggie, bumping him along the bench.

"Hi, guys. You the ones looking for Robert?"

Auggie had gone very stiff, and the color drained from his face.

"Looking for his family," Theo said. "What's going on?"

"Show him, boyo. Nice and slow."

Auggie inched up in the booth to reveal where the guy was pressing the muzzle of a revolver into his ribs.

7

The muzzle of the gun jabbed Auggie in the ribs, and he struggled not to wince. He was hyperaware of every movement. The tremor in his thighs seemed like it might be enough cause for this asshole to pull the trigger. Rolling his eyes, Auggie tried to get another look at the man, but he couldn't bring himself to move his head.

Opposite him, Theo slowly brought up both hands. "Hey, I don't know what someone told you, but we're not looking for trouble."

"No," the guy said. "You're looking for Robert's family. And I seem to recall both of you getting tagged in a video of him getting murdered."

Theo shook his head.

"That's not—"

"Blondie, be quiet."

Auggie worked his tongue over chapped lips and managed to say, "He's just my ride."

"Let's go outside," the man said. "We're going to take a drive."

"Not him," Auggie said. "I'll go with you, but he doesn't know anything about Robert. He doesn't know anything about the night Robert was murdered. He's just my ride, and he was unlucky enough that he got tagged in the video."

"No," Theo said. "Nobody's going anywhere. We're going to sit and talk like normal people. Hell, I'll even buy you a burger."

"Boyo, you're going to have plenty of time to talk, and I'm going to have a lot of questions. Until then, just shut your hole."

"I'll go," Auggie said. Part of him was trying to pass out, panic nibbling away at the edges of his vision. But his voice was loud and hard. "I'll go with you. I'll tell you everything I know about Robert. But he's just my ride; you don't need him. If you leave him alone, I'll walk right out of here with you, and we can go wherever you want."

"Stop it, Auggie," Theo said.

"I hate to break it to you," the guy said, "but that's what we're doing no matter what."

"Or I can scream, kick, fight, and make your life hell until you've got me duct taped in the back of your car. I'll throw my phone away, and then there's no way you'll see what really happened to Robert."

"Make me mad, boyo, and this won't just be about Robert anymore. I loved my cousin. I'd like to know what happened to him. But piss me off, and you and I will be spending some quality time together that has nothing to do with Robert."

"Jesus Christ," Theo said. "He's a kid. Can't you see that? We're here because we're trying to figure out why we got roped into this. We didn't have anything to do with what happened to Robert. We're just looking for answers."

"I think it's time we took this somewhere else," the man said.

"What's your name?" Auggie said.

"Come on," he said, seizing Auggie's arm.

"Tell me your name. What's your name?"

Blowing out a breath, the man looked at Theo. "Is he always like this?"

"Leave him alone," Theo said. "He's a kid."

"It's just your name, that's all I'm asking," Auggie said.

"Les. Now come on. We'll get to know each other a lot better on the ride."

"Les, I know where the flash drive is. Leave Theo here, and I'll get it for you."

"For fuck's sake," Theo shouted. "What the fuck are you doing?"

"Well," Les said, "that's very interesting."

"He's just my ride. Leave him here. He's just my ride, that's all. I just bummed a ride."

"Don't listen to him," Theo said. "Look, if this is about making a deal, we can make a deal. I'm sure we've got things you want, and we can—"

"Mister," Les said, tugging Auggie along the bench. "I think you ought to stay right there and be quiet. And in a few minutes, you can drive home. You have a good night's sleep; your boy is going to be in good hands. We'll have him back in one piece, as long as he's telling the truth."

"This is kidnapping," Theo said. "That's a federal offense. You've got a lot of smart options here, but this isn't one of them. We can sit here, talk about this, for fuck's sake just sit the fuck down and let go of him."

Auggie stumbled out of the booth, and Les tugged him toward the door. They were still alone in the dining room. The girl, Lindsey, hadn't come back. Had she known this would happen? Or was it just bad luck? The rational, critical part of Auggie's brain had locked up; his sneakers slipped on the tile; his shallow breaths brought the taste of raw onion; the muzzle of the revolver dug into sensitive skin. Part of him knew, if he got in the car with Les, he was dead.

Back at the booth, Theo's face was twisted with rage. He was still talking. "Please don't do this. Just let him go; I can tell you what you want to know. Don't do this. Don't fucking do this!"

And then Les had shouldered open the door, and he spun Auggie away from the restaurant and into a blast of snow and cold. The storm had gotten worse; a thick layer of snow had already settled across Frozen King's parking lot, and traffic on the state highway had thinned out, probably because people weren't willing to risk the weather. A little red Geo zipped along the road, and where the highway curved, the lights fishtailed for a moment and almost went off the shoulder.

"Colder than a nun's tits," Les muttered, steering Auggie toward a big, black Ford that was rumbling at the back of the lot. Exhaust drifted over the asphalt. Snowflakes spun and whirled; where the sodium lights caught them, they became mirrors and prisms. The effect dazzled Auggie, whiting out his vision. Get in the truck, you're dead. Get in the truck, you're dead. Get in the truck.

A hard wind cut across the lot, the snowflakes spinning on the new current, and Auggie blinked to clear his eyes. He was breathing through his mouth. He could still taste fries and chocolate malt, but with the mineral taste of snow settling on his tongue. A ringing started in his ears. He slipped.

"Shit," Les said, almost going down with Auggie.

Auggie twisted, broke free, and ran for the empty field next to the Frozen King.

"Get the fuck back here," Les screamed. Running footsteps smacked the asphalt behind Auggie. "Boyo, your ass is going to be—"

A thunk cut off the shouts.

"Auggie!"

Theo's voice.

Auggie skidded to a halt and looked back. Picked out by the sodium lights and the spindrift of snow, Theo was just an outline, that ridiculous bro flow of hair unmistakable. He had a mop over his shoulder like a baseball bat, and light gleamed along the aluminum pole. Les lay on the ground in front of him.

"Car," Theo shouted, and then he lurched toward the Malibu.

Turning, Auggie sprinted toward Theo. When Theo got into the passenger's seat, Auggie shot to the other side and dived behind the wheel. Theo already had the keys in the ignition, and Auggie turned them. The Malibu's engine cranked. And cranked. And cranked.

"Shit," Theo muttered.

Risking a glance, Auggie saw a big guy who had gotten out of the Ford and was jogging across the lot. Les had pushed himself up onto his hands and knees, and the big guy was shouting something to him.

The Malibu's engine was still trying to turn over.

"For the love of fuck," Auggie screamed.

That did the trick.

As the Malibu's engine grumbled to life, Auggie shifted into reverse, backed out of the stall, and then shifted again. They shot out onto the state highway, and only luck kept them from sliding into the drainage ditch when Auggie turned. Tires slewed in the snow, and Auggie pictured the Geo fishtailing as it went around the bed. Panic came for him again, and his brain blinked out.

Auggie was back in Huntington Beach. He had been driving. He'd been trying to make his own version of the "Call Me, Maybe" videos that had gone viral. He'd been holding up the camera, singing. He'd been multitasking—that's what he called it. His attention had slid to the traffic in front of him, then to the rearview mirror, then to the camera, all while he was still singing along with Carly Rae. He'd felt good. He'd felt splintered. His attention everywhere at once. He'd felt unstoppable. Then his light had turned red, and a sixty-eight-year-old woman in a Chrysler New Yorker Fifth Avenue had her light turn green, and she pulled out in front of him.

"Hey, hey, hey, hey, hey," Theo was shouting.

Auggie flinched, came back, and tightened his hands on the wheel. Headlights were coming toward them. His first reaction was to jerk the wheel, but then he remembered the snow. He let the Malibu drift back into their lane; a moment later, a Mack truck shot past on the other side, horn blaring.

"What the fuck was that?" Theo shouted.

"I'm ok."

"Auggie!"

"I'm ok!"

But he wasn't ok. Some sort of essential wiring had come loose in his brain. Input just kept coming at him, and he couldn't put it together. The agonized rasp of Theo's breathing, that was one part of his brain. The flare of lights in the rearview mirror, that was another part. The ache in his side where he could still feel the muzzle digging into him, that was a part. The snow chittering against the glass, that was a part. The blur of the double yellow in front of him, that was a part. A sharp snap of air clearing the storm for a moment, that was a part. The pink-and-blue fluorescent of WESTPHALIA MOTEL – COLOR TV – AC – NO PETS. The hot strength of Theo's hand on his neck.

"I can't," Auggie said. "I can't. I can't."

"Yes, you can."

"I can't."

"Yes, you can."

Auggie cut the wheel hard to the right; they turned onto a frontage road and drove behind a string of brick buildings—ENGINE OIL TIRES said one; THE LADY'S LANDAU TREATS AND OLD-FASHIONED CIVILITY said another. He killed the car. He killed the lights. He put his head on the steering wheel. Once, growing up, he had grabbed one of those vibrating back massagers and held onto it until his hand was numb, and this felt like that, only all over.

Theo's breathing was getting sharper and faster until he finally shouted, "Fuck," and punched the headliner. Then, quieter, "Are you ok?"

Head still on the wheel, Auggie nodded. He waited for Theo's reaction: would he shout? Would he rip Auggie a new asshole? Fer would have asked him why he'd freaked the fuck out. Chuy would have told him he was a fucking screw up, but it was ok, because Chuy was a screw up too. His mom would have . . . what? When he'd hit Mrs. Fay Litten, sixty-eight years old and a lifelong resident of Anaheim, and sent her Chrysler New Yorker Fifth Avenue spinning through the intersection like a Matchbox car, his mom hadn't said anything to him. He'd heard her later having a screaming fight with Tommy G., the current flavor at the time. He'd heard her favorite expression: *making a scene.*

But Theo didn't do any of that. Theo dragged him across the center console, wrapping him in a hug. Theo was shaking. Wild shakes, like he was coming apart. And then he kissed Auggie's neck, right behind his ear, just once, and held him tighter.

8

They left the car hidden behind THE LADY'S LANDAU and walked a quarter mile to the WESTPHALIA MOTEL – COLOR TV – AC – NO PETS. Theo kept looking at the sign. He kept thinking about being back in the car, Auggie in his arms, the poor kid frozen solid. Auggie still looked like that: his face blank, his eyes dull. Theo caught his gaze and looked up at the sign again.

When Auggie followed his glance, Theo said, "Wonder if they'll let me keep you."

A tiny smile cracked Auggie's frozen façade, and he said, "You're the worst."

Annie Rodriguez had owned the Westphalia Motel for thirty years; her husband had bought it when the bank foreclosed, after he'd spent almost eighteen years digging ditches and laying irrigation pipes. He'd restored the place himself, one room at a time, and then he and his wife had run it together until he'd died a few years ago.

Pausing with her pen above the registry, Annie said, "I told him, 'Victor, you never eat watermelon with a glass of milk. You just don't do it. It hits the stomach too hard. And Fourth of July, he had a glass of milk with his watermelon. He went inside, lay down, and he'd passed on before the fireworks started." She touched a knuckle to the corner of her eye. "Bless his heart, he hated fireworks."

"He died of watermelon and milk?" Auggie asked. A little color had come back into his face, but he still looked exhausted and scrubbed out.

"Stroke," Annie said, finishing the registry page with a flourish. "But I warned him."

"But—" Auggie said.

Theo squeezed his arm and gave a tiny shake of his head.

Annie took Theo's money—he had to count out the last dollar with change—and gave them a key attached to a large plastic tag that had the number 3 on it. She asked them if they wanted a wake-up call.

She promised coffee and tea were already in the room. Theo took advantage of every break in the flow of words to nudge Auggie toward the door. When Annie took a breath, Theo shoved Auggie outside and called thanks over his shoulder.

Room 3 looked like every other low-budget motel room Theo had been in, although it was cleaner and smelled better than most. It had particleboard furniture that consisted of two full beds, a table with two chairs, and a combination dresser/TV stand. The bedding was rough enough to put scratch into a cat, and the towels were so thin that Theo could practically see through them, but the bathroom had fresh bars of soap and hot water. After a few minutes of messing around with the window unit, warm air chugged into the room.

"Might want to sleep with your clothes on," Theo said, holding a hand in the current of air. "I don't know if it's going to get much warmer in here. This thing just doesn't put out enough heat."

"In porn, there's only one bed," Auggie said.

"Ok, I guess that's one way to have this discussion. You will be sleeping in that bed," Theo said, pointing to the bed farthest from the window. "I will be sleeping in this bed. Never the twain shall meet."

"You are so weird sometimes."

"You're the one bemoaning a non-porn-conforming motel room."

"I wasn't bemoaning," Auggie said, but a little more color had come back into his face. "I was observing."

"Well, if you do any observing in the shower, please keep it quiet. I already have enough nightmares, thanks."

"God, I hate you." Auggie heeled off his sneakers. "My feet are still soaked, and they are fucking freezing."

"Take a shower," Theo said. "Quietly."

"Fer made a dumb joke about gay porn when I moved into Moriah Court. Something about my hot roommate. And now, with Orlando, it's, like, weirdly real."

"Is that who you—" Theo stopped himself. "Sorry, none of my business."

"Shit," Auggie said, digging out his phone. He placed a call, undid his jeans, and kicked his way loose from them as he hopped toward the bathroom. "Orlando, I am so sorry. Listen, you're not going to believe what happened."

The bathroom door clicked shut behind him. Water ran. A moment later, Auggie's voice rose, and the words became clear enough for Theo to hear.

"I'm not lying to you, and it's not fucking weird that he's my friend, so you'd better let that fucking go, ok?"

Theo thought he was mostly a good person, so he felt like a real shitheel for taking an extra few minutes to try to eavesdrop before he turned on the TV. Then he kicked off his shoes, grabbed Auggie's sneakers, which were some sort of outrageously expensive-looking white high-tops, and put them upside down over the climate-control vents. Grabbing the pocket edition from his jacket, he stretched out on the bed and tried to read *King Lear* and not think about Auggie twelve feet away, naked and wet. He changed the channel to C-SPAN; maybe that would help.

Auggie came out of the shower in nothing but a towel, and God help him, Theo looked. He was lithe, enough muscle to give him tone and shape but not bulk. Dark hair under his arms. Dark hair leading from his navel to the thin white towel. Fine, straight dark hair on his legs. Auggie checked himself in the mirror for a while, and then he walked straight over to Theo and got onto the bed next to him.

"Nope," Theo said.

Auggie squirmed around until he was under the covers.

"I said no."

Auggie propped himself up against the pillows.

After another moment, Theo blew out a breath. "Fine, I'll move. I said no and I meant it."

Auggie caught his arm and pulled it around his shoulders. The skin was warm and soft; Auggie smelled like motel soap.

"Auggie, we just talked about this."

"Please," he said. "I won't make a move, I won't do anything. But some guys just tried to kidnap me, and they were probably going to kill me, and I had a panic attack in the car. My brain feels so fucked up right now, and I started crying in the shower and couldn't stop. Now there's this huge knot in my chest."

Theo blew out another breath, about to tell Auggie that this was exactly what making a move looked like. Instead, he shifted around until Auggie fit inside his arm perfectly and tried to pretend he was reading.

"So, I told you about that accident, right?" Auggie said.

"You did."

"That kind of, um, came back tonight."

"Do you want to talk about it?"

"I don't know. I mean, I just wanted you to know. I couldn't keep driving. I was going to spin off the road or hit another car or something. But I know that's a bad topic for you, so I don't want to dwell on it."

"I can talk about it," Theo said. "I think you want to talk about it."

"I just . . . do stupid things. It's like this pressure builds up inside me, and finally something blows, and I can't help it. I do something stupid. I get so tired of everyone looking at me, seeing this . . . this human poster that I've made out of myself, and not having any fucking idea who I really am, and I do something stupid." Auggie rested his head on Theo's shoulder; his hair, wet and still warm, dampened Theo's shirt. "That's a really first-world-problem kind of situation, isn't it?"

"It's not exactly on the same level as having a warlord attack your village," Theo said, "but that doesn't mean it's not real, and that doesn't mean it doesn't hurt. It sounds like it hurts a lot."

"My mom was dating this guy, Jordan, and he had this insanely cool Ferrari. A 458 Italia. And my mom wasn't really there for us a lot, which I kind of told you about, and it's fine, it's not a big deal, but it used to bother me a lot. So I grabbed his keys, took his car, and crashed it into the wall of this car wash. Oh my God, my mom almost killed me. But at least she was paying attention to me, the real me."

"I'm sensing a theme with cars."

Auggie laughed into Theo's chest. "Yep."

"And the accident, the one last year?"

"I'd gotten in this fight with Logan and Devin. They're the guys—"

"From your videos. Your friends from home; I remember."

"Well, that's kind of the thing. We had this video get crazy popular right before Thanksgiving. And we decided to celebrate. So I got Logan tickets to a concert by this band he's obsessed with, and I got Devin this sweet Buddhist prayer bead thing because he thinks he's Buddhist. And do you know what they got me? They got me a fucking camera. It wasn't even a good camera; the ones on our phones were better."

Dropping his book, Theo combed fingers through Auggie's wet hair. "And the problem is that they only saw you as . . . this guy who makes funny videos."

"Yep. And now I feel really shitty because that is so stupid compared to what you've been through."

Theo hushed him. After a moment, he said, "What would you have liked them to get you?"

"Tickets to Disneyland so we could hang out together. A book of Japanese poetry. A sex doll of Robert Pattinson."

Theo laughed so hard he almost fell off the bed.

"What?" Auggie said, punching him. "He's hot."

"Yeah, well, it's not exactly the kind of gift your buddies get you. You might have to buy that one yourself."

"And they definitely won't buy it for you if you're super secretive about who you are," Auggie said.

"You shouldn't feel bad about that," Theo said. "You're allowed as much time as you want to decide who you are and what you want to share with people." Grabbing up the pocketsize *Lear*, he said, "In the future, though, if you feel the urge to show everybody the real Auggie, please do not ask to borrow my car."

Theo couldn't see it, but he could feel Auggie's grin. "Deal."

"I'm more worried about how we're going to get home. If both of us have panic attacks when we get behind the wheel—"

"I'll be ok."

Theo grunted.

"No, I will. It's just—the gun, and the adrenaline, and then we almost went off the road. I feel better already. We'll just take it slow tomorrow, and it'll be fine."

"We'll see," Theo said. "Maybe I'll call someone to pick us up."

"I'll be fine."

Theo grunted again and tried to get back to *Lear*.

Auggie shifted against him, and then one hand came up and ran through Theo's hair.

"You have really pretty hair," Auggie whispered.

"Thank you."

"Does that sound super gay?"

"Not as gay as telling me Robert Pattinson is hot and you want to own a sex doll of him."

"It's nice to be able to say something like that. It feels good to say something like that out loud." Auggie swallowed. "You're beautiful. You're handsome, I mean. And hot. But you're so beautiful."

Theo put down the book again. He slid out from against Auggie and turned to meet his gaze. A heartbeat passed, and Auggie squeezed his eyes shut and turned into the pillow.

"I'm going to shower," Theo said. "And then I think we should get some sleep."

Auggie nodded.

"Could you switch over to the other bed before I get out of the shower? I'm not asking to be a dick. If those guys find us, I want to be in the bed closest to the door."

Auggie nodded again.

In the tiny bathroom, Theo stripped down, showered, and jerked off, bracing himself with one hand against the wall. Then he saw Ian's face, and he felt sick and dizzy and squatted under the spray, hot water needling his back, until he didn't think he was going to puke.

He cleaned himself up again, but he was shaking now, and he took a long time drying off.

When he came out of the bathroom, Auggie was still in Theo's bed, his chest rising and falling slowly in sleep.

Theo turned off the lights and climbed in next to him. Once, near dawn, Theo woke and realized Auggie had wormed his way into his arms. Then Theo slept again.

9

When Auggie woke, Theo was in the other bed. The air was freezing, although the heating unit was still pumping steadily, and frost rimed the inside of the window. Auggie flopped around for a minute until he was facing Theo and said, "Cold."

Theo, who was fully dressed and wrapped in the blanket on the other bed, said, "It's not that bad."

Auggie groaned and pulled the blanket over his head. "What time is it?"

"Eight twenty."

Auggie groaned again.

"It's not that early," Theo said. "You had morning classes last semester."

"Yeah, and I hated every minute of them."

"Huh," Theo said.

"Except Civ 1, of course."

"Right."

"Because it was taught by the best grad student slash professor ever."

"Ok."

"The handsomest, smartest, bravest Shakespeare professor in the history of the world."

"Foot off the gas, Auggie."

Under the blanket, Auggie didn't have to hide his smile.

Then he sat up, and the blanket fell away, and goosebumps ran across his skin. "Oh shit. Morning classes!"

Laughing, Theo said, "Crawl back inside your cave, Abominable Snowman. They canceled classes today, thank God; there's no way we're getting back to Wahredua any time soon."

"They canceled the second day of classes?"

"Snow day."

Wrapping himself in the blanket, Auggie said, "I've never had a snow day."

"Well, usually they entail sleeping in, binge-watching *Arrow*, and drinking hot chocolate and eating cinnamon rolls. That is, if you don't have kids. If you do have kids, then you spend snow days digging child-sized snow pants out of a box in the basement, putting on snow pants, taking off snow pants, putting on coats, taking off coats, putting on gloves, taking off gloves, and going sledding for a grand total of five minutes before she's too cold and you have to start the whole process with the clothes again." He was smiling, folding open a pocketsize edition of *Lear* against his knee. "And if you have a husband named Ian Moore, you spend almost the exact same amount of time just trying to keep track of that man's gloves. I kept threatening to pin them to his sleeves." For another moment, Theo was grinning to himself, staring off into the middle distance. "Anyway, that's a downer for you to hear about. Sorry."

"No," Auggie said. "You look happy when you talk about them. That makes me happy."

Blowing out a breath, Theo said, "I'm sorry I called you Ian, you know, before break."

"It's ok."

"God, that's so weird. I'm really sorry. I was drunk, and I don't know. Obviously I'm still really messed up."

"You're not messed up."

"Yeah," Theo said quietly, folding the *Lear* shut now. "I think I am."

"*Arrow*?"

"God, yes. Strand me on that island, please."

"So you've got a thing for guys with great abs and showy muscles."

"Of course," Theo said. "Let's go get breakfast."

By the time Auggie had dressed, he decided the room might be habitable. "I think I'm only going to have frostbite in my fingers now," he announced.

"Baby," Theo said, tossing him his high-tops one at a time. "Luke and I shared a loft in the addition my parents built. Totally uninsulated. Well, Meshach and I shared it first. Then he wussed out, and Luke moved in."

"You're joking."

"Nope, Meshie is a total wuss."

"Did you spend your whole life milking goats or something?"

"Not goats plural," Theo said, "just the one."

"Did you dry these?" Auggie examined the high-tops. "When did you do that?"

"I stayed up all night with a hair dryer."

Auggie rolled his eyes, but he said, "This is amazing. I was dreading putting these back on."

"Well, there you go."

"Thank you."

"Breakfast, Auggie. I'm hungry."

Auggie followed Theo to The Lady's Landau, which was open for business against every conceivable odd. The snow had stopped, and a thick layer crusted the roads, the trees, the buildings, the cars. Here and there, chrome or glass blinked out, but everywhere else the blanket of white glowed in the rising sun. It was like liquid light, poured out across the world, everything incandescent. Auggie had to blink to clear his eyes. The world even smelled like snow, which he hadn't known was a smell: crisp and, to his mind, dry, although he knew snow was water.

Inside the Lady's Landau, the aesthetic was pseudo-Victorian crossed with country antique: spindle-back chairs, clawfoot tables, white cotton-sack towels, enameled stoneware jars, one labeled ROCK CANDY – KIDS FREE – ADULTS 35C.

"Maybe we'll get you a treat if you're good," Theo murmured as they stepped inside.

"I honestly think I hate you sometimes."

Most importantly, The Lady's Landau was warm, and it smelled like honey and ginger and pork sausage. When they stepped inside, Auggie immediately felt his fingers and nose begin to defrost. The dining room was empty, so Theo ushered Auggie to the back corner, and he sat so he could face the door. A few moments later, the door to the kitchen swung open, and a woman emerged with a tray of sticky buns.

"WELL, GOOD MORNING," she shouted. That was the only possible way to describe it: a full-on shout. Auggie's ears were ringing. "I'LL BE RIGHT WITH YOU."

She settled the sticky buns in a glass display case, and then she came over. "WHAT BRINGS YOU TWO BOYS TO THIS PART OF THE WORLD?"

"Storm stuck us here," Theo said. "But it might have been luck, because those sticky buns smell amazing."

"PECANS?"

Auggie had to fight a giggle.

"Excuse me?" Theo said.

"DO YOU EAT PECANS? THE STICKY BUNS HAVE PECANS."

Auggie could feel himself slipping. Then Theo kicked him in the shin, and Auggie yelped and bent to massage his leg.

"Love pecans," Theo said. "Do you have coffee?"

"COURSE."

"We'll both have coffee. How about the biscuits and gravy for me? And a sticky bun, definitely. I think that'll be good to start."

"SWEETIE, YOU JUST TELL ME IF THOSE BISCUITS DON'T FILL YOU UP. I'LL EAT MY APRON. AND FOR YOU?"

"Um, a glass of orange juice. Is it fresh squeezed?"

"WHAT?"

"Fresh squeezed," Auggie said, more loudly. Some part of his brain had become convinced that she had a hearing impairment. "And do you have an egg-white omelet?"

"THIS ISN'T A BARN, YOUNG MAN. YOU DON'T HAVE TO YELL."

That was it; Auggie felt himself sliding over the edge.

"He'll have the biscuits and gravy too," Theo said. "And I guess a sticky bun for him as well. Sorry. He doesn't get out much."

The woman sniffed and left.

She had barely cleared the kitchen door when Auggie broke out laughing. He laughed until he was crying.

"She's coming back," Theo whispered, and then he tried another kick. Auggie saw it coming, though, and he just laughed harder.

"COFFEE," the woman announced. She gave Auggie a curious look, glanced at Theo, and shrugged. Then she set down cream and sugar and left.

"I can't take you anywhere," Theo said.

Auggie laughed even harder.

"You're going to get us kicked out," Theo said. He sipped the coffee. "Oh my God, Auggie, it wasn't that funny."

"You. Don't. Have. To. Yell," Auggie got out between gasps. Then laughter overwhelmed him again.

Theo had one of those gentle smiles tucked away behind his beard, and he just shook his head.

Somehow, Auggie managed to pull himself together enough to doctor his coffee: eight packs of sugar, and most of the cream. Then it tasted just right. The biscuits and gravy came, a gray mass slopped over two mounds, with home fries and over-easy eggs on the side. Auggie stirred the gravy with a fork. He ate the eggs. He speared a couple of home fries and looked around for ketchup.

Theo had already finished one biscuit when he glanced over. "What's wrong?"

"Oh, nothing. I just don't really like gravy."

Chewing slowly, Theo watched him. Then he swallowed and said, "Have you had sausage gravy before?"

"It's not, like, something I grew up eating."

"Well, you might not like it."

"Yeah, I don't think it's my thing."

"It's kind of more of a country meal, you know," Theo said. "California kids, yeah, I don't think they'd eat it."

"Well—"

"I should have thought of that when I ordered. Sorry. Just, you know, put it to the side. I'll box it up and take it to go."

"What? Why?"

"I like it. Here just give me this. What do people in California eat? A nice breath of air with asparagus essence?"

"Oh my God," Auggie said. "Oh my God, how did I not realize this before?"

"What?"

"You hate California."

"I don't hate California."

"You do."

"I hate people from California." Theo raised his fork. "Most people."

"Oh my God."

"So just give me your biscuits and gravy, and we'll find something else for you."

"No."

"Excuse me?"

"No, you're like this crazy anti-Californian. And what do you know about me? Maybe I'd like this stuff."

"You won't."

"Maybe I would."

"Don't do this."

"You say it's great, so why wouldn't I like it?" Auggie cut into the biscuit, revealed steaming fluffiness, and popped a piece into his mouth. The peppery heat of the sausage exploded on his tongue, melding perfectly with the buttery flakiness of the biscuit. "It's delicious," Auggie said. "There. Are you happy?"

"This is silly. Just let me—"

"No. I'm going to eat them. I like them. I like biscuits and gravy."

"Ok," Theo said. "Fine."

Five minutes later, Auggie's plate was clear, and he said, "And if you ever fucking brag about using reverse psychology on me, I will go cut a fucking switch and go all country on your ass."

Theo had to cover his mouth with his napkin for almost a full minute.

After breakfast, they scraped snow off the Malibu until their hands were stinging, and then they made their way back to the motel. Auggie wiped away the frost from the inside of the glass, and he studied the state highway.

"There's no way we're getting out of here today."

"They actually are really efficient about clearing the roads," Theo said. "I bet we'll be back in Wahredua by this afternoon."

"So we just hang out here until we can leave?"

"I'm not going to hang out," Theo said. "I'm going to work." He grabbed the pocketsize *Lear*, bundled himself in the blanket, and began to read.

"Theo?" Auggie said.

Theo made a questioning noise.

"Robert's apartment was a dead end. Robert's police record was a dead end. Robert's social media was a dead end. We tried to figure out who else might know him, and we just about got dragged off into the woods and shot."

Theo made the same noise again.

"How are we supposed to find the flash drive?"

"We'll keep working on it," Theo said. "There are other people around here who might know him. That guy last night said he was a cousin; he obviously wants revenge for what happened to Robert. But we might find parents, siblings, friends. We keep looking, Auggie. That's all we can do."

"Yeah, but we have less than two weeks, and we're just sitting here."

"We're snowed in. We can't do anything until we can leave, so I'm going to make use of this time to try to write this thesis before I shoot myself because I have to teach freshmen every day."

Auggie bundled up in the blanket, snapped a few selfies, and worked on his social media presence. Getting snowed in at a motel was actually a fun story, and he was getting a great response. After a while, though, the back part of his brain switched tracks, and Auggie found himself thinking about Robert McDonald and the flash drive.

Everything had started in September. Robert had approached him for some reason Auggie didn't understand. They'd stolen the Porsche, crashed it, and almost killed Theo. Robert had run off into the woods. And as far as Auggie could tell, that was the last time anyone had seen Robert alive. Then the video had surfaced—a video with footage that only Robert could have filmed. Did that mean Robert had made the video and posted it? Or had Robert's killer taken

Robert's phone and used the video clips on it to frame Auggie and Theo? Or was it something else entirely?

Another thing that bothered Auggie was that Lender's timeline had shifted so dramatically. At the beginning, Lender and the Ozark Volunteers had pressed Auggie to tell them where Robert was. They'd been frantic. They'd been desperate. Then Lender had vanished for almost a month, and he'd come back looking rested and relaxed. He'd still wanted to know about Robert, but it had been . . . almost casual. Like Lender just wanted to close the book. And now, Lender and the Ozark Volunteers had a timeline again: two weeks.

What had changed?

Auggie searched the Wahredua Police Department and found Albert Lender. He ran Lender's full name through Google. He found a lot of results for financial lenders, and a few entries about a Modernist architect, and a single news story out of Kansas City, a 2010 piece that listed Albert Lender among participants in an elite counter-terrorist training program the state was running.

"What's the newspaper in Wahredua?"

"The *Courier*," Theo said. "Why?"

"I want to see if they have any stories about Lender."

"They don't have a digitized archive. Trust me: I already checked."

"Do they have a website? Like, a digital version of the newspaper?"

"Yes."

Instead of trying to navigate the *Courier*'s clunky website, Auggie just did a site-limited search on Google. He hit gold on the fourth entry.

"Holy shit," Auggie said. "Read this."

Accepting the phone, Theo studied the screen. After a moment, he said, "So on September 19th, Lender has a big arrest. Supposedly this woman he's picked up is a big player in the Ozark Volunteers, and blah blah blah, everything is finally going to get better. Then a few days later she's released. What am I supposed to think about this?"

"Lender and the Ozark Volunteers are both freaking out about Robert. They're both trying to figure out where he is, because they both want this flash drive and whatever's on it. Blackmail, I guess. Or something along those lines."

"Ok," Theo said. "That's a little bit of a jump, but I don't have a better explanation."

"Then Lender hauls this woman in, supposedly she's a big deal, and she gets out of jail a couple of days later when the charges are dropped. The next time I see Lender, he's not really in a rush. He wants to know where Robert is, but he's not on a strict timeline."

"And you think the arrest was a way to put pressure on the Volunteers. Lender gets them to admit they don't have Robert. He's worried they had the blackmail, or whatever is on that flash drive, but once he knows they don't have it either, he can be more careful, move more slowly."

"The Ozark Volunteers stopped showing up too. My guess is that Lender threatened them and told them to stay away from this."

"So why does it all start up again?" Theo asked.

"I don't know. There's pressure again. A timeline. Two weeks."

"What's causing the pressure? What happens in two weeks?" Theo asked.

"I don't know."

Theo tossed Auggie's phone back onto the bed, picked up his own and placed a call. He spoke in a low voice, laughing occasionally, and then he stood and moved into the bathroom and shut the door. Auggie tried to eavesdrop, but then Theo turned on the shower, and the white noise of the water blocked out the conversation.

Auggie tapped his phone's screen. Hard.

He couldn't find any more local news articles that might explain what had changed recently for Lender, and after a few more minutes, he gave up. He went back to Robert's Instagram account, scrolling through it, checking faces. Les, the man from Frozen King the night before, showed up in several of the posts. And, now that Auggie was looking for patterns in the faces, he noticed a girl showing up in the pictures over and over again. Bottle blond hair, a preference for denim cutoffs and white tank tops. She was probably close to Robert's age, early twenties. She had hard eyes and a hard mouth even when she smiled.

The bathroom door opened, and Theo came out.

"Who was that?" Auggie said.

When Theo looked over at him, Auggie blushed.

"Turns out," Theo said, "there's currently a lot of questions coming down from the State Attorney General's office. They haven't said anything outright, but my buddy thinks a public corruption investigation is already in the works. Unofficially, the word is that someone is coming down at the end of next week to poke around."

"Someone is looking at Lender," Auggie said. "And he's got to find that blackmail and make it disappear. I mean, he needed to do it anyway, but now he's got people that are going to dig up everything in his life. If they find it first, he's in deep shit."

"Sounds about right," Theo said. "Once the machine gets rolling, if this is a real investigation, they'll uproot his entire existence. That's probably why we've got a two-week deadline: they want us to find it before the investigation really gets going."

"And the Volunteers have to move fast because Lender is moving fast, and they don't want him to find it first." Auggie hesitated, tried to make his voice normal. "So that was your buddy, the one who's a cop. What's his name again? Cart?"

"Auggie."

"It's just a question." His face was hot again. "Anyway, look at this: I think this girl might be Robert's girlfriend. Maybe he left the flash drive with her."

"Hold on," Theo said, shoving his feet in his sneakers and grabbing his coat. "I'll be right back."

He was gone maybe five minutes, and as he stomped snow from his sneakers at the door, he said, "Guess who's lived here for thirty years operating the kind of motel where scumbags drop by pretty regularly?"

"Holy shit," Auggie said. "Why didn't I think of that? That's genius."

"I'd like that in writing," Theo said.

"What'd Annie say?"

"Annie says that she knows Robert McDonald pretty well. He rented a room regularly; she didn't come out and say it, but she made it pretty clear he was dealing drugs. His girlfriend came by too sometimes. Blond girl named Jessica Wallen. She's got it written right there in the registry. Those dumbasses didn't even use fake names."

"No way."

"Annie even knows where Jessica lives these days."

"You got an address?"

"Oh yeah," Theo said with a grin. "Jessica is currently staying at the Dore County Correctional Center."

10

"You're a very good student," Dr. Kanaan said. "People here like you. I like you. More importantly, I respect the work you do. And everyone understands that you've had a terrible tragedy in your life. But you've got to understand that this profession has a lot to do with your reputation; what we produce, the way we're evaluated, it's all so subjective that reputation is an enormous factor, and one you have to consider."

"I understand," Theo said. He felt like he'd been understanding for over an hour now, but it had probably only been fifteen minutes.

"That kind of behavior, what we saw at the holiday party, that might not only endanger future career opportunities; it might hurt you here."

"It won't happen again."

The conversation limped on for another twenty minutes, with Dr. Kanaan making feeble inquiries into Theo's progress with his thesis. When Theo finally escaped, he checked his watch, swore, and hurried to catch the elevator.

As he'd predicted yesterday, the roads had been clear by mid-afternoon, and he and Auggie had made it back to Wahredua without any problems. Auggie had seemed fine behind the wheel; apparently he'd been telling the truth that his freak out had occurred more because of the stress of the moment than regular panic at the thought of driving, like what Theo experienced. That was a good thing because, like it or not, Theo needed Auggie to drive again today. Now that Wednesday classes were over, it was time to pay a visit to Robert's girlfriend in the county jail.

When Theo emerged from Liversedge Hall, Auggie was sitting at the curb in the Malibu, the engine groaning and whining. Theo limped down the steps and got in.

"Campus security has made me move the car twice," Auggie said; as soon as Theo was buckled, he pulled into traffic.

"I know. I'm sorry."

"It's past four. Visiting hours end at five today."

"I'm really sorry."

"We're running out of time, Theo."

After a few slow breaths, Theo said, "Auggie, I said I'm sorry. What's going on? Why are you so upset?"

Auggie played with the radio, got nothing but static, and turned it off again. He tapped the mister, ran the windshield wipers, and made grumpy noises under his breath. Theo adjusted his weight in the seat, trying to ease the pressure on his hip, and waited.

"It's about that date I was supposed to go on. And it's weird talking to you about going on dates, so just forget it."

"Try me."

"No, forget it."

"Ok."

"And don't try reverse psychology again."

"I'm not trying anything." Theo turned up the heat. "How were classes?"

"Orlando was a huge dick because I had to cancel again."

"Oh, I'm sorry."

"I told him it was an emergency. He didn't care; he was really an asshole about it."

"Damn. That sucks."

"Who cares? Fuck him."

"How about this? You drop me off, take the car back, and go to dinner."

Running his hands along the steering wheel, Auggie seemed to consider this. Then he shook his head. "He was too big of a dick about it. I don't want to see him today."

Leave it alone, Theo told himself. Back up until you're a mile off and then just leave it alone.

Instead, he said, "Can I offer some unsolicited advice? Just as a friend."

"No."

"Ok."

Theo adjusted the vents. He tried to find a better way of reclining that didn't put so much pressure on his hip. He stretched out the seat belt.

"Oh my God, just say it," Auggie said. "You're about to explode over there."

"I'm a little worried."

"I told you, fuck him. It's fine."

"But it's not fine, Auggie. You live with him." Theo struggled for a moment and added, "It's weird."

"Why is it weird? Just because you're not interested doesn't mean nobody else is."

"That's not what I meant, and you know it. This is not normal. Orlando is acting like you two are caught up in some poorly written gay porn. Your college roommate? And he just happens to be gay? And he just happens to be into you? And he just happens to want to hook up clandestinely?"

"What do you think is happening?"

"I don't know."

"Do you think he's a serial killer?"

"Will you be serious?" To the south, on the river, splashes marked where a Canada goose had landed, just barely visible in the gloom. "What do you even know about him. This whole thing is weird."

"You know what's weird? This. Us. This is weird, ok?"

"You're twisting things around."

"Jesus Christ. He happens to be my roommate. He happens to be bi. He happens to think I'm hot. It's not an impossible coincidence, Theo."

"Fine, ok. Say you're right. Say you just happened to luck into this unbelievable situation. There are still a lot of good reasons people suggest you shouldn't date your roommate. You spend a lot of time together, which can create this illusion of intimacy, and it's easy to think that the way things work between you isn't going to change if you add a romantic element to it. But it does change. And you can't ever undo it. So, if things haven't gone too far with Orlando already, you might want to talk to him about how this is going to affect you as roommates."

The Malibu made a clunking noise as one of the wheels dipped into a pothole. Auggie said, "What do you mean, 'if things haven't gone too far with Orlando'? What does that mean?"

"You know what? I think I've said enough."

"Like, if we've had sex?"

"That's the county jail."

"I know where it is. I'm the one driving; I know where the jail is."

"You've got to turn in here," Theo said.

"I'm going around the block. I'm not ready to turn in yet."

"Auggie, come on."

They passed the entrance to the sheriff's department offices and the county jail; at the corner, Auggie turned right.

"It's just sex, Theo. It's not a big deal."

"So, you have had sex with him."

"That's not what I said. Why does it matter to you? Sex is sex."

"You're trying to get a rise out of me," Theo said. "You're trying to get me to say something I'm not ready to say. I told you the way I feel is complicated. I told you this is as far as I can go right now. We literally just had this conversation; don't do this again."

They turned at the next street. What passed for rush hour in Wahredua was picking up, which meant they were only creeping along. This part of town rolled down toward Market Street and the Grand Rivere; the water was a glossy brown ribbon running through the snow.

"Yeah, well, fine," Auggie said. "But you can't go butting into my life."

"I'm not."

"You can't, Theo. If we're just going to be friends, then we're just friends."

"I'm not. I won't. That's not what this is."

Auggie braked and took the next turn. "Yes, it is. You can pretend it's advice, but I've told you before: I don't need another older brother, I don't need a dad, I don't need anyone to take care of me. My sex life isn't any of your business. If I want to fuck around with Orlando, I will. It's just sex. It's not love; it's not complicated. We both want things simple and fun, and that's all it's going to be."

"That's not the way it works," Theo said. "You can blow smoke up your own asshole if you want, but that's not the way it works. Sex releases really powerful hormones. It affects your brain chemistry. Maybe there's one person in a million who doesn't cross the wires, but you're not one of them."

"I told you," Auggie said as he pulled into the lot, "I do not need a father figure, Theo. I don't need a fucking birds-and-bees talk." He slowed the Malibu, eased into a stall, and shut off the engine. "Besides, you don't know anything about me."

Leave it, Theo told himself. Get ten miles off. Get twenty miles off and just leave it.

But something wild was clawing at the inside of his ribcage.

Grabbing Auggie by the back of the head, he dragged him in and kissed him. It lasted three seconds. Maybe five. When he pulled away, Auggie's eyes were owlish and had a soft glow like polished lead.

"Fine," Theo said, not recognizing the scratchiness of his own voice, not familiar with whoever was taking those huge, furious breaths. "Tell me that was just a kiss."

He gave Auggie another three seconds, with Auggie just staring at him, and then he got out of the car.

The Wahredua Sheriff's Department Offices looked like they'd been built in the 70s, with narrow windows and unadorned lines, everything built low and long, because Wahredua had always had plenty of space. The jail was attached to the back of the building. Theo went in through the front and found government-grade linoleum, the kind that was brown and had lots of yellow and orange flecks in it, perfect for blending in the occasional upchuck or blood spatter. Everything smelled like Cup O Noodles. He asked for directions from the duty officer and followed a hallway toward the jail facility. Auggie caught up with him halfway, and under the light brown skin, his blush was an inferno.

They had to store everything except their IDs in rental lockers, and then they passed through a metal detector. After they'd signed in and listed Jessica Wallen as the inmate they were visiting, they had to sit on a bench; Auggie kept a clear six inches between them.

"Mr. Stratford," a deputy said from a secure doorway. "Mr. Lopez."

Theo followed her into the visiting room, which could have passed for a middle-school cafeteria: plastic-top tables with attached benches, vending machines, a drinking fountain. The only difference, of course, was the presence of the seven inmates, all dressed in the same teal uniform that vaguely resembled scrubs: cotton shirt, cotton trousers, socks, and sandals. A man on the far side of middle age was wearing an inmate uniform, talking quietly to two girls who might have been his daughters—until he leaned over and frenched one of them while the other cooed. A woman with a severe haircut was playing gin with another woman who might have been her mother. A woman and a man, both young, conversed quietly in Spanish. A black woman played with twin boys while chatting with a woman who might have been her sister.

Jessica Wallen was sitting at a table on the far side of the room. She looked like the girl from Robert's pictures, although a little rougher after months in jail. Graying brown roots showed in her blond hair, and fine lines marked her eyes and mouth. They were the same hard eyes, though. The same hard mouth, even when she smiled at them.

"Who are you?" she asked when Theo got close enough.

"Theo Stratford."

"Auggie Lopez."

"And what do you want?"

"We're actually hoping we could talk to you about Robert."

"Last I heard, Robert was dead. Either of you have change for an ice cream sandwich? I just like the chocolate part."

Shaking his head, Theo glanced at Auggie. Auggie shook his head too.

"Next time, you gotta bring quarters," Jessica said. "Anybody in here'd kill for an ice cream sandwich."

"You don't seem very upset that Robert's dead."

"Why would I be upset? That white-trash poon hound finally got caught sniffing around the wrong girl. Or maybe the Volunteers caught up with him. Got himself killed either way. Big loss to humanity. He couldn't keep it in his pants even when we were together; once I got locked up, we were done." She put the back of her hand to her forehead. "The next William fucking Shakespeare got himself killed. Big fucking loss."

"He wrote plays?" Theo said.

"Screenplays. You sure you don't have any quarters? They can make change at the front desk if you ask nice."

"Let me check," Auggie said, slipping off the bench and heading for the door.

Theo was trying to match the young man he'd briefly known as Robert Poulson to the aspiring screenplay writer. He said, "We're looking for something Robert might have hidden."

"What?" Jessica's gaze sharpened, and she leaned in toward Theo. "What are you looking for?"

"A flash drive."

"What's on it?"

"I don't know."

"Bullshit," Jessica said, leaning back and waving a hand in disgust. "Why're you looking for it then?"

"Somebody's twisting my arm."

"Oh yeah? Who?"

"I'd rather not say."

Her gaze sharpened. "You got right in the middle of all of it, didn't you?"

"In the middle of what?"

"You want to know about Robert? Here's Robert in a nutshell: always thought he was meant for bigger and better things. Better job, better life, better pussy. He'd move stuff for some guys he knew. Sold some stuff for them. And then he'd turn around and go to the police, think he could tell them something that would make him important, or make him some easy cash. Then he'd flip and be dealing again, holding meets in that shitty motel out on 50."

"Sounds like a good way to get yourself in trouble."

"He's dead, right? He got himself in plenty of trouble." Jessica leaned back. "The thing about Robert is that he wasn't that smart, and he didn't have any follow-through. He hopped from one thing to the other because he thought he could get there twice as fast if he just cut corners."

Auggie slid back onto the bench and passed over an ice cream sandwich.

"Aren't you a sweetheart?" Jessica said, picking open the paper with long nails. She worked the sandwich free and began breaking off pieces of the chocolate cookie. "It wasn't just the drugs, you know. He'd do it with everything. He was convinced he was hot, you know. Good looks like a movie star or something. He did some coke, but he wouldn't do meth because of his teeth. He was crazy about his teeth. Wouldn't touch a cigarette because he said it ruined your teeth, aged you twenty years or something. I mean, for around here, he was definitely a nice piece of ass. But sometimes he'd go full steam. He'd do *Oklahoma* at the community theater, and I'd have to sit through two weekends of it, and he'd be riding high, next stop Hollywood. Then he'd forget about it. Six months later, he'd be picking up weird Craigslist jobs, pretending to be somebody's boss or somebody's boyfriend, thinking he was Tom fucking Cruise. I told him he'd get a new cornhole if he kept that up." She chewed the last piece of cookie and pushed the stripped-down ice cream bar to the center of the table. "You want some?"

Theo shook his head, and Auggie said, "No, thanks."

"I was in here when it happened, but you know who I think killed him? I think it was one of those weird sex things. Like a three-way. Or a guy who promised to pay him a ton of money. Robert thought he was such hot stuff, and if he thought he could get some good money and feel like hot stuff at the same time, he'd do it."

"Where would he have hidden something?" Auggie said. "We found his apartment, but there wasn't anything there. Did he have a place he liked to hide out? Would he have trusted a friend? Someone in his family?"

"What's it worth to you?" Jessica said. Then she laughed, throwing back her head, and said, "Christ, your faces. Honestly, I've got no clue. If it was something really valuable, he wouldn't have left it with a friend. Robert liked himself too much to really like anyone else, and besides, he was so busy covering his own ass, going to the cops then going back to deal, that he never really trusted anyone. That includes me, I guess. I just stuck around long enough to figure out all his shit. His mom and dad passed a while ago, and his cousins are shitholes." She shrugged. "He didn't really have anywhere he liked to go. Not anywhere I knew about."

Theo struggled to contain a frustrated breath. He shot a look at Auggie, and then he said, "Do you have any idea where we could look? Please. This is life or death."

Jessica shook her head. "You got enough quarters for another ice cream sandwich?"

"Yeah," Auggie said. "Hold on."

When he came back and handed it over, Jessica said, "You know, one time I was on his phone, and that dumbass had a list of every password he'd ever used. You know, in the notes app. He wrote down everything." She tapped the side of her head. "Not smart."

"We can't find his phone."

"Whoever killed him probably sold it. They probably scrapped it or figured out a way to reset it. Too bad. It was a nice phone."

After that, the conversation went nowhere, and Theo finally thanked Jessica. He and Auggie left; they were heading outside when a voice said, "Auggie?"

Theo glanced over and saw two men crossing the lobby; he fought a groan when he recognized Somers and Upchurch.

"Hey Auggie," the blond man said. "I thought that was you."

"Oh. Hi, Detective Somerset. Detective Upchurch."

Somers stretched out a hand to Theo. "Hi, Theo."

Theo shook and nodded. He repeated the process with Upchurch.

"I didn't know you two were acquainted," Upchurch said, his gaze lingering on Theo. "We just met Auggie a couple of days ago."

"What are you doing here?" Somers said, and his gaze and the question were directed at Auggie, but Theo could feel it taking him in as well.

"Civics class," Auggie said. "Next time, we tour city hall."

Somers smiled and let the moment drag.

"We've got to get going," Theo said. "Good to see you guys again." He caught Auggie's arm and tugged him toward the door.

"Theo," Somers said, "I'm really sorry about Ian."

"Thanks."

"Theo, we should talk."

"Have a good night," Theo said, dragging Auggie outside.

11

When Auggie had gotten home Wednesday night, the fight with Orlando had been brutal; Orlando had insisted that Auggie tell him where he had been, and Auggie had insisted on telling Orlando to fuck off. Auggie had left when Orlando wouldn't drop it, and he spent the rest of Wednesday night and all of Thursday avoiding Orlando; he slept in the Sigma Sigma house in a friend's room, and he showered and changed at Moriah Court when he knew Orlando would be at wrestling practice.

Friday morning, Orlando was standing outside Auggie's classroom in Tether-Marfitt. His dark brows were furrowed as he scanned the milling students, obviously hoping to spot Auggie first; his thumbs were hooked behind the straps of his backpack, and he rocked on his heels.

Turning around, Auggie headed the other direction.

"Auggie?" Orlando called behind him.

Reflex took over, and Auggie opened a familiar door ahead of him and dove into the classroom. Theo was at the board, chalking up some lines from *Lear*, while kids settled into their seats and took out notebooks, pens, laptops, and tablets. Some of them glanced at Auggie, but not many; it was still the first week of classes, and the add/drop period ran for two more weeks.

"Professor Stratford," Auggie said.

Theo glanced over his shoulder. "Oh. Hey, what's—"

"I'm considering adding this class. Could I sit in on today's lecture?"

A tiny furrow appeared on Theo's forehead, but he just nodded and waved at the seats. Auggie slid into one in the front, adjusted the tablet arm, and got out a notebook. He'd wait ten minutes and then he'd quietly pack up his stuff and leave; if Orlando was still waiting outside the door to Auggie's classroom, well, Auggie would go to the library.

The only problem with that plan was that Theo was, well, Theo. Today he was wearing khakis and a navy button-up printed with gold pineapples. He had the sleeves rolled to his elbows. He was writing out lines that Auggie remembered from the first act of the play. His butt looked particularly cute today.

When the bell rang, Theo turned around and said, "All right, good morning. Let's go ahead and get started. Today we'll be discussing act one, scene one of *Lear*. We'll be working on this for the whole semester in a variety of adaptations and reimaginations, so it's important to get a solid understanding of the play first. Let's start by listing our characters."

Doodling in his notebook, Auggie let his mind drift while Theo ran through Lear and Gloucester and Edmund; Cornwall and Albany; Goneril, Regan, and Cordelia. Some of the students asked questions for clarification. It was funny, having taken the class once, to hear so many of the questions repeated. It was also funny how easily Auggie could tell which students had done the readings and which ones hadn't. When ten minutes had passed, he flipped his notebook closed, ready to head for Civ 2 down the hall. His phone buzzed.

Orlando: *i know ur in there.*

Auggie: *go away.*

Orlando: *i just want to apologize.*

Auggie: *seriously, go away.*

"I'm sorry," Theo said. "No phones."

Glancing up, Auggie realized Theo was talking to him. "Wait, I'm not—hold on. Are you for real?"

Theo just held out his hand.

"We're doing this again?" Auggie said.

"Class rule."

After a moment, Auggie passed over his phone.

Theo picked up the thread of his lecture, and Auggie slumped back into his seat. He wasn't going to risk leaving with Orlando creepily waiting for him. Once the halls were full during the ten-minute passing period, Auggie could venture out. He grimaced, opened his notebook again, and started doodling.

While Theo banged on and on about the first act of *Lear*, Auggie tried to do something productive: they needed to find where Robert might have hidden the flash drive, but everything they'd tried had been a dead end. Jessica had told them that Robert wouldn't have hidden something valuable with friends or family, and having met some of Robert's friends and family, Auggie thought she was probably right. More importantly, Robert had been double-timing everyone: he'd sold out the Ozark Volunteers to the cops, he'd dealt drugs and

217

probably sold out the cops to the Volunteers, and according to Jessica, he'd been willing to sleep with just about any girl who gave him the time of day. When you betrayed everyone, there wasn't anyone left you could trust—and, Auggie thought, you believed everyone was willing to betray you, too. Jessica had also told them that Robert wasn't very smart. He relied on his phone for everything, which wasn't exactly a fair equation; Auggie depended on his phone for just about everything too, but he considered himself at least as smart as the next person. But the phone certainly would have been nice to have; whoever had killed Auggie wouldn't have kept it, so Jessica was doubtless right when she said it had been sold or scrapped.

Maybe the answer was hidden in Robert's Instagram feed; after all, that was how they'd found his apartment. Auggie tried to think back through the photographs and videos that Robert had posted. Lots of pictures of his apartment, but they'd already checked there, and Lender had torn it apart—if the flash drive had been there, he would have found it. Lots of amateur photography, mostly sunsets and abandoned buildings. Images that Auggie guessed Robert would have described as dynamic or energetic: beer bottles clinking together, a little girl blowing out candles, a rave with glowsticks and party lights. The problem, though, was that there were hundreds of images like that, and no pattern, no recurring places or events.

"So," Theo was saying, "up until now, Lear's plan has been working flawlessly. He's divided his kingdom into three parts. He's got this bright vision of how everything will work so 'that future strife may be prevented.' And all he wants now is proof that he's giving his land to children who love him—'where nature doth with merit challenge.' And then what happens?"

Hands shot up, and students fumbled through sleepy, half-considered answers, but Auggie could have told them: Cordelia screws up the whole thing. That was the problem. Lear had a plan. It wasn't a great plan—giving away your kingdom seemed pretty stupid to Auggie—but at least he'd had a plan. And everything had been going all right until Cordelia messed it up. The problem was that Lear hadn't been flexible, hadn't known how to adapt. Everybody had plans, and the universe made sure those plans rarely worked out the way anyone expected. The secret was to be flexible. Auggie had had a plan; he'd been on track to score at least one major endorsement contract, with some marketing deals still in the works, and then he'd screwed the pooch with that stupid car accident. But he'd been flexible. He'd come here to Wroxall. He'd kept producing content. In spite of the mess with Robert, Auggie had even managed to keep his name out of the news.

Auggie's pen froze on the page. What about Robert? What had been his plan? He'd pretended to add Theo's class. He'd pretended to be a pledge at Sigma Sigma. He'd approached Auggie, and they'd stolen a car together. And then he'd disappeared after that weird murder video showed up. Why?

Well, the answer was that obviously something had gone wrong in Robert's plan. The question that was more interesting to Auggie was, what had he been planning in the first place?

"Everything's going so well for Lear," Theo said. "Goneril says that Lear is 'dearer than eyesight, space, and liberty,' and Regan says that she loves her father so much that she declares herself 'an enemy to all other joys.' Lear is thrilled. Lear is so pleased. And when it's Cordelia's turn, she says, 'Nothing.' And Lear thinks there must be some mistake. He tries again to get her to say how much she loves him."

Auggie was barely listening; his mind kept turning over Robert's actions. What had Robert wanted? Why had he focused on Auggie? What had he thought he could get from him? Had it been blackmail? Some sort of weird obsession? Had he fixated on Auggie? Blackmail seemed the most likely; he'd been filming Auggie in the Porsche without Auggie realizing it. And then what had happened? Like Lear, Robert had seen his plan go sideways, and he hadn't been flexible, hadn't adapted.

"What Lear wants to hear," Theo says, "is exactly what he bemoans at the end, when he is complaining about all the people who have flattered him. 'They told me I was everything; 'tis a lie, I am not ague-proof.' We should be sympathetic with Lear, right? Up to a point, anyway. We all want people to tell us that we're special, that we're important, that we're everything. But that kind of attention has consequences. Even in act one, Cordelia tries to point out how flattery has skewed Lear's ability to understand himself and his relationship with other people. She tries to explain that she loves her father as much as is natural, and that what her sisters have professed is a lie. 'Why have my sisters husbands,' Cordelia asks, 'if they say they love you all?' And then she goes on to explain that when she marries, half her love will go to her husband; Lear can't be and won't be the center of her universe. That's a big problem for Lear; he wants to be told, over and over again, that he is everything to everyone."

You should have had a backup, buddy, Auggie thought at the corner of his brain. You should have had a plan for when everything went wrong, because eventually, everything always went wrong. You got pissed at your friends and you wrecked a car. That was a major one. But little things too. You dropped your phone in the pool, and you lost a month's worth of content because you hadn't turned on cloud backups—

Auggie lurched out of his seat, shoving his notebook into his backpack. He grabbed his phone from the corner of Theo's desk and shot toward the door.

The hall was empty; no Orlando. Auggie didn't even care. He sprinted to the library, took out his laptop, and started searching for the online backup provider that Robert might have used for his phone.

12

The morning's classes had gone well, Theo thought, with the exception of Auggie's strange behavior in the middle of Civ 1. He ran through a mental playback of his lectures as he limped across campus to Liversedge Hall, checking for things he'd tweak next time, jokes that got a laugh, difficult passages that he needed to spend more time parsing. Yesterday had been physical therapy, and he leaned heavily on the cane as he made his way to the elevator and rode up to the third floor. After collecting his mail from the department office and giving Peg and Ethel Anne a quick wave—both of them called him Daniel again—he made his way to his office.

Dawson's computer was on, which was rare, and the small room smelled like pot—which, unfortunately was not rare, at least, not in correlation with Dawson's time in the office. Theo left the door open, powered up his computer, and dropped his satchel on the banker's box that he still hadn't dealt with. He was just settling into his desk when he realized he wasn't alone.

The kid standing in the doorway was clearly an athlete: big shoulders visible even under the winter coat, the sweats branded with Wroxall's seal, the big-man-on-campus air. He had thick, dark eyebrows and heavy scruff. Theo had seen him sucking on Auggie's neck once. He was pretty sure this was Orlando, although Theo didn't think cockblocking this kid counted as an official introduction.

"Can I—" Theo began.

Orlando stepped into the office and slammed the door. The sound was thunder clapping inside the small space. Then Orlando hesitated, sniffed, and said, "Are you fucking high?"

"What's going on?" Theo said. "Who are you, and why are you here?"

"You know who I am."

"What do you want?"

Orlando kept shifting back and forth. He had his hands buried in his coat pockets, and Theo wondered if the kid had a knife or a gun. He smelled like he hadn't showered in a day or two, and now that the initial shock was wearing off, Theo noticed Orlando's pallor, the dark circles under his eyes.

"I'm calling security," Theo said.

"Do that. We'll go over to their office and have a nice chat about what you've been doing with Auggie."

"Get out of my office."

Orlando was still rocking back and forth, his breathing getting harsher.

"Get out," Theo said. "Right fucking now."

"You stay away from him."

"What?"

"Stay away from Auggie. Don't go anywhere fucking near him again. Do you understand me?"

"You're joking, right? This is some asshole jealousy bullshit?"

Orlando's hand came out of his pocket, and he held up something small. Then he lunged forward, slapping it on Theo's desk. "Stay away from him, or I will kill you. And after I fucking murder you, I will bury you in this fucking shit so that you'll never work at a school again."

Before Theo could respond, Orlando threw open the door. It crashed into the wall, and Orlando hurried out. Dawson was standing in the hall, playing with his man bun, eyes wide.

"Dude, what was—"

"Just give me a minute," Theo said. "Close the door and just give me a minute."

"Yeah, but—"

"Jesus Christ, Dawson, shut the fucking door."

Dawson shut the door.

Picking up the flash drive that Orlando had left on his desk, Theo examined it for a moment before inserting it into the computer. Some tiny part of him was hoping this was the flash drive that Lender had been asking about, but he knew that wasn't the case. This was just some bizarre coincidence.

The drive held only a single video: Auggie and Theo sitting in the parking lot outside the sheriff's office, Theo leaning in and kissing Auggie. It was dusk, but you could still see enough to identify both people.

"Shit," Theo said yanking the flash drive from the computer. He got to his feet. He limped a few paces until he came up against the far wall, and then he turned and paced the other way. "Shit," he muttered. "Shit, shit, shit."

He grabbed his cane and his satchel and left.

"Hey, man, are you—" Dawson asked.

Theo took the stairs this time, not caring how it would fuck up his leg, not caring about anything except getting out of this fucking place and away from all the fucking mistakes he'd made. When he got to the bottom of the steps, he had to rely almost totally on the cane to make his way out to the curb. He lucked out; a bus was just pulling up, and it was the one he took to Downing. It seemed like a sign. He heaved himself up onto the bus, flashed his pass, and dropped into the closest seat.

He thought he heard a voice shout his name before the bus doors closed. It didn't matter; he closed his eyes and let his head fall back, and he tried to figure out why he'd let himself fuck things up so badly.

13

Standing outside Liversedge Hall, Auggie watched Theo board the bus. He called Theo's name, but Theo didn't look back. By the time Auggie got to the street, the bus had already pulled away and was too far for Auggie to catch. The decision only took an instant: Auggie opened the Uber app and requested a ride to the opposite side of town, and in less than two minutes, a silver Toyota Corolla was pulling up to the curb. Auggie jumped into the car.

"Afternoon," a young black woman said as she eased the Corolla into traffic.

"Hey, can you follow that bus?"

"Sorry, what?"

"That bus up there. Can you follow it?"

"No, sorry. We've got to drive the route you requested."

"Shit, never mind. I'll figure something else out. Just let me out."

"Hold on, hold on," the girl said. "If you know where it's going, you can put in the destination. That bus goes back to the main terminal near the government complex."

"But it stops other places, right?"

"Well, yeah." She eyed him in the rearview mirror. "What's going on?"

"My friend got on that bus and I've got to talk to him."

"He doesn't have a phone?"

"It's a little more complicated than that."

The girl made a skeptical noise in her throat, but all she said was, "If you put in the main terminal as your destination, the app figures out the best route. We probably wouldn't follow the bus the whole way."

"Hold on," Auggie said. He tapped at his phone until he'd pulled up the Wahredua public transit webpage, and he found a map of the bus schedule. He checked it against the Uber map, and he began adding stops: not all of them, but every stop before the bus turned, so that the Uber route matched the bus's path. "How about that?"

"I can't go as slow as the bus," the girl said. The Uber app told him her name was Imani J. "If it stops too much—"

"I'll make it up to you with the tip," Auggie said.

Imani hemmed.

"Please," Auggie said.

"This is weird. Are you stalking this guy?"

"No. It's just complicated."

"You got that right," she said, glancing at him once more in the mirror.

Imani kept her promise: she drove slowly behind the bus, following it, pausing when the bus stopped to load and unload passengers. Fortunately, it was early afternoon, and the bus passed many of its normal stops without slowing because no one was waiting, and presumably no one needed to get off.

After a few minutes, Auggie drooped against the Corolla's back seat. The car had a pleasant, pineapple-orange air freshener, and soft jazz played quietly through the speakers. Everything was nice and clean; Auggie had been in Ubers that looked like they'd come straight from soccer practice.

No matter how he tried to get comfortable, though, he couldn't unspool the worry he felt in his gut. Getting the Uber, following the bus—those had been irrational decisions, motivated by the sight of Theo looking pale and upset. And, if Auggie were honest with himself, motivated by curiosity. Theo was always going places and not explaining why. He went somewhere every morning if he could, and sometimes he'd go again later in the day. Over the last five months, Auggie had stopped by his house too many times to count, and the pattern had quickly become obvious. But whenever Auggie had tried to get an answer, Theo changed the subject or shut it down completely. He could picture all the times he'd stopped by on Saturday mornings to find Theo dressed like he was going to work. All the times Theo had been late, or been in a bad mood, or been distracted.

Around Auggie, Wahredua was shifting and transforming. They left behind the trendier neighborhoods, many of them in the middle of redevelopment, that surrounded Wroxall. In their place came parts of the city Auggie had never seen before: small houses with asbestos siding or crumbling brick; quarter-acre lots that were well kept but unornamented; cars that were ten and fifteen years old, Chevys and Fords and Pontiacs. The house at the corner had a junker panel van parked at the back of the driveway, blocked in by trash cans, the tires flat, the paint that had once said EXTERMINATOR peeling from the door. In a vacant lot on the right, a trio of kids were having a snowball fight; Auggie was watching when one of the kids, probably eight, got pegged in the eye and started bawling and running home. Winter-brittle stalks of blue grama drooped and bent under the snowfall from earlier that week.

Between glances at the bus, to make sure Theo wasn't getting off at any of the stops, Auggie kept working on the cloud storage account that he had uncovered. He was pretty sure it belonged to Robert McDonald because it had accepted the same ridiculous username that Robert had used for Instagram: mcdaddyr. Auggie had read up about the service and its app. It backed up everything on your phone: contacts, emails, notes, pictures, videos, messages. Anything it could get access to, it uploaded to the cloud. For someone like Robert, who thought of himself as an actor and a photographer and an artist, it made sense that he'd have something like this, a way of saving all those monologues and dramatic Missouri sunsets. The only problem was getting access. Auggie tried to think of what he knew about Robert: self-absorbed, treacherous, not very smart. He tried all the obvious ones: password, 12345, abcde, Robert's birthday (which he'd seen on the pictures Theo had taken of the police report), and even variations on Jessica's name. No luck. He kept trying as they followed the bus across town.

The bus's route took them to what Auggie assumed was a major thoroughfare for this part of the city: Casey's and QuikTrip and Amoco stations, a Walmart, a brick medical complex with thick plastic sheeting over the windows, a Dollar Tree, where two old men were standing in the parking lot, waving their hands at each other. Another half-mile later, the bus pulled to the curb in front of a sprawling compound of single-story buildings. Someone had tried to mitigate the bleak severity of the design—unadorned concrete, obviously built as cheaply as possible—with picture windows and bright yellow paint, but it hadn't worked. The sign in front said Downing Children's Healthcare Center.

Theo got off the bus.

"Here," Auggie said, scrambling upright and unbuckling himself. "Pull over here."

"Look, if he doesn't want you to know where he's going—" Imani said.

"Thanks," Auggie said. "You were great, thank you."

Theo didn't even look around; his shoulders sagged, and he looked twenty years older as he shuffled toward the front doors of Downing. Auggie slid out of the Corolla just as Theo was stepping into the building, and Auggie jogged after him. He could taste the last of the bus's exhaust; the smell of frying chicken came from the VFW Hall on the other side of the street. January wind cut across the sidewalk, levitating a cloud of snow, the crystals flashing like fool's gold. Auggie kept looking at the sign, kept looking at the word Children's, and he had to blink to clear his eyes. The wind kept coming, sharper and colder, and he kept blinking while snow drifted around his ankles.

When he got inside, the warmth and the quiet were a welcome change. The lobby had blond-wood furniture with polka-dot upholstery; everything looked very clean and Scandinavian, magazines neatly held in clear plastic trays on the wall, chrome baskets for toys. Auggie caught a whiff of something that made him think of Salisbury steak, and that took him back to elementary school and the brown slab of something covered with a brown sauce of something else on his tray. He pictured fruit cocktail in tiny cans. Cardboard cartons of milk. The thought running through his head was: Theo comes here every day. Every day.

"May I help you?" a man asked. He was wearing scrubs, but judging by how settled he looked at the computer behind the reception desk, Auggie guessed he was some kind of secretary or administrative assistant.

"Yes, hi. Sorry, I'm here with Theo Stratford. I missed the first bus, so I'm a little late."

The man picked up a clipboard from the desk and examined it. Then he looked at Auggie. "And you are?"

"Auggie. August Lopez."

"And who are you here to see?"

"Oh, I came here with Theo."

"Mmhmm." The man's eyes flicked to the clipboard and then back at Auggie.

Auggie made himself say it: "I'm here to see Theo's daughter. Lana. I guess I don't know if she has Stratford or Moore as her last name. I never asked."

"Mmhmm."

The next part was the hardest: waiting, letting the lie float.

"All right, Mr. Lopez," the man said, passing him the clipboard. "I just need you to sign in here."

Auggie scribbled his information; his hand was shaking so badly that it was mostly illegible, but the man behind the desk barely glanced at it. He passed Auggie a name tag with the word VISITOR printed clearly at the top, and then he pointed. "Lana is in Ridley, which is down that hall. Follow it to the end. You'll have to get buzzed in; just tell them who you are and who you're there to see, and they'll get you the rest of the way."

Nodding, Auggie pasted the name tag onto his chest. Then he headed down the hall that the man had indicated. The building was silent aside from the squeak of Auggie's wet high-tops. Inside Downing, the same effort had been made to soften the aesthetic: brightly painted walls interrupted by murals that had been attributed to Westcott Boys 1997, Cavendish 2002-2003, and so on. The murals looked like they'd just let some toddlers attack the walls with paint and brushes. In other places, framed artwork by children hung on display: Candice Evans had done stick figures, the lines zigging and zagging as she tried to control the pencil; Amber Hamm had painted the sky, powder blue, and clouds; Shaniqua Proctor had traced her hand. But bright paint and children's art couldn't distract from the speckled linoleum, the fire doors, the security cameras, the wire mesh of the safety glass.

At the end of the hall, Auggie stopped at a pair of glass security doors; on the wall next to them was an intercom. Auggie didn't press the button. He just looked through the doors.

On the other side of the glass, a large rec room held chairs and couches upholstered in microfiber, plush rugs patterned with blocks of primary colors, a massive television that was showing *The Land Before Time*, balls and dollhouses and a green John Deere play tractor and a firetruck and a Lincoln Logs set that had been scattered to kingdom come. Children, too. Many of them obviously with disabilities or developmental delays. Some of the children seemed alert and active—a girl with a mass of blond ringlets and no legs was acting out a tea party between two dolls; a black boy with scars from burns over most of his face had one foot on the John Deere tractor, and he was rolling it back and forth with one foot while he watched the movie—but many of the children were strapped into wheelchairs or were propped up on the couches with pillows.

Theo sat with a girl on his lap; he was talking to her, his finger marking his place in a picture book. Next to them was a child-sized wheelchair. The girl was wearing what looked to Auggie like a bike helmet; her dark eyes stared off into the distance, and she didn't seem to register anything Theo was saying to her.

Auggie wasn't sure how long he stood there. He only knew that at some point his legs jerked into motion, and he staggered out of Downing. The wind was still cutting the January day, but he barely felt it. He dropped into a squat at the edge of the cement apron outside the building, and he washed his face with snow while he sobbed. When his hands and face were numb, he called an Uber and took it back to campus.

He thought about Theo. He tried not to think about Theo. He thought about all the ways people hold secret the things they love. He thought about Robert, and something cold and hateful worked through Auggie. He opened the cloud backup webpage and tried Robert's password again.

This time, it worked.

The password for an abysmally selfish fucker like Robert McDonald had been his own name.

14

Theo got home from Downing exhausted; he was always exhausted after visiting Lana, but today was worse because of the cold, because the bus had been late again, because of the flash drive that Orlando was blackmailing him with. In the small brick house in the boonies, Theo messed with the thermostat, which was on the fritz, until he heard the furnace kick to life. He picked up some of the books in the living room, and then he called the whole thing a wash and dropped them back onto the couch. He went upstairs and changed into sweats and a hoodie. He found himself in the kitchen, staring at the two six-packs of Great Lakes Christmas Ale. Or the joint in the nightstand upstairs, he thought. Or the Percocet, and the clarity of that idea was like broken glass.

A knock at the front door interrupted him. Maybe it was Cart again; in just a week, Cart had managed to do some amazing work. The walls were insulated and had drywall in place, although they still needed to be taped and mudded and painted. And the floors were back in usable condition—Cart had replaced some of the broken boards, but most he'd been able to salvage. If it was Cart, Theo thought, maybe tonight they'd drink their way through both six packs. If it was Cart, maybe he'd tell Cart he wanted to get his opinion on something upstairs. Why not, Theo thought, trying to muddle his way through the logic. Why not, when everything else was already so fucked up?

Limping, Theo made his way to answer the door. Instead of Cart, Auggie stood there, his cheeks red with the cold, his eyes red too, shivering with his hands stuck in his pockets.

"We need to talk," Theo said.

The look on Auggie's face was pure panic.

"Come inside," Theo said. "It's freezing."

Auggie followed him into the house, kicking off his snow boots, shedding his coat and hat, tangling himself for a minute with his scarf until Theo caught one end and helped him out of it. Auggie grinned up at him, but the panic was still there, pounding like a heartbeat.

"What's wrong?" Theo asked.

"Nothing. What happened to your house?"

"I told you: those assholes were here looking for the flash drive."

"Yeah, but I didn't know it was this bad."

"It's actually a lot better than it was. Cart's made this shithole livable."

"Right," Auggie said. "Cart."

Theo met his gaze.

"That's nice," Auggie said. Then Auggie rubbed his mouth. "Why do we need to talk?"

"What's going on? You're acting weird."

"Nothing's going on."

With a grunt, Theo limped back to the kitchen. He got one of the Christmas Ales, opened it, and spun the cap into the trash. Then he sat at the table that had somehow survived two break-ins by the Ozark Volunteers—the table Ian had refinished, the table Ian and Theo and Lana had shared God only knew how many meals at.

"Your roommate is trying to blackmail me," Theo said. He grabbed his satchel from the seat next to him, pulled out the flash drive, and set it on the table. "He has a video of us outside the sheriff's office. It shows me kissing you. You can see both of us pretty clearly."

"Oh shit."

"I know you're worried about your business—"

"No, fuck that. That piece of shit is trying to blackmail you? What does he want?"

"He wants me to stay away from you."

Auggie was silent for a moment. "You're joking."

"No, I'm not joking."

"Theo, I didn't—I don't know how he—I'm eighteen, right? So it's legal."

Something about the way Auggie said it made Theo close his eyes and laugh. "Calm down. He can't get me arrested."

"So what'll happen to you if he releases this?"

"Nothing. I mean, people will ask questions, and it certainly won't look good. But it didn't happen while you were in my class, and I won't be the first instructor who's had a relationship with a former student." Theo took a drink, and the ale's honey and cinnamon was cloying tonight. "What'll happen to you?"

"What?"

"If he posts this, what will happen to you?"

"I don't know."

"Is it going to ruin your business?"

"I don't know. I mean, maybe." Auggie squeezed his eyes shut and then opened them again. "I'm going to talk to him."

"Auggie, that's not a good idea. In fact, it's not a good idea for you to be around him at all."

"No, I'm going to talk to him. I'm going to tell him to fuck off and never—"

"He's not right in the head, Auggie. Pay attention. He's obsessed with you. This isn't normal behavior, and you shouldn't be around him."

"We're going to fix this," Auggie said. "We're going to figure it out."

"Ok."

"It'll be fine."

Theo took another long pull of the beer.

"Anyway, I think I've got a break in the stuff with Robert."

"What? Really?"

"Yeah, I got into the cloud backup for his phone. Do you have your laptop?"

After a moment of digging around in his satchel, Theo set the computer on the table.

Auggie navigated through a series of screens, and there it was: the full contents of Robert's phone.

"Holy shit," Theo said.

"I've been looking at it," Auggie said. "There's a few things I think you should see." He clicked into the archived messages and then to a chain of messages with AL. "Albert Lender, right? And look at this."

It was a series of messages from late August escalating in intensity, with Lender demanding that Robert produce some sort of information about the Ozark Volunteers and their drug operations.

"But what does he want to know?" Theo said.

"Nothing. I mean, nothing in particular. He just wants a bust or something. Whatever Robert can give him. Now look at the last message from Robert."

Theo read it aloud: "Don't need your narc money anymore. Pretty soon someone's going to be paying me to be quiet. Got everything I need on one little flash drive." After a moment, Theo said, "Well, that sounds like blackmail. Christ, how stupid was he to blackmail a dirty cop?"

"I don't know," Auggie said. His hands hovered above the keyboard, and then he said, "This next part is going to be weird."

"Oh boy."

"Remember how we couldn't figure out why Robert was so interested in me?"

"Please don't tell me he's another psycho like Orlando."

"No, but I think my ex might be."

"What?"

Auggie clicked into Robert's emails. "My ex-girlfriend, Chan. She posted this Craigslist ad; she wanted to hire someone to get embarrassing pictures of me. Or video, I guess. Whatever. She says, 'Dirt on my ex, pics preferred.' And Robert answered it. We know he picked up Craigslist jobs, especially ones where he had to play a role because he thought he was such a great actor."

"How do you know this is about you? How do you know this is your ex?"

Auggie went back to the archived messages, where a long string of texts between Robert and Chan spelled out the details.

"That is fucking batshit," Theo said.

"She's got an Instagram account built around this kind of material; she was obviously planning it all the way back in August. It's not just good revenge; it's going to make her a fucking fortune."

Theo shook his head. "So that's why Robert wanted to add my class. That's why he pretended to pledge Sigma Sigma. That's why he approached you at the party and suggested stealing a car. That's why he filmed you driving the Porsche. Then what?"

"Then somebody killed him and posted those clips to throw suspicion on you and me."

"Who killed him?"

Auggie shook his head.

"Why us?" Theo asked.

"Probably because we were in those videos from the night of the car crash. They were the most recent videos on Robert's phone."

"Why kill him?" Theo asked.

"I think Lender did it. To silence him, because he thought the blackmail was about him. It wasn't, though; Robert was planning on blackmailing me."

Theo sipped his ale. Then he shook his head. "That doesn't make sense. Lender couldn't have killed him because Lender was desperate to find him. I'll buy the rest of it: Robert sent a stupid text message, and Lender interpreted it as a threat against him. Robert had this plan with Chan. Robert decided to double dip and use the pictures and videos that he was going to sell to Chan to blackmail you, which is a stupid plan because the blackmail would have been worthless after Chan posted the videos and photos to her account. But who killed him? And why? It wasn't the Ozark Volunteers, either; they were desperate to find him too. We're missing something. This doesn't make sense."

"It was all a misunderstanding. Lender thought Robert had some sort of blackmail; once Lender got worried, the Ozark Volunteers were interested too."

Theo shook his head again. "I don't know. It doesn't feel right."

"Why are you being stubborn about this? We can take this to Lender. We can explain the whole thing. We can be done with it."

"He's not going to believe this story. Not without some sort of proof that Robert was intending to blackmail you. Without that, it just reads like two separate events in Robert's life. It could piss him off."

"I'm going to tell him."

"No, that's not a good idea. If he thinks we're trying to pull a trick, he could decide to teach us a lesson. Provide motivation. Make an example."

"I'll call him and explain—"

"No," Theo shouted, slamming the ale down so hard that foam ran down the neck, the bubbles fizzing against his fingers. "What don't you understand? I'm saying no. No. That's the fucking end of it."

"Why are you getting so angry?" Auggie said. "I think if we—"

"Oh my God. Do you really not understand what I'm telling you? No, Auggie. We keep looking, and we find the flash drive that Robert hid, and then we're done. Then we're safe."

"You don't get to talk to me like that." Auggie slid out of the seat. He snatched up the flash drive that Orlando had given Theo and held it up. "This isn't just about you. I want to be done with Lender so we can take care of Orlando. I'm going to—"

"If you say it one more time," Theo said, "I'll call Lender myself and warn him you're going to spin him a bullshit story."

"Why are you being like this?"

"Because I'm fucking terrified!"

The transformation in Auggie's face was so sudden that Theo almost didn't understand what he was seeing; it took him a moment to recognize compassion in the kid's face.

"Did he threaten Lana?" Auggie asked. "I know the care center isn't the most secure facility, but I don't think she's in danger."

"What did you say?"

Theo could see in Auggie's face the knowledge that he had made a mistake.

"Never mind," Auggie said.

"What did you say about Lana?"

"Nothing. It's none of my business."

"You're right it's none of your business." The sound of the ale sliding across the table was the only noise in the room. Theo managed to get to his feet. "Did you follow me?"

"No, I—"

"Get out of my house."

"Ok, yes, but Theo, I didn't mean to. I mean, I did, but it just kind of happened. It's not like I planned it."

"Get out."

"I'm really sorry. I didn't know. You looked so upset when you got on the bus, and I thought maybe I could help, and—"

"Get." Theo was struggling to get enough air; his knuckles were white around the ale. "Out."

Something in his tone or his face must have convinced Auggie, because the kid stumbled back. He hurried toward the door, shoved his feet into his boots, and grabbed his coat.

"Theo, please, please, please. I am so sorry. I wasn't trying to spy on you."

Limping into the front room, Theo circled Auggie and pulled open the front door. Cold air rushed in; tracings of snow powdered the floor and melted into a shining fan of water.

"We're done," Theo said. "Do you understand that?"

"I made a really big mistake," Auggie said. "I know that. I know I messed up, Theo. Please tell me how I can make this right."

"Easy," Theo said, smiling because the night was cold and the snow was glowing under the streetlights and for the first time since June he felt at peace. "Never show your fucking face around here again."

15

Wroxall's library was one of the oldest buildings on campus, built from stone, with carvings of fauns and nymphs on the tympana of the south entrance and sculptures of Aristotle and Plato on the north entrance. It had verdigris copper flashing, and the windows were leadlights with geometric patterns of red and white. On the inside, though, it had been gutted and completely redone five years ago, and everything was glass and blond wood and chrome. Auggie sat on a bench near the north entrance; he needed to be as smart as possible for the next ten or fifteen minutes, and he figured Aristotle and Plato might be a little more help than the fauns trying to bang one out with the nymphs. On Saturday morning, the library was quiet. Auggie waited, his knee bouncing.

When Lender arrived, the detective stood for a moment in the entrance, scanning the lobby. Then, adjusting the thick glasses, he sauntered over and sat next to Auggie.

"August, my boy," he said, clapping him on the shoulder. "How the heck are you?"

"All right," Auggie said. He pulled out his laptop and opened it. "I've got what you wanted."

"Do you? Now, isn't that interesting? Because I didn't ask you for it. I asked your pal Theo."

"We're helping each other. Anyway, it was my decision. You'll see what I mean in a minute."

Lender made a rumbling noise in his throat; he smelled like garments that had been in storage for too long, a stale, closed-up odor that reminded Auggie of visiting his grandfather.

"Here's what happened," Auggie said, clicking to the first tab he had open. He explained all of it: the nasty breakup with Chan, the Craigslist ad, Robert's texts negotiating with Chan, the ways Robert had tried to infiltrate Auggie's life, first in Theo's class, then at the Sigma Sigma pledge party, and then by stealing the car.

Lender said nothing.

"Two things went wrong," Auggie said. "First, he sent you that text, bragging about blackmailing someone, but he was too stupid to realize you'd misunderstand it. Second, he got himself killed. If he'd been alive and you'd caught up with him, you would have figured it out pretty fast. Once he was dead, though, everybody was operating under the same mistaken assumption."

"But you don't have any proof he was talking about blackmailing you," Lender said. "I have good reason to believe I understood him perfectly well when he sent me that message."

"Actually," Auggie said, "I do. He was putting together footage of me. Video clips that would humiliate me and ruin my social media platform. Chan was going to post them on her feed."

"That's silly," Lender said.

"Chan is making five figures from an account that is mostly just stories about how awful I am. In a year, if she keeps adding content and followers, that'll be six figures. And she's got other accounts too. It's a lot of money, and all she needed was for Robert to get her some fresh material."

For a moment, Lender seemed to consider it. Then he shook his head.

"I have proof," Auggie said. "I found the flash drive you wanted. It has one video on it. And it's of me." He drew from his pocket the flash drive that Orlando had given Theo and held it out.

Lender took it and said, "How did you find it?"

"We talked to his ex-girlfriend, Jessica Wallen. She's in the county jail right now, so she had plenty of time to chat. He'd taped it to the back of the mirror in the Frozen King bathroom."

"Really?" Lender said, turning the flash drive in his hand. "I have to point out, Auggie, you've been much too trusting, giving it to me."

"I want you to leave me alone. And I want you to leave Theo alone. You've got what you wanted: Robert was planning on blackmailing me, and now you have the flash drive with the video."

"I thought he was going to sell it to your friend Chan."

"From what I hear, Robert had big plans. He obviously decided to score something on the side."

"Very interesting," Lender said. A tiny smile puffed into existence and then vanished. "Can you imagine? All this chaos over a misunderstanding. I don't suppose you know who killed the little cunt."

Auggie shook his head.

"Well," Lender said, "I'm going to think about this, August. And if I'm not satisfied, I'm going to come back, and we'll talk again. And, of course, I think we'll need to discuss the value of this video you've given me. I understand your little internet star is rising; I'd like to be a part of that success."

"No," Auggie said.

"You should have thought about that before you handed this over."

"That video isn't worth anything," Auggie said, clicking to his Instagram feed. "I've already posted it."

And there it was, at the top of his feed: the clip of Theo leaning over and kissing him, their faces clear in the light spilling into the car. Thousands of comments were displayed under the video; Auggie couldn't look at them. It was bad enough seeing that his followers had dropped to forty thousand—less than half of what he'd had a couple of hours before.

"Well," Lender said with another of those momentary smiles. "Well, well, well."

"We're done, right? And you'll make sure the Volunteers know, so they'll leave me alone?"

"I suppose so."

"And Theo? You're done with Theo? And you won't hurt him, you won't hurt his daughter, you won't go anywhere near them?"

Lender bared huge, yellow teeth, and it took Auggie a moment to realize it was a grin. "August, if I may, I'd like to offer you some fatherly advice. You're a young lad, just a callow youth sailing into life's storms of adversity, and so on and so forth. In the future, here's something it might help you to remember: watch your own fucking ass. Nobody else will do it for you."

"You won't go anywhere near Theo or his daughter?" Auggie asked quietly.

"Of course not," Lender said. "We're finished here."

16

Theo was halfway through the article on Lear and hadn't understood a word of it. He flipped back to the beginning and tried again.

Two days had passed since that brutal fight with Auggie. Theo had regretted everything, every word of it, almost as soon as Auggie was out the door. But the combination of shock that Auggie knew about Lana, the humiliation of his situation, and the pain that never went away had made it impossible to think clearly in the moment.

He picked up his phone, flipped it open, scrolled to the messages, and stopped. He shut the phone and tossed it onto the cushion next to him. Then, grabbing a highlighter, he started the article once more from the beginning.

When a knock came at the door, he mumbled, "Thank God," around the cap of the highlighter, and got to his feet. It was late afternoon on Sunday, the light coming through the windows in fat, golden beams, and the house still smelled like the pancakes Theo had made that morning—not as good as Auggie's, instructions on the bag or not. Theo knew how it was going to go: Auggie would be out there, a knit cap pulled down, his big, dark eyes soft, and Theo would apologize, and Auggie would get that lightbulb glow in his face, and they'd have some excuse about studying on the couch and then they'd order Chinese and somehow things would be normal again.

Only, when he opened the door, it wasn't Auggie. It was Cart, and his ears were red with the cold. He pushed into the house without saying anything, dropping the rigger bags on the floor, and stripped off his gloves and his coat.

"Hey," Theo said. "I didn't know you were coming over."

"Why?" Cart said, squatting to dig through the bags. "You got somewhere to be?"

"Not really."

"You got some sort of busy schedule I need to know about?"

"No. I'm just saying I didn't know you were coming over."

"If it's a bad time, I can come back." Cart stood, and he kicked one of the rigger bags. It rattled, and the smell of metal and oil drifted up. "Is that what you want? When's convenient for you, Mr. Stratford? You want me to shuffle on out of here and come back when you're ready for me?"

"Jesus Christ. What's the matter with you?"

"Fuck you."

"Yeah, fuck me. What'd I do?"

"Aw, fuck off. I'm going to work in the basement."

"What the hell?"

"I said fuck off. I'm in a bad mood."

"Kind of got that."

For a moment, Cart just stood there, running his red, chapped hands over his buzzed hair. Then he grabbed the rigger bags and headed for the stairs; he'd set up a saw down there, and he was cutting boards to finish a few final places where the floor had been damaged.

When he got to the stairs, though, he dropped the rigger bags with another clatter, and he put his hands on his hips.

"I mean, were you going to tell me you were fucking that teeny-bopper, or was I just supposed to figure it out on my own?"

"What are you talking about?"

"You want some eighteen-year-old to swing on your pecker, that's fine. That's great."

"What the fuck are you talking about? Are you talking about Auggie? He's just a friend."

"But you know what? It's really fucking pathetic that you let me go on and on and make a fucking fool out of myself. You could have just fucking told me."

"Told you what?"

"Don't play me like I'm stupid," Cart shouted. "I'm not as smart as you, but I'm not a fucking idiot."

"I don't know what you're talking about. Jesus Christ. You know what? Get out of here."

Cart just stood there, shaking his head.

"Go. I appreciate what you did. I'll find a way to pay you. But I want you to go."

Grabbing out his phone, Cart came across the room so fast that Theo limped back a step. Cart didn't touch him, though. He just held out the phone.

A video was playing on Instagram.

Auggie had posted that goddamn video: Theo leaning in, clear as day, and kissing him.

Over ten thousand comments.

Auggie had posted it. And Theo knew that Auggie had done it out of some sense that he was protecting Theo, which only made Theo angrier.

"That is not what it looks like," Theo said, knowing it was the wrong thing as soon as it came out.

Cart shook his head and put the phone away.

"You know what you are?" Cart asked quietly. "You're a fucking joke. Everything that happened with Ian, and you go running off for some teenage boy pussy. Have some fucking self-respect."

Theo threw the punch without even thinking about it. He caught Cart on the jaw, and Cart stumbled. Then Cart came back at him, catching Theo around the waist in a bear hug, both of them crashing into the wall and sliding to the ground. Theo kicked, used his elbows, fought as close to dirty as he dared. Cart, who was country-boy skinny and all wiry muscle, just kept grabbing him and pinning him until Theo was exhausted and his leg was on fire.

"Fuck you," Theo said.

"Fuck you right back," Cart said.

"No, fuck you. You are a fucking coward. Fuck you. You're so fucking scared of what people say that you kissed me when I was wasted, when I'm so fucked up in my head about my dead husband that I don't know what's going on, and you used that fucking opportunity because you're so afraid somebody might think you like dick. You're the worst fucking person I've ever met."

"You dragged me out of my chair, dumbass. You pinned me up against the wall. Your fucking lips were a half an inch away. You did that. You. Don't fucking tell me I took advantage of you, you stupid piece of shit." Cart grabbed double handfuls of his shirt, lifted him, and then slammed him back against the floor. "Christ, I ought to kill you."

"Get the fuck out of here," Theo said, but the words were woolen, and he couldn't think straight. He was vaguely aware of Cart crawling away, and then the chaos of his thoughts went to Ian, went to Auggie, went to Cart, went to Lana, and then back to Ian again, and all he could do was lie there, staring up at the cracked plaster ceiling, hearing his own breathing from a mile off.

Then, from downstairs, he heard the whine of the saw.

Somehow, Theo rolled onto his side. And then somehow he got to his feet. He grabbed his cane, and he used it to hobble into the kitchen. The rigger bags were at the top of the stairs. Below, the whine of the blade cut off, and the smell of sawdust drifted up. Theo eased his weight down one step at a time until he was at the bottom.

He'd brought all the shit he couldn't handle down here, Ian's stuff, Lana's stuff, everything wrapped in plastic and boxed and stacked against the wall. Cart stood at the table saw, measuring a board and marking it. One of his ears was huge and puffy, and Theo realized he'd gotten in one or two blows that were harder than he'd thought.

"What are you doing?" Theo said.

"What does it look like?" Cart said without looking up. Instead of waiting for an answer, he ran the saw again, and the end of the board clattered to the ground.

"I want you to go," Theo said.

"Wishes in one hand," Cart said, grabbing another board and measuring it. "Your dick in the other."

"Cart, Jesus, please. What are you doing?"

"For fuck's sake, you stupid redneck son of a bitch," Cart shouted, throwing down the board and the carpenter's pencil and the square. "What the fuck does it look like? I said shitty, awful things, and I don't know how to make it right, so I'm going to fix your fucking floor because I care about you. Jesus Christ. Is that so fucking hard for your fucking redneck brain to understand?"

From outside came the soft hoot of an owl. Theo leaned against the railing, working a splinter with his thumb.

Slowly, uncertainly, Cart's shit-kicking grin spread across his face.

"Christ, you're a hillbilly," Theo said.

"What kind of beer you got up there?"

"Christmas ale."

"More of that girly stuff."

"Do you want one or not?"

"Course I do."

17

By Wednesday, Auggie's followers had dropped to thirty thousand. He hadn't posted anything since the video. He couldn't bring himself to read the comments. But every day, he pulled up the numbers and saw how bad the damage had gotten. Logan and Devin didn't respond to his messages. His circle of friends from Sigma Sigma had evaporated. Chan was probably gloating across all her different accounts, but Auggie didn't want to see what she was posting. And the genuinely most awful part was that Theo hadn't reached out, hadn't asked what had happened, hadn't even tried to contact Auggie.

The weather had warmed a few degrees, and Auggie slushed across the quad, his high-tops soaked through again, his feet frozen. He'd never had to deal with snow outside of skiing, and although the first few days had been pretty, he was quickly realizing that he hated it. Hated pretty much everything, in fact. And the thought of spending the rest of the semester here, months and months of trying to dodge Orlando, wanting to see Theo, sounded unbearable. He'd just move back home. The whole point of being here had been to save his platform and get those endorsements and marketing deals. Now he wasn't going to get jack shit. Not with thirty thousand followers.

"Auggie, wait up."

Orlando was sprinting across the quad toward him, heedless of the snowmelt and the skin of ice coating the cement in places.

"Jesus," Auggie said, lowering his head and hurrying toward Moriah Court. He could go to the library instead. Or find a table in the student union. But the thought of running away again made him exhausted.

"Wait," Orlando called. "Please wait."

Auggie got through the security door and took the stairs two at a time. His high-tops squeaked on the steps. The second floor smelled like burnt popcorn. The third floor smelled like gym socks. The fourth floor smelled like Glade and vanilla incense. Jimmy Parvis was standing halfway down the hall, and when he saw Auggie he turned bright red and tried to run away so fast that he crashed into a fire extinguisher mounted on the wall. Jesus Christ, what did he think Auggie was going to do? Run after him and kiss him before he could get away?

Auggie let himself into the room and locked the door behind him. Leaning against it for a moment, he tried to figure out how to handle what was coming: how to act, how to play it all off, how to be cool. And then he thought fuck it and grabbed a duffel bag from under his bed. He opened the top drawer of his dresser, grabbed an armful of clothes, and shoved them in the bag.

Orlando's key rattled in the lock.

Grabbing another armful of clothes, Auggie tried to focus on packing.

"Hey," Orlando said, shutting the door behind him.

Auggie gave a jerk of his head.

"I tried to catch up with you," Orlando said. He stood between Auggie and the door; under the thick scruff, his cheeks were red. "I wanted to talk to you. I thought maybe, um. Maybe you'd be more comfortable if we talked somewhere public."

Laughing, Auggie grabbed more clothes.

"Would you like that? Somewhere more public? We could walk over to Hobbs and get a coffee or—"

"Doesn't really matter what I like, does it? Say whatever you want to say."

"I hope you don't mean that."

When the first drawer was empty, Auggie shoved it shut and opened the middle drawer. Part of his brain knew he had to be more selective now—he'd packed exclusively underwear and socks so far, and the duffel was filling up—but he couldn't seem to keep his attention on anything. He just kept grabbing and shoving.

"I care about you a lot, actually," Orlando said. "I know I have a lot to apologize for, and I want to start by making sure we do this the way you want to do it, you know, so you're comfortable."

"Comfortable?"

"Yeah, maybe the union—"

"Fuck off, Orlando. I don't want apologies. I don't want to talk. I will never feel comfortable around you, you blackmailing treacherous stalker psycho piece of shit."

"You don't understand. I was really worried."

Auggie laughed again. It came from this weird place inside him that didn't feel like laughter at all, and he was slightly worried that he didn't know how to turn it off.

"Don't laugh at me," Orlando said.

Grabbing more clothes, Auggie turned toward the duffel.

"Will you stop for one fucking second?" Orlando said, seizing his arm, spinning him.

"Fuck off," Auggie said. He tried to wrench himself from Orlando, but Orlando was bigger and much, much stronger. When Auggie couldn't get free, he stumbled back. Orlando came with him, still grappling. "Get the fuck off me or I will scream," Auggie said.

Orlando released him so abruptly that Auggie stumbled two more steps, and his hip connected with the bed. The clothes spilled from his arms; he vaguely saw two packs of Parliaments and a pack of Kools tumble under the bed, and Auggie realized he hadn't thought about rolling a pack in his sleeve for months, had forgotten completely why he'd ever thought that was a good look. Then the thought passed, and he grabbed the clothes.

"I made a big mistake," Orlando said, his chest heaving. He was starting to cry, and his thick brows were drawn together as he tried to control himself. "I made a huge fucking mistake, and I am so sorry. I never thought that video would get out. I just wanted him to leave you alone."

"Oh my God." Auggie shoved the clothes in the duffel and sat on the edge of the bed, staring at Orlando. "You are so fucking pathetic."

"I care about you so much—"

"Stop. Just stop."

"I do. I know you don't believe me, but I do. You're the only person I think about. You're funny and you're smart and you're kind. You're gorgeous. You're this incredible person that I lucked into meeting, and I know I messed things up, but if you'd just let me show you—"

"You don't know me."

"Yes, I do." Orlando was trying hard to firm his jaw. "I do. I know there are things about your life you don't want everyone to—"

"Oh my God. That part's over, Orlando. Everybody saw a dude kiss me. No matter what I say, that's out there. You. Don't. Know. Me."

"I do know you." His lip trembled. "And I love you."

"You're insane. You need to understand that. You are legitimately batshit insane." Hopping off the bed, Auggie, opened the bottom drawer of the dresser. "I'm going to stay somewhere else the rest of the semester, so—"

"He's a creepy old fuck," Orlando shouted. "What the fuck is the deal with him? You don't realize how weird that is?"

Auggie laughed again. "You're jealous of Theo? Jesus. He told me he never wanted to see me again, Orlando, so don't worry about that. But you know what? I'm feeling really fucking self-destructive right now, so I might as well go nuclear. Here's the thing about Theo: he's pretty fucked up, and I realized that early on, but at least he never wanted me to be anything but myself."

"Neither do I. I want you to be you. I'll do whatever you want. We can figure out a way to make better videos. We'll find the right girls. There's a girl in my chem class who's really funny. We can make a joke out of the whole kiss thing."

The idea was so tempting that Auggie felt it viscerally, a hook lodged in his gut. More videos. More jokes. More pictures and smiles and filters. And every day, becoming cardboard by inches.

"Please," Orlando said, touching Auggie's arm again, but softly. "Please. And we can . . . we can maybe give us a try, in secret, like we talked about. I can take care of you."

Auggie shivered. He pressed the clothes firmly into the bag, but he left it open, not bothering to zip it shut. He turned and faced Orlando.

"Keys," he said.

"What?"

"You want to see what you're dealing with? Keys. We're going to take a ride."

After a moment, Orlando handed over the keys. They went downstairs; it was late afternoon, and the sun set early in January. Another half hour, and dusk would be settling over everything. Orlando gave directions until they found his car, a BMW 335i, slate gray, probably a year or two old. Auggie slid behind the wheel; the smell of leather made his heart pulse a little faster, and when the engine roared to life, the pounding in his ears drowned out everything else. He played with the radio until he found some sort of screeching death metal, and then he turned it up until Orlando winced. He found a way to turn off the automatic headlights, and then he stepped on the gas.

"Jesus," Orlando yelped.

Ten miles over the speed limit, on a street bordering a college campus, felt like a lot. A pair of girls in ski caps backpedaled out of a crosswalk and shouted at Auggie as he blitzed past them. He dropped the pedal and slid around a bus idling ahead of them. The light at the intersection was yellow, and he slewed into the turn. When he spotted an elderly man in the crosswalk, Auggie just goosed the car into the oncoming lanes, which were clear for a moment, and zipped around him. Then they were shooting west out of the city.

"What the fuck are you doing?" Orlando screamed. "My dad will fucking kill me."

Auggie hit the gas again. Fifty in a thirty. A massive, illuminated red sign for HAROLD'S FRIED CHICKEN screamed past them on the right. Half a mile ahead, the next traffic light flipped to red, and the road was empty. Auggie kept accelerating. Cars shot through the intersection on the cross street. He wondered if he had timed this correctly.

"Stop," Orlando shouted. "Stop, you're going to—"

The light winked green, and they shot through the intersection.

"I told Theo," Auggie said, "that I liked to fuck things up every once in a while. I got tired of everybody seeing the same fucking cardboard cutout."

Wahredua was dissolving around them. Seventy in a forty. It was like special effects in a tornado movie, everything coming unglued, particles whirling away in an updraft. Pretty soon there'd be nothing left but the dark.

"Slow down," Orlando was shouting, "slow down, slow—"

"But here's what I didn't tell him," Auggie said.

They were a rocket clearing the atmosphere: Wahredua had disintegrated behind them, and now they blasted into full dark. Ninety in a fifty. A hundred. A hundred and ten. Without the headlights, it was like driving in a world of silhouettes: the trees and hills clipped out of the relative lightness of the horizon; the moon; the snow; a barn, its white paint skeletal.

To their left, a steel cattle guard bridged the drainage ditch, and then six feet of gravel drive ended at a split-rail snake fence. Auggie cut left, hard. For a moment, the bars of the cattle guard sang under them, and he kept turning, the tires drifting over snow and gravel, still turning, the rear of the BMW connecting first with the fence, still turning, the car whipping around, knocking the rails into the air like matchsticks, still turning, the tires biting deep into the ground and chewing up thick, muddy strips, still turning, and Orlando screaming the whole time.

Then the car stopped. Auggie goosed the engine, and the tires spun in the mud, splattering the snow behind them. After another minute, when he was sure the car was stuck, he shifted into park. He turned off the radio.

"What I didn't tell Theo," Auggie said, "is that I like fucking around with cars because sometimes it feels really good not to know if you're going to live or die." Clicking on the hazard lights, Auggie slid out of the car. "Have a good night, Orlando. Guess I'll see you back in the dorm."

Orlando's face was pale as he stared at Auggie.

Then Auggie shut the door and started walking. He squished along the shoulder of the state highway, heading back to campus. He paused at the edge of town, at Theo's street, and squinted, but he couldn't see the little brick house. Then he walked on again. He stopped for a second time at the stretch of road where he'd driven the Porsche into the drainage ditch. He remembered sitting on the asphalt after Theo had punched him. He remembered the heat of the road on the September night. Grabbing up the pack of smokes that had fallen out of his sleeve. Wanting so badly to be cool, to be popular, to be liked, even after some asshole had just loosened his teeth.

Well, so long and fuck off to that kid, Auggie thought, and he kept walking.

18

By Thursday night, Theo knew he had waited too long; he had made a mistake. He sat in his kitchen, the last Christmas ale on the table in front of him, the Percocet just far enough that he'd have to stretch to reach it. He liked the ale's ginger and cinnamon and honey. He liked how the taste complemented the lingering scent of sawdust; Cart had been here earlier, and the floor was almost finished. He liked how his classes had gone that day. He liked that he'd biked to campus and back and still didn't feel like he needed the cane, although he thought he might pay double for it tomorrow. He liked everything except for the fact that he was a low-down, shitty coward, because he still hadn't tried to talk to Auggie.

Theo took another long drink of the ale, felt distant panic at the realization that the bottle was almost empty, and told himself it was just a normal response when you were almost out of beer. He reached for the Percocet without getting up; his fingertips fell short of the plastic bottle. He'd biked to and from campus today. He'd done really well without the cane. He didn't need a pill, maybe not technically. But maybe—maybe he could think of it as preventative. Maybe taking one tonight, he'd sleep better. He wouldn't feel it when his leg stiffened up. He'd wake up tomorrow refreshed and ready to go. Sure, yeah. That sounded like the way a normal person thought.

But he just took another drink and sat there.

The problem was that he had waited too long. If he'd sought out Auggie the day after their fight, if he'd made Auggie sit down and talk to him—and Theo knew he'd have to force him to talk, because he knew how badly he'd hurt Auggie—if he'd done any of that, they could have figured it out. But instead, Auggie had gone and posted the video. And that meant that Auggie had gone to Lender and made some kind of deal. Theo hadn't been able to stop himself; since Cart had shown him that video, Theo had gotten on his computer every day and checked Auggie's social media accounts. Radio silence on all fronts. The numbers dropping by the tens of thousands every day.

Auggie had thrown his whole life away for Theo. And Theo knew he should feel grateful. Theo knew he should head straight to Auggie's dorm and thank him on hands and knees, thank him for putting an end to this madness, thank him for sacrificing himself to protect Theo and Lana. But Theo didn't feel grateful. He felt so shitty he wanted to die, and the only times he didn't feel that bad were when he was teaching, or when he was drinking, or when he was limping around the house doing gopher jobs for Cart. And how many times could Cart ask him to clear the nail gun or check the compressor before the joke got old?

A sound came from the front of the house, and Theo tensed, his fingertips white on the Great Lakes bottle. Not a knock. But a footstep, maybe. Not Cart; Cart had picked up a swing shift because two patrol officers had called in sick. Auggie?

Theo was up and moving before he could reconsider. He was limping more than he expected, and he checked the front room as he moved through it. Cart had brought over an old TV to replace the one that had been destroyed, so that was all right, because sometimes Auggie wanted to watch basketball. And the pile of books and papers on the couch would have to be moved. And thank God Theo had taken the pills into the kitchen.

When he opened the door, though, the porch was empty: just a dusting of snow and the yellow glare of the porch light. A raccoon, maybe. Or just the wind knocking something around. Theo was closing the door when he saw a single pair of footprints in the snow on the porch. Their shape was fresh and distinct. He hesitated, shut the door, and bolted it.

For a moment, he stood there. Auggie had cut a deal with Lender. The running clock wasn't running anymore. Nobody wanted anything from Theo. Lender had been dealt with. Lender would have gotten the Ozark Volunteers to back off. The whole thing was done and over.

A board creaked.

An old house, Theo thought. Just an old house. Cart said the joists need serious work. And you thought maybe he was just making up reasons to hang around, but maybe he was right. An old house, and the floors creak, and that's all, the end of it.

He spent ten more seconds telling himself that before he limped toward the stairs, already picturing the pistol hidden in his bedroom.

"You can just stop right there."

It was a woman's voice, and when he glanced over, at first he didn't recognize her. She'd found time to get her hair done. She'd even taken care of her nails. But the hard eyes and the hard mouth were the same, and after a moment, he recognized Robert's ex-girlfriend, Jessica, standing in the opening to the kitchen. She was holding a Bowie knife as long as her forearm. Behind her stood the woman with the swastika tattoo on her cheek—Mae, one of the thugs the Ozark Volunteers had sent to intimidate Theo and Auggie.

"Guess we should have asked you how long you were going to be in jail," Theo said quietly.

"Trespassing in the first degree," Jessica said. "Six months tops." Waving the tip of the blade at the couch, she said, "Have a seat."

"Why are you here?" Theo asked.

"Have a seat, Theo. We're going to have a nice, long talk. Mae and her friends are going to make sure nobody interrupts us."

As though that had been her cue, Mae nodded and left.

"Why are you here?" Theo asked.

"Sit down on the fucking couch."

"No," Theo said, and he eased himself up onto the first step.

"You are one dumb son of a bitch."

"Ask just about any man in my life," Theo said, easing himself up onto the next step. "Ask Ian, if you can. I think you'll get a consensus."

"I'll cut you up. You don't want that."

Theo nodded. The hardest part was turning away from her so he could make a mad dash up the stairs.

"Shit," Jessica shouted.

Ignoring her, Theo launched himself up the steps. His bad leg gave out on the second push-off, and he hit the steps hard, landing on his chest, his ribs creaking. He scrabbled at the next tread, trying to pull himself up, but his leg was ablaze with pain. After a few more frantic seconds, he managed to plant his other foot and push up with his good leg. He caught the railing, dragged himself another few feet, and his hand cleared the top of the stairs.

The first blow connected low in his back, and the pain was so shockingly crystalline that Theo could hear himself think, *That bitch paralyzed me.* But he wasn't paralyzed, and he flopped over, trying to defend himself. She had picked up his cane, and she was swinging it like a baseball bat, big slugger swings that were ridiculous in the cramped stairwell, cracking him in the arm, the head, the legs. She kept hitting until he stopped moving. Taking him by the ankles, she dragged him downstairs. Theo's head bumped on the steps. Fractals of light multiplied in his vision. He was in the hayloft. He was nudging aside the needle and the rubber tubing. He was trying to wave away the flies, so many damn flies he couldn't hear anything for all their buzzing. He thought about how disappointed Luke would be; this was the second fight Theo had lost in two weeks.

Too late, he came back to himself and realized she had taped his hands behind his back. Then she kicked him until he rolled over. He blinked, trying to clear his eyes, realizing now that he was bleeding from a head wound.

Jessica stood over him, the knife drawing an S in the air.

"Now," she said, "let's talk about where you put Robert's flash drive."

19

By the end of Thursday, Orlando still hadn't said a word to Auggie, and Auggie was fine with that. Orlando just played Xbox or messed with his phone, occasionally shooting looks at Auggie from under those thick eyebrows. He obviously was waiting for Auggie to break first. Auggie hoped he liked waiting.

Auggie was digging into a Com 2 assignment, an analysis of a social media platform's success. He'd picked Chan's thisisurex2 account. He knew about people who cut themselves; he'd never really understood it, but he'd known Christian Johnson had cut the inside of his thigh before every lacrosse game. But suddenly it all made sense. When everything hurt his much, when everything hurt everywhere, he could control this one thing and fine tune the pain, make it hurt exquisitely.

His phone buzzed. It was Theo.

Running his thumb along the aluminum frame, Auggie made himself release a slow breath. Then he answered.

"Where is it, fucktwat?" a woman's voice said.

"What? Who is this?"

"This is your buddy Theo," the woman said. "Where the fuck is it?"

"I don't know what you're talking about. Where's Theo? Is he ok? Let me talk to him."

After a moment, the woman said, "All right."

The sound of the call changed slightly, as though she had set down the phone or moved away from it. In the background, Theo shouted, "The Volunteers are here, Auggie, don't—" Then, from a distance, came muffled thuds cutting off Theo's voice. More blows. And then, at the end, a wheezing grunt that sounded a lot like Theo.

"Did you hear that?" the woman asked when she came back, a little breathless. "He says hi."

Auggie squeezed the phone so tightly that one of his knuckles popped. He forced the next words to be slow: "Please tell me what you want."

"Well, you're so polite. That's just so nice and refreshing. I want Robert's fucking flash drive. I know one of you two dongblowers has it. Where the fuck is it?"

"I don't—"

"Now, I know Robert had that fucking flash drive when he went to the Sigma Sigma party. And I know he didn't have it when I saw him later that night. In between, the only thing out of the ordinary were you two dickbags. So I want to know where that flash drive is."

"I don't know!"

"Let's see if Theo has anything to say about it."

"No," Auggie shouted, but she had already moved away from the phone.

The distant sound of the blows resumed and went on longer. This time, when it ended, Auggie could hear Theo struggling not to sob, his breathing high and panicked and frayed.

"Theo says he thinks you have it. Did you hear him?"

"Please," Auggie said. "I don't—"

"I'll ask Theo again."

"No, no. Don't. Ok. I have it. Yes. I've got it. But it's not here. It's going to take me time to get it."

"Auggie," she said, and suddenly he recognized the voice, a sliver of clarity in the chaos: Jessica Wallen, Robert's ex-girlfriend, whom they had spoken to in prison. "Time is about the only thing I don't have. You've got an hour. And don't do anything stupid like call the police, sweetheart. Theo's right: my friends are here."

"No, I need more time, I need—"

The call disconnected.

"Shit," Auggie screamed, hammering the phone against his leg. "Shit, shit, shit."

"What did that asshole get you into?" Orlando said, sitting up and swinging his legs over the side of the bed. "It's him, isn't it? I knew he was going to be trouble for you."

"Shut up," Auggie said.

"This is what I was trying to keep from happening. I only ever wanted to—"

"Shut the fuck up, Orlando. I am trying to figure out where the fuck this fucking murdered asshole lost his fucking magical flash drive, and I can't do it while you're patting yourself on the fucking back for being a psycho stalker."

Orlando pulled his knees to his chest and wiped his eyes.

Auggie screamed again, getting off the bed so he could pace.

Orlando sniffled.

"Stop," Auggie snapped.

"I just wanted to help."

Auggie ignored him and tried to think. The room was too small for really good pacing; by the time Auggie got going, he had to turn and start over again. So he tried to compensate by going faster. He was wearing a tank and gym shorts, and he chafed his arms, cold even though the dorm was always roasting. Where had Robert hidden the flash drive?

Smart, thorough, lucky. Wasn't that what Theo had said about solving difficult problems? Start by being smart. Ok. So, assume that Jessica is telling the truth. Robert had the flash drive with him when he went to the Sigma Sigma party. And he didn't have it when she saw him again later that night. Auggie considered the problem again and tried to be a little smarter. He only had an hour, so he had to snip off even more of the timeline. In theory, Robert could have hidden or lost the flash drive inside the Sigma Sigma house, but Auggie would never have time to search the frat house thoroughly. The same logic applied to the end of Robert's night: after Robert ran away from the crashed Porsche, Auggie had no idea where he had gone or what he had done. Searching the stretch of woods near the crash would be pointless, especially in the dark, with less than an hour.

"Can I please help?" Orlando said, sniffling some more.

Auggie wanted to say something brittle and cutting about big, butch wrestlers who haunted his life and ruined everything and then cried too much, but instead he just said, "Call the Sigma Sigma house and see if they have a lost and found."

Orlando looked pathetically grateful, offering Auggie a huge, teary smile as he placed the call.

Auggie considered what he remembered from the one night he had known Robert. Auggie had sat on a low wall outside the Sigma Sigma house. Robert had approached him. They had talked. Auggie had offered a cigarette. He'd said something about wanting to fuck things up. Robert had suggested stealing a car. Robert had come back from the Sigma Sigma house with the keys, and they'd taken the Porsche. Then Auggie had almost hit Theo, driven off into a ditch, and Robert had run away. It was probably twenty minutes total. Thirty minutes at the outside. And what were the odds that Robert had lost the flash drive in those thirty minutes?

"They've got a lost and found," Orlando said. "What did you lose?"

"A flash drive."

Orlando repeated the item, then shook his head. "They've got a spindle of blank CDs."

Auggie spread his hands.

"You're sure?" Orlando asked into the phone. Then he shook his head again. "Ok, thanks."

Auggie started pacing again.

"You know what they say," Orlando said. "It's always in the last place you look."

"How is that supposed to help me?"

"You just jump ahead and look in the last place. Where's the last place you'd ever think to look?"

"I don't know, Orlando," Auggie said through gritted teeth. "That's why it's the last place I'd ever think of."

"I'm just trying to help," Orlando said, a new variation on his phrase of the day.

"Stop trying."

"People say you should retrace your steps. What about that? Where was the last place you know you had it?"

Auggie shook his head.

"Well," Orlando said, "you're just pacing, so we might as well try it."

Auggie decided to accept his earlier premise: if Robert had lost or hidden the flash drive either before or after he'd been with Auggie, then Auggie wouldn't be able to find it in an hour, and he needed to come up with a backup plan. Blowing out a breath, Auggie said, "Outside the Sigma Sigma house."

"Ok, good. And then what did you do?"

Trying imagine the night's events from Robert's perspective, Auggie said, "I walked down to the wall and talked to this guy."

"Who?" Orlando said a little too quickly. "What was his name?"

Auggie pointed a finger at him.

"I'm just saying maybe he has it."

"No," Auggie said. "He doesn't."

"Ok, then what?"

"We talked. I asked for a cigarette."

"You don't smoke."

"But I was acting like a fucking poser back then," Auggie could hear himself mixing his point of view with Robert's, but he couldn't slow down, "and I had that pack rolled in my sleeve."

"Ok. Then what?"

"We talked. I said we should steal a car."

"Wait, what?"

"I went back inside the house. I grabbed somebody's keys. I came back outside, and we took the car."

"It could have fallen out of your pocket," Orlando said. "My keys fall out sometimes when I'm driving."

Auggie nodded, a sick heat clenching his stomach. The car presented the same problem: there was no way Auggie could get to the Porsche, get inside it, and search it for the flash drive before his hour was up. Maybe he could offer Jessica a list of possible places. Maybe she'd let him barter for more time.

"What next?" Orlando said.

"We crashed. I ran away."

"Oh. Shit."

"No," Auggie said, and he forgot again that he was supposed to be imagining it from Robert's perspective. "Wait. Hold on. I didn't. Not right at first. Theo punched me. And then Robert came around the side of the car, and they were wrestling. And then he heard the sirens and ran off, and I grabbed the pack of cigarettes that had fallen out of my sleeve." Auggie stopped walking. "Except they weren't mine. They were Kools. And so they had to be Robert's, but he said he didn't have any smokes. That's why he bummed one from me."

"I thought you bummed one from him?"

"Why did he ask me for a cigarette if he had a whole pack?"

"I do that sometimes. It's an ice breaker. I don't even smoke."

"But we'd already started talking," Auggie said. "He didn't need to break the ice. He'd stolen a sash and said he was a pledge; that was his icebreaker."

"Augs, what are you talking about? This is some crazy shit."

Ripping open his drawers, Auggie tossed his clothes on the floor.

"Come on, man, you're not going to stay with this guy, right? This Theo guy? I mean, he's trouble. He's getting you in trouble right now."

"Where are my cigarettes?" Auggie said, dumping out the middle drawer.

"This is the kind of stuff I was trying to protect you from."

"Orlando, for the love of God, where are my cigarettes?"

"I don't know. I didn't touch them."

Tossing clothes from the bottom drawer, Auggie let out a growl of frustration. Nothing. Were they gone? Had someone stolen them? Had someone thrown them in the trash?

"Oh," Orlando said. "Remember when, um, we kind of had a disagreement, and you had your clothes, and—"

"What are you talking about?"

"Some of your stuff fell under the bed," Orlando said, drawing his knees to his chest, an injured expression crossing his face again.

Dropping onto his knees, Auggie dug through the clutter. His hand closed over a plastic-wrapped package, and his heart pounded, but when he drew it out, it was a pack of Parliaments. He crawled deeper into the mess. Found the second pack of Parliaments. Then his hand closed over a small cardboard package. He sat back on his heels, staring at the Kools, and then he opened it. No cigarettes. The flash drive lay at the bottom of the pack.

Auggie grabbed his coat, not pausing to change into warmer clothes, and sprinted toward the stairs. Behind him, Orlando was calling his name. Auggie ignored him, pulling the phone from his pocket. He had two very important calls to make.

20

The knock at the door roused Theo from the haze of pain. At some point in one of the beatings that Jessica had administered, he had tried to crawl onto the couch. He wasn't sure now why it had seemed like a good idea—he guessed it was animal instinct, a need to get away, get to higher ground—but he had only made it halfway. He knelt there, his torso supported on the cushions, his hands still taped behind his back. One eye was swollen shut, and there was a ringing in his right ear that faded and grew more intense in waves. She had used the cane on him until she had broken it, and then she had found the broom and used that. And at some point, she had called Auggie.

Please, Theo thought, please don't let Auggie come.

Jessica's footsteps clipped across the room, and the door opened.

"I've got it," Auggie said.

Theo moaned and tried to tell Auggie to run, but he couldn't get the word to take shape.

"Good job," Jessica said. "Let's have it, and then fuck off."

Instead, though, Auggie's steps moved into the house, and the door swung shut. Auggie gave a sharp intake of breath, and the steps hurried toward Theo before stopping abruptly.

"I know you want to play with your jerkoff buddy," Jessica said, "but I'll put four inches of this Bowie knife in your gut if you try to get any closer. Flash drive. Now."

"What the fuck did you do to him?"

"He wasn't playing along," Jessica said. "Give me the flash drive."

"Theo?" Auggie called. "Theo, are you ok?"

"Ok," Theo managed to mumble.

"Give me the drive," Jessica said.

"Not yet," Auggie said.

Groaning, Theo tried to stand. Pain crackled in his hip and lanced down to his knee. He flopped back down onto the cushion.

"You're a dumb shit," Jessica said. "Why shouldn't I just cut you open and take it?"

"I didn't say I wouldn't give it to you. I just want some answers first."

"Well, aren't you a regular Hardy boy?"

"Why did you and Robert agree to help Chan ruin me?"

A beat passed, and Jessica said, "What?"

"Why did you take the job to humiliate me? I know she was going to pay you, and it was a lot of money, but that's some pretty low-down work."

Jessica's answer was too stilted. "Money is money."

"Oh my God," Auggie said. "You didn't even know."

"I knew." Then Jessica shifted her weight. "What are you talking about?"

"You didn't know about the ten thousand dollars Chan paid Robert. Oh my God. You were just . . . you were just his sidekick. What'd he do? Tell you it was one of those fifty-dollars-a-night shitty acting jobs? You missed out on ten thousand dollars because you were too fucking stupid to pay attention to what was going on."

"I'm not stupid," Jessica shouted. "Robert, he was the fucking retard. Who had the idea to blackmail that motherfucker Lender? Me. Who had the idea to string along the Ozark Volunteers, squeezing them for cash and promising them the recording, as if those dumb fucks would have any idea what to do with it if they ever got it? Me. And Robert couldn't see it. Robert was just such a fucking man, such a fucking man about everything, his dick doing all the thinking for him. He two-timed everyone. He played Lender against the Volunteers. Played the Volunteers against Lender. And then he thought he was going to play me. Showing up that night, telling me he didn't have the flash drive, wouldn't say a fucking word about where he'd stashed it. I couldn't stand it anymore." She cut off, her breathing ragged.

"You killed him."

"I smashed the back of his fucking head in, princess. While he was watching his fucking *SportsCenter* on his fucking stolen Magnavox."

"Did you record the blackmail that night?"

Theo tested his balance, pushed up with his good leg, and managed to twist himself into an upright position on the couch. He could see Auggie now, dressed in a coat, a tank top, and gym shorts, his bare feet shoved into high-tops. His dark eyes were hard and glittering. He was barely taller than Jessica, but everything about Auggie was power: the lithe lines of his body, the set of his jaw, his voice. Theo was pretty sure he had a concussion, but he still thought Auggie was fucking fantastic right then.

Jessica was trying to control her breathing. "Asshole wouldn't even take five minutes to make a backup. He wanted to rush off to the Sigma Sigma party. Said he had another job to do. That's when I started to get worried. We'd just recorded a city cop on the take, and instead of making a million copies for insurance, Robert wanted to go play dress-up. When he got home that night, when he wouldn't tell me anything, wouldn't show me the flash drive, wouldn't tell me where it was, I knew that fucker was trying to cut me out. So I cut him out first."

"But you didn't know where the flash drive was."

"All I could find on his phone were those fucking videos of you and your jerkoff rag over there. So I put together that video, posted it, and got the hell out of his place."

"And you made sure you got caught trespassing so you'd be locked up when Robert's body was found. Nobody would even think about you for the killing."

Her breathing had gotten even more ragged; the tip of the Bowie dipped and bobbed in the air. "Storytime's over. I want the flash drive."

"Ok," Auggie said. He held out a pack of Kools. "It's in here."

"Show me."

Opening the package, Auggie displayed it for her. After a moment, Jessica nodded and held out a hand.

"Take a few steps toward the door," Auggie said. "And I'll take a few steps toward Theo."

"Nice try."

"What am I trying? You've still got the knife. I'll toss you the pack, you head out the door, and we're done."

Jessica shifted her weight; after a moment, she shuffled toward the door. Auggie rotated with her, inching closer to Theo. For one, wild moment, Theo thought it was going to work.

Then the door flew open, and Orlando stumbled into the house. "Auggie, watch out," he shouted. "She's got a knife!"

Jessica turned and drove the Bowie into his stomach.

Orlando screamed, dropping against the jamb and sliding down. The knife came free with a squelching sound, and blood spurted out. Orlando clasped his hands over the wound, and more blood trickled between his fingers, soaking his t-shirt and jeans.

"Fuck, fuck, fuck," Jessica shouted. "Give me the drive, give me the drive."

Auggie tossed it to her. She snagged it out of the air, and she took a step toward the door. Then she stopped, staring outside, and took a step back. When Auggie moved, she slashed in his direction.

"Stay the fuck out there," she called through the open door, speaking to someone Theo couldn't see. "I've got hostages. I'll cut their fucking throats. Mae, where the fuck are you?"

"Mae's gone," Auggie said. "Les and some of his brothers decided to stop by and say hi. They were really interested to learn who had killed Robert."

Jessica bared her teeth at him as she stumbled closer to Theo.

"Get away from him," Auggie shouted, lunging.

Jessica was closer and faster. Theo lurched up from the couch, trying to get away, but his leg wouldn't support him, and the beatings he'd taken slowed him. Grabbing a handful of Theo's hair, Jessica yanked his head back and put the blade of the Bowie against his throat. Theo could smell Orlando's blood.

"Everybody calm down," Auggie said. "Orlando, Orlando, we're going to get you some help."

"Get over here," Jessica said to Auggie.

"You're making a big—"

"Get over here," she screamed, jerking on Theo's hair, and Auggie stumbled over to them.

Sirens played in the distance. Steps moved on the porch. Theo recognized a familiar voice from the doorway when a man called into the house, "Jessica, my name's Detective Somerset. I'm with the Wahredua PD. I'd like to come inside the house."

"Go the fuck away."

"It's too late for that, Jessica. You hear those sirens? Everybody's on their way. Pretty soon, this house will be surrounded by cops."

"Anybody comes in here, and I'll kill these two."

Theo was wavering, held up more by Jessica's grip on his hair than by his own strength. Auggie must have noticed because he slid an arm around Theo's waist, taking some of his weight, and whispered, "It's going to be ok."

Theo almost laughed.

"You hurt this kid pretty bad," Somers said from the doorway. He stepped over Orlando, his heel clicking as he eased into the house. He had both hands in the air. "If he dies, that's on you. Right now, this is bad, but it's not murder. Let's not make things any worse."

"I said nobody comes in this house," Jessica screamed.

"Too late for that too," Somers said. "I'm here, and we're talking. So let's talk. Let's talk about how we can fix this. The first thing you've got to do is let those guys go. The next thing is you've got to let me get help for this kid before he bleeds out. Those are the things we've got to do right now, Jessica, or I can't help you with anything else."

"Fuck this," Jessica muttered, giving another vicious tug to Theo's hair. "We're leaving. You try to stop me, and I'll cut his fucking head off."

"Slow down," Somers said. "We're just talking—"

"Shut the fuck up." Jessica gave another jerk, trying to force Theo toward the door, but Theo could barely hobble.

"He can't walk," Auggie said. "I'll go with you."

"No," Theo said, trying to move faster.

"Stop," Auggie shouted. "He's slowing you down. Just leave him, and I'll go with you."

"No," Theo said, but the word was mumbled. He couldn't seem to string anything more complicated together.

Jessica's breathing whistled in Theo's ears. She grunted and swore under her breath as she dragged Theo toward the kitchen. Theo yelped as his weight came down on his bad leg, and he started to fall before Jessica yanked on his hair and he managed to right himself.

"Just stop," Auggie said, stumbling after them. "You're hurting him!"

"Don't fucking move," Jessica screamed. She came unhinged, shoving Theo aside, turning on Auggie, the knife slashing out.

Theo saw the knife, only the knife, the knife that was spearing toward Auggie's belly. Theo half fell and half threw himself into the path of the blade. He felt it connect, felt the impact first like someone shoving him, and then a sharp, stinging heat in his side.

He landed on his back. He was staring up at Jessica when a bullet struck the side of her head, and bone and brain erupted. Then blackness rolled in, and Theo felt hands turning him, hands on his cheeks, Auggie's voice saying, "Theo, Theo, hey, stay with me."

In the distance, Renard Upchurch, who had played softball with Ian on the department team, was saying, "I had to do it; she was going to kill them."

And it was raining; Theo felt the drops, hot, falling on his face. His last thought before darkness towed him under was that the fool in *Lear* was right: the rain it raineth every day.

21

On Friday, they wouldn't let Auggie see Theo at all, so he spent the whole day pacing the floors of Wahredua Regional. He wasn't sure if he said a single word that whole day. He just remembered fragments of it: speeding up so he could pass a middle-aged man on a walker; the smell and crinkle of the paper towels as he dried his hands in a public restroom; the fluorescent lights becoming a headache that flickered just behind his eyes. His phone buzzed from time to time; most of them were alerts from Instagram and Facebook, which he ignored. One was a text from Fer: *Dickcheese, how were the first two weeks of school?* He ignored that one too.

On Saturday, they moved Theo out of the ICU and into a step-down unit, where visitors could only stay for an hour at a time. Theo was asleep for the whole hour; the nurses wouldn't tell Auggie anything, and on the way out, he bumped into a wiry guy with buzzed hair who glared at Auggie like he wanted to murder him. Auggie was pretty sure this was the infamous Cart. He hung around for the next hour until they kicked Cart out, and then Auggie tried again. They wouldn't let him back in the room. Sometime in the afternoon, he got another text from Fer: *Cumbreath, answer my text.* Auggie just put his phone back in his pocket.

On Sunday, they moved Theo into a shared room. When Auggie finally was allowed into the room, Theo was asleep again; Auggie didn't care. He dropped into a chair. He figured out what he was going to do if anyone—in his mind, anyone looked a lot like Cart—tried to make him leave. Auggie figured he'd go for the nads first. And then he fell asleep, shivering and uncomfortable in the molded-plastic chair.

He woke once when he thought he heard the door open and close. Then, later, he woke partway to a pained grunt and the realization that he was warm. He opened his eyes.

"Oh my God," Auggie said.

Theo was leaning over the railing of his bed, trying to adjust the blanket he'd thrown over Auggie. He was pasty and sweaty, his face covered in bruises and bandages from the beatings Jessica had administered. He had huge dark rings under his eyes, and he looked like he needed to sleep for a week, but he just kept fussing with the blanket and grunting when he moved the wrong way.

"Oh my God," Auggie said, surging up from the chair and knocking the blanket to the floor. "You're awake."

"Do you know how long it took me to get that on you?" Theo said with a roll of his eyes. "It was like playing ring toss."

"Oh my God," Auggie said, his eyes stinging. He stepped forward, stopped, examined Theo for some sort of sign.

Theo waved him forward, and when Auggie was within range, he pulled him into a one-armed hug. He grunted again when Auggie tightened the embrace and whispered, "A little less enthusiasm, please."

Auggie thought he was laughing at Theo's comment; then he realized, after a few seconds, he was crying, crying so hard he thought he was coming apart.

Theo just held him and said, "It's ok, it's ok, I'm fine," laughing awkwardly between rounds, his arm never loosening around Auggie.

"Ok," Auggie finally said, standing up and wiping his face. "Ok. Oh my God. You're awake."

"Uh huh," Theo said with a smile. "Hi."

"Hi." Auggie wiped his face again. He was grinning so hard it hurt. "You dumbass! What the hell were you thinking? You could have gotten yourself killed."

"Yeah, well," Theo said, "I was thinking about all the Dorito crumbs I needed to clean out of my couch. Getting stabbed with a knife seemed like a better option."

"Don't joke about this," Auggie said. "No jokes. This is not funny!"

Theo shrugged; he still had that small smile almost hidden by his beard. "Did you get it on video? Or a picture? I bet you could make an awesome meme out of it."

"You saved my life," Auggie said. "You don't get to joke about that."

"I can joke about whatever I want."

"And you don't even know what a meme is."

"I read the Wikipedia entry."

Auggie started crying again.

"Oh no," Theo said, "come on, everything's ok."

"If I hadn't messed everything up," Auggie was trying to say. "If I'd made sure Orlando wasn't following me, if I hadn't called the cops, you wouldn't be hurt."

It took him about fourteen tries, between sobs, to get the message across. By the time he finished, he was sitting on Theo's bed, mashing tissues against his face while Theo rubbed his leg.

"You know that's not true, right?" Theo said. "She'd already killed once. What was going to stop her from killing both of us once you gave her the flash drive?"

"She was leaving—"

"Auggie, we don't know what she was doing. She was dangerous, and she was a killer. You couldn't have stopped Orlando, and you did the right thing calling Somers and Upchurch." Then Theo smiled. "Calling Les was a stroke of genius."

Auggie sat there, drawing in shuddering breaths.

"Did you hear me?" Theo asked, squeezing his knee.

Auggie nodded.

"So," Theo said, squeezing again, "this is officially me thanking you for saving my life."

Shaking his head, Auggie pressed the tissues harder against his eyes.

"Give me an update," Theo said. "What happened after, well, you know?"

"You know Jessica's dead?"

"I kind of remember that."

"After they took you and Orlando, I had to go down to the station and answer a million questions."

"How's Orlando?"

"He's still in the ICU."

"Shit."

"A nurse told me he's looking better," Auggie said. "But he's not stable yet."

"And what happened with you at the station?" Theo asked.

"Just questions."

"What did you tell them?"

Auggie lowered the tissues; his eyes were red, but his gaze was clear as he met Theo's look. "I told them the truth," he said. "Robert gave me a pack of cigarettes; he didn't tell me he'd hidden a flash drive inside. Jessica targeted us because of the video footage from the night she killed Robert. When she called me, she told me to bring the pack of Kools. I didn't know anything about a corrupt cop; I had no idea what she was talking about. I didn't know what was on the flash drive."

Theo blew out a breath and squeezed Auggie's leg again. "Good. Good. Oh Jesus, Auggie. Good."

"They didn't believe me. Somerset and Upchurch."

"That's ok. That doesn't matter. That's the story we keep telling."

After a moment Auggie nodded. The other patient in the room, hidden behind a curtain printed with tulips, gave a deep, rasping cough, and then the television kicked on. A grainy episode of *Hollywood Squares* was halfway over. Auggie didn't recognize any of the celebrities.

"So," Theo said, "this is kind of a perfect opportunity for me to apologize for being a huge dick."

"What?"

"I kind of overreacted the other day."

"What? When?" Auggie said.

"About Lana."

"Oh. Oh my God. No, you didn't overreact. I can't believe I did that. I'm sorry, again. Really. It was—"

"Ok, ok, it's my turn to talk."

"—totally out of line, and I should have respected the boundaries you were—"

"Ow, ow, ow," Theo said, pressing a hand to his side. "Auggie?"

"Yes, what? Are you in pain? What do you need? Do you need a nurse? I'll get a nurse."

"No, you can do it."

"Yes, yeah, I can do it. What do you need? What should I do?"

"I need you to take your hand, like this." Theo demonstrated.

"Ok."

"And put it over your mouth like this." Theo sealed his hand across his own mouth to demonstrate.

Somebody on *Hollywood Squares* was cackling about the best joke in the universe.

Glaring, Auggie said, "You're on morphine or something, right? Is that why you think you're a comedian all of a sudden?"

Theo just raised his eyebrows.

"Only because you got stabbed," Auggie grumbled, but he put his hand over his mouth.

"That's perfect," Theo said. "We should practice that."

Auggie flipped him off.

"Blessed silence," Theo said.

"I'm not—" Auggie said, pulling his hand away.

Theo raised a finger.

With a wounded expression, Auggie clapped his hand down again.

"Ok," Theo said, "here we go. I am really . . . embarrassed about my situation."

Auggie made a questioning noise.

"Embarrassed isn't the right word," Theo said, dropping his eyes to the thin sheet that covered him. "Humiliated. Ashamed. So fucking ashamed I can't, well, even really talk about it. But I'm going to do this because I treated you awfully, and you didn't deserve that." He squeezed his eyes shut. "Lana was hurt really badly, and she'll get better, a little, but she's not ever going to really get better, if you understand me. She needs full-time care. And I can't afford that; Ian's life insurance, when it comes in, will barely cover the bills we already have. And I can't just stay home and take care of her because, well, money. And I can't afford to pay someone to take care of her at home because, well, I have no fucking money. And my parents won't have anything to do with me. My brothers, Christ, I don't even know. And Ian's parents hate me, so they've made it really clear that they will not pay for Lana to have in-home care with me."

Auggie still had one free hand; he took one of Theo's and squeezed.

"And I'm the worst father in the entire world. The worst. I'm a fucking . . . I'm a fucking monster, to leave her there. Not to be able to be with her, take care of her, even though she doesn't recognize me or know who I am anymore or, Jesus, just hold on a second." He had to take a few harsh breaths; Auggie tightened his grip, and Theo was squeezing back just as hard. "Anyway, I said fuck it, I was going to have her at home with me, and I'd do some sort of online work, something just to make ends meet, and Ian's parents threatened to take me to court. Missouri doesn't recognize that Ian and I were married. She's his daughter, biologically, and they say that they have custody rights now. I guess I could fight them on it, but, fuck, money. And Jesus, it's just been such a fucking nightmare that I don't even know what to do or how to talk about it or how not to feel like the shittiest human being in existence."

Auggie counted out the seconds. Theo's nails bit into his hand, and it hurt like hell, but Auggie knew Theo was hurting even more. After almost half a minute, Theo exhaled sharply and opened his eyes.

"Anyway," Theo said. "That's that. And I shouldn't have treated you the way I did. I'm sorry about that. Oh shit, your hand." He released Auggie, and then he turned Auggie's hand, exhibiting the white crescent marks his nails had left. "Christ, Auggie, why didn't you say something?"

Auggie made a questioning noise and wiggled the fingers of the hand covering his mouth.

With a groan, Theo dropped his head back onto the pillow. "Please, can we not talk about this anymore? I really don't think I can talk about this."

Auggie held up one finger.

"No, Auggie, please."

Auggie made a pleading noise.

After a moment, Theo nodded, but he looked away.

Dropping his hand from his mouth, Auggie said, "You're a great man and an amazing father, and you're doing the best you can in an impossible situation. When you're ready, I want to do whatever I can to help you, but I promise I won't bring this up again until you want to talk about it."

Theo gave a jerky nod, still staring at the tulip-print curtain.

Auggie might have made a mistake, might have said more, because the anguish on Theo's face was still so raw, but the door opened, and Auggie shot a glance over his shoulder.

"Hi, Auggie," Detective Somerset said quietly. "Theo, how are you?"

"Ok," Theo muttered, wiping his face and coughing hard once.

"I know you've both been through a lot," Somerset said. "I'd like to get your account of events, Theo, but that can wait. I need to ask you both something else first, and it's very important that you tell me the truth."

Auggie tensed, waiting for the questions about corrupt cops, about Lender, about everything that had really been happening over the past five months.

Somerset frowned. "We can't find the flash drive anywhere. We know it was in the house; I saw it in Jessica's hand when I went inside. We've searched the house a couple of times since then, full sweeps. It's vanished. Do either of you have it? Maybe you just picked it up by mistake?"

In the words, Auggie could hear the offer: Somerset would let it slide, would let them take the easy route by claiming it had been a mistake. He shook his head. Theo shook his head.

"Damn," Somerset said, riffling his hair. "Here's the real question, then: do you have any idea who might have taken it?"

22

Theo was exhausted by the time Somers left; Somers hadn't exactly interrogated them, but he'd come pretty close. He'd pressed Auggie pretty hard about contacting Les and his brothers; Somers had wanted to know if Robert's cousins had killed any Volunteers when they cleared a path for Auggie, but Auggie had just shrugged and said he didn't know anything. After Somers had finally left, it had taken even more time to send Auggie home. The poor kid had been a wreck, physically and emotionally, and he needed food and sleep in a real bed, even if he hadn't been willing to admit it. After Auggie left, Theo closed his eyes and tried to sleep; the room smelled like old cigarette smoke and liniment, which Theo guessed was probably courtesy of his roommate. The guy's cough had gotten steadily worse throughout the afternoon. Theo could barely hear *Wheel of Fortune* over his hacking.

Theo felt like his eyes had barely been closed for five minutes, though, when the door opened again.

"Well," Cart said, "you look like shit."

Theo studied Cart, trying to make sense of what he was seeing. Cart was wearing a button-up that was shockingly trendy: the fabric was printed with old-fashioned Christmas lights, and it looked good on Cart's compact frame. He had on khakis and loafers. He was carrying flowers.

"Oh my God," Theo said.

Cart blushed. "I wouldn't have gotten all dressed up if I knew you were going to be in your panties."

"You look like you're fourteen years old and picking up your first date."

"Fuck off," Cart said. Then that huge, shit-kicking grin exploded. "So I look good, huh?"

"You don't look like a reprobate who only owns gym shorts."

Cart came across the room and settled into the chair that Auggie had recently left. With that same crazy-ass grin, he held out the flowers.

"These are nice," Theo said.

"I don't know how to pick out flowers, so I just got a big one."

"They're really nice. I like carnations."

"My first date, when I was fourteen, was Alexis Lind," Cart said. "But I'd gotten a handjob the summer before from Joey Ridenhour at Scout Camp. So maybe that was my first date."

"You want to count getting a handjob in a canvas A-frame as your first date?"

"Joey was a sweetheart. And I think tents are romantic."

"God, you're a certified hoosier. You understand that, right?"

Cart just grinned and stretched out in the chair. He looked around and said, "Where's your boytoy?"

Theo looked at him and waited.

"It's just a joke," Cart said. "Don't get your panties in a wad."

"If you've got any more jokes, get them all out of your system."

"Did your preschool buddy give you a little . . ." Cart mimed jerking off.

Theo rolled a finger.

"Did he kiss it and make it better?"

"You get one more, so make it good."

"Did you show him just how adjustable that hospital bed can get?"

Theo shook his head. "I don't even know what that means."

"It means he rode your dick while you—"

"Jesus, Cart." In spite of himself, Theo was grinning. "Who the fuck was in charge of civilizing you?"

"I don't know," Cart said, "but they did a shit job." Then he rubbed his face with both hands and his eyes got bright and wet.

"Oh no," Theo said, "I can't handle two crying men in my hospital room in one day."

"I'm not going to cry, you big cooz. I'm just really glad you're ok. Christ, when I heard—" He broke off, and his adam's apple bobbed.

After a moment, Theo said, "Well, I'm ok. I am."

"Good."

"Yeah."

"No thanks to your jailbait."

"Cart."

"Ok, ok. I'm just saying, no thanks to your teenybopper."

"You don't have any idea what happened, Cart, so don't get started. That's my last warning."

Cart rubbed his cheeks again, blinking his eyes clear. His smile this time wasn't quite as crazy-ass, but it was still a Cart smile. "So are you going to date him or something? He's pretty. I saw him around here a couple of times."

"Nope," Theo said. "I'm not talking to you about this."

"I'm your friend, right? You can talk to me."

"That's not why you're asking."

"Come on," Cart said, waving one hand. "That's in the past. I'm just your buddy. I'm just asking if you're going to date him. He likes you. More than likes you, I think. And he's gorgeous."

Theo made a noncommittal sound.

"Are you freaking out because of Ian?"

Theo shook his head. Then he said, "Christ, it's barely been six months. How fucked up is that?"

For a while, neither of them said anything; Vanna was turning letters on *Wheel of Fortune,* smiling when Brittany from Biloxi got three E's. Cart was wearing cologne, Theo realized. It smelled like the Drakkar Noir knock-off from CVS. It was kind of nice on Cart.

"You know what I think?" Cart said.

"I guess you're going to tell me."

Cart flashed him that grin again. "I think people are always telling us how we should feel and what we should feel, who we should love and when we should love. I guess I kind of think that's bullshit now. You love somebody, and you just love him, and there's nothing you can do to change it or explain it or make sense of it. You shouldn't feel bad about that."

Theo nodded.

"Besides," Cart said, "you could fuck your way through a whole frat house and Ian still wouldn't be as mad at you as he was that one time he caught you cheating on him with a donut. You know, when you both went gluten free."

Theo gaped for a moment. "He told you?"

"Damn near divorced your dumb ass. Eating donuts while you thought he was at work. Theo Stratford, you are one stupid son of a bitch."

"Yeah," Theo said, smiling in spite of himself. He'd forgotten about the donuts. "Yeah, I am."

Something changed in the air. Vanna was still turning letters—two L's—and the man behind the tulip-print curtain was coughing up a lung, but now Cart was staring down, straightening his khakis, his heels bouncing.

"Hey Theo," Cart said, looking up.

The door opened, and Dr. Kanaan, Theo's adviser, stood there in a track suit and a hijab. She glanced at them and said, "I'm sorry, I'll come back."

"No," Cart said. He took the flowers from Theo. "I should get these in some water. Be back in a bit."

When he'd left, Dr. Kanaan took a seat.

"Theo, we're all so glad you're ok."

"Thank you."

"You are ok, aren't you?"

"Yes. How are you?"

The question flustered her; she touched the hijab, stared at the foot of the bed. "Oh, I'm fine. Thank you. And you're ok? How are you?"

"Still ok," Theo said slowly.

"And do you have everything you need? Can the department do anything for you?"

"I'm fine, thanks."

"That's really wonderful," she told the foot of the bed. "I'd say this is a miracle."

"Dr. Kanaan, I think you came here for a reason."

"Well, Theo, there's no easy way to say this."

He waited. He had no intention of making it any easier.

"After a lot of discussion," Dr. Kanaan said, "we, the department, all of us, we really feel that you've had a difficult year."

"I see," Theo said. "It took a lot of discussion to figure that out?"

"And a video has surfaced of you with a . . . with a former student, I understand. So of course, if you have anything to say about that . . ."

"No," Theo said. "I don't have anything to say about that."

"Well, extenuating circumstances, Theo. Everyone understands." She risked a glance at him and then mumbled, "Because of the tragedy."

"I think it'd be best if you told me whatever you came here to tell me," Theo said. "I've had a long day."

"Of course, of course. I just want you to understand—we just want you to understand—that this is for your own good. I really hope that's clear. We care about you, Theo. We want what's best for you."

"Am I being kicked out of the program?"

"What? No, of course not."

"Then what?"

"You've been under unusual strain, and—"

"You're taking my classes."

"The teaching requirement can impose a lot of undue stress," Dr. Kanaan said. "It might be better to take a semester off. Or a few semesters."

"I'm being blackballed from teaching, is that it?"

"Don't be ridiculous."

"Because I kissed a former student."

"Well, I really don't know why you're taking that tone, Theo. Yes, you kissed a former student. An eighteen-year-old. And then you were attacked in your home, and this same student was there. It's . . . it's not good, Theo, however you look at it."

"He's an adult."

Dr. Kanaan tugged on her track suit.

"Nothing happened when he was my student."

"That's really not the point."

"And because you're worried about the department's image or the school's image or whatever you're worried about, I'm getting cut off."

"The teaching stipend—"

"And how am I supposed to pay my mortgage? How am I supposed to buy groceries? How am I supposed to get a job in five years, when my CV is totally blank?"

"You're being dramatic, Theo. We'll certainly look into other funding opportunities, of course, but you understand that the department and the college are still under financial strain."

After that, whatever Dr. Kanaan said was white noise; Theo could barely look at her, and she spent the rest of the time talking to his feet. When she left, he lay back, breathing in the old cigarette smoke and the liniment and trying to figure out how the fuck he was going to make it through the end of the day, let alone the end of the week.

Then the door opened, and steps came closer, and Theo smelled drugstore cologne and seared meat. Paper rustled.

"You awake, dingdong?"

When Theo opened his eyes, Cart was holding out a burger.

"Thought you might be hungry and not want whatever circus-animal shit they're feeding you."

Theo started to cry.

"All right," Cart said, and he set aside the burger and rolled up his sleeves and sat next to Theo, not touching him until the end, just talking nonsense, and then, when Theo finally had himself under control again, tucking Theo's hair behind his ears.

"How about that burger?" Cart said.

"Yeah," Theo said.

They ate for a while in silence; it was the best burger Theo had ever tasted.

"Cart," Theo said. "Thanks."

"Somebody's gotta keep you from getting into more of your peckerbrained fuckery."

23

Two weeks passed, and Auggie went to see Theo every day. Sometimes it was just for ten minutes. Sometimes he'd stay curled up in one of the chairs, pretending to do homework while Theo pretended to work on his thesis. More than once, he crossed paths with Cart, and Auggie would smile and say hi. Cart wouldn't smile, but at least he'd say hi, and they both found reasons to leave when the other one showed up.

And then Theo went home, and the next night, Auggie stood on the porch and knocked. Snow crunched under his boots as he shifted his weight. His stream of breath seemed to catch fire in the cold air, passing in front of the yellow porch light. Down the street, a cat yowled, and then trash cans crashed against each other as something, probably the cat, burst into a flurry of movement.

When the door opened, Theo was wearing joggers and an 80s-era Blues sweatshirt. The bruises that covered him were finally starting to fade, and the cuts were healing nicely. The only thing the doctors were still cautious about was the stab wound, the one that he had taken for Auggie, but even that seemed like it was on the mend.

Theo just smiled, ran his hands through that bro flow of strawberry-blond hair, and motioned for Auggie to come in.

"Home sweet home," Auggie said, unlacing his winter boots, stripping out of his coat, getting tangled for the millionth time in his scarf and Theo not missing a beat, catching the end of it and spinning him out of it.

The house looked really good. The walls had been finished and painted, and it was quite a bit warmer inside than Auggie remembered. Theo had even hung a few pieces of art that hadn't been there before: some were obviously done by Lana, while others were watercolors of nature scenes. The toys had been cleared out, the couch had been replaced, and the TV looked old but functional; the Blues were playing the Devils, and they were up by one.

"Do you want something to drink?" Theo asked. "Or something to eat? Cart picked up groceries before I came back, so I actually have stuff."

"That was nice of him," Auggie said.

Theo raised an eyebrow.

"What?" Auggie said.

"No way," Theo said, limping over to the new couch. "Don't start."

"Did Ian do these?" Auggie asked, studying the watercolors. One of them showed a deer at the edge of a pool of water. Another showed a barn. The level of detail made Auggie think these were real places—the crumbling foundation under one corner of the barn, for example. Another showed the Gothic skyline of Wroxall's campus.

"I'm trying to watch this," Theo said.

"These are really good," Auggie said. He moved slowly from painting to painting. At one of them, which showed a valley with what Auggie thought were crabapple trees in blossom, he stopped and said, "God, I'd love to go somewhere like that."

"Auggie," Theo said. Then the goal buzzer sounded, and he shouted, "Hell yeah!"

"Is this around here?"

"Ok," Theo said, "commercial break. Yes. Those are real places around here. Yes, that's part of a state park, probably an hour away. And no, Ian did not do those."

"Oh my God," Auggie said.

"No, do not turn this into a whole thing. When this commercial break is over, I'm watching the game."

"You did these," Auggie said.

Theo rolled his eyes, but he blushed behind the beard. "I hit a rough spot after my family cut me off. One of the things my therapist suggested was trying new activities. Anything artistic was a waste of time for my parents, so I'd never even tried. Anyway, I found them when I was putting some of Ian's stuff in the basement, and I thought I'd hang them up."

"They're beautiful."

"No," he said laughing, "they're not. But thank you. They're just a reminder that, you know, things get better."

Auggie studied the crabapples in blossom.

"Come sit down, would you?"

"Theo, I think I'm going to move home."

"What?"

Auggie leaned in a little closer; Theo had painted the faintest hint of blossoms tumbling away on the wind, and Auggie realized that at some point, Theo had stood in that valley, had seen those crabapple trees, had seen the breeze carrying the petals.

"Hey, what are you talking about?"

"I think I'm—"

"Uh uh. Sit your ass over here and talk to me."

On the TV, the game came back on, and Auggie heard the thwack of a stick slapping a puck.

"Commercial break's over," Auggie said.

Theo turned off the TV. "There, done, permanent commercial break. Are you going to sit down, or do I have to hobble over there, every fucking cut and scrape and bruise screaming at me?"

"Hey," Auggie said, glancing over.

Theo shrugged. "Your choice."

After Auggie sat on the couch, he said, "You fight dirty."

"What are you talking about, Auggie? Moving home? What, because of what happened with Jessica?"

"No."

"If you're still blaming yourself, then we need to talk about that."

"I mean, I do blame myself. A little. But that's not why."

"Ok. Why?"

"I don't know why I should stay here. The whole reason I came here was to get a clean slate, focus on building my brand, and leverage that into some endorsement and marketing deals. That's over. That's dead. I don't even want to tell you how many followers I have now, and whatever, that's fine, but there's no point in staying here."

"You'll rebuild. You're smart and funny, and you've got charisma. You rebrand and you rebuild, and you'll be even more successful this time."

"I don't know if I want to."

"I know things look bad right now, but you shouldn't throw away everything you worked for."

"Right," Auggie said. "Stupid videos of me dancing, stupid videos of me with my shirt off, no nips. Stupid videos that nobody remembers five minutes after they watched them."

"My favorite one is the one where you keep trading shirts."

In spite of himself, Auggie snorted. "Are you serious?"

"You've got the three blue polo shirts, and one is sized for a little kid, and then there's one that fits you, and then there's the huge one. And you and Logan and Devin keep passing them around, and somehow, you keep ending up with the tiny one."

"Yeah," Auggie said. "That was one of our earliest videos."

"Like the eighth time you end up with the little shirt, you get this look on your face. I don't know. I've seen the real version of that look on your face so many times, and it made me laugh. It still makes me laugh, actually. I'll think of it at the weirdest times and just start laughing out loud."

"Ok, thanks."

"That's a pretty big deal. Making people laugh, brightening their day, that's a gift."

"It's not a gift. It's a . . . it's a fucking defense mechanism. I'm so fucking sick of it. Do you know why I do it? Jesus, this is so pathetic, but I can still remember the exact moment I figured out how it works: my mom had brought home her boy of the week, and he was actually a decent guy, and I wanted him to like me. Back then, I just wanted somebody to like me, pay attention to me. So I balanced this cup on my nose like a seal, and the guy thought it was the funniest thing he'd ever seen. And when he left, the next guy thought it was hilarious watching me slide down the stairs on a cardboard box. And then the next guy. And at some point, I started hating all those fucking guys, but I liked how it felt, having people look at me, like me, and it just kept going. And I'm tired of that."

Theo was quiet for a moment. "There are people who see you for who you really are. People who like you, care about you, and you don't have to perform for them."

"Ok."

"Fer does."

"Fer's my brother."

"I do."

Auggie nodded; he couldn't look at Theo right then, so he stared at the couch and blinked.

"I think you could find a way to use this talent and still be honest about who you are," Theo said quietly.

"I don't really want to talk about this," Auggie said, which he thought sounded pretty stalwart until he wiped his nose with the back of his hand.

"Ok," Theo said slowly. "Another reason you should stay is that you're getting a great education."

"That Fer is paying a ton of money for. I could get a good education at home. I could just go to community college for a couple of years."

Covering his face, Theo said, "Auggie, I think you're being hasty."

"I didn't come here to have you talk me out of it. I came here because I wanted to tell you in person. You mean a lot to me, and you saved my life. I can't ever pay that back. So, I just wanted you to know."

"Auggie, let the semester play out. See how you feel. Give everything some time."

Auggie scrubbed his hands on his jeans, and then he moved, sliding along the cushion until his knee bumped Theo's, stretching up, kissing Theo. For a moment, it was perfect: one of Theo's hands moved to the small of Auggie's back, holding him; the other cradled the back of Auggie's head. The kiss was strong and soft and sweet all at the same time. Theo kissed back, and there was something so erotic about his tongue teasing the opening of Auggie's lips without ever sliding into his mouth that Auggie ached to know what it would feel like to have Theo kiss him deeply.

Then Theo planted a hand on Auggie's chest and pushed him away.

"Theo," Auggie said, "I love you. Ok? I love you."

When he tried to kiss him again, though, Theo kept him at a distance. He didn't say anything. He just fended him off.

"Auggie, hold on."

"Oh my God," Auggie said, his face heating. "Oh my God."

"It's ok."

"Now I have to leave. Now I have to leave the country, I think."

Theo surprised him by laughing. Then his hand slid up, and he caught a handful of Auggie's collar, and he said, "Nope. You're not going anywhere for a few minutes. We're going to talk."

"Please no talking," Auggie said, blinking furiously. "You can stab me if it'll make you feel better. I owe you one anyway."

"I really care about you, Auggie," Theo said.

"Oh God, not the soft letdown."

"Damn it," Theo said, jerking on his collar. "Will you listen?"

"Yeah," Auggie said. "Yeah, I'm sorry. Ok."

"I really care about you. And I'm really messed up right now. I asked you once if that could be enough, but that wasn't what I should have said. What I should have said was this: I'm not at a place where I can date someone. Anyone. But I could really use a friend. I would really like you to be my friend."

Auggie wiped his eyes. Struggling to control his voice, he said, "You don't know how to text."

"I can text perfectly fine."

"You don't have any social media presence."

"I know how to get on Instagram on my computer."

"Oh my God, sometimes I wonder if you can even hear yourself. You don't watch any good TV shows."

"I would be willing to make some sort of television compromise."

"All my friends have to be in my videos."

"That's a hard no."

"Please, Theo. You'd get final say, and you're so grumpy sometimes that you'd be perfect."

Theo was making a strangled noise, and finally he gave Auggie another shake and said, "We can discuss it further."

"Friends with benefits," Auggie said.

"That's also a hard no."

"Cuddles."

"Oh my Christ," Theo whispered. "It's like opening Pandora's box."

"I'm taking that as a yes," Auggie said with a smirk. "Fine, we can be friends. Now it's my turn to say something." He pried Theo's fingers from his collar, and then he took Theo's hand in both of his own. He forced himself to meet Theo's eyes. "I know I kind of sprang that on you, but I meant it. I love you. I'm not going to chicken out. I'm not going to cheapen it by telling you I was just turned on by the kiss, although, um, yeah. I love you. And I understand that right now, I'm not who you want to be with. But I want to be the person you want to be with."

"No, Auggie, that's not what I meant. It's not about you."

"I know. But you deserve someone amazing. I'm going to try to become that person."

"You shouldn't change who you are for someone else."

"I don't want to change who I am," Auggie said, smiling. "I just want to be better. And hey, look, I got through this whole ego-shattering rejection without crying. That's a step in the right direction, don't you think?"

"You can cry whenever you want," Theo said, his voice wobbly for some reason Auggie didn't understand. "Crying doesn't bother me."

"I'm going to walk back to Moriah Court," Auggie said, standing. "And then, tomorrow, I'm going to come over and do my homework on your new couch and get Dorito crumbs everywhere. And we're just going to be friends."

"Friends," Theo said.

"With cuddles," Auggie said.

"Platonic, completely nonsexual cuddling."

Auggie rolled his eyes.

"No wandering hands," Theo said.

"Yes, Mother Superior."

Theo followed him to the door. While Auggie pulled on his boots and his coats, Theo stood in silence. Then Auggie looked around for his scarf, and Theo was holding it. Theo put it on him carefully, adjusting it a few times, his eyes never meeting Auggie's.

When Theo looked up, he said, "Auggie, when my life blew up, making something beautiful gave me a new way to go forward. Even if it was just stupid watercolors that nobody else would like. Even if it was just something beautiful to me."

Auggie nodded.

"And when the plague came to London," Theo said, "do you know what Shakespeare did?"

Auggie smiled. "I got a 98.5% in your class. Of course I know. Goodnight, Theo."

"Goodnight." Then Theo caught his sleeve. "Auggie, you're not moving home?"

Auggie just grinned and said, "Better stock up on Doritos."

He headed out into the night, not feeling the cold, buoyed up on the brightness of the stars and the silver flood of the snow. He could feel Theo watching him from the porch all the way to the end of the street; when he turned onto the main road, he heard from a distance the thunk of the door shutting. Auggie walked another block until he was sure he was safe, his eyes burning hotter and hotter, and then he pulled out his phone and placed a call.

"What, asshat? If you tell me you fucking failed that first fucking finance exam, I'll personally fly out there and beat your fucking ass."

"Fer," Auggie said, gulping around the sobs that were choking him. "I just really need to talk to someone right now."

The sounds on the other end quieted; Fer was moving into another room. "All right, jizznuggett," he said. "Talk to me."

24

Saturday, Cart came over to finish the floors. Theo did what he could to help. They'd already sanded and swept and vacuumed, working at night when Cart was off duty, and now they were applying the stain. Cart had shown up in nylon shorts and a tuxedo t-shirt; Theo kept getting glimpses of those skinny-boy abs with their dusting of dark brown hair. And that butt. He definitely didn't remember Cart having a butt like that.

At lunch time, Theo ran out and got sub sandwiches and a couple of six packs of Big Wave. When he got back, Cart had finished the front room, so Theo went around the house and met Cart in the kitchen. Tossing him a sub, Theo grabbed the bottle opener and hooked two of the Big Waves by their necks.

The rattle of pills against plastic interrupted him. Cart held the bottle of Percocet, and he shook it again.

"Come on," Theo said.

"Right now, big boy. What's it going to be today?"

"I could just go refill the prescription. You know that, right?"

"Yeah, but then I'd have to whip your ass. What's your poison today? Pills or booze?"

"Pills don't really go with a sub sandwich."

"You sure? Last chance."

"Yes, I'm sure."

The bottle of pills went back into Cart's pocket, where they'd been for the last week.

"I got stabbed, you know," Theo said between bites of the sub. "I deserve a little compassion."

"I've got plenty of compassion," Cart said, pausing to slurp up a slice of salami that had almost slipped out of the sandwich. "Just not for fuckwads who do stupid fuckwad shit like they've got no fucking brains and never learned how to read a fucking warning label."

"Fuck off," Theo said.

Cart shot him the finger.

"Mayo," Theo said, touching the corner of his mouth.

Cart found it with his tongue, grinned, and shot Theo the finger again.

When they'd finished the sandwiches, Theo opened two more beers, and Cart moved over to the chair next to him. This had become part of the routine too: Cart's thigh pressed along Theo's, Cart's shoulder leaning in from time to time, Cart's redneck laugh making the muscles in Theo's back and chest pleasantly tense. This part of the routine involved more of the same bullshit talking. It was also totally different.

"Your boy know he can't come over today?" Cart asked.

"Try again."

"Your fucktoy."

"Come on, Cart. You can do it."

"Your teenybopper."

"I know that fucking one-room schoolhouse you went to didn't give classes beyond the third grade, but I've got faith in you."

"You pretentious piece of shit," Cart said, "I'd already finished college and the academy while you were still sucking off lumberjacks or whatever the fuck you were doing."

Theo hid his grin.

"Now you've gone and ruined the whole thing," Cart said.

"Try it one more time."

"No, fuck you. You think you're special cause you get to jerk off in your ivory tower now."

"Let's hear you talk about Auggie right, and then I'll apologize."

"Is your friend," he laid his disgust on the word, "coming over today?"

"I'm sorry for the joke about school," Theo said, "And no, he's not. I told Auggie I was staying at your place because of the floors."

"I bet he didn't like that."

"I don't care if he likes it. But I did tell him I'd be sleeping on the couch. By myself." Theo watched Cart over the rim of brown glass. "And all I'd be doing was sleeping."

"Message received."

"By myself."

"I said message received."

"Let's hope so."

"Christ, you're a cocky piece of shit," Cart said with that huge grin. "What the fuck did Ian ever see in you?"

"He kept me around because I'm so handy."

"Fuck," Cart said, drawing the word out an extra ten syllables. Then he burst out laughing.

When they'd finished the floor in the kitchen, they locked up the house. At Cart's insistence, they drove to the Mighty Street Taproom, and Cart got chicken-fried steak and Theo got a burger. They talked. They watched the Blues lose like shit. They drank a few beers.

"Did you see this?" Cart asked when the game was over. He pulled out his phone, tapped the screen a few times, and held it out.

Theo took the device and watched the video load on Instagram. It had been posted by aplolz that morning, and it was the first post since Auggie had outed himself with the video that showed Theo kissing him. The video began with words on a black background: WHEN YOUR FRAT BROS FIND OUT YOU'RE GAY. What followed was a series of clips of Auggie being approached by what looked like every hot guy in Sigma Sigma, all of them asking Auggie if he could help them out with a personal problem. They cornered him in the kitchen. They followed him into the bathroom. One guy was hiding in the closet, and Theo wasn't sure if that was irony, but he knew how smart Auggie was, and he thought it was probably intentional. The video ended with a horde of hot guys chasing Auggie down the Sigma Sigma lawn. The video had a hundred thousand views.

Theo glanced up to see a look he couldn't parse on Cart's face.

"What?" Theo asked.

"He looks happy, doesn't he?" Cart said.

"Yeah," Theo said, smiling as he started the video again. "He does."

YET A STRANGER

Keep reading for a sneak preview of *Yet a Stranger*, book two of The First Quarto.

1

Auggie and Fer had been driving for three days when they reached the Sigma Sigma fraternity house, which sat on Frat Row on the south side of Wroxall College's campus. For the last hundred miles, the Civic had been chugging and croaking, and it made a shrill, despairing noise every time they went up a hill—which in this godforsaken corner of the Midwest was about every fifty yards. Auggie was pretty sure he could smell plastic burning. It was better than the day and a half of Fer's cheesy-tater-tot farts, though, that he'd experienced in the middle of the trip.

"Be fast, dick drip," Fer said as he pulled into the Sigma Sigma parking lot. "Or I'm going to miss the shuttle."

"I know."

"So be fast."

"I know, Fer."

"So don't sit there scratching your pubic lice. Get a fucking move on."

"I hate you so much," Auggie said as he jumped out of the car and ran toward the move-in tables set up in front of the fraternity house. It was mid-afternoon because they'd left Amarillo later that morning than they had planned, and Auggie guessed the rush of move-ins had happened that morning. A couple of guys around his age—they were sophomores too, he guessed—were lugging plastic totes toward the red-brick house, and another guy was folding bedsheets while he argued with a girl—sister? girlfriend?—at the back of a station wagon. No parents. No older brothers.

Fer laid on the horn, which was actually pretty pathetic because the Civic just kind of squeaked a few times. Then he shouted, "For fuck's sake, imagine some dude is jackrabbiting your hole and move your ass, Augustus!"

Auggie's face was hot as he approached the move-in tables. He found the L-R sign and felt his face get even hotter. The guy sitting there was gorgeous: big, brawny, in a tank and shorts and Adidas slides, with blond curls spilling over his forehead. He was grinning as Auggie moved forward.

"Lopez," Auggie said.

"Hi," the guy said, shuffling the papers. He glanced up. He had blue eyes. "Dylan."

"No, August. But I go by Auggie."

The guy laughed.

"Oh," Auggie said. "Got it. Hi."

Dylan laughed again. He had a nice laugh. He had very white teeth. When he handed over the paperwork and a key, he said, "You know everybody's talking about you, right?"

"No, I definitely did not know that."

"Yep," Dylan said. "They are. I like your videos. You're super funny."

"Thanks. I'm always looking for people who want to be in them."

"Nah, man," Dylan said. "Not really my thing. It's cool, though. I'm following you on Instagram and Snapchat. dylan_j199. Add me back."

"Cool," Auggie said.

"You want a tour?" Dylan glanced at the other guys manning the table, who were all trying incredibly hard to pretend they were doing something else while obviously fixated on the conversation. "Someone can cover for me."

The Civic squeaked again, and Fer roared, "Jesus Christ's bloody tampon, Augustus, either go down on him or don't, but hurry it the fuck up!"

"Maybe another time," Auggie said.

"Hit me up."

"Do you live here?"

"No, man. Senior. Some buds and I have a place off-campus. You should come over sometime. Hang out."

"That'd be cool."

"Hit me up," Dylan said again, but this time with a lazy smile that Auggie felt low in the belly.

As Auggie jogged back to the Civic, he could hear conversation buzz to life behind him. One guy said, "Jeez, Dyl, let the kid take a breath before you bend him over," and another guy said, "Dylan, you are such a fucking perv," and Dylan just laughed—a low, rumbling sound.

"Did you get your complimentary scissoring?" Fer asked as he got out of the car. They had different dads, and Fer was taller, darker, and bigger—muscle that was softening as Fer spent more and more time at business lunches and meetings. The taller part, that was what irked Auggie. Of course, sometimes the bigger part was pretty fucking annoying too.

"For the millionth time," Auggie said, "I didn't need you to drive out here with me."

"And let you go by yourself and give blowjobs to truckers for almost two thousand miles? Yeah, right, Augustus. Great idea."

"And for the millionth time, I didn't want you to drive out here with me."

"Pay for your own fucking education then."

"Just unload the stuff in the parking lot, and I'll get some guys to help me carry it inside."

Fer ignored him. He was working the biggest piece of luggage out of the trunk, grunting at the weight. "What the hell do you have in here? Your stainless-steel dildo collection?"

"Oh my God," Auggie said, covering his face.

The unloading and moving-in process went relatively smoothly. The Sigma Sigma house was a massive, three-story Colonial with red brick and gleaming white pillars. It was relatively new construction, with high ceilings and big windows. Auggie's room was on the third floor. The walls were a grayish brown, and someone had clearly patched and painted over the summer because there were no nail holes or broken plaster. Bunkbeds took up one corner of the room, and matching desks took up the rest of the space. One wall had been given over to two closets, which was where Auggie was going to have to store all his clothes—apparently, a dresser was not part of the standard package.

"This is worse than your last place," Fer said on their third trip upstairs.

"No, it's way better."

"Do you have a roommate?"

"I don't know; if I do, he hasn't moved anything in yet."

"He better not be a fucking psycho like your last one."

"I think that's everything, Fer."

Fer grunted, hands on hips, still studying the room.

"I guess you can go now," Auggie said.

"I want to see the bathroom. Your last place, you had that private bathroom."

"You can't just wander around the bathroom."

"I'm going to take a leak."

"You can't."

"I can't take a leak? Jesus, Augustus, I don't even know if you hear yourself sometimes."

Fer left, and Auggie considered whether or not it would be better just to die right now rather than dragging it out for the rest of the time Fer insisted on staying. Instead, he rearranged some of his luggage and the moving boxes, snapped a selfie, and pushed it out on Instagram with the caption: *The eagle has landed at Bro Central. Wish me luck!* He repeated the process with Snapchat—he was still feeling out the relatively new platform, but he felt like it had a lot of possibility. Almost immediately, he got a snap back: it showed a quarter of Dylan's face and mop of blond curls, and then grass, trees, and a swatch of asphalt. Dylan was grinning, and he'd scrawled a message on top of the picture: *welcome to Bro Central, little bro!*

Auggie added him as a friend so fast that he almost sprained his finger.

"Private showers," Fer reported, adjusting his junk as he came back into the room. "But it's just curtains, so you could still get ass raped."

"Go home, Fer. Go catch your shuttle. Go stand in the middle of the street until someone runs you over."

Instead, Fer shut the door. "You and I are going to have a talk right now, Augustus."

"Oh God. Hold on. I should probably film this."

Fer pushed Auggie's phone down and shook his head. Then he said, "Condoms."

"What?"

Taking a foil-wrapped condom from his pocket, Fer said, "Condoms." He pronounced each syllable distinctly, wagging the packet for emphasis. "Your fuck-up father isn't around to give you the talk—"

"Fer, no. Please. No. Please. You already gave me the talk. You gave me the talk when I was thirteen. You used a cucumber. Please don't make me go through this again. I'll never earn enough money to be able to pay for the therapy I need to get through this."

"That was the straight Auggie talk. This is the flaming homo Auggie talk. I've been doing some research because I wanted to get this right."

Auggie groaned.

"You're young. You're an ugly little fucker, but you're still probably going to get some dick."

"I will use a condom. I will be safe. End of discussion."

With his free hand, Fer jabbed a finger into Auggie's chest to punctuate each word. "Every. Dick. That. Goes. In. Your. Ass. Suits. Up. Do you understand me?"

"Suits up?"

"Rubbers up. Learn the fucking lingo, Augustus. And I'm not fucking kidding with you right now. I don't care if he's your little fancy man and you think you're head over heels in love. Rubbers. Rubbers. Rubbers. I will buy you a lifetime supply if you want, but you use a rubber every fucking time. Same goes for you if you decide to stick your Vienna sausage somewhere."

"What do I have to say so that you will leave? What do I have to do? Is it money? Do you want money?"

"Save it for your fancy boys," Fer said. Then he wrapped Auggie in a huge hug, squeezing him tighter and tighter until Auggie grunted.

"I can't breathe."

"I love you. You're basically just one really fucking annoying snipping of ball hairs, but I love you, and I want this year to be better for you. I want you to be safe, and I want you to find some stud who can cornhole you all night long."

Black specks danced in front of Auggie's eyes, which was probably why he had such a hard time fighting off Fer when Fer started kissing him all over the face like a lunatic.

"Go home," Auggie said, shoving Fer away, laughing and wiping his face. "God, you are so weird sometimes."

"Fine. I'm going. Now you can hunt down that guy you were throwing a bone for and deepthroat him or however you gay guys say hello to each other."

Auggie found a sneaker and pitched it; it caught Fer in the shoulder, and Fer stumbled back, laughing.

2

Theo sat in Dr. Wagner's office, flip phone at his side, trying to look like he was paying attention to whatever Dr. Wagner was saying. The office was cramped, and it felt even smaller because the walls were lined with books. They made the space smell like moldering cloth and old paper. Dr. Wagner currently had his red, bulbous nose in the Riverside Shakespeare; he was looking for a specific passage that he had suddenly decided to add to the lesson plans.

Tell him you've got a sister you want to set him up with.

The text was from Howard Cartwright. Cart was a police officer, and he had been partnered with Theo's husband, Ian, before Ian died in a car accident. In the year since that accident, a lot had changed between Theo and Cart—some of it good, some of it . . . well, Theo couldn't quite tell. One thing that hadn't changed was that Cart was a redneck pain in Theo's ass. Sometimes.

Aren't you supposed to be working? Theo had gotten pretty good at texting on the flip phone; he still didn't understand the rush to get a smart phone. He was just barely getting the hang of this one.

I am working.

Really working.

I am really working, dumbass.

"Mr. Stratford," Dr. Wagner said, lifting himself up from the pages of the Riverside Shakespeare with what looked like a great deal of effort. The booze on his breath, when he faced Theo directly, was strong enough to overpower the smell of the old books. "It's lost to me now. I suppose I'll have to find it later."

Then he stared at Theo, his head bobbing on his neck, his eyes cloudy with cataracts and drink. Theo wouldn't be surprised if the horrifying old fossil just dropped dead—and the female grad students would probably have a parade out of pure relief.

Wagner was still staring.

"We were going to talk about grading expectations," Theo said.

"Well," Dr. Wagner said, his jaw working soundlessly for a moment. "I don't know if that's really necessary."

Tell him you've got an eighteen-year-old cousin who will do things to his limp little lizard that Shakespeare never dreamed about.

Theo fought to hold back a smile.

"It was your idea, sir."

Last year, at this time, Theo had been planning his own class. Last year, Theo had worked out an entire semester's worth of material exploring adaptations and versions of *Lear*. Last year, he'd gotten some major work done on his thesis, and he'd also had the highest instructor evaluations in the department—for graduate students and professors. He'd turned some of his course materials into an article that was in the second-round review at *Shakespeare Quarterly*. This year, though, Theo was a teacher's assistant. He was going to shuffle papers, sit in on discussion groups, make photocopies, and scratch his balls. He'd be lucky if he didn't have to carry Dr. Wagner's briefcase and mop up his drool every time a co-ed bent over.

"I believe I do have a rubric," Dr. Wagner said, hoisting himself out of the seat and tottering toward the filing cabinet.

Stop a crime. Shoot up a bank robber. Get in a car chase. Rescue a kitten from a tree if you've got nothing better to do than bother me.

Gotta leave the kittens up there or the FD won't have anything to do.

Theo smiled in spite of himself.

"Here it is," Dr. Wagner said, holding a yellowed sheet of paper between two fingers. He waved it around and then blew dust off it. "Yes, I remember this. '59 was an excellent year for rubrics."

Kill me.

Not until you buy me that burger you owe me.

Mother. Fucker. You are one miserable son of a bitch. I was joking. It wasn't a real bet.

A bet's a bet.

"You can take a look at it for yourself, but I think you'll find it's perfectly up to snuff. I don't understand why there's all this rush to innovate these days. I really don't. Edwin Markle developed the six-point rubric in 1959, and it's just as good in 2009."

"Or 2014," Theo said.

"I'm very well aware of what year it is, Mr. Stratford. I was waxing poetic."

That wasn't all he was waxing.

Ok, I kind of cheated, Cart texted. *I already knew you were ticklish.*

Bastard.

Can't help it. You're just too cute when you laugh.

That one sentence was evidence of how very far things had shifted between them.

"Mr. Stratford, there is one thing that I think we need to discuss."

"Yes?"

"I understand that in the past you were found to be having inappropriate relationships with students."

Theo tried as hard as he could to keep his face smooth. His first year as a graduate student at Wroxall, the evening of the department's welcoming social, he had watched Dr. Wagner pursue Grace round and round the cheese table. Finally Grace had retreated to the bathroom. Dr. Wagner had followed. Theo had pushed open the door, rapping loudly, asking if anyone was in there. Dr. Wagner had stumbled out, his cheeks almost as red as his nose, smelling like he'd been swimming in a distillery. He'd mumbled something about getting turned around. Grace had been holding a can of pepper gel, so she would have been fine, but Theo hadn't forgotten.

Now, looking at those cloudy eyes, the glint in them, he realized Dr. Wagner hadn't forgotten either.

"No," Theo said.

"Excuse me?"

"I said no. That's not true. I had a relationship with an undergraduate student who had been my student previously. There was never any suggestion that the relationship had taken place while we were teacher and student." Theo struggled for a smile. "And relationship is really too strong of a word. We tried something, and it didn't work."

Wagner huffed. "Well, that's certainly not how I heard it."

"You're hearing it right now. From me."

"Yes. Well."

"And I'm sure you understand how appearances can be misleading."

Wagner huffed some more. "I certainly hope there won't be any further misunderstandings, Mr. Stratford. No more misleading appearances. As instructors, we have a sacred trust to shape young minds. We are responsible for their wellbeing. I hope I make myself perfectly clear when I say that nothing less will be tolerated."

Gin, Theo thought. He couldn't be sure, because all he was getting was the reek of alcohol, but Theo would have put money on gin being the drink of choice.

"Of course," Theo said.

"I think that will be all, then."

Dismissed, Theo limped out of the office, collecting his cane as he went. His knee was much better, and he had been consistent with his exercises even after physical therapy ended. He carried the cane, though, because his knee stiffened after he sat too long, and it still gave out at the weirdest times. And, if he were honest, because he found the cane comforting. You could really mess somebody up with a cane if you needed to.

He was unlocking the door to the office he shared with Grace and Dawson, a cubbyhole of a room at the far end of Liversedge Hall, when his phone buzzed again. He fanned the door back and forth to clear the toxic musk of weed (Dawson) and chai (Grace) from the closed-up room. Another message from Cart.

Have you talked to him?

Just got out of the old fuck's office.

Theo was just settling in at his desk, cane propped against the window, when the phone buzzed again.

You know that's not what I meant.

Theo looked at the message for almost a full minute. Then he closed the phone, put it in his pocket, and started up the ancient desktop computer. It was none of Cart's fucking business if Theo had talked to Auggie yet.

3

Auggie ran into Orlando, literally, on his second day in the Sigma Sigma house. He was naked except for a towel around his waist, and he was rushing because he'd overslept and they were having a house meeting in half an hour. He yanked open his door, charged into the hallway, and crashed straight into his roommate from freshman year. They both went down in a tumble.

"Oh my God," Orlando was saying, "I'm so sorry—Augs?"

Auggie grabbed the towel, which had ripped free in the fall, and covered himself awkwardly as he stood. Orlando picked himself up too. He'd been carrying a box, and now it lay on its side, spilling sneakers and tie-dyed jockstraps across the carpet squares. Auggie forced his eyes up, away from the jocks, to meet Orlando's eyes.

His former roommate hadn't changed much. The same thick eyebrows, the same heavy scruff, the same strong jaw. He looked both thinner than Auggie remember and like he'd packed on even more muscle. It seemed impossible but made sense in a way—Orlando was a star on Wroxall's wrestling team, and he'd doubtless worked hard over the last six months to recover from the terrible stab wound he'd taken in the winter. He was staring at Auggie, and Auggie had to fight the urge to cover his bare chest.

"Hey Augs," Orlando said. "Umm. Hi. Hello."

"No. Absolutely not. Whatever this is, go away."

"This is crazy, right?"

"Yep. Crazy. Totally batshit. Bye, Orlando."

Then the door next to Auggie's opened, and Ethan Kovara, a junior and one of the few other Cali boys in the frat, poked his head out. "Hey, Auggie. You met my new roommate? Orlando, this is Auggie. Auggie, Orlando."

Orlando smiled uncertainly. "How have you been?"

"You guys know each other?" Ethan asked.

"Could you give us a minute?" Orlando said.

"Yeah, man. Oh, dude, raunchy," he said, laughing as he looked at the jocks, and then he shut the door.

Orlando stooped down, gathering up the jocks and sneakers. Auggie grimaced and struggled with a growl and then squatted—which was weird as hell in a towel—and helped. It had been his fault, after all.

"I, uh, didn't know you were going to live here. You said you thought you were going to get a place with Tyler and Chris."

"That didn't work out."

"I wasn't trying to, you know . . ."

"Stalk me?"

A huge grin broke out on Orlando's face. "Something like that."

For some reason, Auggie found himself smiling too. "God, I'm an asshole. I'm sorry. I just didn't expect—I mean, it's good to see you, but things just ended kind of weird."

"Yeah, I didn't like how they ended. I'm really sorry, Augs. About all of it. I—I'm on a new med, and I'm seeing a therapist, so, you know, you don't have to worry."

"I wasn't worried." Orlando's smile got a little bigger, and Auggie heard himself adding, "I could have handled things better too."

"Nah, man. It was all me. Sorry again."

They were still hunkered down, and Auggie was still in a towel, and Orlando's dark eyes were staying painfully fixed on Auggie's face like he was fighting the desire to look.

"Are you ok? I mean, the recovery and stuff."

As they both stood, Orlando tugged up his tee to expose dense muscle covered by dark hair. Low on his stomach, a shiny scar ran for four inches; it still looked inflamed

"Shit," Auggie said.

"I might be out this season. The doctors really don't want me wrestling; they already think I might have to have another surgery, and they're worried I'll do more damage."

"I'm so sorry."

"It's ok. If I creep you out again, just don't punch me in the stomach."

"Orlando, you didn't creep me out. It just . . . it just didn't work."

"Yeah," Orlando said, "well, you're a nice guy for saying that."

Down the hall, somebody was blasting Korn, and two guys stumbled out into the hall headbanging and screaming.

Over the blare of music, Auggie said, "I guess we're neighbors."

"I'm not going to bother you, Augs."

"That's not what I meant."

Orlando's dark eyes fell, and he fiddled with the flaps of the cardboard box. "Ok, well, I gotta finish bringing up my stuff."

"By yourself?"

"Yeah, I mean, sophomore year. Last year, my parents, my brothers and sisters, they were climbing all over each other to help. This year, I guess I'm an adult and I'm supposed to handle things myself. You know how it is."

"Yeah," Auggie said, but he was thinking of Fer driving halfway across the country with him. "Let me put on some clothes and I'll help you."

"No way."

"Yeah, it'll just take me a minute."

"Augs, that's weird. You don't have to be nice to your psycho ex-roommate."

"I'm not being nice. I mean, I guess I am. But you're not psycho. And you're not just my ex-roommate. I thought we were friends."

Orlando played the cardboard flaps. When he looked up, his eyes were dark and heavy. "God, you want me so bad, don't you?"

Auggie stared at him.

A tiny grin played at the corner of Orlando's mouth.

"You are such a dick," Auggie said.

Orlando burst out laughing.

"Let me change. Oh, hold on. Do you want to do something fun? Like a move-in video? We could do like . . . well, let's see if Ethan wants to be in it. We could have him move your stuff every time we bring up more boxes. Or something like that."

"And I have to pretend to be mad," Orlando said.

"You're shit at being mad. Maybe you should just pretend to be dumb."

"Hey!"

Auggie grinned.

"Go change," Orlando said, "before I forget how generous I'm being by providing you with free content."

Over his shoulder, Auggie flipped him the bird as he went back into his room. He changed and went next door. As soon as Ethan heard their plan, he wanted in on it. He was good looking, too, which helped—dark brown skin, huge eyes, a nervous smile that Auggie's audience would eat up. Not as good looking as Orlando, and that was a good thing too. You had to balance that kind of thing, or it started looking like a Gap commercial.

They were on their third trip up, both of them with arms full of boxes, when a familiar voice called out, "Little bro, you're missing the house meeting."

Dylan was leaning against one wall, blond curls spilling over his forehead, an unreadable smirk on his mouth as he watched Auggie. He was in a blue paisley tank top that showed blond stubble on his chest. He had massive legs.

"Hey," Auggie said, smiling—too big of a smile, he realized. Then he stumbled, and he would have fallen except Dylan caught his arm and steadied the tower of boxes. Dylan's grip was solid. He still had that smirk that Auggie couldn't decipher.

"Careful," Dylan said.

Sweat beaded on Auggie's nape.

"Augs," Orlando said from the stairs.

"Yeah," Auggie said. "Coming."

"See you around, little bro," Dylan said, releasing Auggie's arm.

"Who's that douche?" Orlando said when they were passing the second-floor landing.

"He's actually pretty cool. His name's Dylan."

Orlando shook his head.

"What?"

"I just forgot that sometimes you're kind of dumb."

About the Author

For advanced access, exclusive content, limited-time promotions, and insider information, please sign up for my mailing list at www.gregoryashe.com.

Made in the USA
Monee, IL
28 September 2022

14782644R00177